The Unmaking

Jane Glatt

The Marriage

Jane Glatt

TYCHE BOOKS LTD.

The Unmage
Published by Tyche Books Ltd.
www.TycheBooks.com

Print ISBN: 978-1-928025-51-1
Ebook ISBN: 978-1-928025-52-8

Cover Art by Niken Anindita
Cover Layout by Lucia Starkey
Interior Layout by Ryah Deines
Editorial by M. L. D. Curelas

Author photograph: Eugene Choi
Echo1 Photography

This book was funded in part by a grant from the Alberta Media Fund.

Alberta
Government

Writing is a solitary endeavor so I want to thank friends and

family for cheering me on. You're the best ...

-Jane Glatt

Chapter 1

"She's not supposed to be here!"

His mother shook with anger and Timo took a step back, thankful that for once the venom in her voice wasn't directed at him. Her hand tightened on his arm as he stood on his toes and peered over her shoulder, ignoring the fine, purple mist that swirled about her.

Timo's eyes slid past Mage Guild Primus Rorik, who stood in front of them, shaking his head in apology. An older man stared at him with ice blue eyes.

That must be Santos Nimali, the one who had insisted on this meeting. A grassy green mist circled the fingers of his right hand. And there—that must be *her*! She met his eyes and smiled a wide, warm smile.

"Timo?" The woman stepped forward. "I've been asking to meet you for years but your mother . . ." The woman paused, and her gaze flicked to his mother. "*Our* mother forbade it."

"To protect him," his mother, Arabella Fonti, said. "From the woman who killed his father."

The woman—Kara Fonti, his sister—turned her sad gaze to him. "I had no choice. He was trying to kill me."

"After *you* tried to have Kara killed." A man detached himself from a shadow and strolled up to stand beside Kara Fonti.

Timo couldn't supress a shudder. The man seemed relaxed—

his arms hung loose by his sides and his shoulders were slouched—but from the quiet, controlled way he held himself Timo sensed that he was dangerous.

"You tried to contract me to assassinate her."

"No!" Arabella replied. "I deny it. What proof do you have?"

His mother's grip on him relaxed, and Timo took the opportunity to step out from behind her.

Kara Fonti smiled again. Not the warm welcoming smile she'd directed at him, no, this was a sad, bitter smile full of old pain.

"Reo never formally accepted the commission," she said. "But the official request for an Assassin is in Warrior Guild's Hall of Records. Santos put a protective spell on it."

Timo felt his mother stiffen beside him, and he had to hide his surprise. Had his mother tried to assassinate her own daughter? She was capable of that?

"And," Kara continued, "although you sent many, many spells in the years afterwards, it's still there." She looked directly at him, ignoring his mother. "I believe Warrior Guild will make the record available to you if you wish to see it for yourself."

"It's a lie," Arabella said, turning to him. "Don't believe them."

Timo simply nodded, his heart sinking. He wanted to trust his mother, he truly did, but there was no chance Warrior Guild would fabricate something like this. She had tried to assassinate her own daughter. What other horrible things had she done and then lied to him about?

"But you did kill my father?" Timo asked, speaking for the first time. He'd desperately wanted this meeting, had hoped that the woman who was his sister would be there, but he'd always thought that his mother had lied about this.

"Yes," Kara said. "I've always regretted that I had to but he was trying to kill me—kill us." She reached out and clasped the hand of the man beside her, the man who had implied that he was an Assassin.

"Rorik." The old man, Santos Nimali, spoke up. "I thought this had all been explained to the boy."

"We explained as much as we thought prudent, yes," Rorik replied.

"Prudent?" The other man frowned. "You lied."

"No," Rorik said, shaking his head. "We may have omitted a few details that both Arabella and I thought might cause undue stress for Timo, but it was never our intent to lie."

"But that's what you did," Santos replied. "And I think that it *was* Arabella's intent. The truth about Valerio Valendi's death must be a matter of Mage Guild record, how did you expect to keep that from him? Surely he's studied the records?"

"I have not been allowed access to the records," Timo said, tired of everyone talking around him. "I've been told that I can study them when I'm sixteen."

"Sixteen!" Santos said. "That's ridiculous. When did you find your Mage talent?"

"I was eight, Primus Nimali," Timo replied, giving the elder Mage his true title. Rorik used the title but he wasn't the rightful Primus of Mage Guild.

Santos Nimali grinned, and Timo revised the man's age downward. He grinned back, briefly, wondering if Santos could outlive Rorik and deprive him of ever having the title he so desperately wanted. Timo was apprenticed to the acting Primus but he didn't trust the man any more than he trusted his mother.

"You're fourteen now?" Santos said. "Six years and you've never studied the records, the history of Mage Guild?" The old man shook his head. "Rorik, that is shameful. Timo Valendi is your Apprentice. It's your duty to educate him."

"Yes," Rorik replied. "And despite what you think, I take his education very seriously. Although we fear his talents do not reflect the promise of his parents."

"What about the promise of his sister?" Kara asked. "Does he have unmagic?"

Timo heard his mother's indrawn breath. There it was, the question Arabella Fonti never wanted an answer to, the question she'd told him to never, ever answer, no matter who asked it, not even if she herself asked him. Not that she ever would.

"No," Arabella said, so loud it was almost a shout. "He has a small talent for casting spells, but none for . . ." she paused and gripped his arm. "For whatever unnatural talents you have."

"Unmagic," Kara replied calmly. "It is not unnatural. We think it's probably hereditary, like any other magical talent. I see magic spells. I can distinguish the signature colours of the Mage who cast them, I can undo them, I can read the intent of them to determine whether they are malicious or benign, and I can redirect them." Kara fixed her gaze on him again. "Which is how

I came to kill your father. It was his spell, one he'd sent to kill me and Reo. I turned it back on him and it killed him."

His mother's grip was almost painful now. Timo concentrated on keeping his face blank and emotionless but his heart was racing. Something that made sense, finally! She couldn't create spells, he'd been told that over and over, yet his mother had always insisted that somehow she'd killed one of the most powerful Mages in the Guild. It *wasn't* her spell that killed his father—she'd turned his father's own spell back onto him in order to save herself.

He searched Kara's face. There was no trace of any mist around her—all he saw was sadness and pain and concern. Concern for him? Had that been another of his mother's lies? When she'd first spoken, Kara had said that she'd been asking to meet him for years. His mother and Rorik always claimed that Kara and Santos wanted to use him to corrupt the Guild.

"Why did you want to meet me?" he asked.

Kara smiled again. "You're my brother. My family."

"Family is very important to Kara," Santos Nimali said. "Her other half-brother, Osten, lives with us, as does your own half-brother, Giona Valendi."

"You have a Valendi boy?" Rorik asked. "You had no right to take him."

"He wasn't being treated very well when I found him," Reo, the Assassin, said. "Besides, you know as well as I do that he wouldn't have survived his father by more than a few days. None of his other children did."

"I have other siblings?" Timo asked in shock. Neither Rorik nor his mother had ever mentioned any siblings, but his father had been a man in his prime when he died. Of course he'd fathered other children. "Where are they?"

"Dead," Reo said flatly. "Except for Giona. I assume Mage Guild Council took care of them. That's the usual practice, isn't it, Rorik? Assassins weren't hired—we don't kill children—but by the time I searched they were already dead. Three girls and two boys. They died in falls and drownings—except for one poor child who was burned alive."

Timo swayed and would have fallen if his mother hadn't been clutching his arm so tightly. Brothers and sisters, all of them dead, and he hadn't even known they'd existed.

"They did not die by Guild Council order," Rorik said.

He faced his accuser calmly, so calmly that Timo knew he'd known about this, about these deaths, all along.

"Of course there was no order," Santos said. "Just as there was no order to kill my children when I went mad. But they're dead all the same. I'm surprised you were able to save Timo."

"He's my son," his mother said. "Of course he was safe."

"You knew?" Timo said. He shook his mother's hand off his arm. "You knew that I had siblings and yet you let them be killed?"

"No," his mother said. "They all died accidentally." She lowered her voice. "We can discuss this later, in private."

"So you can tell me more lies?" he replied. He looked across to Santos Nimali. Pain lined his face. He was telling the truth, Timo was sure of it. "And my brother—Giona you said his name was. Does he know of me?"

"Of course he does," Santos said. "He wanted to come but someone with power needed to stay behind with Kara and Reo's children." Santos smiled. "Your niece and nephew."

"You have a whole family wanting to meet you," Kara said. "You are welcome anytime you wish to visit." She directed her gaze at his mother, at *their* mother. "Or stay. You can live with us for as long as you want to. Santos has been offering to take you on as his Apprentice for years. He's getting desperate now that Giona has completed his Journeyman training."

"He's never going to visit you," his mother said. "Let alone stay."

"I'm not sure that's your decision to make, Arabella," Santos said. "In a few years, Timo will be of age." Santos smiled at him again. "He will *always* be welcome on Old Rillidi."

Timo looked across at his sister. Just a few steps separated them. If he took those steps he could change his life. But his mother would not let him go without a fight. His eyes moved from Kara to her husband. And if his mother tried to hurt Kara, Reo would kill her, or die trying. His new life would start with death instead of hope. It was less than two years until he was sixteen. He could wait that long, couldn't he?

A long, green trail of mist detached itself from Santos' left hand. Timo tried to ignore it as it slithered across the floor towards him. It wrapped itself around his mother's legs and started winding its way up her body. Timo took a step away from his mother when it slid down her arm towards him. It pooled on her hand, wrapping itself around her arm faster and faster, before it suddenly disappeared. Startled, Timo looked up directly into the eyes of his sister, Kara. She gave him one tight nod, that was all, a movement so small that it was barely noticeable. But it told him that she knew. Knew what his mother didn't want to know, *was afraid* to know because it would put him in danger. That he could see spells, see magic. That he had . . . what had Kara called it? Unmagic.

"Now you've seen the boy," Rorik said. "I think we can conclude this visit."

"One more thing," Kara said, and Timo held his breath. She wasn't going to tell, was she? "Acting Primus Rorik, you seem to have some malevolent spells about you. If you wish I will try to undo them."

"Malevolent . . ." Rorik paused, his face white. "Someone has cursed me? Are you sure?"

"Yes," Kara said. She glanced over at Santos and smiled. "I have quite a lot of experience lifting curses. Valerio Valendi was very thorough with Santos."

"I'd accept her help if I was you," Santos said. "Kara might not offer again."

"Yes, thank you," Rorik said.

"Rorik," his mother said. "You can't trust her."

"Apparently I can't trust anyone," Rorik said. "At least she's being open about what she's doing."

Kara stepped over to Rorik. She walked slowly around him, her eyes focussed. Timo leaned closer, fascinated. Rorik had always had multi-coloured mists swirling around him and Timo had never given them a second thought, until now. But Kara said that they were curses and that she'd dealt with such spells with Santos. Spells cast by his father. Had his mother known that? Had Rorik?

Kara raised a hand and gently waved at the crown of Rorik's head. A pale blue strand of mist unwound itself and then dissipated. Timo didn't recognize the colour of the spell but he'd look for it from now on. It was unlikely that Rorik's enemy was a friend to his mother. And that could be dangerous for him as well.

Frowning, Kara poked a finger at a gossamer wisp of gold.

"Sss." Rorik winced and sucked in a breath.

"Sorry. It's a nasty spell," Kara said.

She poked again, and Rorik clamped his eyes shut. The gold clung to Kara's finger, and she made a face as she pulled her hand away. The gold thread seemed to tighten around Rorik's head before it loosened and trailed away from him, following Kara's hand. She walked a few steps away from Rorik and shook her hand. The gold thinned and finally faded completely.

"Someone really doesn't like you," Kara said.

Timo knew who; he recognized the colour of the mist. It was Master Mage Inigo, one of the most vocal and powerful council members. But Timo had never once considered that it was harmful, or that Inigo had actually cast a spell. How long ago had he cursed Rorik? Timo couldn't remember a time when Rorik *hadn't* had that gold mage mist swirling around him.

"My thanks," Rorik said. "I feel clearheaded. It's as though a minor headache is gone, one I'd lived with for so long that I forgot it was there." He shook his head gently. "Do you know what it did?"

"Sorry, my talents don't allow me to read the spell, just the intent with which it was cast." Kara stepped back over to Rorik. "There's one more that should be removed." She poked her finger at another pale blue strand. It twitched away from her and Kara frowned at it. "Hold still," she said and slapped Rorik's shoulder. The pale blue mist puffed out, then thinned and drifted away.

Rorik shrugged his shoulders.

"Again, my thanks," he said, nodding at Kara.

"Time to go," his mother said abruptly. She grabbed Timo's arm and spun him around.

"Bye, Timo," Kara said.

He looked over his shoulder and met her warm smile.

"Remember, you're welcome any time. We're on Old Rillidi, at the old manor house. Any Warrior can help you find us."

"Seyoyans too," Reo said. "Although they might be harder to find."

And then Timo was being dragged through the door and out into the hallway. Acting Primus Rorik caught up to them and closed the door behind him.

"Why couldn't we stay?" Timo asked his mother. "They were nice."

"Nice!" His mother stopped and whirled to face him. "They are *not* nice. They're dangerous. She killed your father, and that Assassin, who knows how many people he's killed in his life."

"But Kara helped Primus Rorik."

"So she says," his mother replied. She turned and started walking again, dragging him behind her.

"I do feel better," Rorik said.

"Santos probably spelled you to make you think she was helping," Arabella said.

Timo pressed his lips together. He knew that Kara had removed some spells but he couldn't say it, not without revealing that he could see magic, just like his sister. At least he knew where to go to learn how to use his unmagic. And they *were* nice—especially Kara. Which was more than they could have hoped for, considering that Arabella had tried to kill her.

Silently Timo followed his mother and Primus Rorik out of the council chamber and through the halls of Mage Guild Island. Despite the brevity of the meeting, many of his questions had been answered. But now he had even more. Would either his mother or Rorik tell him the truth?

"Did my father curse Santos Nimali?"

"I have no idea," his mother replied. "And if he did, I'm sure he had good reason to."

"Primus?" Timo turned to Rorik. "Did he?"

Rorik sighed and looked over at Arabella, who frowned and shook her head.

His mother had led them here, to her apartment. As soon as they'd closed the door to her sitting room Timo had asked his question. Now he glared at his mother, who ignored him and went to sit in her favourite chair. Rorik shrugged and sat on the settee across from her.

"Who exactly is the Primus here?" Timo said.

Rorik stiffened and turned to him. "When it concerns you, I defer to your mother," he said.

"How exactly does this concern me? It happened years before I was even born."

"It's about your father," his mother said. "So it concerns you." She looked up at him, her mouth a thin line. "Go and tell Annya that you and Primus Rorik will be dining with me. And have her bring tea."

"Then you can practice the spell I taught you yesterday," Rorik said. "I'll expect you to show me before we dine."

Timo clenched his fists. He knew that look on his mother's face—he would get no answers from her. Not today and probably not ever. And Rorik, that spineless old man, did whatever his mother told him.

"Practice your magic in your old room," Arabella said. "There's nothing in there that I'll miss if you ruin it."

"Yes, Mother," Timo said. Of course she didn't care about anything in his old room. He wasn't even sure she cared about *him*. He turned and left the room so his mother and Rorik could discuss the meeting, so his mother could instruct Rorik to tell her son nothing.

"You let her stay!"

His mother's voice and she was very angry. Timo paused and took a step back towards the open door.

"She was already there," Rorik said. "Was I supposed to tell her to leave the room?"

"Yes! I told you I never wanted Timo to meet her. She's clever and devious and will try to use him against us—against Mage Guild."

"Are you worried that if Timo realises he has another option he might not do what you want?" Rorik asked. "I don't think she was being devious when she helped me."

"You have no idea what she did to you," his mother replied. "She might have cursed you."

"Arabella," Rorik scoffed. "That's too weak an argument for even you to use. You know she has no magic. Just this . . . unmagic. Besides, in fourteen years not once have any of them—Kara Fonti, Santos Nimali, or Reo Medina—ever tried to attack us. I believe Santos has told us the truth. They simply want to live in peace. Why can't you let them?"

"She killed Valerio. I will *never* forgive her for that."

"In self-defence," Rorik said. "Even the witness accounts state that."

Timo frowned. This was why he wasn't allowed in the Hall of Records.

"They were manipulated," his mother said. "Probably by Inigo."

"Arabella, I saw to them myself. The witness accounts are valid."

"I won't let her have him."

"In a few years he'll make his own decision," Rorik said. "There is nothing you can do about that. But if you keep lying to him, he will never choose to become your Journeyman."

"He will. I will make sure he has no other choice." There was a pause. "Why is it taking Annya so long to bring our tea?"

Guiltily, Timo found Annya and relayed his mother's instructions, hoping his delay didn't get her into trouble.

He stepped inside his room and closed the door, leaning against it.

His mother expected him to be her Journeyman! He couldn't imagine anything more unappealing. With almost two years before he had to choose, he hadn't thought about which Mage he might select. Or who might accept him. But his mother had been thinking about it—*planning* it.

He waved a hand at the mage lights that hung along the back wall, activating them so they bathed the small room in bright, white light. Carefully he scanned the room, looking for purple mage mist, looking for evidence that his mother was spying on him. Nothing. Good.

Timo crossed to the chair and sat down. The bed was bare, the mattress rolled up at one end to reduce dust, but his desk and book case were clean and polished, no doubt thanks to Annya. The Server Guild woman had been in his mother's service as long as he could remember, and she knew better than to neglect anything, even the unused room of her employer's son.

He would not be Journeyman to his mother. She'd told Rorik that she would make sure he had no other choice, but he would *not* let her control his life. He didn't know Santos Nimali—wasn't sure he could trust him—but he would take that chance. Because he *knew* he couldn't trust his mother. If he was her Journeyman, it would be for her benefit, not his.

Two years, that's all he had to wait. When he turned sixteen he would be considered a full Guildsman, even if Rorik deemed him not ready for Journeyman status. If Santos Nimali agreed to teach Timo, he would have to give compensation—that was Guild Law—but after today Timo thought Santos would be willing. He was rich, richer than almost anyone else in Mage Guild—he'd heard his mother complaining about it to Rorik.

What's more, he owned the island of Old Rillidi. He was the only Guildsman in all of Tregella who didn't have to rely on the Guilds, any Guild, for the place he called home.

Timo's old room was where he'd lived until he was apprenticed but it was not his home. He hadn't even spent a single night here since he'd moved to Rorik's over six years ago. A move his mother had arranged, just as she and Rorik controlled his education. But he had a right to see the Mage Guild records.

He stood up, pushed the chair against the wall and lifted his right hand, watching as the soft mauve mist collected around his wrist.

He would learn what he could from Rorik—he was duty bound to teach Timo, after all. But Timo vowed to do everything he could to learn what Rorik *wouldn't* teach him. Things he believed were beyond Timo's power and skill level, because just like unmagic, his mother and Rorik didn't want to know he had strong magic.

He concentrated, and the mist spiralled out from him towards the chair. There was a small puff of mage mist and the chair disappeared. A second puff and the chair re-appeared in the centre of the room. He grinned. The chair was much bigger than the stone Rorik had given him to practice relocating with, but the stone hadn't seemed like any effort at all. Even the chair hadn't taxed him. Timo eyed the bed, letting the power build and curl around his wrist again. He'd play with the stone later and he'd use that when Rorik tested him, but for now, he wanted a challenge.

"YOU'VE BEEN TOO lenient on him." Arabella glared at Rorik. Annya had left, closing the door behind her. A steaming cup of tea sat ignored beside her chair. "I do not like the insolence Timo demonstrated today. You need to drive that out of him, I don't care how."

"He needs to ask questions," Rorik replied. "I need him to trust me if I'm to teach him the magic he needs."

"But not about his father," Arabella replied. "He can learn all he needs to know about Valerio Valendi from me!"

"Can he?" Rorik asked. "You knew the man for a brief time. I knew him for years. I knew him when he *was* Santos Nimali's Apprentice."

"Are you implying that you knew the father of my child better than I did?" Rorik may have the title of Primus but they both knew who kept the council in check.

"Not better," Rorik said quickly. "But in a different light." He touched a hand to his head. "It's probable that he cursed Santos."

"I don't care," Arabella replied. "As I told Timo, if he did, he would have had good reason to. You are not to tell him anything." She was fairly certain that Valerio *had* cursed Santos—she was only sorry that the old Mage was no longer mad. What had that witch she'd given birth to done to him?

"All right," Rorik agreed. "But surely he can see the records now. Santos was right about that—six years is far too long to keep the boy away from them."

"No! I forbid it."

"He is my Apprentice," Rorik replied. "I am the one who decides on his training."

"But he is my son." Arabella stared at Rorik until he looked away. She smoothed her hands along her skirt. "Now. We must not tell anyone about our meeting. No one must find out that Santos is no longer insane." She wished she'd known just how lucid the man was and had come prepared with her own spells to use on him. She would never again get close enough to him to curse him. Although . . . would the woman have seen any spell she'd cast? That was what she'd claimed: she could see spells and determine their intent. Once Timo was her Journeyman, she would see if he had some of the same talents. But not until then. She did not want Rorik to control her son's other abilities. They would be hers to use—and she would.

"It is not in my best interests to tell," Rorik assured her.

"Not if you want to remain Primus," Arabella agreed. "Make sure Timo doesn't mention this to anyone. Can you at least do that? We can't have anyone on council insisting Santos take up his duties."

"Timo has no friends to tell," Rorik replied. "Besides, telling would not be in his best interests either."

"How do you mean?"

"If I'm no longer Primus then you're no longer Secundus. Any protection he has because of that, he will lose." Rorik paused. "Although he would be Apprentice to the Secundus—me."

Arabella pasted a smile on her face and pretended that Rorik hadn't just threatened her. But it was true. If Santos was to resume his responsibilities as Primus, then Rorik would become Secundus. And she would become just another council member—unprotected and vulnerable to attack. She and Rorik would have to make sure that never happened.

KARA STUDIED THE mage lights that dotted the underside of Mage Guild Island and shivered. She knew the island wouldn't fall on her, knew that it had been kept aloft for years—decades—by the myriad spells that wisped around it, but she still felt in danger. The small boat parted the water silently, as silently as Kara parted the mage mist that swirled around.

"They haven't sent any spells after us," Kara said, turning around to face Reo and Santos.

Reo nodded before he resumed scanning the small docks they passed. He wouldn't ease off until they were on Old Rillidi, back behind their barriers—both magical and non-magical. Even then she knew he wouldn't feel completely safe. A result of his early training, he'd told her years ago. A relaxed Assassin was a dead Assassin and he had too much to lose now that he had her and their children.

"I didn't expect it," Santos said. "But it's better to be sure." He flung his right hand out and grass green mist surrounded the small boat. Santos turned to face her.

"He looks like you," the old man said.

"Do you think so?" Kara asked. "I thought he looked like Arabella."

"Yes," Santos replied. "And so do you."

"Already fourteen and I only now get to meet him," Kara said. "I hate her for that."

"Only for that?" Reo asked. "She tried to hire me to kill you, and when I refused, she tried to kill us both, and you hate her for keeping you from your brother?"

Kara sighed. She'd made her peace with her mother's actions years ago, although Reo never would. She'd tried to explain to him that she'd expected nothing other than betrayal from her mother. How could she be angry when that was exactly what happened?

"At least he looked well," Kara said, grateful that her brother seemed fit and healthy. She'd tell them the other news—that he could see magic—once they were home and safe. It was too dangerous to mention here, where any of the spells that swirled around them could be listening to them. Timo seemed to realize that as well. He'd tried to ignore Santos' spell but Kara had seen him react. "Even if he didn't seem happy," she finished.

"Happy," Santos said with a chuckle. "What child that age is happy? But he did not seem to trust either Rorik or your mother." In the flickering mage light, the old mage's face looked eerily solemn. "Which is a good thing for the boy."

"What do you mean?" Kara asked.

"I grew up here on Mage Guild Island," Santos said. "It's a dangerous place for even the youngest with power. Your position in life is secured by strength, both magical and political. Trust is not something you can give safely, even to your own mother."

"You think she would sacrifice him to further her own ambitions," Kara said flatly.

"She's done it before," Santos said. He referred to the way Arabella had traded Kara, her daughter—leaving her behind in the small villa where she was born—in order to go to Rillidi and the seat of the Mage Guild. "I've seen others—men and women— use their children for their own gain. No matter the cost to the child."

"That's why they kill the children a Mage leaves behind."

"Yes," Santos said, and sighed.

Kara knew he was regretting the loss of his own children, children who had been killed after Santos had been cursed to madness by Valerio Valendi. She didn't understand how they could do it, how the council could condone—even order—the deaths of innocent children. It explained why her mother was willing to assassinate her own daughter, but not why she seemed so attached to Timo. Although to Kara, it looked more controlling than caring.

After half an hour of travelling in silence, the boat edged out from under Mage Guild Island. A few minutes later they were in bright sunlight. Kara turned and stared at the hulking mass that floated above the surface of the sea. She never wanted to go to Mage Guild Island again but she'd go everyday if she could see Timo, her brother, and let him know that there was someone out there who cared. Growing up that was all she'd hoped for—that wherever she was her mother missed her, wanted to see her, wished her well. Her hope had been shattered once she met her mother, of course, but for years that hope had sustained her. Looking back she was glad she'd had that dream—that hope—even though it had been extremely painful to learn the truth. But Timo wouldn't find the truth painful. Kara *did* want to know him, *did* want him to live with her. And she wanted him to have that hope.

Chapter 2

Timo leaned across the library table, his shadow falling across the book that Barra Eska was reading.

"Will you help me?" he asked.

"Why should I?" Barra replied. She tugged the book into the light.

Annoyed at being disturbed, a few other Apprentices glared at them from other tables scattered around the library. Timo ignored them and leaned closer to Barra.

"I helped you when you needed to find that book Inigo was looking for."

Barra looked up at him with a frown. "That was a year ago," she whispered. "And it's hardly the same thing. An Apprentice is only allowed access to the records when they're with a Master Mage."

"Or his Journeyman," Timo said. "We could go with Hestor. If Rorik had a Journeyman I'd ask him, but he doesn't. There's just me."

It had been a week since he'd approached Barra with his request. He'd chosen her because although not his friend, at least she didn't seem to hate him, like some of the other Apprentices. And he was desperate to see the records—he had to know what they said about his father. The truth would help him know who he could trust.

"That's not my problem," Barra said. She was a small girl,

about Timo's age but half a foot shorter than him. Her dark hair was tied back with a pale blue ribbon that almost matched her eyes, a gift from her parents, Timo knew, on her last birthday. She'd been very proud of it.

"I can get you more ribbons," Timo said. "Any colour you want." He couldn't actually *buy* her ribbons, but he could *make* them. All he needed to do was look at the one she was wearing, so he could use it as a pattern. Then he'd be able to duplicate it from any scrap of twine or rope. He'd been practicing all week.

"Any colour?" Barra asked. "I have a dress that I plan on wearing on Founders Day. It's a grey-blue silk—at least it looks a lot like silk. I need a ribbon the exact same colour." Absently she reached up and touched the ribbon she was wearing. "This one is just a little too blue."

"I can get one, I promise. All you have to do is get Hestor to let me join you in the records room." Timo wasn't sure why Barra was dressing up for Founders Day—Apprentices were only invited to the day events, not the formal evening party—but if she wanted the ribbon he could get it for her.

"I can talk him into an hour," Barra said. "That's all. And you don't get to ask him any questions. He hates you."

"I know," Timo said. "But it's not my fault that Rorik didn't accept him as his Journeyman. He should have." It *was* his fault, in a way. Rorik's Journeyman would be expected to teach his Apprentice, teach *him*. It would be harder for Timo to hide his true magical abilities from someone not deliberately ignoring them. That meant his mother and Rorik would no longer be able to pretend he was weak.

"Yes, he should have," Barra said. "It's not right for the Primus to have a single Apprentice." She frowned at him. "Especially when you have such a small talent. At least you realize it's wrong even if your master doesn't. That's the only reason Hestor might consider helping."

"I appreciate it. I'll need to see the colour of your dress if I'm going to find ribbon to match it."

"I'll bring a piece of fabric next time," Barra said.

Timo nodded and settled in his chair and picked up a book.

"There's one more thing I want from you." Barra leaned over the table. "Mention me to your mother."

"My mother?" Timo asked, surprised. "What do you want me

to say to her?"

"Tell her that I'm a strong and accomplished Apprentice. I know there's time still, but a posting as Journeyman for the Mage Guild Secundus would suit me."

"I'll do what I can," Timo said. And he would, since it would keep Barra in his debt. He might need more than an hour with the records, after all. But he didn't think his mother would value his opinion of Barra—she didn't seem to value it for anything else. Besides, his mother seemed to think *he* would be her Journeyman.

CREATING THE RIBBON was even easier than he'd thought it would be. Not wanting to make too close a match, Timo had decided to pattern his ribbon on the velvet material that edged the curtains in Rorik's dining hall. Barra had slipped him a swatch of fabric during their next library session and it had taken only one small spell to create a ribbon that matched the colour perfectly. He'd taken a gamble that the velvet would do but still, he'd been surprised at her squeal of excitement when he'd given it to her.

"I couldn't find silk," Timo lied. "I hope this will do."

"It's perfect," Barra breathed. "I didn't even hope for velvet." She ran her hand along the plush fabric, a smile on her face. "What do you think?" She lifted the ribbon up to her hair.

"It brings out the colour of your eyes," Timo said, repeating something he'd heard Annya tell his mother years ago.

Barra nodded. "That's why I chose this colour for my dress." She wound the ribbon around her hand before gently packing it into her satchel. "Come on, Hestor's waiting for us at the Hall of Records. You need to keep quiet. Don't say anything unless Hestor asks you a question. I'll do what I can to keep him happy, but it won't be easy."

No, Timo thought, keeping Hestor happy would not be easy. He'd never even seen the man smile.

The Hall of Records was adjacent to the Council Chambers where Timo had met with Kara Fonti, Santos Nimali, and the Assassin Reo. Hestor, pacing in front of the double doors, frowned when he saw them.

"You're late," he said.

"Sorry," Barra said. "It was my fault. I completely forgot how long it would take to get here from the library and I insisted that we go through the garden. It's so pretty this time of year, don't you think?" She beamed a smile up at Hestor, and to Timo's surprise, the man relaxed and smiled back.

"No harm done," Hestor said. "It was only a few minutes." He turned to Timo and scowled. "Let's go."

Hestor stopped directly in front of the double doors that led into the Hall. A line of topaz mage mist unwound from his wrist and traced a pattern on the doors. The mist sank into the wood of the doors, and they swung open.

"You have one hour," Hestor said. He let Barra enter the room before he reached a hand across to the door frame, blocking Timo's path. "If you do anything to get either me or Barra in trouble you'll regret it, Apprentice," Hestor whispered in Timo's ear.

Timo nodded and followed Barra in. His eyes followed the line of shelves up and up, each shelf lined with books and scrolls. Far away he saw a skylight and beyond it, white clouds. He heard a soft click and looked behind him. The door had closed.

"I forgot that you'd never been in here," Barra said, studying him. "Why is that? I don't want to do anything to get me in trouble." She paused. "Or that would make your mother angry with me."

"Don't worry, she'd be angry with me, not you. Besides, Rorik should have brought me here, but between his Council and Primus duties, he just hasn't had time. Everyone is allowed in here once they find their talent."

"That's true," Barra agreed. She nodded, and her shoulders relaxed. "Do you need help finding anything? In case the spells are beyond your talent?"

"Thanks." Timo nodded. "I should be fine." He ignored the pitying look Barra gave him and instead headed down the aisle towards a work table he saw.

Barra went in the opposite direction. She, like everyone, believed he was weak, that his magical abilities were almost non-existent.

Timo shook his head. He wasn't even sure why he was supposed to hide his talent, though he was certain it was what Rorik and his mother wanted. The one time he'd tried discussing it with Rorik the man had been emphatic that he should accept his limitations. And it was pointless trying to talk to his mother—

Arabella Fonti didn't tell her son *anything*. At least not the truth. Which was why he was here, looking through the records.

Timo whispered his father's name and pointed up, towards the distant skylight. Mauve mage mist sped from his finger and trailed up, twisting around a bookshelf. It stopped moving, and Timo snapped his fingers. The mage mist rushed down, a leather-bound book trailing it. After a few more searches, Timo had a stack of books piled up on his desk, each with a date etched into its spine.

There, that book had the most recent date—the year he was born, the year his father died. He opened the book to the last page and peered at the script. He flipped back a few pages and started reading, his fingers tracing the words on the page.

It was an account from an eyewitness, one of the guards who helped his father track down Kara and Reo.

Mage Guild Secundus Valerio Valendi had led the search for Kara Fonti and the Assassin, Reo Medina. According to the guard, the Secundus told him that those they pursued had no magical talents but that the Assassin was a danger if they got too close. The guard and his partner defended one end of an alley while the Secundus secured the other, trapping the two suspects.

The guard said the suspects ducked and then his partner was hit and killed by what he assumed was a spell. In the next few minutes, the buildings and fences that lined the alley were damaged in magical attacks. Then the Assassin ran forward, the girl shouted and waved her arms, and the Secundus was blown all the way to the mouth of the alley. The guard viewed the body—it was in exactly the same state as his partner. There was no doubt in his mind that the same type of spell killed both men. Spells that could not have been created by the suspects.

Timo leaned back, his hand on the page in front of him. This was Mage Guild's official account of Valerio Valendi's death, and it matched what Kara Fonti had told him. It seemed—unlike his mother—his sister had told him the truth. But did that mean everything else she'd said was true?

Timo picked up another book, the one with the earliest date. He hoped to find out if his father had cursed Santos Nimali.

"ARE YOU FINISHED?" Barra asked.

Timo dropped the book onto the table, startled.

"Uh, yeah," he said. "I got caught up in what I was reading."

Barra peered at the book's spine. "Huh, sounds pretty dull. I thought you might be trying to find the secrets of Primus Santos Nimali."

"Why would I do that?"

"Because everyone does that the first time they come here," Barra said. "He had a book, a journal that he wrote all his spells in—that's what I've heard." She leaned closer. "Some say that's what drove him mad. He had too many spells, too many dangerous, evil spells all kept in one place, all in that journal. He got them confused when he was trying to use them against someone and ended up cursing himself." She straightened up. "At least that's the rumour. Now he's mad and they keep him on Old Rillidi so he can't cause any damage." She turned towards the entrance to the room. "Come on, Hestor will be here soon."

"All right," Timo said. "Just let me return these." According to Santos and Kara, Santos went mad because he'd been cursed, not because he had a journal full of dangerous spells. But Valerio Valendi had been Santos' Journeyman, his best and most powerful student. He would have known about the journal. Had he wanted it for himself? Nothing he'd just read proved Valerio cursed Santos but his actions showed him to be ruthless and ambitious—a man Timo thought capable of cursing his Master in order to steal his spells.

Barra was out of sight so Timo flung his right hand out over the books. Mage mist raced from his outstretched hand and passed over the books that were stacked on the table. He flicked his hand up, and the mage mist split, each strand now returning a book to the shelf it had come from. Once the books were in place, he lowered his hand and sighed.

A mother who'd tried to have her own daughter assassinated and a father who'd probably cursed the man who'd trained him. Would he end up like them? Consumed by his own ambition? Threatened by the people closest to him?

"Hestor's here," Barra said from the aisle. "Let's go."

"Coming," Timo said. After one final glance to make sure he hadn't left anything out of place, Timo hurried after her.

Hestor frowned at him as he joined them. A flick of the older boy's wrist sent mage mist spinning around the door. It opened and Barra stepped through. Hestor followed her. Timo was about to fall in behind him.

"Barra, Hestor, I trust you are well today?"

It was his mother's voice, coming from the hallway, just outside the doors. Timo quickly slipped behind the open door, trying to hide. His mother would be furious if she found he'd been in the Hall of Records.

"Yes, Secundus," Barra said. "We're quite well. Thank you for enquiring." Timo cringed at the fawning tone in Barra's voice, but his mother would probably welcome it.

"And hard at work I see," Arabella Fonti replied.

Hestor stopped in the doorway, beside Barra. Timo sidled away from the door, backed down an aisle, and crouched beside a shelf.

"Of course, Secundus Fonti," Hestor said. "It's important to make sure Apprentices keep up with all aspects of their studies. Although Barra is so diligent that she hardly needs my encouragement."

"Very good," Arabella said. "I won't keep you. No doubt you have more studies to attend to."

"Yes, of course," Hestor said.

From his vantage point Timo saw him hesitate and then look behind him, into the Hall of Records.

"Good day to you, Secundus," Hestor finally said, bowing slightly.

"And to you," came the reply, this time from further away.

Timo straightened and headed towards the door.

"Sorry," he said when he reached the others, holding up his satchel. "I forgot this and had to go back for it."

"Did you?" Hestor asked.

"You missed your mother," Barra said. "I mean the Secundus." She frowned. "You could have told her what a fine student I was." Barra turned to Hestor and smiled. "Although Hestor very generously praised me to her. It may even work out better this way. Once Timo compliments me she will have heard two good opinions."

"I think mine would carry more weight than Timo's," Hestor said, sending a dark look Timo's way.

"Of course," Barra said. "But it wasn't something I could ask you to do. The fact that you did it is wonderful, though."

Timo followed the other two out into the hall. Would Barra be able to get Hestor to help him again? He wanted to find out what the records said about Santos Nimali. He needed to know more about the man he was planning his future around—the man who would hopefully conduct his Journeyman training.

"HOW DARE YOU disobey me?"

Timo looked up from his work table. His mother stood in the doorway, glaring at him. Rorik hovered behind her. She stepped into the room, and Timo sighed and placed his pen on the table.

"What have I done now, Mother?" He knew though. She'd found out about his trip to the Hall of Records.

"You were told not to," she said. "And yet you entered the Hall anyway. By recruiting a pair of unwitting accomplices." Arabella walked over to the table, leaned over, and smiled grimly. "Don't count on either them or anyone else helping you in the future."

"It wasn't their fault," Timo said.

"No, but they will both pay a price nonetheless," Arabella said. She sat down in the chair opposite him. "By not asking enough questions, they helped you do something that both Rorik and I had forbidden."

"It's not fair to refuse me entry," Timo said.

"That's not your decision," Arabella replied.

"It shouldn't be yours either," Timo muttered.

"What did you say?" His mother straightened up and raised her eyebrows as purple mage mist swirled around her.

"You heard me," he said louder. "My studies should be a matter between me and my Master, but somehow every time Rorik should be giving me instructions, there you are, telling me what to do as if it's your right. Well, it's not your right. It hasn't been your right since I was eight and found my talent. Why don't you get your own Apprentice and leave me alone?"

Arabella's eyes narrowed, and she leaned back into the chair. Rorik glared at Timo from behind her, but he didn't say anything, and Timo shook his head in disgust.

"You will not visit the Hall of Records again," his mother said.

"I think that should come from my Master, don't you?" Timo said. He met Rorik's gaze. "Does she speak for you, Rorik? Even in this?"

The older man held his gaze for a few seconds. "She does. It's for your own good."

"An Apprentice should be able to respect his Master," Timo said. "But I can't respect you, not when all you do is follow my mother's directions."

Rorik's face paled slightly, but that was his only response. His mother's lips tightened, and she stood up and turned to leave.

"You're too late, you know," Timo said. "I read all about my father, the great Valerio Valendi. He was not a man to be proud of."

Arabella whirled and leaned over the desk, her face inches from his.

"You have no idea what you're talking about," she snarled. "He was brilliant."

"Maybe so," Timo said. His mother's mage mist swirled violently around her upper body. "But he had no morals. He used everyone around him, even those who meant him no harm."

His mother's smile chilled him.

"Then you are truly your father's son," Arabella said. "Because you used Barra and Hestor though all they wanted to do was help. Poor Barra. With this type of indiscretion it will be hard for her to find anyone willing to take her on as Journeyman, when the time comes. And it certainly won't be me." She glanced over her shoulder at Rorik. "Hestor could find himself placed in a small villa somewhere. Perhaps in the dung heap that I was born in." Arabella swept out of the room, followed by Rorik.

Timo stared after them. With a wave of his hand, he sent mage mist flying towards the door. It slammed shut with a satisfyingly loud thud, and he flicked his hand again, letting the spell trace the door and lock it from the inside.

Let his mother and Rorik try to get through that spell, he thought. He was much more powerful than either of them even suspected. Then his fury drained away, and he had to place his hands flat on the desk to stop them from shaking.

Less than two years. That was all he had to wait before he could make his own decisions. Not even the Primus and Secundus of Mage Guild could circumvent the Guild Law that said that at sixteen, with talent, he was an adult. Let Rorik claim he wasn't ready to be a Journeyman. That would only matter if he stayed here. He would have to trust that his sister—the only person who'd told him the truth about the death of his father—meant it when she'd said he was welcome. And he would have to trust that Santos really did want to teach him.

He sighed. He hadn't meant to get Barra into trouble but he hadn't worried about it either. Did that make him like his father, as his mother suggested? He didn't think so. He was stupid and Barra had paid a high price, might even pay a high price for the rest of her life, but he hadn't done it on purpose. He'd try to explain it to her. He doubted she'd give him a chance, but he would try. He doubted anyone would speak to him now. But it wasn't as though any of the other Apprentices had been particularly friendly before this.

Timo leaned over his desk and flipped to the last page in his notebook. Ever since he'd met *her*, his sister, he'd been trying to work with his unmagic. When she'd described her talent, she'd said that she could tell if spells were benign or malevolent—and he'd seen her remove the curses from Rorik. Ever since, he'd been trying to teach himself how to do the same. Most of the time, he could remove small spells, and he'd had a few successes distinguishing between harmless and malevolent spells. But now he *needed* to be able to use his unmagic.

Barra wouldn't be a threat, but Hestor? If he lost standing with Inigo, he would retaliate. Some Journeymen liked to humiliate Apprentices. They would set magical traps—pranks—that had no true ill will and caused no real harm. In order to keep his unmagic a secret, Timo had to walk into these traps. But Hestor might try to really hurt him. Would he try to kill him? At least if he could tell which spells were malicious, he could avoid them. He wanted to live long enough to make his own choice.

"ARABELLA, YOU CANNOT say anything." Rorik softly closed the door to his workroom and sat across his worktable from her.

"Of course I can," she replied. "I want to make certain that no one else helps Timo disobey me."

"He won't ask anyone else," Rorik replied. "The boy has no friends and now will have few—if any—allies. Humiliating Barra, and particularly Hestor, could have serious consequences."

"Like what? Will they make him trip or spill ink? I lived through worse." Much worse—and it had made her work even harder in order to become someone they wouldn't dare humiliate. It would do the same for Timo.

"Do you forget who Barra and Hestor call Master?" Rorik

asked. "Inigo will use any means to hurt you, including allowing his Apprentice and Journeyman to harm Timo."

"He wouldn't dare," Arabella said. "It's against Guild Law to deliberately hurt a student. He would risk his own position if it was proved."

"But it would have to be proved," Rorik replied. "And Hestor might be willing to take the blame. In the meantime, Timo would be hurt. Or worse."

"Rorik, I think you are making far too much of this," Arabella said. "Timo's life will not be in danger. He'll have to deal with a few bruises and some shame, that's all. Nothing he doesn't deserve after going against my explicit direction."

"I hope you're right," Rorik said. "I believe Inigo will do almost anything to get what he wants. He cursed me, after all."

"So says the non-Mage I gave birth to." She didn't believe any curses were removed from Rorik despite what he thought. Kara Fonti had put on a good show but *she* hadn't been fooled.

"I believe her," Rorik said. "She made a difference to how I feel and think."

"I know you believe that," Arabella said. "But that doesn't mean it's true."

"I am worried about Timo," Rorik continued. "Perhaps I should have accepted another Apprentice or Journeyman. They would have offered the boy some protection."

"More likely they would have helped him break more rules," Arabella said. "It would have been more difficult for me—*for us*—to manage him."

"Making this public will make things even more difficult and dangerous for him."

"A few pranks will be played on him and in a few weeks it will be forgotten." Arabella stood to leave. She had some reports to read before the next council meeting.

"If you're wrong?"

"I am not wrong," she replied.

"But if you are?" Rorik paused. "You might want to consider Santos Nimali's offer to train Timo. He would be safe with them, you know it."

"What?" Arabella couldn't believe it. "Are you suggesting that I send Timo to Old Rillidi? Never! Timo will be *my* Journeyman, *not* the mad mage's. You will not suggest that ever again. Not to me and especially not to my son. Are we clear?"

She glared at Rorik until he nodded his head and looked away. How dare he make such a suggestion! He *knew* what she wanted for her son. Had the girl somehow meddled with his mind? Was that what she'd done when she claimed to be helping him?

She wrenched the door open and strode out into the hallway. Rorik was investing far too much importance into this one small lesson she was giving her son. He would see—Timo would suffer wounded pride along with a few bruises, and in a few weeks all would be forgotten.

"THEY'VE REFUSED OUR request again, of course," Santos said.

Even though she'd expected it, Kara's shoulders slumped in disappointment. She, Santos, and Reo were in Santos' study. A mage light hovered overhead, softly lighting the cluttered desk they sat at.

Reo reached over and grasped her hand, squeezing it gently. Kara closed her eyes for a moment and sighed.

"Nothing we weren't expecting," she said. "Gyda even knows why they let us visit Timo two months ago."

"Because Arabella thought only Santos was coming," Reo said. "And despite what she would like to think, even she can't ignore a request from the true Mage Guild Primus indefinitely. My sources are limited but so far there is no indication that our visit has caused either Rorik or Arabella any political problems." He paused. "At least no more than usual."

"Inigo?" Santos asked.

Reo nodded.

The Mage pursed his lips. "I barely knew him. He was just an Apprentice when I was Primus, and because he didn't have an extraordinary talent, he was never brought to my attention."

"I'd say his talent is political manipulation," Reo said. "From what I've been able to learn, he controls the council. I wish I knew what was going on inside those doors."

"I wish I knew what was going on with Timo," Kara said. "Although he's apprenticed to the Primus, he appears to have only minor magical abilities. And he can see spells but tried to conceal it. He didn't want anyone to know."

"I still think Rorik and Arabella are hiding his true abilities, including his ability with unmagic," Reo said. "Why else would he be the only Apprentice to the Primus and the Secundus has neither Apprentice nor Journeyman? Nothing else makes sense."

"No," Kara shook her head. "If Rorik could have had Timo remove those curses he would have." She shuddered. "One was almost as bad as the curse Valerio put on Santos—the one that almost killed him when I tried to remove it."

"I have to agree with Kara," Santos said finally. "If Rorik knew Timo could see spells, he would have known he had been cursed, even if the boy couldn't remove them. Rorik doesn't know Timo has unmagic. Which means Arabella doesn't know either."

"Why not?" Kara asked. "Timo knows."

"Maybe he's been hiding it," Reo said. "Or maybe, like you, he didn't know what he was seeing."

"He knows now," Santos said. "I do think it safer if he keeps it a secret."

"I don't think he'll tell Arabella," Kara said. "He didn't seem very happy with her."

"She and Rorik have kept a lot from him," Santos said. "Maybe Timo's retaliating by keeping secrets from them?"

"He is fourteen," Reo said. "A rebellious age. If no one finds out about his unmagic, he should be safe enough until he turns sixteen."

"Yes," Kara said. She ran a hand through her long dark hair. "I just wish we knew that he *was* safe."

Distracted, Kara let Reo lead her through the manor house to the kitchen to gather their children, Lisha and Nando, before heading home to the cabin.

Reo teased her about collecting people, surrounding herself with those who felt like family, but when it came down to it she couldn't protect Timo, her own flesh and blood.

Reo stopped so abruptly that Kara bumped into him.

"You can come out now, Mole," Reo said. "I know you're there. You've been spying on us all evening."

Mole stepped out from a shadow and grinned. "What gave me away?"

"Nothing obvious," Reo said. "But I am the one who taught you."

Mole shook his head and shrugged. "The clammers are here."

"How long?" Kara asked. "Have they been here the whole time

we were with Santos?"

"Close," Mole said. "Pilo sent me to fetch you."

"She'll be furious," Kara said. Pilo hated the clammers. She made them stay outside rain or sun until Kara dealt with them. She glared at Mole. "You left her alone with them so you could spy on us?"

"You were having an interesting conversation," was all Mole said. He shrugged again and headed in the opposite direction.

Kara paused. Mole wouldn't tell anyone what he'd heard. As a boy he'd never talked much. Then he'd spent hours following Reo around, soaking up everything he was willing to teach him. But Assassins needed to be able to talk—to lie—convincingly, which took practice. So Mole learned that as well.

He wasn't a true Assassin since he wasn't Guild, but he'd had all the training, as well as a few Guild commissions. They could put his training to use.

Reo tugged her forward. "Let's deal with the clammers so we can go home," he said.

Kara gripped his hand and nodded, following him to the kitchen. Later she'd talk to Reo about sending Mole to watch over Timo. But first, the clammers.

"They're all here?" Kara asked.

"Mole says yes," Pilo replied. Her fists were clenched as she stared out the kitchen window with narrowed eyes.

"Good," Kara said. She only wanted to do this once. She followed Pilo's gaze to the group of dirty men and women sprawled on the back lawn. Getting even this close to the clammers made her skin crawl. "You stay here with the children." She smiled at four-year-old Lisha and six-year-old Nando. "Reo and I will handle this."

Reo nodded before preceding her out the door and into the garden. Kara shivered when she stepped outside, despite the warm evening.

Over twenty pairs of eyes turned towards her all at the same time, and Kara shivered again. The clammers, with matted hair and clothed in filthy rags, all sat up a little straighter. Kara felt Reo's hand on her shoulder, and she took a deep breath.

This was one of her least favourite tasks. Every six months the clammers came for her help, and she gave it willingly with the understanding that they would stay on their part of the island and not harm anyone who stumbled into their midst. But it still made her skin twitch.

"It's time," one of the clammers said.

Kara nodded. She wasn't sure if the man who was their leader was one of the clammers who'd captured the docks all those years ago. She thought it might be, but if she dwelt on the past, on the terror of their escape from the clammers, she might not be able to do what she needed to do.

She straightened up and lifted her head. "I'm ready." Kara took a deep breath and raised her hands towards the group then *pulled* at the magic with all her might. Slowly at first and then faster and faster, wisps of mage mist were drawn out of the clammers until streams of multi-coloured mist circled the lawn. Once all the magic had been drawn from the clammers, Kara concentrated on dissolving the mist. Soon there was nothing left but a blank patch of grass.

"We will return," the clammer said, and the whole group silently rose to their feet and headed off into the night.

Kara slumped against Reo.

"I hate that," she said softly.

"I know," he replied. "But it's for the best. We can't afford to have Mage Guild suspect that some unguilded have traces of magic. No one would be safe."

"Including Pilo. I just wish there was another way, a way that didn't involve me." She always felt tainted after draining the clammers of their magic. She knew it made her family and friends safer, and she herself never actually touched their mage mist, but it left a stain, somehow. She glanced at the patch of lawn where the magic had pooled. There wasn't a trace of magic left but she knew she'd avoid this area for a few days just the same.

"Let's get the children and go home," Reo said.

Kara nodded and let him lead her into the kitchen.

Among the warmth and smiles of her family, she felt some of the taint wear off.

Chapter 3

TIMO SAT DOWN at his work table and winced as he rubbed his hand along the bridge of his nose. Not broken, at least not this time, but there would be a bruise.

He'd been dodging attacks like this last one for the past year and a half, ever since he'd persuaded Barra and Hestor to take him to the Hall of Records. He knew who had set this spell—he always knew—that was one of the hardest things about his unmagic. He knew whose magic made him fall, or spill ink on his notebook, or interfered with his own spell casting. He knew, but had to pretend he didn't. No retaliation, no dark looks sent the offender's way, nothing that would reveal that he knew who was to blame. The only thing worse was deliberately walking into the traps.

He'd become very good at determining not just whether a spell was meant to harm or humiliate, but how much power was behind it. It had taken one bad fall, one fall that had been meant to kill him—that *would have* killed him if his own magic hadn't been so strong and he hadn't practiced relocating so diligently—for him to realize that his life depended on knowing which spells to avoid. He'd spent every waking hour for a month on that task, but now he could read spells with a single glance. After he'd mastered that, he'd concentrated on learning an invisibility spell. It was advanced—far beyond most Apprentices' skills. If they couldn't see him coming they wouldn't set a trap in the first place.

He'd startled more than one person by turning up in the library when they'd been watching for him.

"They're a despicable lot."

Timo froze. Then he let his breath out slowly and readied a spell, mage mist wrapped around his fists. Slowly he turned in the direction the voice had come from, a voice he didn't recognize.

"Who are you?" he asked. There, in the corner, was something moving? He peered into the darkness, cursing himself for not bothering with a light. But he'd been humiliated enough for one day. There'd been no need to see the bruise he knew was forming. Eventually he made out the faint glow of mage mist. Grass green, a colour he'd seen once before.

"Santos?" he whispered.

"Hah!" came the reply. "Kara said you were the same as her."

A shadow detached itself from the corner, green mage mist softly weaving around the figure. A boy, no, a man—shorter than Timo but half a dozen years older than him—stopped in the middle of the room, his stance relaxed and his arms hanging loosely at his sides. Somehow that didn't make Timo feel any less nervous. He'd seen someone move like that before, with dangerous, calculated, barely leashed energy.

"I'm Mole," said the figure. "I'm not gonna hurt you." He frowned. "Unlike them burro-spawned brats you study with."

"You know Reo," Timo blurted, then wished he hadn't when the man, Mole, narrowed his eyes and crossed his arms across his chest.

"What have you heard?"

"Nothing . . ." Timo stammered. Mole *seemed* calm but the menace in his voice said otherwise. "I've never heard of you . . . it's just . . . you move like him."

"You only met him once?" Mole's tone was skeptical but he let his hands drop to his sides again. They were fisted though, Timo noticed, so he wasn't really at ease.

Mole's gaze followed Timo's, and he laughed and loosened his fists. "Sure, sure, you'd notice a thing like that." Mole's lips tightened. "Your life depends on it."

"What have *you* heard?" Timo asked. He'd been so careful to keep up the pretence of being a fumbling, inept Apprentice with little magic and less intelligence. Who might know the truth?

"Not what I've heard," Mole said. "What I've seen." He padded over to the chair in front of Timo's work table and sat down across from him. "The stumbles, the ruined books and clothes, always walking into tables and doors." Mole shook his head. "Don't worry, none of them suspect. I only know because I'm trained, like you guessed, by Reo." Mole leaned back in his chair and frowned. "But that older one with the pinched face?"

"Hestor," Timo said. There was only one Journeyman who still set traps for him.

"Yeah, him. He's getting frustrated. He wanted you dead long ago and he doesn't know why it hasn't happened."

"I was hoping he'd start to doubt his own skills," Timo said.

Mole grunted then laughed. "That's working then." Mole nodded. "And likely part of why he's so furious. Which makes him unpredictable."

"I know," Timo said. He slumped in his chair, defeated.

"No," Mole said quietly. "I don't think you do."

Timo looked up and met Mole's eyes, and he felt the blood drain from his face. "That's why you're here," he whispered. "He's done something, or he's planning something."

"Yes." Mole nodded. "He's trying to contract an Assassin." He put his crossed feet up on the corner of the work table.

"Gyda," Timo said. "How do I outsmart an Assassin?" He tugged his notebook from underneath Mole's soft-soled boots. He'd run—would Mole take him to Old Rillidi? He eyed him. He only had the man's word that he was a friend of Kara's and Reo's. For all he knew, Mole *was* the Assassin Hestor hired to kill him.

"You don't. But you don't have to." Mole paused. "I can kill him for you if you want," he added softly, so softly that Timo almost missed it.

"Hestor? I, no, no I don't want that." Timo looked at Mole. He was serious.

Did he want Hestor dead? Timo wouldn't mourn Hestor's death, but he didn't want it on his conscience. It was too much like something his father would do. But he didn't think Mole would offer to kill Hestor if he'd been hired by him. Mole might be who he said he was. But he was still a stranger to Timo.

"No?" Mole seemed almost disappointed. "Your decision. But you don't have to worry about Assassins. None will take this contract. Warrior Guild has an arrangement with Kara and Reo.

They notified them the minute they realized that you were the target." Mole shrugged. "Not exactly Guild Law but they want what Kara offers them."

"Which is?"

"She visits Warrior Guild Island once a month to clear out any spells Mage Guild has cast." Mole smiled. "There's always a few."

"There would be," Timo agreed. "Mage Guild hates Warrior Guild. Did Kara send you?" Maybe he *could* leave with Mole.

"Yes," Mole said. He dropped his feet to the ground and leaned over the table. "After you met, Kara and Reo asked me to keep an eye on you. To keep you safe."

"What?" This Assassin had been trailing him, spying on him, for close to two years? "How?" As unnerving as it was to think of being spied on for so long, Timo was a little relieved. He hadn't been as alone as he'd thought—his sister had been trying to look out for him.

"It wasn't hard." Mole ran a hand down the front of his shirt. "Santos gives me a little keep away spell, and you magic wielders think so highly of your power that you forget that there are other ways to do things."

"Like what?"

"Unhappy people are often willing to look the other way. Server Guildsmen are unhappy, but the Mage Guildsmen who have little or no magic? They are miserable."

"You've been spying on me," Timo said. "Did you learn anything?" How many of his secrets did Mole know? Could he trust him—and Kara—with them? Did he have a choice?

"Yes." Mole's tone was serious. "I'm impressed. You've managed to avoid serious injury while letting minor spells hurt you." He gestured towards Timo's bruised face. "Like today. You get hurt just enough that no one suspects you know what's happening or that you can do anything about it."

"I've managed to stay alive," Timo said. "Good for me."

"Yes, good for you," Mole said. "But I don't understand what you're waiting for, why don't you leave?"

"I'm only half-trained and am not yet an adult." Timo dropped his eyes to the desk. "I would be considered a dangerous runaway."

Mole shrugged. "You'd be safe on Old Rillidi."

"Would I?" To Timo it seemed far too close to Mage Guild

Island for safety—especially if he ran away. Would his mother try to kill him the same way she'd tried to kill her daughter?

"Kara has been safe there for years," Mole said. "It can't be more dangerous than staying here."

"I suppose," Timo said. He met Mole's gaze. He seemed sincere, but Timo would expect an Assassin to lie convincingly.

"Every month Kara and Santos request that Mage Guild allow you to visit."

"They do?" Timo asked. "I assumed they didn't want to anger Mage Guild and were waiting for me to turn sixteen." He didn't want to be a Mage Guild runaway. They would never stop trying to kill him.

Mole snorted. "Kara angers Mage Guild just by being alive. If they can get you to Old Rillidi returning here would be optional."

"I didn't know," Timo said and frowned. "My mother kept this from me."

"Sure, sure," Mole said. "But she's also been keeping you alive."

"She has?"

"You study a lot," Mole said and smiled.

"So?"

"When you're studying I go looking for more . . . interesting things to watch."

"You spy on my mother?" Timo asked. Then his curiosity overcame his surprise. "What does she do?"

"Mostly tries to control council," Mole replied. "But none of them trust each other, and they especially don't trust Arabella Fonti. Not with her daughter sheltering on Old Rillidi and Mage Guild unable to kill her after years of trying." Mole's smile was grim. "Then there's you."

Timo forced his hands flat on the table, hoping they wouldn't shake and betray his fear. "Do they know?" He looked up and met Mole's serious gaze. "That I'm like Kara?" If the council knew he had unmagic he wouldn't live long. He wouldn't be dodging traps and tricks set by Apprentices and Journeymen—he'd be dealing with deadly spells created by powerful and experienced Master Mages.

"No, thanks to your mother," Mole said. "They've used spells on her to make her tell them the truth. She doesn't know. She suspects but she doesn't *know*."

"She never *wanted* to know," Timo said. He dropped his gaze to his hands. She and Rorik had made it clear that he was never to mention if he had anything like his sister's talents. And he hadn't. But the council had used magic on the Secundus. That frightened him.

"Smart," Mole said, and Timo looked up in surprise. "She made sure she could pass their tests. And you've helped," Mole continued. "Council argues about you. They know about the magical pranks—some of them encourage them. But because you don't avoid all the traps, and often are hurt by them, the majority on council believe that even if you are like your sister, your magic is so weak that you can't affect the spells."

"You said the majority," Timo said. How by Gyda's star had Mole managed to listen in on the Mage Guild Council? "Who doesn't believe it?"

"Inigo," Mole said.

"Of course," Timo said. "He's behind Hestor's request."

"Yes," Mole agreed. "A worm like Hestor wouldn't have the courage to contact Warrior Guild on his own. Inigo doesn't believe you're what you seem to be."

"He cursed Rorik," Timo whispered. "Kara removed it."

Mole nodded. "I'm not surprised. He's ambitious. He's very obvious about that in council. And he hates that your mother—a woman—is Secundus over him. Blames your father for that."

"Is he to blame?" Timo asked.

"Probably," Timo said. "Rorik too."

"Rorik?" Timo asked, surprised. Rorik always followed his mother's direction—but she wasn't the first Secundus Rorik had appointed. Had Valerio Valendi engineered Rorik's ascendancy to Primus? He *had* cursed Santos, the previous Primus.

"Santos trusted Valendi," Mole said. "But the council at the time was divided—he felt he couldn't appoint him Secundus. Rorik was Valendi's suggestion."

"My father cursed Santos and had Rorik appoint him Secundus," Timo said. Even after decades as Primus, Rorik was weak. If Valerio Valendi had helped him become Primus he would have done whatever was asked of him. Including ignoring the sudden madness of the previous Primus. Now Rorik took direction from his mother. He leaned his head on his hand and sighed. "Knowing why Inigo hates me doesn't help me decide what to do."

"Come to Old Rillidi," Mole said.

"Now?" Timo asked. "I'm not sure."

Mole nodded. "You don't trust me."

"I don't *know* you," Timo said. "You claim to be a friend of Kara's but I've only met her once."

"And my name never came up." Mole grinned. "Sure, sure. You haven't stayed alive this long by trusting easily." Mole eased himself to his feet. "I've said what I came to say. No Assassin will take Hestor's contract and you will be welcome on Old Rillidi anytime." Mole peered out the door before slipping through it. "I'll come back as soon as I can." He winked at Timo just before he shut the door.

Timo sent a flash of mage mist to secure the door. He would be a lot more careful in the future. Not against Mole—he didn't trust him completely, but he believed he'd come on Kara's behalf and wouldn't hurt him. But Hestor and Inigo had tried to hire an Assassin. When Warrior Guild refused, they might try to hire someone else. Mole was proof that not everyone with the skills to kill him was Guild.

Two months. He had to stay alive for two months. Then he would go to Old Rillidi—he didn't really have another choice—but it would not be as a runaway. Even his mother wouldn't be able to stop Mage Guild from trying to kill him if he was a runaway.

ARABELLA GLARED AT Inigo's retreating back, plastering a smile on her face when he reached the door and turned to look at her.

"Was there something else, Master Mage?" she asked sweetly.

"Just wishing you a good day, Secundus," Inigo said. He tilted his head and left Rorik's sitting room.

Arabella wanted to throw something, preferably a spell that would kill that devious fiend. Her only consolation was that he was just as angry as she was.

"He used a spell on me," she hissed. "To try to make me speak the truth."

"Are you certain?" Rorik leaned close and peered at her. "He could be put to death for that."

"I'm sure," Arabella said. She drew in a deep breath, trying to calm herself. "I had already set a defensive spell. It was triggered by whatever mischief Inigo flung at me." He'd tried to hide his fury from her but he'd known his spell had been deflected.

"Shall I convene the council?" Rorik asked. "To try him?"

"No. He will deny it and ask for proof." She shook her head. "And none exists. It will be my word against his. He has enough council votes to win if we put it to a vote. We must do nothing." At least until Timo was her Journeyman. She should never have let him Apprentice to Rorik, but at the time it had seemed the safest thing to do. Inigo had just gained control of council, and of all of them he was the most suspicious of Kara Fonti's continued existence. It hadn't been long before he'd realized the truth and accused her of keeping secrets about the girl's magical talents. So she'd had Rorik take Timo on as his Apprentice. But it meant she'd had to keep her distance or risk even more scrutiny than she was already under.

"Do you really think Timo's accidents are a result of his clumsiness?" Rorik asked.

"No," Arabella said. "There are too many and they have been going on far too long. They are using my son's humiliation to shame me. But continuing to blame it on clumsiness lets them believe we don't know they are behind them."

"You should talk to the boy," Rorik said. "He should know that he's in danger."

"He's not in danger!" Arabella said. "They will not seriously hurt him. They wouldn't dare." They would—she thought they had already tried—but Timo had survived. It gave her hope that he had his sister's talents—unmagic that she would use against Inigo once Timo was her Journeyman.

"But—" Rorik began.

"I said no! You will not tell him anything." She smoothed a hand across her hair. "In a few months he will be ready for Journeyman status. This will all end then." It wouldn't end until Inigo was dead . . . which would be soon after Timo was under her control.

TIMO PRESSED HIS ear to the partially open door.

He'd caught sight of Inigo leaving Rorik's study. Inigo wanted him dead—what Mole had told him confirmed it—so he needed to know why the Council Mage was here.

What he'd overheard confirmed something else Mole had told him: Inigo was using magic on his mother. Worse—she knew but had no way to make him stop.

His mother could no longer offer him any protection. She couldn't even protect herself.

Mole had thought his mother had been smart in the way she'd fooled the council, but Timo wasn't so sure. He thought she was so intent on believing the lies she told herself that she was blind to the real truth.

Inigo wouldn't wait until he was old enough to become a Journeyman. He would try to kill Timo—he'd already been trying kill Timo—before then.

Timo stepped away from the door and returned to his room. He took a few moments to secure it, magically and physically, before he relaxed.

Would Mole come back to spy? Could he tell him he'd changed his mind? Timo could probably leave Mage Guild Island but gaining safety on Old Rillidi was a different matter.

"YOU TOLD HIM Inigo wants him dead?" Kara asked.

"Sure, sure," Mole said. "He already knew."

He was sitting across from her at the small table in her and Reo's cabin. Reo had taken the children to the main house and promised to return with Santos.

"The boy's smart," Mole continued. "It's not Gyda's luck that's kept him alive this long."

"You didn't tell us he was *already* in danger." Kara heard the panic in her voice and took a deep breath.

She glanced up to see Reo and Santos enter the cabin. Reo took one look at her and sat down beside her, wrapping his arm around her shoulder and pulling her into his warmth.

Santos pulled up another chair.

"Someone tried to contract an Assassin," Reo said. "Of course he's in danger. If they could have killed him themselves they wouldn't need to pay an Assassin."

"Warrior Guild hasn't given their answer yet?" She'd told Warrior Guild Primus Rualla that if they fulfilled a contract on Timo she would never clear their Guild Hall of magic again.

"No," Reo assured her. "They won't until they hear from us."

"Unless Inigo and Hestor can make Timo's death seem like an accident." Mole paused and looked at her. "Which will be difficult considering how good he is at avoiding the most dangerous spells. They'll wait for the Assassin."

"Will he change his mind?" Kara asked. "And come before he turns sixteen?" Mole had explained Timo's decision, but she didn't understand it. Runaway or not, Mage Guild would try to kill him once he joined them on Old Rillidi. Arabella Fonti didn't have enough control over the council to stop that, not when Inigo already wanted Timo dead.

"Maybe," Mole said. "He doesn't trust you, not yet—or me—and I can't blame him for that, but he *knows* he can't trust his mother. She expects Timo to be her Journeyman, which won't be a good thing for him."

"What?" Santos asked. "Mage Guild has never allowed a parent to formally teach their own child. How does she expect to get council approval?"

"She didn't seem concerned about that," Mole said.

"Does she know that Timo has unmagic?" Kara asked.

"She suspects," Mole replied.

"Maybe she's counting on Timo to help her control council," Kara said.

"It's risky," Santos replied. "The boy isn't trained."

"Is she desperate?" Reo asked. "Is Timo her last chance to beat Inigo? She might try anything."

"She still has Rorik," Santos said. "Even if Inigo can convince council to move against Arabella, most of them won't tolerate all-out war against both the Secundus and the Primus."

"That sounds right," Mole agreed. "The attacks against Timo, as well as the Assassin contract, have all been done by Inigo's Journeyman."

"So nothing out in the open," Santos said. "Inigo needs his name kept out of this—at least for now."

"We need to warn Timo," Kara said. "He's in more danger than he knows." She wanted Timo here now. It was the only place in all of Tregella where he'd be safe.

"Founders Day is in two weeks," Santos said. He glanced out the window before shaking his head and meeting Kara's gaze. "I think it's time the true Primus attended. I will, of course, require an entourage."

"One of whom will meet Timo," Kara added. "And convince him to leave with us."

"Arabella won't let him go without a fight," Reo said. He

gripped her hand and squeezed it. "Especially if she's been planning to use him to save herself."

"I've learned a lot about my talents since I last battled my mother," Kara said. "I'll manage her." Timo would get to choose—Kara would make sure of that—and what her mother wanted didn't matter.

Chapter 4

Timo shifted the stack of scrolls he held and eyed the door. He'd been able to stay inside Rorik's house for two days. Two days when he'd been reasonably safe from attack, safe from Hestor and Inigo. But now Rorik had signed these scrolls and they had to be delivered—*he* had to deliver them. And to the council! The last place Timo should go, knowing what he knew, knowing that Inigo wanted him dead.

His mother would be there. Could she keep him safe? Would she? She didn't even understand the danger he was in.

Timo hadn't seen her since he'd overheard her conversation with Rorik. Mole was convinced his mother had been protecting him from the council for years, and maybe she had, but that didn't mean she would continue to. Especially if the choice was between protecting her son or saving herself. He'd be wise to remember that she'd tried to kill her own daughter. That wasn't a mother he could rely on.

There were two traps that had been set for him, neither of which were particularly dangerous, so by the time he reached the hall leading to the Mage Council chambers, Timo was dishevelled and a couple of new bruises were starting to form, but he wasn't really hurt. Before he approached the clerk, he paused to re-order the scrolls he carried.

"Mage Guild Primus Rorik sent me," Timo said when the clerk finally raised his eyes to him. "I have documents to deliver to the council."

The clerk's eyes narrowed. "You're his Apprentice?"

"Yes," Timo replied. He leaned over to drop the scrolls onto the desk. "I'll just leave these here?"

"No," the clerk said. The smile he gave Timo had no hint of humour in it. "I'll let them know you're here." He waved his hand, and a puff of orange mage mist headed towards the door.

"But there's no need . . ." Timo's voice trailed off when a second, golden puff of mage mist raced from the door to the clerks' desk. A small bell that sat on the desktop rang once.

"Go right in," the clerk said. This time his smile held humour, but Timo was certain that *he* wasn't going to find anything to laugh about.

Timo stepped up to the door. Multiple threads of mage mist swirled around it, no doubt put in place by distrustful council members. He recognized his mother's purple and Mage Master Inigo's gold. And there, that pale blue colour. He'd been looking for that ever since he'd met Kara, ever since he'd understood that Rorik had been cursed. The door opened, and Timo had no choice but to enter.

The room was smaller than he'd expected—a room for working, not for show. Inigo sat at the head of a rectangular table, its wooden top scattered with scrolls and open ledgers. His mother sat to Inigo's right, her small frown of surprise disappearing almost as soon as it had appeared. She eyed him coolly, purple mage mist wafting around her head.

Another man, soft with middle-age, sat on Arabella's other side, and across from his mother, beside Inigo, a slightly thinner man of the same age stared at Timo with a bored expression. But the man on Inigo's left leaned over the table for a better view of the intruder. Younger than the rest, with blond hair and fine, almost pretty features, Timo didn't recognize him. But he did recognize the colour of his mage mist. The man straightened and with a flick of his wrist, a trail of pale blue mist slowly headed towards Timo. The blond Mage looked over at Inigo and nodded.

"Sorry to intrude, Secundus, Councillors," Timo said, trying to keep his voice calm and his eyes off of the mist that was now only a few feet from him. "Primus Rorik asked that I deliver these to you." He motioned with his chin to the scrolls he carried.

"Yes, of course," Inigo said. "You can set them on the table, we'll sort them out."

Timo took a step towards the table, towards the mage mist. They wouldn't kill him here, right in front of his mother, would they? He glanced at the spell, but it was complex, too complex for him to get a feel for any danger so quickly. His next step would put him in the middle of it.

"Good of Rorik to send his trusted Apprentice," Inigo said. "He must think highly of you since he has no Journeyman."

"Yes, sir," Timo said. Then he stepped into the mage mist, and his feet skidded out from under him. The scrolls flew into the air, and Timo landed on his back, his breath knocked out of him. It took him a few moments to regain it.

"Sorry," he said, scrambling to his knees, panting, scared to look up at them, especially his mother. He bent to gather the scrolls, reaching over to set each one on the table. Once they were all on the table, Timo slowly stood up, keeping his eyes on the scrolls in front of him. He heard a snicker, then his mother's voice.

"Faron," she snapped.

"Arabella is quite right," Inigo said. "We shouldn't laugh at another's misfortune. No doubt the boy will grow out of this clumsy stage." He paused. "In time."

"I do apologise," a smooth male voice said.

Timo lifted his eyes a fraction. The blond Mage didn't look even a little bit sorry.

"Poor Arabella," the man, Faron, continued. "I completely forgot that this . . . Apprentice of Rorik's is your son." He leaned back in his chair and smiled. "How very motherly of you to come to his defense."

Timo heard his mother's indrawn breath from where he stood. Why was it an insult to want to protect her child? And why wouldn't she even look his way? He risked a glance at the rest of the council and met Inigo's piercing gaze. Timo quickly looked at his feet, trying with all his might to supress a shudder.

He knew that Hestor loathed him but the depth of hatred in Inigo's eyes scared him. He quickly created a spell of protection and relaxed slightly when mauve mage mist enveloped him. He had his answer though. Inigo *would* dare to kill him here, in front of his mother. He thought Inigo would dare anything.

"He looks very much like his father, doesn't he?" another of the council members said, the bored one. "But with Arabella's colouring. Too bad his power isn't as strong."

"Yes, and much unexpected," Faron said. "It's almost unheard of for two such powerful Mages to produce a child with so little power."

"It does happen," Arabella said.

"So you keep telling us," Inigo replied. "No matter. You've carried out your Master's request, you may leave, Timo Valendi, Apprentice to Mage Guild Primus Rorik."

Timo nodded and backed away, all the way to the door. He didn't care if they all laughed at him, he didn't care if they knew he was terrified. The way Inigo had intoned his name and title had sounded far too much like the Founders Day Call to remember those who had died in the past year. As he hurried to Rorik's house, all Timo could do was pray to Gyda that Mole came for him soon. One man in that council chamber didn't believe that he was weak, didn't believe that he wasn't a threat. And he didn't believe he should let Timo live.

Once in his room, Timo spent a few hours reinforcing the safeguards he'd placed around it. When he'd done everything he could think of magically, he spent a few moments setting non-magical traps. Mole had told him that no Assassin would take the contract, but that didn't mean someone else wouldn't. He lay down on his bed and stared at the ceiling. How long could he barricade himself inside his room, inside this house?

He should have gone with Mole when he'd had the chance. It wouldn't matter to Inigo if Timo left as a runaway or as a Guildsman—he wanted Arabella Fonti's son dead.

Timo had never been off Mage Guild Island. Rorik and his mother had never even allowed him to step into one of the many small boats that dotted the underside of the island.

He got up and stood in front of his book shelf. There it was. Rorik had given it to him when he was young, before he'd found his magic. He'd learned how to read using this book, but it also had drawings—maps—of Rillidi. It wasn't accurate but it had the basics—which islands were connected by bridges and where the ferry docks were. Things he'd need to know in order to get safely to Old Rillidi.

He sat down at his desk and opened the book. He had no idea if Inigo knew Warrior Guild wasn't going to send an Assassin.

Mole might not return in time. Timo wasn't about to die waiting for him.

Timo wasn't going to pretend anymore. He couldn't afford to. On his visit to the council chambers and his encounter with Faron's spell, he could have walked right into his own death. He could not, *would not*, let that happen. From now on his goal was to stay alive long enough for either Mole to return for him or for him to leave on his own. And that meant he had to use every skill and talent he had available. It also meant he had to tell Rorik. His Master could not send him out into danger again.

"Master Rorik?" Timo tentatively stuck his head into Rorik's workroom. There was no sign of the Primus, but the work room was a mess. Scrolls and papers and books were scattered over every surface. Shelves lined every wall, leaving only tiny rectangles of light where the windows weren't fully covered by books stacked on the ledges. Mage mist swirled across everything. Mostly it was Rorik's tan colour but there were smatterings of purple and some of the dustiest stacks had a dark, grey-black tint to them. Timo had always kept well clear of those. Although the spells were old and almost faded they still felt threatening.

He sighed. He really should try to create some order in his Master's workroom. It was one of his duties as an Apprentice, after all, but he'd never been comfortable in this room. Generations of Mages had committed spells to the paper and books in this room, and to Timo it felt as though all that magic had saturated the air until he could hardly breathe. He shook his head and squared his shoulders. A deep breath told him that he was imagining things—the air was dusty but perfectly fine—so he set to work.

Two hours later and the work room was presentable. All except for two stacks of books on the top shelf of the book case that was the furthest from the door. He peered up at the shelf. Grey-black mage mist covered the books, almost obscuring the thick layer of dust. He dragged a chair over and climbed up, stretching to reach the books with the dusting cloth. The threat he felt emanating from the mage mist made him hesitate for a few moments, his hand hovering just out of range of the sluggish mage mist. He heard the door to the work room open.

"What in Gyda's name are you doing?" Rorik said from the doorway. "Get down from there!"

Timo almost tumbled as he stepped off the chair. "Sorry, Primus," he said. "I was just trying to dust the top shelf."

Rorik peered at him, and Timo took a step back, horrified to see a new spell swirling around the Mage Primus' head. A new *golden* spell.

"Do you feel all right?" Timo asked. "I mean . . ." He stopped, eyeing the open door.

"What do you see?" Rorik whispered. He flicked a hand, and tan mage mist flew to the door, closing it tight. "Come here, lad. I need to know what you see."

"So you do know," Timo said. "You and Mother, you both know." He stepped up to Rorik and studied the new curse.

"No," Rorik said. "It's too dangerous. We don't talk about it even between ourselves, but we suspect. *I* suspect. But I haven't felt well at all today, not since meeting with key members of the council." He sat down heavily behind his work table. "And now I suspect something else." He lifted tired eyes to Timo. "I've been cursed again, haven't I?"

Timo nodded.

"Do you know by whom?"

Timo nodded again, and Rorik rubbed a hand over his eyes and sighed. "Inigo?"

"Yes," Timo replied. He grabbed the chair he'd been standing on, dragged it in front of the table, and sat down. "He set the other curse on you—the one that Kara said was nasty when she removed it."

"Do you think you could remove this one?" Rorik asked. "It feels like it means me real harm."

Timo leaned over the table top and stared at the gold mage mist that circled Rorik's head. He reached out a hand and tentatively poked at the mist. It recoiled from his touch slightly and then it started to circle faster.

"I don't know," Timo said. "I don't have any experience doing this." Because no one would even acknowledge that he had unmagic, he wanted to shout, so of course he didn't know how to properly use it. "But it feels like a malicious spell."

"Yes." Rorik gave him a half smile. "It feels like a malicious spell from this side as well." He sat back in his chair. "Perhaps I'll see how I feel in a few days. Maybe I'll recover." Rorik didn't seem very hopeful, and Timo couldn't blame him.

Rorik pulled his journal over to him and picked up a pencil. "Was there anything else?" he asked.

Timo looked down at his hands and then met his teacher's gaze. "Yes. Please don't send me on any errands for a while. It's not safe for me outside of your quarters."

Rorik stared at him for a few seconds. "No, I suppose it isn't," he said quietly. "Not when they're brazen enough to curse me. You're to stay inside my walls until Founders Day. As your Master, I order you."

Timo nodded and stood to leave. He was two steps from the door when he turned around to face Rorik. "Those books up on the top shelf, the ones I was going to dust. Whose were they?"

Rorik looked up towards the shelf in question. "I think you already know, lad. They belonged to your father."

Timo nodded and left the room. He had known, of course, but he'd wanted it not to be true. Sixteen years after his death, Valerio Valendi's mage mist still felt so menacing that his son didn't even want to touch it. What did that say about the man who had fathered him? What did it say about *him*? He'd inherited his magical abilities from his parents—had he inherited their ruthlessness and cruelty?

No. He would not become like his mother—or worse—his father. He would escape to Old Rillidi and live with Kara and his half-brother Giona and Santos Nimali. But Santos had mentored Valerio Valendi. Had his father been taught to be so cruel by his master?

Timo shook his head. Santos had been cursed by his own Journeyman. If he'd taught Valerio Valendi to be evil, he would have expected that, been prepared for it. Santos had trusted his student, too much as it turned out, but he had trusted him.

"I'm TELLING YOU that it's not natural."

"So you keep saying," Arabella said. She poured more tea into Rorik's cup and frowned when he closed his eyes and pressed his hands against his temple.

"The Healer could not help," Rorik said. He opened his eyes and stared down at his cup.

"Then try another Healer," Arabella said. "Surely there's at least one who is an expert at getting rid of headaches."

"Yes, the one I went to." Rorik looked up and met her eyes, and Arabella shrank from the pain she saw there. "She couldn't help because it's not natural."

"There's no proof."

"Not that *you* would believe," Rorik said. "But Timo is my Apprentice."

"Stop it!" Arabella said. "Don't you dare involve my son."

"He saw it," Rorik mumbled, as though he was talking to himself. "I didn't have to ask—he saw it, and it startled him. Scared him, even. Inigo cursed me."

"Shhh, quiet," Arabella said. "You don't know that. And you can't say things like that here. This room isn't shielded."

"Who else could it be?" Rorik asked. "Inigo has always wanted more than the council—it seems he's tired of waiting."

Arabella shook her head and sipped her tea. If Inigo wanted to be elevated from council he would target her—not Rorik. She set her cup into its saucer. Rorik was weak; Inigo knew that. With the right incentive, Rorik could be persuaded to select Inigo as Secundus if her position were to become . . . vacant. She, on the other hand, would never choose Inigo for anything. He knew that too.

"I fail to see how targeting you would benefit Inigo," she said.

"Make sure you are shielded," Rorik said. "And Timo . . ."

"What about my son?"

"We should warn him," Rorik said. "Or better yet send him away. He's in danger."

"Send him where?" She met Rorik's gaze.

"There's one place where he'd be safe," Rorik said. "One place we've never been able to attack successfully."

"What? No! I will not send him there," Arabella said. She couldn't believe Rorik was even suggesting it—not after all these years of trying to destroy them. "I forbid you to say anything to him. The boy belongs here—as my Journeyman—not on some pile of rocks with his witch of a sister and the mad mage."

"They can keep him safe," Rorik said. "They may be the only ones who can."

Arabella followed his gaze to his hands. To her horror they were trembling. She looked up and studied Rorik's face. She'd always thought of him as a Mage in his prime but now he looked broken and old. Perhaps he *was* seriously ill, too far gone for the Healers to help.

She leaned back in her chair, worried. She'd assumed Rorik would live for many years yet, that there was plenty of time for Timo to be her Journeyman and then become a full Mage. It would only make sense that she would appoint him as Secundus when she became Primus, even though he was her son.

But if Rorik died now . . . Who could she trust? She closed her eyes and breathed out. There was no one. Inigo controlled the council. There may be a few Mages who weren't as loyal to Inigo as they professed, but that didn't mean she could trust them.

She'd always thought she'd manipulated Rorik into choosing her as Secundus, but she'd be grateful if she had someone as trustworthy as she'd been. Rorik had wondered if he hadn't made a mistake by not having a Journeyman and perhaps another Apprentice. Now she wondered if she hadn't made an even bigger one. Inigo hated Timo almost as much as he hated her. She'd been counting on his unmagic to protect them both, but who knew how strong and reliable that was?

If . . . she looked at Rorik . . . *when* Rorik died she would have no political allies. Was it too late? There was no one on council she could cultivate, and she wouldn't be able to offer newly minted Mages anything. There were a few Apprentices ready to move to Journeyman. Could she take one on? Would they become her ally or another threat?

Maybe the girl—the one who had helped Timo get into the Hall of Records. What was her name? Ah, yes. Barra Eska. She was Inigo's Apprentice. It might be a delicate matter to gain her trust, but she could always appeal to her as a woman, couldn't she? Would the girl be loyal to her, or had she already been poisoned by Inigo?

Hours after Rorik left, Arabella remained in her sitting room. She had to try to cultivate allies as soon as possible. When Rorik died she would be alone.

REO SET THE map on the table, and Kara leaned over his shoulder to look at it.

"We should wait until dusk," Reo said. "Santos will spell us invisible but a boat carrying all of us will produce a noticeable wake." He turned to her. "Have you talked to Giona?"

"Yes," Kara said. "I'll reinforce the barriers before I go. He's adding a spell to notify him if anyone uses magic against it."

"I still don't like risking both you and Santos," Reo said. "You're his heir."

"And the children are mine," Kara said. Years ago Santos had discovered that Kara was related to him through her mother. Only a living heir ensured that Old Rillidi Island remained free from the guilds. "He's my brother."

She looked down and met Reo's eyes. His lips softened into a sad smile, and she knew he agreed.

"My skills will be needed," she added.

"I know," he said. "But I don't have to like it." Reo sighed and turned back to the map.

"Can we make sure Timo's there?" Kara asked. "Mole's contacts say he hasn't been outside of Rorik's quarters in almost a week."

"I'll tell him," Mole said. "Next time I see him."

He lounged on the opposite side of the table, and Kara gritted her teeth and stifled a retort. He seemed too relaxed—and so unconcerned about this trip to Mage Guild Island that she wanted to slap him.

Mole had been stealing onto Mage Guild Island for over a year without being noticed but Kara wanted—*needed*—them all ready for anything. Until Timo was safe she'd be uneasy. Mole's description of her brother's life made her desperate to help him.

"Kara, you'll be with me. Once I enter the Guild Hall, all eyes will be on me," Santos said.

Kara wanted to slap him too, for grinning like he was a kid going on a great adventure. Her brother's life was at stake!

"We'll leave Mole invisible and hope that Timo will be able to see him," Reo said.

"I can," Kara said. To her, someone with an invisibility spell was simply covered in mage mist. "We have to assume he can too."

Santos was going to proclaim himself—truthfully—as the Mage Guild Primus and insist on giving the greeting. He didn't really expect to be allowed to speak but very few people outside of the Mage Guild Council knew he was still Primus. His announcement would cause an uproar.

"Once Mole has Timo we'll need to form up," Reo said. "As

small a group as possible for Kara to shield. Then we make our way back to the boat and home."

"You don't expect fighting," Kara said. She'd been told that it would be quick and secretive. No one would realize Timo was gone until he was safely away.

"There will be verbal fighting," Santos said. "I don't expect magic to be used. We'll be so covered in defenses that nothing will be able to touch us anyway." Santos looked across the table and met her gaze. "I don't think anyone in this room cares if Mage Guild destroys itself."

"Not once Timo's out," Reo said. Then he looked over his shoulder at Kara. "Unless you want us to warn your mother?"

"No." Kara shook her head. "My mother made her choices long ago. I don't owe her anything." Nor would Arabella Fonti thank her daughter for her trouble, Kara thought darkly. She probably wouldn't even miss Timo once he was gone.

"That's it. We all know what to expect," Reo said. "In two days, Mole will talk to Timo, and in five days, we'll be on Mage Guild Island."

"And in six days, we'll be home with Timo," Mole said, and Kara hoped he was right.

Chapter 5

FOUNDERS DAY WAS less than a week away, and Timo hadn't heard from Mole. He hadn't said when he'd return so it was up to Timo to get himself to Old Rillidi. He hoped Kara really did want him there.

As he shuffled out of his workroom into the long hallway, he glanced towards Rorik's workroom door. It was closed, as it always was these days, but he knew the Primus wasn't working. The man could only stand for a few minutes at a time anymore—his health had failed that quickly.

The door to the workroom suddenly opened, and Timo met his mother's frown as she exited the room.

"Get your Master some broth," she said as she strode down the hallway towards him.

"He can't swallow it," Timo whispered. "He chokes."

His mother stood in front him, her frown deepening as she stared at him. "Then do something else useful," she finally said. "I'll be at home if anything . . . happens."

"Yes, Donna," Timo said. He knew she meant if Rorik died. The Healer hadn't been able to do much for the man except keep him comfortable, and now he couldn't even do that. Rorik was in constant pain and each breath was a struggle.

His mother strode down the hallway to the door that led outside without a single glance at him.

What had she meant about him doing something useful? Was

that a request for him to try to remove the spell? Did she know that Rorik was cursed? Rorik could barely speak—soon he would no longer be able to ask Timo for help. Had she been urging him to use his unmagic?

If he did nothing, Rorik would be dead in a few hours, a day or two at the most. The man wouldn't live to see Founders Day, not at the rate he'd been deteriorating. If Timo was to have any chance to save him, he'd have to do it now.

He pushed open the door to Rorik's workroom and entered. One small mage light hovered overhead, but Timo didn't need that light to see into the room. The hunched figure of Rorik was illuminated by a thick swathe of gold mage mist. It lazily circled his neck and upper chest, throwing his face into stark relief. The man's eyes had sunk into their sockets, and his once robust face was gaunt and etched with pain.

"Arabella?" Rorik whispered. He started to turn his head but the small movement sent him into a convulsion. He doubled over in his chair, coughing and gasping for breath.

"No, it's me," Timo said. He sidled over to stand in front of the man. "I came to see if there was anything you needed, anything I could do to help."

"Timo." Rorik's voice was barely audible, and one papery hand lifted off his lap for a moment before it dropped back down in defeat.

"I want to try," Timo said, and Rorik's head came up. Timo met his watery eyes. "I don't know what to do, but I want to try, if you'll let me."

Rorik sighed softly, and his chin dropped onto his chest. "Yes." The word was spoken so quietly that Timo had to lean over to hear it.

"Then may Gyda guide me," Timo said. He straightened up and looked around the room. Was there anything he needed? Anything that would help him? He shook his head. Kara hadn't needed anything when she'd removed Rorik's curses almost two years ago, but she had walked around Rorik studying and testing the spells. Would that help him?

He stood behind Rorik. The mage mist seemed just a bit thinner at the back of his neck. He poked at it with a finger, and the gold mist eddied away from him. He shivered. The closer he came the more strongly he felt the malevolence of the spell.

Timo peered at it. Was the mist moving faster? He waved at it with his hand. Rorik grunted, and surprised, Timo leaned away. The mist was definitely moving faster. He stepped in front of Rorik and met the Mage's pain shrouded eyes. The Primus blinked once then closed his eyes, his mouth set in a firm line.

All right. Rorik wanted him to proceed.

Timo nervously watched the mage mist. It circled Rorik's neck and chest so quickly that he could no longer tell where it was thinner. Tentatively he reached his right hand towards the mage mist, which collapsed away from him, tightening around Rorik's neck. Timo snatched his hand back but the gold mist continued to contract.

Rorik choked and his eyes flew open. Weak hands scrabbled at his neck. His eyes met Timo's, the panic in them igniting Timo's fear. Rorik opened his mouth and gasped, futilely trying to suck in a breath.

Panicked, Timo pushed his hand into the mage mist—through it—until he touched Rorik's neck. Where his hand met the mage mist his skin felt cool and damp, but the gold mist continued to circle Rorik's neck, sweeping over his hand. He felt pressure as the mist constricted even more tightly around Rorik's neck. He pulled his hand off of the Primus' neck, hoping that he could lift the mage mist, but the mist parted to let his hand pass through and continued tightening around Rorik's neck. Timo tried to *grab* the mist but there was nothing to grasp, nothing solid to hold on to.

Rorik's head slumped to his chest, and Timo stared in horror. The man was dying. Frantically, Timo placed his hands around Rorik's neck and tried take the force of the mist on his hands but it slid beneath his fingers.

"Gyda," he whispered hoarsely. "Don't let him die, please, let me help him." The spell felt even more ominous now, clammy and cold where it touched his skin. Concentrating, Timo tried to *force* the spell away. It wavered for a second, and he redoubled his efforts.

"Go away," he screamed, willing the spell to leave. It shimmered, briefly, but then it collapsed until it was one, single, tight band of gold circling Rorik's neck.

"No, no, no," Timo moaned when he saw the way the spell now bit into Rorik's skin. It tightened until a thin line of red appeared beneath the gold. Rorik sagged forward and slid off the chair onto the floor. Timo slid down beside him, weeping.

"I'm so sorry," he said to his Master. "I didn't know how to do it." Angry, Timo lifted Rorik's head up and looked into his lifeless eyes. "You were my teacher but neither you nor my mother wanted to help me learn." He gently settled Rorik's head down on his chest. "And you wouldn't let me get help from my sister, the only person who could teach me."

Timo drew his knees up under his chest and set his chin on top of them. He should do something, tell someone, but he felt numb. Why couldn't Mole have come to take him away before he'd killed Rorik? He wiped the tears from his cheeks and breathed in deeply. He had no time to feel sorry for himself. Rorik was dead, in part because of him, and there were things he must do. Tell his mother, for one.

Timo started to rise but stopped when something moved.

"Rorik?" he asked. But it wasn't Rorik's movement he'd noticed—it was the mage mist that had killed him. Slowly it unwound from Rorik's neck and snaked across the room towards the door.

Timo scrambled to his feet. "What in Gyda's name . . ." He followed the mage mist through the workroom door and out into the hallway. The spell was still active—there must be a second part to it. Inigo must have embedded an alert, something that would notify him when Rorik was dead. Timo stopped, unable to take a breath. Would the alert tell Inigo that the spell had been tampered with? That someone had tried to remove it? Timo watched the spell seep under the door and out of Rorik's house. He had to find his mother.

"Is Rorik dead?" Arabella Fonti asked.

She was sitting in her workroom, reading from a journal. She'd barely looked up when Annya had announced him.

"Yes, Mother," Timo said. "Just now." He paused. "I . . ."

His mother looked at him now, her dark eyes boring into him. "You what," she said. "Did you do something? I must know."

"I," Timo started again. He stopped and stared down at his feet. "I tried to help him."

"No," his mother said. She stood up and the journal fell to the floor with a thud. "How could you? After all these years, how could you expose yourself, *expose me*, in this way?" She stood in front of him.

"How could I?" Timo replied, angry now. He stared into her face, inches away from his own. "He was dying! You're the one who told me I should do something useful. I thought you meant . . ."

"I never would have meant that!" Arabella said. She stepped back. "How could you even think that?"

"But he was dying," Timo said, his voice faltering.

"Yes," Arabella said, more calmly. She paced a few steps in front of him, clearly under control now. "He was dying. He needed no interference from you."

"I was trying to help." And he had been, no matter the result.

"But you didn't, did you? No, all you've done is complicate things." Arabella turned and stared at him, her arms crossed over her chest. "You've forced me into a position I never wanted to be in." Her lips tightened. "Rorik told me it was Inigo."

"You knew!" Timo said. "You knew that Rorik had been cursed and you did nothing!"

"I *suspected*," she corrected him. "I only knew what Rorik had been told by you. Without a way to *prove* he was cursed or who cursed him, there was nothing for me to do."

"It was Inigo," Timo said, and his mother nodded. "And . . ." his voice faltered.

"And what?" Arabella demanded. "I must know everything."

"I think he set a spell to notify him," Timo paused to take in a deep breath. "I think it might have been triggered because I tampered with the original spell."

"Worse and worse," Arabella said. "Of course it was Inigo, but we still have no proof. Who to tell?"

"Not Faron," Timo blurted out.

His mother turned to stare at him coldly, and he faltered a moment. "He cursed Rorik himself. Kara removed his spell."

"Faron." Arabella nodded. "He would be part of this. The man will do anything to gain power."

And you haven't? Timo wanted to shout at his mother. *You left one child behind and bore another in order to tie yourself to a man—all in pursuit of power.*

"I am still Secundus," Arabella continued. "I have the upper hand, no matter that Inigo controls the council. He cannot strip me of my position. It's mine for life until I become Primus."

"What about Santos Nimali?" Timo said. "He's the true Primus."

"Nimali doesn't want it," Arabella said. "I actually think he's still a bit mad but he might support me. I want the title of Primus—I would be the first woman Primus in generations." She looked at him. "You must run away."

She turned and started pacing again, and Timo thought she'd already forgotten that he was her son. Now he was just a game piece to be moved to her advantage.

"Yes." Arabella turned and flashed him a smile full of danger. "You will run, and so Inigo does not think I know what he did, I will blame you for Rorik's death."

"But I . . . ," Timo started to say that he didn't kill Rorik, but he *had* killed him. He'd been trying to help, but that didn't matter. He'd killed the Mage Guild Primus. "Where will I go?" He wished again that Mole had come for him already.

"You'll find your way to Old Rillidi," Arabella said. "Once you're there you can convince them to support me as Primus." She nodded. "Santos Nimali's support will still hold weight with some Mages. Inigo will not risk alienating those he does not yet control."

ARABELLA HAD TOLD him to make his way to Old Rillidi, but she hadn't told him *how*. He paced his mother's workroom. She'd left a few minutes ago, giving Annya instructions to tell anyone that she'd been out when Timo came to advise her of Rorik's death. Timo was to wait a few more minutes and then leave. But how? He had no idea how to get off of Mage Guild Island—or how to make his way to Old Rillidi.

His mother's Server hovered close to the door, her face a mask of calm. Timo thought of Mole's remark that the Server Guild was unhappy. Did that include Annya? He met her eyes. Yes, that included Annya.

"Annya," Timo said. "I know I have no right to ask." His heart fell when Annya frowned. "But I need to get away. It doesn't really matter where I go right now, I just need to get off Mage Guild Island."

Still frowning, the Server stared at him for a moment. Finally, she nodded.

"You were always kind to me," she said. "And Donna Arabella?

No matter how mean she was to me, she was always worse to you."

"Why do you stay?" Timo asked. He had no choice, but surely Server Guild would place Annya somewhere else if she asked? He was startled when she grinned.

"You think Mage Guild is the only Guild with politics? This position assures me of a fine retirement within Server Guild." Her smile faltered. "If I live long enough. Come," she grabbed Timo's arm. "Servers have been coming every day to prepare for Founders Day. The man who's in charge owes me a favour."

ARABELLA TOOK A deep breath and entered the council chamber. She'd been to her home—ostensibly to receive the notice of Rorik's death—and had immediately rushed to Rorik's house. It was what the others would expect her to do—but she'd also done a few things they wouldn't expect. Then she'd come directly to the council.

"I have terrible news," she said. She pushed a stray hair off her face and tried to look shocked.

Inigo and Faron, their heads bent together, looked up at her with blank looks. A few other councillors set aside whatever ledgers they'd been reading.

"Secundus," Inigo said, rising and coming to stand in front of her. "What is it?"

"Primus Rorik is dead." She hung her head. "I fear that his Apprentice had a hand in it."

"Primus Rorik has been progressively ill for some time," Castio said. "Are you sure the Apprentice is to blame?"

"He may be my son but he has never appreciated the opportunities I have provided him," Arabella said. "Inigo, he has used your own Apprentice and Journeyman for his own gains. I believe he may have tried to force Rorik to do something similar. When the Primus refused, it's possible the boy poisoned him."

"Poison! Are you sure?" Inigo asked. He exchanged a look with Faron, and Arabella knew they were both party to this.

"I can't be certain," Arabella said. "But I went to check on Rorik as soon as I heard the awful news. He is dead, and there were some potions near him. A Healer might be able to say what they are, but the Apprentice does not have enough talent to kill any other way."

"I must see," Inigo said. "Castio, contact a Healer, one who is a master at potions. Better yet, find the one who has been treating Primus Rorik. He will know if these are medicines he prescribed to help or something someone else has employed to do harm."

Castio frowned but he left on his errand. That one, Arabella thought. She'd disregarded him as an ally because he never seemed interested in choosing a side—but he had not liked that Inigo had sent him on an errand.

Inigo took her arm and escorted her out into the hallway. She smiled gratefully and leaned on him as he steered them towards Rorik's house, Faron and a handful of other councillors trailing them.

Inigo's Journeyman, Hestor, stepped away from a wall and fell in behind them. Arabella glanced at him, and her eyes tightened when a small sneer flitted across his face.

Hestor had interfered with her plans to talk to the Eska girl. Now she knew it was deliberate. Had he done it on Inigo's orders?

It didn't matter. Once she had Santos' support, she would wipe that sneer off Hestor's face. It would be humiliating to accept Santos' help—to accept *Kara Fonti's* help—but she would do it to remain in power. Just a few years—that was all she needed—then Santos would return to being nothing and she would appoint her own Secundus. And during those few years, she would have every council Mage trying to please *her*, trying to secure *her* trust in order to become Secundus.

Sprawled on the floor, his face a mask of pain, Rorik was just as she'd left him. The group huddled by the door to the workroom.

Inigo stepped into the room and walked around Rorik before taking a bottle from the desk and sniffing it. "It seems harmless," he said. He picked up another bottle, one Arabella had brought from her own workroom and set amongst the remedies. This time he grimaced and quickly stoppered the bottle. He turned to Arabella. "I fear you may be right and the Apprentice is involved."

She hung her head. "I am deeply saddened that I must agree."

"Where is your son?" Inigo demanded.

Arabella looked up and met his gaze. "I do not know. He delivered the news of Rorik's death to my Server while I was out. He was not at my home when I returned. Nor was he here when I came to see to Rorik."

"You've always protected him," Inigo said. "I don't believe you have given up on him."

"He's betrayed the trust of his Master," Arabella said. "Why would I want to protect such a boy?"

"And yet he is not here," Inigo said. "Hestor, contact the guards. The brat has so little magic he can't have gotten far."

Hestor raced from the room, and Arabella looked from Inigo to Faron. She knew Inigo didn't believe her—his curse had killed Rorik—but did Faron know?

"We will need to convene the council," Arabella said. "And discuss this further. I will stay until the Healer comes."

"As will I," Inigo said. He nodded to Faron, who turned and gestured to those peering into the room from the hallway. Faron closed the door and leaned on it.

"Faron will make sure we are not disturbed," Inigo said. He looked over at Rorik. "It does not look like a pleasant death."

"Betrayal never is," Arabella said. She met Inigo's narrowed eyes and shrugged. "To think he sheltered the boy for so many years. One can only hope he never knew who had betrayed him in the end."

"But you are certain?" Inigo asked.

"Very," Arabella replied. "I will not fall to the same betrayer as Rorik." She'd already covered herself with the most powerful protective spells she knew—Inigo would *not* be able to curse her. "From this day on Timo Valendi is no longer my son." She glanced at Faron and caught a smug smile on his face. It vanished as soon as she looked at him, but it was enough to convince her that he knew Inigo had cursed Rorik.

"It must trouble you," Inigo said. "To have only two children and have them both turn on you. It makes me wonder . . ."

"Wonder about what?" Arabella asked. "I did not raise my first child and Timo has been under Rorik's care longer than he was under mine. You cannot possibly blame me."

"Not blame," Inigo said. "But your children had different fathers, so one must think that there is a streak . . . of instability . . . in your bloodline."

Arabella sucked in a breath, and then let it out slowly. "Children of Mages are often unpredictable. When they find their talent—*if* they find a talent—as well as the strength of magic they can wield—these cannot be predicted. Why else do we test them for years?" Inigo may not have fathered an untalented child, but others on the Council had.

TIMO WHISPERED A spell, and mauve mage mist settled over his face. He hefted his small pack onto his back. Now he was ready. Annya glanced at him, and her eyes widened in surprise, then she nodded. Despite his fear, Timo felt a surge of satisfaction at her approval. She gestured towards the hallway. A line of Servers shuffled down it, their voices hushed as they chatted about their plans for the evening or the past day's work.

Timo stepped out into the hallway and immediately bent down and pretended to fuss with the sturdy work boot Annya had provided him. Along with the clothes, and now his own magical disguise, he should pass for a Server. After a moment, he straightened up, and with his heart pounding, he joined the line for the ferry that would take him off the island.

Soon the gates to the ferry dock came into view—along with the Guildsmen who manned them. Always secretive, Mage Guild had strict rules about who was allowed on their island—overnight stays were discouraged for anyone not Mage Guild—and that included day labourers. Every single one of the Servers who had arrived this morning had to be counted when they left. If the numbers didn't match, a Mage would be called to investigate.

Annya had said he should not worry, that a favour was owed to her, but Timo still had to force himself to stay calm as he slowly shuffled towards the front of the line. Finally, he stood in front of a stern-faced Guildsman. The Server Guild crest was sewn onto his shirt with what looked like real silver thread.

As Annya had instructed, Timo caught the man's eye and then deliberately looked down at his hands. He made the signal Annya had shown him, and after a brief pause, the Guildsman grunted and waved him through. Timo hurried past him down a short walkway. A fresh breeze cooled the sweat that dampened his neck, and he breathed in salty air.

MOST OF THE passengers looked ahead, towards their destination, but Timo couldn't keep from looking behind, staring at the only land he'd ever set foot on as the ferry drew further and further away from Mage Guild Island. Mage mist swirled around the vessel, the magic drawing him to safety.

He'd been to the underside of the island, and of course, he knew that it floated, but he was still awed by the enormous mass that hovered above the water. It was dusk, and here and there lights flickered on as darkness enveloped the buildings. The mage mist was beautiful! Rainbows of illuminated mist swirled around the towers and houses, bathing almost all of Mage Guild Island in soft strands of light.

Then he realized that every single wisp of mist was a spell, and he shuddered. How many of those spells were actually curses? How often did Mages use their magic against one another, like Inigo had used his against Rorik? No wonder the council wanted Kara dead, no wonder his mother had refused to acknowledge his unmagic. He and his sister could tell who was being cursed, and what was worse for the Mages, they could tell *who* had laid the spell. They could reveal the treachery of a ruthless and ambitious man like Inigo with a single glance.

The ferry jerked and slowed, and nervous, Timo looked ahead. Arts Guild Island also glittered with light. Mage lights lined the dock and the street leading from it, and the land gave off its own muted glow of mage mist. Like all islands except Old Rillidi, this too was created by magic. What was on the island, however, was not, and the flickering light of torches cast shadows across the faces of buildings.

Timo had assumed they were heading for Server Guild Island when he'd boarded the ferry but overheard that their destination was Arts Guild. The group of Servers closest to him planned on enjoying themselves for a few hours before heading back at dawn to finish their work preparing for Mage Guild Founders Day.

The crush of Servers pushed towards the front of the ferry, carrying Timo along with them, their excited chattering lifting his mood.

He was here! He was finally off Mage Guild Island. He took a deep breath and felt his shoulders relax.

Arts Guild was the most informal of the guilds, from what Timo knew, although in truth he'd never met an Arts Guildsmen.

Now he planned to lose himself in the crowd visiting Arts Guild Island. Singers, actors, dancers, jugglers, and prostitutes—so he'd overheard—all performed nightly. Guildsmen from all across Tregella came to Arts Guild. Strangers were the norm and rooms could be rented with little explanation required.

TRYING TO LOOK like he belonged, Timo picked his way through the crush of people. Night had fallen hours ago, and the streets, instead of emptying, were even more crowded. The crowd surged to one side, and nearby voices rose in wonder. Timo automatically looked ahead. In a space between buildings, a trio of tumblers somersaulted through hoops that were ablaze with flame. A woman dove head first through two hoops and hit the ground and rolled. The crowd cheered as she danced back up onto her feet.

"Hey." Someone tried to drag his pack from his shoulder, and Timo clutched it to his chest. He scanned the crowd but no one seemed to be paying particular attention to him. It was the third time someone had tried to rob him. He settled his pack under his arm after making sure that the flap was tied closed. It was the third time that he'd *noticed* someone trying to rob him. He'd checked his pack earlier—the string he tied the flap closed with had been half undone. Mole would probably have caught the would-be thief, but Timo hadn't felt a thing. But no one would actually try to steal from Mole, not if they watched him for a few moments. Timo wished he looked as capable and dangerous as Mole—it would save him some trouble.

Besides a few guilders, the pack only contained his clothes and a small journal. But they marked him as a Mage Apprentice, so losing them to a thief could compromise his disguise. He needed to stay dressed as a Server until he reached Old Rillidi. Timo glanced around before quickly muttering a spell. A puff of mage mist settled around his pack. That should keep the thieves away.

Half an hour later he'd left the largest crowds behind him. He studied a small sign above a brightly lit door. He had to assume that the picture of a cot tucked into one corner of the sign, beside the mug of ale, meant that there were rooms to let. He pushed the door open and entered a small vestibule. An older woman with a Server patch on her shirt stood behind a counter. A noisy rumble came from the left, where a door no doubt led to a tavern. Across from the woman was a narrow set of stairs.

"Can I help you?" the woman said. She looked up and smiled. "A fellow Guildsman. Are you looking for a meal or a room?"

"Both," Timo said. "A private room, if you have one." He didn't dare share with anyone in case he said or did something to give himself away.

"A private room?" The woman studied him for a moment, taking in his rough clothes and small pack.

"With a lock," Timo added. "I'm about to start my Journeyman placement, and my new Master wants me to get a taste of Arts Guild." He smiled, hoping she didn't see how nervous he was. "He wants me to experience excellent service."

The woman nodded. "You've come to the right place for excellent service. We're known for it. And you won't find a cleaner establishment in all of Tregella. How long are you staying?"

"My Master suggested four days," Timo said. He untied his pack and reached in and pulled out three guilders. "But he only gave me this much to cover food and lodging."

The woman leaned over the counter and frowned down at his outstretched palm. She sighed and nodded. "Four nights plus two meals a day," she said. "It's not one of my best rooms but it's big enough for you."

Timo placed the coins on the counter, and she scooped them up before she reached under the counter and pulled out a few items.

"Here's the key. And a token for your meals." She dropped a metal key and a greasy, carved, wooden cylinder on the counter. "Don't lose them, you won't get more. The room's at the top of the second set of stairs." She nodded her head towards the tavern door. "Best get supper first. Kitchen shuts down when the food's gone, and it won't last much longer tonight."

Timo grabbed the key and the token. "Thank you. I'm sure my stay will be one I remember always." He nodded and headed for the tavern.

The air inside the tavern smelled of smoke, old grease, and unwashed bodies. He sat at the empty end of a long table, cautiously waving his token at the Server. She set a pitcher of ale down in front of a group of stocky men and came over and stood in front of him.

"All's we got left is fish stew," the Server said. "And bread."

"Thank you," Timo said. "And an ale, if you please." As he waited for his meal, he surveyed the other guests, happy enough to have found a place to stay. They were noisy, and he thought there might be a fight or two before the night was over, but no one did more than glance at him. And no one looked like Mage Guild. When his meal arrived, he ate quickly. The stew was at least filling. Not up to Mage Primus Rorik's standards, but he'd been the most important Mage in Tregella—he could afford the best. Timo could not.

As he passed from the tavern to the stairs, Timo nodded to the Server who'd rented him his room. A mage light lit the second flight of stairs, which ended at a locked door. He fit his key into it and pushed the door inward. The light from the stairs illuminated a small lamp and flint beside the door, and despite Timo's lack of practice with a flint, the lamp soon sputtered to life.

He closed the door and looked around the tiny room. The narrow bed was tucked under the eaves and a dormer window glowed with the light from the streets. He dropped his pack on the bed and crouched by the window.

The Server had been truthful—the room was clean. And private. He put the key and the token on the window sill and smiled. He doubted she could rent it out to anyone other than an inexperienced Apprentice, though. He paused, his smile faltering. Except he had nothing to compare it with. He'd grown up living with two of the most powerful people in Tregella. He had no idea how other Guildsmen lived or what their homes looked like. Maybe they would consider this small, private room extravagant.

Timo stared out across the rooftops of Arts Guild Island. He would explore the island tomorrow and look for the safest way to Old Rillidi and the protection of his sister. He only hoped that now that Rorik was dead and his mother was blaming *him* he could find a way there.

He frowned. He knew he wasn't the true cause of Rorik's death—he would not have lived even if Timo hadn't interfered. Inigo's spell was meant to kill him—*had* been killing him. And his mother was right, the only thing Timo's interference had done was put himself in more danger.

Chapter 6

"THAT'S ALL FOR tonight, Annya," Arabella said.

"Yes, Secundus." The Server took the empty tea cup to the kitchen.

A few minutes later, Arabella heard the door that led down to the corridors close. She waved a hand, and the lock clicked. It wasn't quite midnight. Early for her to send Annya away, but Arabella hadn't had any visitors—didn't *expect* any visitors—not since Rorik's death.

And that troubled her.

Her attempts to talk to the Eska girl had been thwarted by Hestor, and a message she was certain was received by Castio had been ignored. She hadn't bothered to try to contact the rest of council. Inigo controlled them.

She was still Secundus, although no one else seemed to care. The council meeting to discuss Rorik's death had devolved into an attempt by Inigo to take control of Mage Guild. Arabella had thought she'd retained her power, but she may have been wrong. If so, it could be a costly mistake.

Absently, she removed all of her defensive spells.

She could barricade herself in her workroom—it was the most easily defended room in her house—but to what end? Even if Timo succeeded in reaching Old Rillidi he still had to convince Kara Fonti and Santos Nimali to come to her aid. She wasn't even certain Timo would even go there, let alone plead on her behalf.

She knew what she would do. She would stay as far away from the political upheavals of Mage Guild as possible. But perhaps that's why she was here, alone. She'd never risked herself for anyone—not even her children.

She didn't expect rescue and her options were exhausted.

She might be able to reach Old Rillidi herself. She grimaced. She would not run away from the guild she'd given her life and talents to. Nor would she beg those she'd tried to harm for a safe haven. She would accept their help to remain in control of Mage Guild, but she would not become an outcast.

No, she would wait for Inigo or whatever lackey he sent to kill her and know that she was beaten not by Inigo, but by herself. She could see the ways she had failed—but they were *her* failures, not someone else's successes.

Arabella sighed and rubbed her hand along the worn fabric of the chair. It was her favourite place to sit. She didn't quite mind dying in it, if it came to that.

It was almost dawn when they came. Hestor entered first— from the door that led down to the dock.

"I see Inigo has sent you to take the first blow," she said. She lit a mage light, and it flared to life overhead. Hestor stopped mid-stride, his face a mask of fear. She chuckled. "I'm not going to hurt you," she said. "What would be the point? But another might have."

"He's shielded," Inigo said. He stepped out from behind the Journeyman. "I would not let anything happen to him."

"Ah, Inigo, surely you don't have uses for a Mage who believes *that*." Arabella smoothed a hand over her hair. "No one is safe, not in Mage Guild. Come, sit, I will not make this difficult. You've won—there is no need to be uncivil."

"I want the boy," Inigo said. He made some hand motions before he sat down opposite her.

"I have no dangerous spells lying in wait," Arabella said. "That is your method, not mine. Rorik said you wanted Timo dead—I should have listened to him, shouldn't I?"

"He *should* be dead," Inigo said. He glanced at Hestor, a scowl on his face. "We've been trying for years."

Arabella sighed. "If my Journeyman had failed so miserably for so long they would not have my trust." Hestor's face grew red, and she smiled.

"He has his uses," Inigo said.

"Don't we all," Arabella murmured.

"Except you." Inigo leaned over and smiled. "I no longer have any use for you, Mage Guild Secundus. Just as I no longer had any use for Rorik."

"I'm sure that at some point you'll no longer have a use for Hestor either," Arabella said. The door to the docks opened again, and she swiveled her head to see Faron step into her hallway. "Ah, there we are. Secundus to your Primus. Where does Hestor fit in, Inigo? I'm sure we're all wondering."

"He knows his place," Inigo said. "Now tell me where the boy is."

"I don't know," Arabella said. "You can try another truth spell on me." She smiled when Inigo glared at her. "Yes. I know what you've been doing. A word of caution, Faron. Inigo feels it appropriate to use magic to force the Secundus to tell him the truth."

"I don't believe you," Inigo said. "You know where he is."

"Truly I don't." She paused and watched his anger grow. "I do know where I told him to go."

"Where is that?" he demanded.

"Old Rillidi. I told him to join his sister on Old Rillidi."

"You lie," Inigo said. "She hates you."

Arabella's laugh startled even her. She was going to die—she hadn't expected to have anything to laugh about.

"Oh Inigo, you think you know all my secrets but I think you've overlooked a few."

"I know you were nobody until you bedded Valendi," Inigo said. "I know you took my rightful place as Secundus when he died. Because you were carrying his child."

"Rorik chose me because he trusted me, as did Valerio," Arabella countered. "I think Rorik would have died years ago if he had selected you—because you need to be Primus."

"I deserve to be Primus!" Inigo yelled. "I'm the only one who deserves it."

"And the only one who believes *that*." Arabella had to stifle a smile. "Unfortunately there already is a Primus."

"Santos Nimali?" Inigo scoffed. "He's insane."

Arabella laughed again. "Have you seen him? Talked to him? I have." She smoothed her skirt, wondering if there was a way to live through this after all.

"When?" Inigo asked.

"Almost two years ago," Arabella said. "The daughter who hates me wanted to see her brother Timo. It was a tender meeting, if you are the sentimental type."

"Which you are not."

"No, but she is. As is Santos. He was very lucid. It seems his madness was caused by curses." She looked over at him. "Something you apparently are quite adept at. My daughter claimed to have removed the curses that caused his madness. She also did something very interesting, something I was less inclined to believe than I am now." She paused to study him. "She removed curses from Rorik." Inigo didn't react so she turned her eyes on Faron. "I learned later who put them there." Faron blanched, and she smiled.

"You can't prove it!" Inigo yelled.

"Not to you," Arabella said. "But the moment Santos Nimali and my daughter see you and your accomplice, they will know. I doubt Santos will be inclined to approve you as *Acting* Primus."

"I won't be acting anything," Inigo said. "And he doesn't have to approve me—council will do that."

"Perhaps you're right. But Santos *did* approve me. Rorik and I visited shortly after I was selected as Secundus." She wasn't going to tell Inigo they'd gone to kill Santos and the girl. "For all that he's been absent, Santos Nimali is a powerful Mage—more powerful than any other Mage alive—and he *is* Primus. You must be very confident that council will support you. Especially after the Acting Primus and Secundus both mysteriously die."

"Inigo," Faron said.

"Be quiet!" Inigo shouted, and Faron snapped his mouth shut.

Inigo would *never* be Primus if Santos was against it. He knew that. Arabella sat back in her chair, waiting. She knew the exact moment when he realized that he needed her alive. He looked up, met her steady gaze, and looked away.

"What do you want?" he asked.

"To live," Arabella replied.

Inigo sighed. "All right. It's you who have won. For now. You have a plan?"

"Yes." Arabella looked at Faron. "You will have to wait to become Secundus." She stared at him for a moment before turning to Inigo. "Do we need them?" she said, referring to Faron and Hestor.

Inigo's eyes narrowed but then he signalled to the other two. Hestor looked like he would have said something, but Faron shoved him out the door before he had a chance.

Arabella sighed. "It must be nice to have such dutiful and trusting friends." Hestor was Inigo's creature—she would have to kill him—but Faron? She might be able to turn him.

"Your plan?"

"Yes. I will invite Santos to Founders Day," she said. "We can ask him to pay respects to Rorik. While he's here, we can have him accept me as Acting Primus and you as Secundus." She paused. "I know it's not what you've waited all these years for but it's a surer bet than a war."

Inigo scowled. "I will agree to this only if we agree to kill Santos once this is done."

"Of course." She didn't think Inigo would have any more success than she and Rorik had had over the years—and now she was grateful. Santos alive would be her small bit of protection against Inigo attacking her. All she needed was enough time to convince some allies she had more to offer.

"Will he come just for that?"

"Perhaps not," Arabella said. "So I will tell him he can visit Timo. He's been asking for that for years."

"You said you didn't know where Timo was."

"I don't—but neither do they. This will ensure that they all come—Santos, the girl, her husband."

"I see," Inigo said.

Arabella smiled as Inigo rose and left. She was sure that he was already plotting ways to kill Santos and his party—which was precisely what she wanted. If he succeeded, she was rid of them. If he failed, he would be to blame and she could select her own Secundus. Preferably one who didn't want her dead.

KARA TUCKED HER arms around her body, trying to ward off the chill. Reo knelt beside the hearth in the estate kitchen, adding wood to the banked fire, trying to coax more heat out of it. It was dark, middle-of-the-night dark. Santos muttered at a pot of water to spell it hot enough for tea. Mole paced the room and that frightened her. She shivered. She had never seen Mole so agitated.

"Enough," Santos said. He waved a hand and the fire flared, startling Reo, who rocked back on his heels. "Let's hear it."

Santos crossed the room and sat down at the table, beside Kara. Reo padded over and sat on her other side, and Kara shivered again. They all knew it was bad news, news she wouldn't want to hear.

"All right," Mole said. He stopped in the middle of the room, facing them. "Timo's disappeared."

"Why?" Kara asked.

"When?" Reo asked at the same time.

"I don't know," Mole said. "Rorik is dead. The council says Timo killed him and ran away."

"No," Kara said. "He wouldn't." She looked at Mole. "Rorik. Are you sure he's dead? There's been no news—*Santos* has not been told."

"He died two days ago," Mole said. "Timo disappeared that same night."

"Two days?" Santos looked at Reo and then Kara. "I don't like it."

"Neither do I," Reo said. "Has Arabella Fonti been declared Primus?"

"No," Mole said, and Kara sucked in a breath. "There's been no word of a successor to Rorik. Master Mage Inigo seems to be in charge."

"Where is my mother?" Her mother would have declared herself Primus if she'd been able to.

"By blaming Timo, Inigo and the council are discrediting Arabella." Mole shrugged. "I didn't want to wait until dawn, when I could learn more. I thought you should know as soon as possible."

"You did the right thing," Santos said. He rose and set out four mugs, then filled them with tea from the pot.

Kara grabbed one and wrapped her hands around it, staring down at the steaming liquid. "We need to find him," she said.

Reo put an arm around her and pulled her into his warmth. "We will," Reo said. "Mole will return at nightfall and find out more, and Santos has his own channels."

Kara looked up to see both Mole and Santos nodding.

"We'll find him," Santos assured her. "Someone knows where

he went."

"Yes," Kara said. She didn't want to think that he might be dead. She wanted to believe that if Arabella Fonti was alive, then Timo was too—but her mother had sacrificed her first child to her ambition, and Kara wasn't sure she wouldn't sacrifice her second child as well.

"WHAT DO YOU see?" Santos asked her.

It was mid-afternoon, and Kara was with Santos and Giona in the small covered loggia that Santos had built at the top of his house. From here they could see in all directions. As always, mage mist swirled at the edges of the barrier Kara had erected years ago to keep spells from reaching Old Rillidi. Far away she could see Mage Guild Island, the bright afternoon sun reflecting off the many spells that circled the tallest towers.

"The spells sent against us seem weaker," Kara said. She lifted her hand to shade her eyes and squinted. "I think Rorik's spells died with him."

"Hmm." Santos stepped back under the roof and out of the hot sun. "He did that on purpose." Kara glanced at him, and he continued. "If all spells died with the Mage the islands would have fallen into the sea long ago. Rorik must have had some doubts about Arabella's desire to hurt you."

Kara stepped into the shade and continued to stare out at the barrier. It wasn't anything she could see, since it wasn't a magic spell, at least not in the way Santos and Giona created magic spells, but she could feel it, as though it was an extension of her will to keep everything bad out.

"Do you feel your spells once you've created them?" she asked. "Can you tell if they've been activated or if they're weakening? Do they keep drawing power from you?" Even after living beside two Mages for years, there was still so much she didn't know about magic. And even more that she didn't know about her own unmagic.

"They don't keep drawing power," Santos said. "Not unless they've been created that way. The same applies to spells that have been triggered. You have to create it to alert you when it's completed what it was fashioned to do."

"That would not be pleasant if it was a destructive spell," Giona said. "I wouldn't care to be notified that it had been successful."

"But you wouldn't set that type of spell in the first place," Kara said and smiled up at him. Soft-spoken and gentle, Giona was the least likely Mage to ever use magic to hurt anyone. Her smile faltered. But that was exactly what she and Santos were asking of him.

"I can if I have to," Giona said.

Kara met his eyes and nodded. Yes, he wouldn't want to and he would never start a fight, but neither would he run away from one. She smiled again. That was something he'd learned from her brother Osten. They'd been inseparable ever since Reo had found them together all those years ago. At twenty-two, Osten, her father's son, seemed to have finally grown out of most of his belligerence. But some of it had rubbed off on Giona.

Kara looked out at the barrier. "I think we should set a few more spells to dissipate magic," she said. "In case Inigo decides he doesn't think we should live."

"I'll do that," Giona offered. "It shouldn't take more than a few hours."

"Mole should have returned by then," Kara said. Gyda, she hoped he was home soon, and with good news.

TIMO CLUTCHED HIS pack close, his head down, as he trudged through the open square. It was quieter than it had been last night, but there were still a few groups of people dotting the square. A woman approached a couple of men who lounged by the fountain. They waved her off with a laugh. When she turned away from them, she spotted Timo hurrying across the square.

"Where are you going in such a rush, love," the woman called to him. She took a few steps, her hips swaying, until she stood directly in his path. Timo changed direction but she grabbed hold of the strap on his pack.

"Ow," she yelled and snatched her hand away, cradling it against her chest. "What'd you do to me?"

Timo stopped. She'd reacted to the spell he'd set on his pack, the one to keep thieves away, but here, in the daylight of the open square, he didn't want anyone to notice him.

"Sorry, Donna," he said and bobbed his head. "A trick I learned in my home villa, to keep the pickpockets away."

"What'd you do?" she asked. She massaged her hand a

moment more then she dropped it to her side and smiled widely at him. "I've got some tricks of my own I could show you." She leaned close, and he smelled her stale perfume and last night's garlicky stew.

"Just a bur stuck to the strap," he mumbled and took a step away from her. "I have no guilders to spare."

She flicked him a now disinterested look. "Come see me when you have some," she said. "I am a true Artist, I can tell you. I'm here every day from noon until midnight." She turned to walk away. "Unless I'm entertaining."

Timo sighed and looked around. No one was staring at him, no one appeared suspicious of him—the lounging men and a couple of women traversing the square seemed engrossed in their own business. He set off across the square again.

Although the island was small, it had two bridges connecting it to other guild islands. Timo had already investigated the one that crossed to Mason Guild Island. That island had a bridge to Old Rillidi but he'd felt uneasy about using that route. It was too direct, too expected. Mage Guild would be looking for him by now—he couldn't afford to do the obvious.

Now he was on his way to the bridge that led to the island Server and Producer Guilds shared. It was the smallest of the guild islands, since most of their Guildsmen lived where they worked, but with his disguise he would blend in.

There were no other bridges from Server and Producer Guild Island so he'd need to get to Old Rillidi by boat. His old picture book showed a ferry dock but he doubted they went to Old Rillidi. Goods and people would travel to Merchant Guild Island though. If he could get that far he could cross the bridge to Old Rillidi. His only other option was to hire a boat. But from whom? Who could he trust to not report him to Mage Guild?

Movement caught his eye and when Timo glanced over, his heart stopped. Someone—a Seyoyan—was staring at him. As Timo got closer, the Seyoyan's eyes flicked down to the mauve mage mist that traced the flap of his pack. Then his eyes were back on Timo's face. A grim smile flashed in his dark face and his long white braids fluttered when he nodded.

Even when Timo was past him he could feel the Seyoyans eyes on him, and he knew he'd seen *something* about Timo that he'd found interesting.

At the edge of the square, Timo ducked into a lane and out of sight of the Seyoyan. The last thing he'd wanted was to be noticed. Should he be worried? Seyoyans had their own reasons for doing things—so Primus Rorik had told him—but they didn't meddle in guild politics. He'd look at the bridge and then head straight to his room. And keep out of sight of the Seyoyan.

"ARABELLA IS ALIVE," Santos said. "I received a message from her advising of Rorik's death."

"Timo?" Kara asked.

She and Santos were in his workroom, waiting, they hoped, for Mole's return. He'd been gone since before dusk last night and now it was just a few hours before midnight. Reo was off making arrangements. Exactly what that entailed, Kara wasn't sure, but he was keeping himself busy, which meant he was worried. And that worried her even more.

"She implies that nothing has happened to him."

"Thank Gyda," Kara said.

"I'm not sure he's safe," Santos said. "Mole heard he'd been accused in Rorik's death."

"Maybe my mother was able to convince them he's innocent?" She paused. "Would clearing his name help her?"

"Yes." Santos tapped his fingers on the desk. "But she would have had to offer something to Inigo in return."

The door to the workroom opened, and Reo and Mole entered. Mole's expression was serious, and Kara's heart dropped.

"Timo?" she asked.

"No word," Mole replied. "No one I talked to has seen him."

"Interesting," Santos said. "I've been telling Kara that I had a message from Arabella. She seems to be in control."

"You don't think she is," Reo said. He pulled a chair to Kara's side and sat down. Mole leaned against a bookcase.

"Not by herself," Santos agreed. "She's invited me to Founders Day. In my official capacity as Primus."

"She never wanted to acknowledge you." Kara frowned. "Why now?"

"She's in trouble," Reo said. "Mole, did the rest of the council know about Santos? That he was no longer mad?"

"No," Mole replied. "They mentioned him a few times, but more as an irritant than a threat."

"So I'm either a surprise or a bargaining chip," Santos said.

"Or it's a trap," Reo said. "What does she want from you?"

"She's asked me to pay respects to Rorik." Santos paused. "And she's offered access to Timo."

"She has him, thank Gyda," Kara said. Her shoulders slumped in relief. "Arabella won't hurt Timo will she?"

Reo placed a hand over hers. "We can't assume that. Rorik's death has changed things. Arabella might not be in control. More than before, I think this is a trap."

"Of course it is," Santos replied. "But we have to go anyway." He smiled. "No matter what, my arrival at Founders Day will cause a commotion. That's our opportunity to find Timo."

"If he's there," Mole said. "No one's seen him, including Arabella's Server."

"We have to go," Kara said. "If there's even the smallest chance of finding him we have to take it."

"Which is why Arabella offered to let us see him," Reo said. "She knew we wouldn't refuse." He met Kara's gaze and nodded. "I don't see any reason to change our existing plans. We'll go in secret and make ourselves known at the last moment. Mole, have you found a place for us to hide?"

"Sure, sure," Mole said. "Rorik's Servers were dismissed—his house is empty."

"Timo lived there," Kara said. "If he's not there and he's not at my mother's, then where is he?" She heard the panic in her voice. Reo must have as well because he looped an arm around her and pulled her close.

"We'll find him," he said. "We will."

"All this for power," Kara said. She shrugged off Reo's arm and stood up. "My mother is setting a trap for us, and we don't know what happened to Timo." She paced in front of the window, her hands balled into fists. "I want to go there and create a *storm* of unmagic until I know what they did to my brother. I'll undo every spell keeping that Gyda-cursed island aloft and watch it sink into the sea." Reo stepped over to her, and she crumpled into his arms.

"We'll find out what happened to them," Reo said softly. "But you should not react out of anger or hurt or rage."

Kara took a deep breath and looked up into his grim face. "You're right. You've always said that anger is dangerous for an

Assassin, and I think it would be dangerous for us, for me, to act out of emotion. But I *will know* what happened to my brother."

"Yes," he agreed. "You will."

TIMO ATE HIS gluey porridge in silence, trying not to think about what exactly was in it. And he was definitely trying not to think of the fresh fruit and warm-from-the-oven bread that had been his usual breakfast as Apprentice to the Mage Guild Primus.

The tavern was mostly empty this early in the day—there was a surly Server who no doubt had expected to have a better station in life than this and a few drunkards left from the night before. Timo still wasn't used to the old smoke, stale ale, and ripe body odours that seemed to have permeated every single inch of the tavern. In the few days that he'd been here, he'd experimented a little, trying to find the best place to sit. Eventually he'd decided that here, in the middle of the room, was the least repugnant.

"Just one more day for you, is it?" the Server asked as she poured more hot water into his mug.

"Yes, Donna," Timo replied. His already weak tea would be even more diluted but at least the water had been boiled. "I'll have the morning meal tomorrow and then I'm away." He just wasn't sure where to. He hadn't been able to cross the bridge. There were extra guards, and even more ominous, both times Timo had investigated, a Mage had been with them. Would Mages be looking for anyone other than him?

"Well, good luck in your posting," the Server said. "You're a polite one so you should do well enough. You could maybe get a placement at a Guild House if you work hard."

"Yes, Donna," Timo replied. His disguise of being Server Guild hadn't been questioned even by those in the guild. He smiled up at her, deciding to take a chance. "Would you know where I might rent a boat?" he asked. She frowned at him, and he continued. "I thought I might get a closer look at Mage Guild Island, you know, maybe even go *under* it."

"Don't you go meddling with Mages," the Server said. "It doesn't pay for the likes of us."

"Oh, of course." Timo knew better than she did that meddling with Mages was dangerous but he needed a boat. "I just thought . . . well . . . I won't be back here . . ."

"I understand." The Server's face softened into a smile. "It could be years before you have another chance." She cocked her head. "It is a sight to see, I'll tell you. But don't you go under the island, hear me? There's all kinds of spells and magic under there. Mages," she said sternly. "They don't trust."

"Who? Strangers?" Timo asked.

"*Anyone*. Not even each other—especially not each other." She leaned closer. "Go to the ferry docks and ask for Guther. But be quietlike. He don't want folks to know he has a sideline. Get him into trouble with one of the other guilds."

"Don't worry," Timo said. "I'll be very careful." His life depended on it. He thanked the Server, and she moved off to tend to a new customer. Timo finished his breakfast and headed out the door. If all went as planned he wouldn't be eating here tomorrow morning. Instead, he'd be on his way to Old Rillidi.

THE FERRY DOCKS were crowded, too crowded for him to even attempt to talk to Guther. Timo leaned against the building, his face turned towards the shadow that he cast on the brick wall.

So many Mages! Mage mist swirled and eddied throughout the crowd as they jostled for a place on the ferry. This was the last ferry before the Founders Day ceremonies started. Anyone who missed this would miss the first part of the festivities.

Timo hunched further into the shadow. He could tell by their actions that these Mages were minor talents. Powerful Mages would never shuffle onto a ferry like cattle, would never allow such threadbare cloaks to bear their guild crest. But as unlikely as it was that any of these Mages had ever met him, he had to assume someone in the crowd could recognize him. An ambitious, politically astute Mage without a lot of options or talent might know who the Apprentice to the Primus and the son of the Secundus was. That was exactly the type of person who would try to gain favour with Inigo and the council in exchange for news about him.

With one last glance at the crowd, Timo turned and headed down a side alley. He was not going to get a boat today, maybe not even tomorrow. Unconsciously his hand slipped to his pack. He had only enough guilders to secure a boat, and after tonight, he'd have no place to stay, no way to buy food, unless he used them. Without a boat, he'd be forced to risk using the bridges.

Timo walked out of the alley and almost directly into

someone's path.

"Sorry," he mumbled. He looked up, distracted, and sucked in a breath. The Seyoyan from the other day stood in front of him.

"No offense taken," the Seyoyan said. He bowed and stepped aside. "You are obviously troubled."

Timo bent his head and took a step forward.

"You are not who you seem to be," the Seyoyan said softly.

Timo's step faltered, just for a moment, but it was enough.

The Seyoyan continued, "But neither am I. Perhaps we can help each other."

Timo concentrated on keeping his steps even and sure despite an almost overwhelming urge to run and hide. He'd been found out! Somehow he'd been found out. He slowed a little, resisting the impulse to turn around and see if the Seyoyan was watching him, and took a deep breath.

Discovered, maybe, but not by anyone who was likely to expose him to Mage Guild. No, it was well known that Seyoyans hated Mages almost as much as Mages hated Seyoyans. So what had the Seyoyan meant by saying that they could help each other? Seyoyans were seafarers—he might have access to a boat. But what could he want from a Mage Apprentice?

When he'd met his sister she'd said that any Warrior would know how to find her. Her husband had added that Seyoyans would as well. He didn't feel safe walking up to a Warrior and asking to be taken to Kara Fonti—especially not when they were guarding the bridges with Mages. Could he trust this Seyoyan? Not right away, he'd need to find out what the foreigner wanted, but if he could do him a favour, he might take Timo to Old Rillidi.

"I DON'T LIKE this," Reo said.

Kara blinked and looked up. Reo had been scanning the bridge as they passed under it while she'd been concentrating on the swathes of mage mist. She was deflecting it away from their small boat, trying to determine if any of the spells were directed at them.

"What don't you like?" she asked, peering up at the bridge that linked Mason and Merchant Guild Islands. Spider webs of mage mist traced the brickwork, and again she wondered if the Masons were magically gifted.

"There are too many Warriors on this bridge," Reo replied.

"And there's a Mage with them."

"Looking for someone," Santos said. He sat beside Kara in the prow of the boat, his rich robes shimmering in the late afternoon sun, his Mage Guild crest sewn onto the right chest with gold thread.

"Yes," Kara agreed with relief. "Which means they don't have him." The silk of her dress rustled when she turned to catch Reo's eye.

"Pull into the first dock after the bridge, Mole," Reo said. Mole, dressed in plain, dark clothes, turned the tiller, and the boat swept towards the right bank. A few moments later, Reo stepped out onto Mason Guild Island.

"I won't be long," he said, and he wasn't. Kara barely had time to smooth the skirt of her midnight blue, silk dress before he was back.

"Four Warriors at each end of the bridge and a lesser Mage with them," Reo said softly as he stepped into the boat. "Warrior Guild has been hired to ensure Mage Guild Founders Day is peaceful but the Guildsman in charge said they were told to watch for an Apprentice. They were told he killed the Primus."

"When we've returned from Founders Day, I'll talk to Warrior Guild Primus Rualla," Kara said. She'd threaten to never help Warrior Guild again. She would not allow her brother to be taken back to Mage Guild Island.

"No need," Reo grinned. "The Warrior I spoke to knows who we are. I've asked him not to catch this Apprentice. I told him that if they can get him to us we will look favourably on both him and his guild."

"They'll do that without hearing it from Rualla?" Santos asked.

"Yes," Reo replied. "You still don't understand the contempt Warriors have for Mages. By nightfall Warriors will be trying to help Timo, not hold him for Mage Guild."

"Thank you," Kara said. She settled back into the boat, and Mole steered them into the bay. Mage Guild Island loomed ahead, mage mist crawling over it, making every structure visible to her. Kara stared at it. *Gyda keep Timo safe*, she prayed. *Until we can find him, please keep him safe.*

The boat swept into the shadow of Mage Guild Island, and a few moments later, they were underneath the hulking mass, mage lights glinting as far as she could see. Kara concentrated on the mage mist that eddied around the boats and docks of the underside of the island. Nothing seemed dangerous so far, so perhaps, as Santos had said, Inigo hadn't expected them to attend. Did he know they were here now?

THE DOCK THAT Mole steered them to was in a well-lit area near the island's centre. Reo stepped out of the boat first, followed by Santos, mist from Santos' invisibility spell covering them. Blindly, Reo reached a hand out, and Kara clutched it, letting him help her onto the dock.

Mole joined them. Now that they were out of it, Kara was the only one who could see the boat. She grabbed the rope attached to the bow and secured it to the dock.

"All right," she said.

Reo headed up the stairs, Santos trailing him. Mole stood on the dock, scanning the area below the island. Kara touched his shoulder, and he twitched.

"Sorry," she whispered. "Just going past."

Mole nodded, his lip curled in a half-smile as she squeezed by him. When she reached the bottom stair, a slight breeze ruffled her skirt.

"They're in," she called to Mole. He nodded and took a step toward her.

"Three minutes," Mole whispered. "Then we'll follow them."

Kara tried to relax while Reo and Santos made sure Rorik's house was unoccupied. Worried that entering the house could trigger a spell, Kara had wanted to go with them, but she'd been outvoted. Santos didn't think there was danger—it was possible Servers were still around so any spell they triggered would likely only notify the Mage who had set it, not attack someone entering. Once they were sure no one was there, then Kara would clear away any spells.

A small ball of grass green mage mist flew down the stairs and hovered in front of her for a moment before disappearing.

"There's the signal," Kara said. She touched Mole's shoulder and headed up the stairs.

A mage light floated at the top, illuminating Reo.

"House is clear of people," Reo said when she reached him.

"All right." Kara edged past him and into a small vestibule. "I'll take a look."

She didn't come across any spells as she wandered through the rooms, but there were traces of mage mist. Mostly tan—Rorik's colour—and a few traces of her mother's purple.

She opened a door. This must be Timo's room. Mauve mist blanketed the walls, floor, and ceiling. She smiled at finally discovering the colour of his mage mist. Her smile faltered. He'd been worried enough that he'd barricaded his room with magic. She wished she'd realized earlier just how dangerous his life had become. She would have insisted Mole drag him out of here whether he wanted to leave or not.

She sighed and trailed a hand along the desk. She might have kept him safe, but she would have taken away his choice. He might not have appreciated that. She wouldn't have.

She left the room and headed down a short hallway to one last closed door.

It was a workroom—most likely Rorik's. Books littered the floor, and a chair was overturned. Tan mist covered every surface but traces of gold mage mist clung to the overturned chair. Kara moved to get a closer look.

Two years ago she'd removed a curse of this same colour from Rorik. She'd look for this Mage. Whoever he was, he had not been a friend of Rorik's. She looked around the room. There was no more of the gold mist but there—at the top of the book case. She closed her eyes. The mist was still there when she opened them. She didn't have to get closer to know that was Valerio Valendi's mage mist. Now that she knew it was there she could feel the malevolence of it. She shivered and left the room to find the others.

"Mole's not back yet?" Kara asked. Reo and Santos were in the parlour of Rorik's home. They were no longer invisible so Kara swept the spell off her as well. Santos would need to replace it in order for them to get safely to Founders Day.

"Not yet," Reo replied.

Kara nodded and sat down beside her husband. Mole was going to track down his contacts to see if any of them had information about Timo. Not only did Kara want to know if he was safe—they needed to have as much information as they could before they met with her mother.

She turned to Reo. "Should we be worried?" Just as she said that there were sounds from the hallway.

A moment later, Mole stuck his head into the room.

"Kara, come to the kitchen," he said, then disappeared.

Kara met Reo's gaze. He shrugged.

"It's Mole," was all he said.

The door to the kitchen was closed, and Kara knocked softly before entering the room.

Facing the door, Mole leant against a long table. A middle-aged woman with short dark hair sat beside him. When the woman looked up at Kara, surprise flitted across her face.

"I thought Annya should meet you," Mole said.

"Annya. My name is Kara Fonti. You're my mother's—Arabella Fonti's Server, aren't you?"

"Yes, Donna," Annya said. "I mean, I am Arabella Fonti's Server. You look like her so it must be true, but I didn't know she had a daughter."

"She prefers not to acknowledge me," Kara said. She shook her head. "I cannot help her rise in the Guild."

Annya pursed her lips. "Yes, that would be like Donna Fonti."

"Do you know where my brother is?" Kara asked. "I understand he's staying with our mother."

"No, Donna Fonti," Annya said. "He left the day Rorik died."

"She helped him," Mole said. "He took a ferry disguised as a Server."

"Thank Gyda," Kara said. Timo was off Mage Guild Island. That meant he was still alive. "The day Rorik died?"

"Yes, Donna," Annya said.

"Thank you for helping my brother." Kara met the other woman's gaze. "In return we will help you if you want to leave Mage Guild Island."

Annya's shoulders slumped, and she sighed. "I will accept."

"I'll take care of her," Mole said. "Let Santos know that Inigo and your mother are now allies."

Startled, Kara looked at Annya. The Server nodded.

"That is why I will go," she said. "I have been in Donna Fonti's household for years but now that she is allied with Master Mage Inigo, I fear for my life."

"He has a very bad reputation among Servers," Mole said. "Come Annya, let's get you off this polluted rock." He turned to

Kara. "Give me half an hour."

Kara headed to the parlor.

"We'll be late for Founders Day," she said when she entered the room. "Mole has another errand." She sat down on the settee. "And I have news. Timo is not on Mage Guild Island and my mother is allied with Inigo."

"Hmm." Santos nodded. "Interesting."

"More like unbelievable," Reo said. "According to Mole, Arabella and Inigo are enemies. What's changed?"

"Nothing," Kara said. "They are using each other to go after another target."

"Us," Reo said. "That's why Santos has been invited tonight. Arabella hasn't been able to kill us on Old Rillidi."

"So she enticed us to leave it," Santos replied. "Well, we didn't think this would be easy."

"No," Kara replied. "At least Timo is safe. We only need to worry about the four of us surviving."

"I think it's the other way around," Santos said. He stretched out a hand. He closed it into a fist and mage mist pulsed. "They need to be worried about surviving the four of us."

Chapter 7

TIMO OPENED THE door to his room and sighed with relief as he stepped inside and pushed the door closed. It was his last night here, the last night he could afford a safe place to sleep.

"Do not make a move," a voice said from the darkness.

Timo sucked in a breath and spread his arms wide, his palms facing up. He readied a spell and mage mist illuminated his hands.

"Don't try it," the voice said. "I'll kill you if you use magic. Now turn around."

They knew he was a Mage. He let the spell swell as he turned around.

"Release that spell and you're dead," the voice said. "I mean it. Now light the lamp." Timo raised his hand to light it with magic but a harsh "No," stopped him.

"Use the flint."

The only light was the one his mage mist cast. How had the intruder known he had a spell ready? Or that he was going to light the lamp magically?

Nervously, Timo headed towards the small table. The oil lamp and flint were clearly lit by mage mist. It took a few tries but eventually he got the lamp lit.

"You magic users," the voice said. "Can't even do simple tasks."

The glare from the lamp made Timo blink so it was a moment

before he could clearly see the Seyoyan who was speaking.

"What do you want from me?" Timo asked.

The Seyoyan perched casually on the bed, a knife balanced in one hand.

"I told you that we could help each other," the Seyoyan said. He eased off the bed in a single motion, an echo of how Mole moved. "At least *you* will help *me*."

"Why should I?"

"Because otherwise I will take you to a bridge and hand you over to the Warriors and Mages who are looking for you." The Seyoyan stepped close to Timo, staring into his eyes, the knife pointed at Timo's chest. "You don't want that, do you?"

Timo stared at the Seyoyan for a few more moments, but he saw nothing but determination in his face. "No," Timo said. "I don't want that."

"Good." The Seyoyan took a step back but kept the point of the knife trained on Timo's chest. "And as I said, I can help you as well. You want off Arts Guild Island without going past the Warriors, and I have a boat. Once you've helped me, I can take you anywhere you want to go." The Seyoyan grinned. "I can even arrange for passage on a ship to somewhere other than Tregella, if you desire. Do we have an agreement?"

"All right," Timo said. "But I'm not sure I can help you."

"I am sure you can," the Seyoyan said. "You are a Mage, yes?"

"I'm a Mage Apprentice," Timo said. "I have not yet completed my training." He looked down at the knife and then up to the Seyoyan. "I will not use magic on you."

The Seyoyan laughed and let the knife drop to his side. He sat down on the edge of the bed. "I would see it coming if you did."

"You would see it coming," Timo repeated, trying to sound surprised. He'd thought the man had seen something in the square. Did he know Timo could see magic too?

"Yes," the Seyoyan said. He leaned back on the bed and casually waved the knife in the air above him. "It is a trait some Seyoyans have. It's very useful."

"Yes, it would be," Timo agreed. "I've never heard that Seyoyans could do that." Timo leaned against the wall. Should he tell this Seyoyan that he knew Reo? That Kara Fonti was his sister? Would he help him?

"You wouldn't," the Seyoyan said. He grinned again, and Timo realized that he wasn't much older than he was. "We've worked hard at keeping this knowledge secret." The smile on his face faltered, and when he spoke again the determination was back. "Which is why I need your help. Someone must have uncovered the secret and now my younger brother has been taken."

"And you want my help finding him," Timo said. "Magical help." He nodded. Finding someone was relatively easy—he just needed something that he owned. Or a blood relative.

"I *know* where he is," the Seyoyan said. "I need your magical help in freeing him."

"All right," Timo said. "I can be of help in that as well."

"Yes," the Seyoyan smiled again. "You can. But we need to leave now, tonight. It's our best chance of getting to him without being noticed."

"Now?" Timo asked. "Where is your brother being held, and why must we go tonight?" Even as he asked the question, Timo knew what the answer would be. And by the look on the Seyoyan's face there was no chance Timo could talk him out of going. Or not making Timo go with him. If he *was* willing to help Timo find Kara and Reo it wouldn't be until his brother was safe.

"Mage Guild Island," the Seyoyan said. "We can slip in while they are celebrating Founders Day." The Seyoyan sat up, aware now of Timo's distress. "Do not worry. I know you have no wish to be noticed by Mages. I assure you that neither do I. You will protect us magically, and I will protect us from physical threats. It's a perfect combination."

"YOU NEVER TOLD me your name," Timo said. The Seyoyan's small boat cut through the water silently, its dark sail blotting out the view of Gyda, the guiding star. "I should know who I might die helping."

"I am called Yash Samma," the Seyoyan said. "And my brother is Wuls. And we are not going to die, at least not tonight."

"And I am Timo," Timo said. He wished he had Yash's confidence, but he was only partly trained, and he knew what Mages were capable of. "Do you know where your brother is being held?"

"Yes," Yash replied. "He is being held by a Mage called Inigo."

"The head of Mage Council," Timo said softly.

"You know him."

"I know him," Timo said. Should he tell Yash Samma that he was sailing with one of Inigo's enemies? Would it matter?

"Good. So you'll be able to counter the spells he has created," Yash said. He sounded confident even though he was talking about an Apprentice besting the head of the Mage Council.

"I'm not sure I can," Timo said. He hadn't been able to disable the curse Inigo had put on Rorik, so there was no reason to think he'd have better luck with spells Inigo had set up to protect his home.

"Don't worry," Yash said. "I'll let you know where the spells are. And we don't have to concern ourselves about anything until we're close to where my brother is being kept." He paused. "I've been a few times. At least as far as the door that leads to where Wuls is being held."

"Then you don't need me," Timo said.

"But there's magic there. Magic that I can see but can't get through," Yash said. "So I do need you. I am worried about the boat, though. It's always been here when I returned, but it's still a worry. Can you spell it to stay here no matter what? Even if someone tries to steal it?"

"No one will steal it," Timo said. "In case it belongs to a Mage."

"That would be bad?" Yash asked. "Stealing from a Mage?"

"If caught, they would be sentenced to death," Timo said. He met Yash's eyes. That would be their fate too, if caught trying to free his brother.

Yash nodded. "We won't be caught. And I'll have to trust that the boat will be here."

"No," Timo said. "I'll spell it invisible."

Yash looked up at him and grinned. "And us too?"

"Us too," Timo agreed. He hoped he could do it. He'd had some practice staying invisible himself, but this would be the first time he'd used the spell on another person. And he was afraid that he'd have to keep them invisible if any of them were to get off the island alive.

He looked up at the bright lights and swirling mage mist. Sounds of revelry wafted on the cool breeze and then they were beneath the island. Yash busied himself taking down and storing the sail while Timo weaved a spell of invisibility around them and the boat, wrapping them all in a thick coat of mauve mage mist.

Yash grunted his approval, and Timo slipped past him to sit in the prow. When he heard the soft splash of an oar in the water, he turned from scanning the docks that lay ahead of them. Yash nodded and bent his head as he used the single oar to paddle the small boat forward.

Mage lights and mage mist lit the way as they wove through the docks and boats that dotted the water under the island. A few times they had to stop as a straggler to the festivities sped past them, magic propelling their boat.

Finally, Yash pulled up to a dock that was almost mage mist free. A dull mage light showed warped and splintered wood, and along the water line there was a thin green line of slime.

"It's safe," Yash said when Timo huddled close to him. "I've used this dock before. I don't think anyone lives here but there is a small spell near the stairs that we'll need to step over."

Timo scrambled onto the dock, holding the boat for Yash, who stepped lightly from the bobbing boat to the planks. Yash quickly tied the boat up and headed towards the stairs.

"Right here," Yash pointed to a wispy spell that covered the first stair. "Don't step on that stair."

Yash leaped up to the second stair, and Timo followed, making sure he stayed well clear of the mage mist. It wasn't a colour he recognized but that didn't mean it wouldn't recognize him. The council would be watching for him—who knew how many Mages were tasked with that.

"You will announce me," Santos repeated.

Kara looked at Reo. He was shrouded in mage mist, as were she and Mole. Though Reo couldn't see her, he nodded in her direction and rolled his shoulders.

"But Master Mage, I have no knowledge of your rank," the Mage said again. Santos' eyes narrowed, and the Mage took a step back.

"Have I been forgotten in the years since Rorik was named Acting Mage Primus?" Santos said. "Does no one remember that I, Santos Nimali, was named Mage Primus before him?"

"No, I mean yes," the Mage stuttered. "Of course the name Santos Nimali is well known, but if you are the current Mage Primus I have no knowledge."

"Enough," Santos said. "I am not dead so I am the *only* Mage Primus. I will announce myself." He waved a hand, and green mage mist pushed the other Mage to one side.

Holding onto Reo with one hand and Mole with the other, Kara trailed Santos into the hall and paused at the edge of the crowd.

When Santos strode to the middle of the Guild Hall, conversations faltered and all eyes turned towards him.

"I am Santos Nimali, Mage Guild Primus," Santos said, his voice booming, enhanced by a small spell. "I have come to Founders Day to pay my respects to Acting Primus Rorik."

Shocked voices sounded throughout the room, and some of the Mages closest to them turned to look at a Mage near the back of the room. Her mother.

"Santos, welcome." Smiling, Arabella swept towards him, the rustling of the silk dress loud in the now silent room. "I am so glad you accepted my invitation. But surely you did not return alone? Was I not clear that your friends were welcome as well?"

"By my friends you mean your daughter and her husband?" Santos asked. A few gasps sounded in the room, and Kara saw more than a few heads turn towards her mother.

"I think mourning a Mage Guild Primus is guild business," Santos continued. "I am the only Mage Guildsman in my house."

"Mage Guild Primus." A man walked towards them, trailing gold mage mist. Those near him quickly retreated out of his way. "I am not sure if you remember me. I am Master Mage Inigo." He bowed slightly. "Head of Mage Guild Council."

"I remember," Santos said. "You must be very astute to have turned such a middling talent into head of the council."

The crowd stilled, and an uneasy silence settled over the room. Inigo clenched his hands, and a ball of gold mage mist formed around one. Kara saw her mother frown at him and shake her head. Inigo relaxed his hands and pasted a wide smile on his face.

"It's a position I earned, Mage Guild Primus," Inigo said, not quite able to keep a sneer from his voice.

"Of course," Santos replied. "Isn't that what I implied?"

Kara grasped Reo's and Mole's hands tight, twice confirming that her mother and Inigo were planning on using magic against Santos.

"It is very good that you are here," Arabella said. She attempted to grab Santos' arm but frowned when her grasp slid away from him. "I am hopeful that just as you did for Rorik and me, you will appoint me as Primus and Inigo as Secundus." She tried to grab Santos again, and again her hand skidded away from him.

Santos ignored her, instead circling the space, staring out at the silent Mages who ringed them.

"I can either appoint another Acting Primus and Secundus or take up the reins of Primus again with you as Secundus," Santos said. "It's my choice."

He stopped before a middle-aged man with a receding hair line and a substantial belly.

"What say you, Jinaro? Should I stay and be Primus? You must have a good opinion of me—you asked to be my Journeyman enough times."

"I, well, I," the Mage mumbled, and a reddish mist twisted around his hand. "It's been so long."

"Yes, it has," Santos said and clapped a hand on Jinaro's shoulder. "And who knows if I can trust you." Santos continued to walk around the centre of the room, scanning the crowd. "And there's Castio," he said, and the crowd parted to reveal a thin, grey-haired man. "It was my recommendation that put him on council—would you help me run the guild?" He frowned and turned his back to Castio. "You never did like hard work."

Santos stopped in front of Arabella. "I do not want to be Primus. Nor do I want to approve you and Inigo in my stead. But I will if you fulfill your promise. I want to see Timo Valendi."

"Yes, just as soon as you approve us," Arabella replied. "Inigo and I are ready."

Santos shook his head and sighed. "You don't know where Timo is. We suspected as much."

"He's my son," Arabella said. "I know where he is." She looked around. "And who is *we*. Who did you bring?"

Kara gripped Reo and let go of Mole, who slipped away before she swept the invisibility spell from her and Reo. She met Santos' gaze, and he nodded. Green mage mist sped from his open hand, and protective spells settled on her and Reo. She looked over at the still invisible Mole. He saluted and headed for the door. Mole would follow Timo's trail—try to find out which island he went to and follow him.

"Only those you invited, Mother," Kara said. She looked around the room. A few Mages were readying spells but the rest seemed engrossed in what they were witnessing. She met Inigo's gaze, and he glared at her.

There was a blaze of gold as he launched a spell. Kara reached out and *pushed* the spell back towards him. There was a blast when the spell hit, and Mages screamed. Shockwaves buffeted Kara but Santos' protective spell kept her safe. She felt Reo's steadying hand on her shoulder.

She'd only smelled this odour once before, but she would never forget it. Inigo had meant to kill her, and she'd deflected the spell onto him. Just like Valerio Valendi.

"You witch!" a man screamed. "Gyda-cursed witch!"

A charred body lay crumpled on the floor and crawling out from under it, his hair scorched and his face blackened, was Inigo.

"She killed the Secundus," Inigo yelled. "Kill her!"

Kara felt Reo pull her against his chest as what the Mage had said sunk in. Her mother! She'd killed her mother!

"Kara," Reo whispered in her ear. "Kara! We need you."

"Yes." She nodded and took a deep breath as she pushed her grief and guilt away.

"Quiet!" It was Santos, looking every bit the Mage Guild Primus, and most of the people in the room automatically responded to him. "Stay calm. We will not hurt anyone else unless they attack us."

"But she killed the Secundus!" Inigo yelled.

"Your spell killed her!" Kara replied, shaking off Reo's hand. "You attacked me and then you hid behind my mother." She looked around the room. "I am not a Mage. That's why my mother, Arabella Fonti, rejected me. But I can manipulate a Mage's spells." She leveled her gaze on Inigo. "I suspect that there is a report in the Hall of Records that indicates that."

"Kill her!" Inigo called out, his eyes travelling past Kara to the ring of Mages surrounding them. He raised his hand, mage mist collecting on it.

Dozens of other Mages now gathered their power, and Kara stepped into the centre of the room. Glaring at Inigo, she *pulled* with all her might at the magic being amassed around her. She heard gasps and grunts as the power was literally ripped from the Mages in the hall.

She felt Reo's steady hand on her arm, and she relaxed and

met his solemn gaze. She nodded and looked around. Mage mist in every colour streamed from the crowd up towards the ceiling. Inigo looked shocked, and a few people stumbled to their knees, their magic already depleted. But other, stronger Mages stared at their hands as they felt their power being sucked away.

Inigo screeched with rage and lunged towards her—then Reo was in front of her and in an instant Inigo was writhing on the floor. And still gold mage mist streamed from him.

Reo fell back beside her, scanning the crowd.

"Are you all right?" he asked her, and she nodded.

"Santos?" Reo said over his shoulder.

The older Mage turned towards them and raised his hand. Grass green mage mist circled his fist.

"I have not been affected," Santos said. "Although I can feel the power moving in the room."

A crack of thunder sounded, and Kara looked up. A river of mage mist swirled around the ceiling, flashes of light crackling from within the pool of power. A few strands of mist still streamed from the crowd, but after a few moments, they trickled and stopped. Then there was only the mage mist spinning ever faster around the ceiling of the room.

"What's it doing?" Reo asked.

Kara shook her head. "I'm not sure. The clammers never had this much power to pull out of them. I'll try to dissipate it." She reached a hand up and waved at the mist, trying to make it go away, but instead it spun faster and faster. Her hands clenched into fists, Kara threw her arms up into the air. Concentrating, she opened both hands and *pushed* at the magic. There was a thunderous rumble, and the walls shook, and then with a sound like rushing water, the magic collapsed into itself and was gone. Kara sagged against Reo, her breath ragged. Around her, the crowd of Mages was silent as they stared upwards. Kara followed their gazes. The ceiling was rimmed with a black, smoky stain.

THE WALLS SHOOK, and the floor seemed to jump. Thunder crashed, and Yash bumped into Timo, grabbing him to keep them both from stumbling.

"What was that?" Yash asked.

"I don't know," Timo replied. The sky had been clear on their way to the island so why was there thunder?

"It's stopped, whatever it was," Yash said. "Let's go." The Seyoyan scanned the hallway ahead of them before he moved forward.

Timo followed, keeping to the shadows even though they were invisible. Yash had pulled a dark hood over his white braids, and Timo could barely see the Seyoyan's dark skin in the faint glow of the mage mist that covered them both. Mage light flickered in the lamps that lined the hallway.

Yash had led the way ever since they left the boat, taking a path little used by anyone but Servers. He'd been to see his brother more than once in the week since he'd been taken, using this same route, he'd said.

Timo knew these paths too—he'd used them often enough when trying to evade traps set for him. He'd never been to Inigo's home but he knew it was around this corner.

Yash hurried forward, fast enough that Timo had to run to keep up. He grabbed Yash's cloak, pulling him to a stop.

"We have to be careful," Timo hissed.

"My brother is in here," Yash said. He tugged his cloak, dislodging Timo's hand.

"And this is where Inigo lives," Timo said. "I thought he would be kept in the council jail. If your brother is here then this must not be Council business." What could Inigo want with a Seyoyan? Was he keeping this a secret from council? "Inigo is very powerful. And dangerous."

"Which is probably why he stole my brother," Yash said. "And it makes stealing him back even more notable." He grinned, and Timo sucked in his breath.

"Is this a game to you?" he asked. "Because Inigo will kill us if he finds us here."

"He won't find us," Yash assured him. "We're invisible. Besides, he hasn't killed my brother. Come on." Yash turned and trotted down the hall.

"He'll kill all of us if he finds you with me," Timo said quietly, but he followed Yash just the same. He'd given his word to help him and he would. As soon as they were off this Island he'd have Yash take him to Old Rillidi. Then he'd never set foot on Mage Guild Island again.

"He's in here," Yash said. He had stopped at a door that writhed with magic. Gold mage mist—the colour of Inigo's spells—washed over the door while pale blue mist swirled around the edges.

Yash leaned up close to the door, careful not to touch the mage mist. He whispered loudly in a language Timo assumed was Seyoyan. He heard a faint response from the other side of the door, and Yash relaxed.

"You see," he said. "My brother is fine. Now you can open this door."

"I'm not sure I can," Timo said. He crept up to it and looked at the mage mist. "It's pretty heavily spelled."

"You can see it too?" Yash asked. "But you have magic yourself—I have seen you cast spells."

"Yes," Timo replied absently. He was studying the magic, trying to determine if it was dangerous or not. He stepped away. It *felt* like a simple spell to keep the door locked. He poked at the mage mist and it swirled away from his hand. "But I don't need a spell for this." Concentrating, he waved his hand at the mist. Slowly at first, and then more quickly it started to fade. In a few moments the mist was completely gone.

"That looked like a spell to me," Yash said. He grabbed the door handle and tugged. The door opened, and he flashed Timo a smile before he ducked through it.

Timo followed more slowly. After all these years pretending that he couldn't see magic, he felt exposed, vulnerable, now that someone knew what he could do. But Yash could see magic too, he told himself, his secret would be safe. He hoped. He followed the sounds of foreign whispers to find Yash standing beside a thick wooden door. The Seyoyan grabbed the handle and rattled the door.

"It's locked," Yash said when Timo joined him. "But there's no magic. Can you get it open?"

"Yes," Timo said. "Tell your brother to stand back."

Yash leaned into the door and spoke. There was a muffled response and then he turned and nodded to Timo before stepping away. Timo raised his right hand towards the door and concentrated. A puff of mauve mage mist enveloped the door and then the doorway was empty. The door settled against the adjoining wall with a soft thunk.

There was a blur as a figure rushed out and into Yash's arms.

"Wuls," Yash said. He embraced a Seyoyan boy a little younger than Timo. They exchanged a few words in Seyoyan, and then Yash turned to Timo.

"Thank you," Yash said. "This is my brother. Wuls, we owe Timo a great debt."

"Yes," Wuls agreed in accented Tregellan. "We will strive to repay you."

"We need to get off this island first," Timo said. Now that Yash's brother was free, he was nervous. Inigo would be at the Founders Day celebration but Apprentices and lesser Mages didn't always attend. Someone could come at any moment.

"You're right," Yash said and grinned. "But I have never had any trouble getting away before." He headed over to the door to the hall, Wuls trailing him. "Let's go."

"Yes," Timo said. He trotted out into the hall, following Yash and Wuls.

THE QUIET WAS pronounced after the thunderous noise of a moment ago. The only sound Kara heard was her own laboured breathing. Her mother was dead. She didn't mourn her, not exactly, but she was angry.

Inigo crawled to his feet, his face red with rage.

"Do not move," Santos said. He lifted his hand, and grass green mage mist flowed up over his head. A ball of mage light coalesced and then drifted a few feet higher. Pale faces in the crowd stared up at it, bathed in the white light.

"Proof that I still have my power," Santos said. He took a step towards Inigo. "And it was always greater than yours. Now, where is Arabella's son Timo?"

"I don't know," Inigo said. "That useless brat killed Rorik."

"No," Kara said. They *thought* Timo had escaped off the island, but if there was even the smallest chance that Inigo had captured him, she needed to know. She took a step towards him and smiled when he shrank away from her. "I think you killed him."

"There's no proof of that," Inigo declared.

"No," Kara replied. "But there might be an eye witness—my brother. You wouldn't have believed him, but my mother might have." She leaned closer. "And I know you'd cursed him in the past. Two years ago I undid a spell that was the exact same shade as your magic."

"Which is nonsense," Inigo said. "Not proof."

"Your Journeyman tried to contract an Assassin to kill Timo Valendi," Reo said.

"I didn't . . ." a man standing behind Inigo said. He tried to move away but in seconds Reo had a grip on his tunic and had brought Hestor's face up to his.

"It probably wasn't your idea," Reo said, staring at the now ashen Hestor. Reo glanced over his shoulder at Inigo. "And it's not against Guild Law. Inigo has experience with Assassins, don't you?" Inigo glared at him, and Reo laughed. He let go of Hestor's tunic and pushed him away.

"Warrior Guild Primus Rualla asked me to inform you that Warrior Guild rejects your request for a contract."

"Why would he have you deliver this message?" A blond Mage sidled towards Inigo. "Who are you?"

"Why don't you ask Inigo?" Reo asked. "He and I go back quite a few years."

"You can't say anything," Inigo hissed. "It's in your contract."

"Yes," Reo agreed. "My Assassin's contract." He looked around the room. "Although I'm not Guild anymore. But Inigo does have a habit of getting rid of people."

"I don't care," the blond man said flatly.

"You probably should," Santos said. "It might be you next." Santos surveyed the room and stared at someone across the hall. "Or you, Jinaro. I don't expect Inigo has become overly dependent on you for anything." Santos turned back to Inigo.

"What's the brat to you anyway, old man," the blond said with a smirk. "Valerio Valendi may have been your Apprentice but if his actions are anything to go by, he hated you."

Kara took a calm step towards the blond man. "He's my brother," she said.

"If I knew anything I wouldn't tell you." He started to sneer but Reo's hand closed on his neck and his breath was cut off.

"I advise you to cooperate," Reo said. He looked over his shoulder and met Kara's eyes. "Do you want me to kill him?"

For a moment Kara was sure she wanted this man dead. He may not have Timo now but she had no doubt that he'd added to her brother's misery. She met the gaze of the man Reo held. He wasn't sneering now.

"No," Kara said finally. Reo let go, and the Mage dropped to his knees, gasping for breath.

"We need to question Inigo," Reo said calmly.

"Yes," Santos agreed. "Then the Journeyman." He waved a hand and mage mist flew out in all directions. All the doors to the room slammed shut, and the mist settled at the edge of the hall, slowly circling the outer walls.

A few people rushed into the mist only to find themselves a few steps away. She smiled. A relocation spell—it was how Santos had protected Old Rillidi for years.

"Inigo first," Santos said.

Reo grabbed the Mage and dragged him over to Santos. Kara watched the crowd. There were a few huddles of people and some furtive glances sent their way, but no one moved toward them.

She glanced behind her. A thread of grass green mage mist wrapped around Inigo's head, and the Master Mage started to choke.

"What did you do to Timo after Rorik died?" Santos said.

"Nothing," Inigo said.

The mage mist tightened, and Inigo fell to his knees.

"I swear. We looked for him but couldn't find him." Inigo's face twisted in hate. "No doubt that bitch he had for a mother helped him. She was always trying to protect him, though he has such a small talent."

Kara laughed, she couldn't help it. "You have no idea what Timo's talents are." Santos nodded—Inigo was telling the truth. He didn't know here Timo was. "And you forget that Arabella was my mother too."

This time it was Inigo who laughed. "It's not like she ever wanted you. She was willing to work with me to kill all of you!"

Kara nodded. It confirmed what they'd thought: her mother and Inigo had been planning something. "Nevertheless she *was* my mother. What were you two planning?"

Because of Santos' spell he'd be forced to tell her the truth. Inigo's eyes bulged with the effort to try to keep from speaking. He sputtered a few times, and when he would have rolled to the floor, Reo dragged him up to his knees.

"To get Santos' approval," Inigo said. "For her and I to be Primus and Secundus."

"Why?" Reo asked.

"So there would be no questions about our right to rule." He glared at Santos. "The great Santos Nimali could still gain support on council. We needed his approval."

"And then what?" Reo asked quietly.

Inigo shut his mouth and closed his eyes tight, straining to not answer.

"Then what?" Reo repeated. He pulled Inigo up off his feet. "What were you planning to do once Santos had approved you?"

"We were going to kill you!" Inigo spat. "All of you! Arabella said there was no way to kill you when you were on Old Rillidi. That's why she lied about her brat being here."

Reo dropped him to the floor, and Inigo started to laugh. "It was her idea—that bitch. Get you here and kill you all. But she didn't know," he dragged himself to his knees, "that I was going to kill her in a week, maybe a month. She had to die. She was in the way."

"Of what," Santos said. "What was she in the way of?"

"Of me becoming Primus," Inigo said. "Of me having the power I deserve."

"Yet you are not Primus—*I* am," Santos said. He nodded at Reo. "Bring the Journeyman."

Kara faced Inigo. She was aware of Reo, striding through the crowd in search of Hestor Galina, but she kept her eyes on Inigo.

"What are you looking at?" the Mage said.

Santos' spell was fading, and Kara waved it away. "My mother's killer," she said angrily. "I deflected your spell but *you're* the one who put her in its path. You *planned* on killing her."

She reached towards him, and he flinched away. But she wasn't trying to touch him, she was searching for his magic. She could feel a tiny kernel still within him. Was it left over from when she'd drained all the Mages in the room or had he replenished it already? The clammers had little magic, and it renewed itself slowly, but was that because she didn't dig deep enough to root it all out?

Kara pulled at the magic buried inside Inigo with all her strength. A tiny thread answered her, and slowly, slowly it spooled out of him. She swept her hand out, and the mage mist writhed on the floor between them. Inigo gave a strangled cry and toppled over. He reached his hand to his head, his breathing laboured.

"What have you done to him?" Hestor asked when Reo pushed him forward. "Is he dead?"

"No," Kara replied absently. She was concentrating on Inigo's prone form, searching for even the faintest spark of magic. She straightened up and looked first at Reo and then at Santos. "But his magic might be. At the very least it will be a long time before he has any power, and it may never return, at least not completely."

Santos' eyebrows went up but he didn't say anything.

"Let's see if this one knows where Timo is," Reo said. He pulled Hestor's arms together behind his back and spun him to face Santos.

This time when she turned to watch the crowd there was fear in the faces of some of the Mages. She balled her hands into fists—Reo would probably chastise her later—but she'd been angry. Even though Arabella had been planning on killing them all, Kara hated that *she'd* had a part in her mother's death. And she'd wanted Inigo to pay for that. And now he would.

Living without magic would be worse than dying for a man like Inigo. He'd be at the mercy of every Mage he'd ever offended. It was probably a very long list.

But she'd given in to her anger, her need for revenge, and in the process had given their enemy information about what she could do, information it might have been better to keep secret. She closed her eyes for a moment. This was why Reo said Assassins could not afford to kill in anger, kill with emotion—it made you forget what was important. Her mother was dead—finding Timo alive was the only thing that mattered. She would not do anything else that might jeopardize that.

When Kara opened her eyes, her gaze fell on the blond Mage who'd spoken up for Inigo earlier. He was staring at Inigo's prone form with what looked like speculation. He glanced her way, and their eyes met, and she smiled. She *did not* regret that Mages like this one would scheme against Inigo, maybe even kill him.

"The Journeyman doesn't know where Timo is," Reo said. He pushed the man to his knees and stepped over to stand beside Kara. "Is there anyone else who might?"

Kara looked out across the crowd and shook her head. Someone in the crowd might know something but with such little knowledge of her brother's life, finding them would take time they didn't have.

"Then we need to go," Reo said. He took her hand.

"You're right, there's nothing more we can do here," Kara agreed. They had to get home. Mole would try to reach them there, hopefully with word that he'd found Timo. If not, Santos would try to pinpoint which island he was on. Her brother was almost the same age she'd been when she'd been thrust out on her own, urged to run away by her mother. Inigo was right—Arabella Fonti had never wanted her, never loved her. But Timo knew there was a place where he *was* wanted, where he would be welcome. All she could do was hope that he made it to Old Rillidi safely.

Chapter 8

"THIS WAY," YASH called softly. He was crouched beside the wall, peering down an intersecting hallway. Mauve mage mist eddied around him—Timo's invisibility spell.

"No," Timo said. Despite Yash's confidence, he'd gotten them lost in the hallways. For most of an hour, Timo had been trying to convince Yash to retrace their steps to try to find the hallway that led back to the boat but the Seyoyan was one of the most stubborn people he'd ever met. Timo was almost ready to take his chances on his own. Maybe he could slip out with the Servers again. The Founders Day events would be over soon, and the extra helpers would be leaving once the clean-up was done. He looked down at the Server crest sewn onto his tunic. He was still dressed for the part, though he looked a little disheveled now.

Timo sighed and followed Yash and Wuls around the corner. He still needed the Seyoyan's boat to get him to Old Rillidi.

Yash stopped and signalled with his hand, and Wuls dropped to the floor. Timo, a few steps behind, did the same. Footsteps echoed in the corridor ahead. Yash crab-walked towards a door, opened it, and waved Timo and Wuls forward.

"WE'RE GOING THE wrong way," Timo protested. They were huddled inside a small storage room. Dusty chairs and a table with broken leg were piled up against one wall.

"I know what I'm doing," Yash insisted. "I've done this a few times already."

"And I've lived here my whole life," Timo said. "Right now we're underneath the library. If we ever hope to find your boat, we need to return to Inigo's."

"No," Wuls said. "I do not want to go back. They want to hurt me."

"We're not going back," Yash said to his brother. He glared at Timo. "And if you know so much about this island then I suggest you find a way to get us off it."

"I can but it will be without your boat," Timo said. He glared at Yash. The Seyoyan's boat was the only reason he'd come to Mage Guild Island, the only reason he'd put himself in such danger.

Yash shrugged. "I can get us another boat." Wuls said something to him in Seyoyan, and Yash laughed.

"My brother says that stealing a boat from a Mage is worth the loss of my own boat," Yash said to Timo. "I will gain much esteem in the eyes of my people." Yash leaned into the door. "I do not hear anyone in the hall. It is time for you to lead us to a boat."

THE CORRIDORS WERE busy far sooner than Timo had expected. He'd planned on taking them to his mother's house not because he thought she'd help, but because Inigo didn't control her—Arabella Fonti was Secundus, most likely Primus by now. Besides, she'd be at Founders Day. But even though the celebrations weren't scheduled to end for hours, Servers were already in the corridors.

Timo led them into another storage room. This one was larger, with shelves stacked with goblets and dishes. He headed to the back of the room and tucked himself in beside two shelves. Yash and Wuls followed him.

Timo peered around the shelf. He could just see the door.

"Something's wrong," Timo said. "The Servers shouldn't be stirring for hours, not until the Founders Day celebration is over."

"Maybe it's because of the noise we heard," Yash said. "And the way the walls shook."

"Maybe," Timo said. He'd almost forgotten about that—was it part of a special service because the Primus was dead? "We need to find a safe place to hide. At least until the Servers are finished cleaning up."

"Can't we stay here?" Yash asked. "It seems pretty safe. And we are invisible."

"No," Timo replied. "We're too close to the Guild Hall. Too many Servers will be in these corridors. One of them could stumble into us and alert the Mages." But these corridors would be the perfect place for him to become visible and blend in with the Servers. Could he abandon the Seyoyans?

Timo leaned against a shelf. No. He'd been left alone too often to be able to do that to anyone else. Besides, he'd given his word to Yash. He couldn't renege.

"We need to get a little further away," Timo continued. "And find something to eat and drink."

THE BOAT RIDE back to Old Rillidi was even more stressful than the one to Mage Guild Island had been. Santos spelled them invisible, and Kara concentrated on keeping any other mage mist away from them. Reo sat in the stern, tiller in hand, scanning the waters that surrounded them.

Her mother had planned on killing her only daughter in order to stay in power.

Kara had always assumed that her mother was in control—she was Secundus. But within a few days of Rorik's death she'd schemed with a man who'd planned on killing her—who *had* killed her, though it was Kara who had deflected the spell.

But she'd protected Timo—probably helped him escape. Gyda knew Arabella Fonti had never shown her daughter anything close to the concern she'd shown Timo.

Roughly, Kara wiped her eyes. Maybe her mother truly had loved Valerio Valendi. She'd seen him drain magical power from the mother of his unborn child, but Arabella Fonti had refused to believe her—had continued to think that Valerio cared for her. Kara turned and caught a quick glimpse of Reo.

What if Reo wasn't as true and good as he was? Would she want to know or would she want to believe the lie? What if he died before she could be sure? Valerio had been Secundus at the time of his death—perhaps that had afforded her mother a small amount of safety? Maybe even then she'd been afraid for her life and the life of her son?

Giona Valendi had been saved by Reo, but other than Timo,

the rest of Valerio's children were dead, as were the children Santos had fathered before he was cursed into madness. Arabella had known the fate in store for young children left behind by a powerful Mage.

Kara would do anything in her power to save her own children—but could she tell herself lies so often that she came to believe them? Had that been her mother's choice?

Finally, the boat passed through the first magical defence that surrounded Old Rillidi—a line of dove-gray mage mist. Giona would know that they'd returned.

He met them at the dock.

Reo tucked the boat in close, and Kara scrambled out of it, taking Giona's outstretched hand.

"You're all here?" Giona asked.

"No," Kara replied. "Mole is trying to follow Timo's trail. We were told he was helped off Mage Guild Island."

"Come," Santos said once he'd joined them on the dock. "There is much to discuss but I need to sit somewhere warm. I'm too old for this." He headed off towards the house with Giona.

Kara waited until Reo had tied the boat up and joined her on the dock before she collapsed into his arms. He held her in silence for a few moments but finally she eased away enough to meet his gaze.

"I am sorry about your mother," Reo said simply.

"Thank you," Kara said. She sighed and looked towards the house. She knew she had to go, had to meet with Santos and Giona and Reo to decide what their next steps were, but right now she had no energy.

"Mole will find him," Reo said. "Or *we'll* find him."

"Then let's find him," she said. She stepped out of Reo's embrace and led the way up the path to the manor house.

TIMO PEEKED OUT the door. The corridor was silent and empty, as it had been for the past few hours, and he didn't like it. It was early yet, but not too early on this part of the island for Servers to be up and about their duties despite the late night of Founders Day.

He eased the door closed and crawled back to the others. They were in yet another storage room, this time far enough away from the Guild Hall that they didn't have to worry about Founders Day revellers.

"No one," he said. "Not one single soul."

"Good," Yash said. "Let's go. Maybe we can find something to eat."

"No. I don't like it," Timo said.

"You've been saying that all night but you haven't given us a good reason to stay here," Yash said. "I say we go. Wuls?" His brother nodded, and Timo sighed.

The truth was that he didn't have a good reason. All he had was an uneasy feeling that things weren't right.

"All right," Timo said. "We have to leave some time." It was still early enough that they should be able to travel without being detected. If they lingered much longer they'd have to hope no one entered this storage room all day. "We're not far from my mother's house. We can get something to eat there and use one of her boats."

"But I want to steal a boat," Yash insisted. "That will help build my reputation."

"Don't worry," Timo said. "We can't afford to let my mother see us so we will be stealing a boat."

"Good," Yash asked. "I will be much admired."

They'd only travelled a few minutes when they heard people talking. Timo waved a hand, and the blanket of mage mist that covered them thickened, keeping them invisible. The three of them silently crept along the wall—the sounds were coming from around the corner. Timo paused.

"He wants tea," a woman said. "Very hot."

"Yes, Donna, right away," another woman replied.

"See that it *is* right away," the first woman said. "He has less patience today then yesterday."

"Yes, Donna."

Footsteps retreated down the hall, and Timo leaned around the corner. A woman stood with her back to him, her hands on her hips as she watched a Server disappear through a doorway. The woman turned, and Timo sucked in a breath. Barra Eska! What was she doing here? They were a long way from Inigo's quarters. Frowning, Barra swept past him, and Timo realised that it was *after* Founders Day. She would have a new placement, just as he was supposed to.

Without thinking, he dropped his concealment spell and

stepped towards her.

"Barra," he whispered. He motioned behind his back for Yash and Wuls to remain where they were. Barra turned. Her mouth dropped open, and her blues eyes widened.

"Timo," she said. "Where have you been?"

"It's better if I don't tell you," Timo said. "Do you know if my mother is at home?"

"Your mother?" Barra asked. She closed her mouth and studied him for a moment. "She's not at home," Barra said. "Why?"

"I can't let her see me," Timo said. "She thinks I'm already gone." He met Barra's cool gaze. "You won't tell anyone, will you?"

"Me? Who would I tell?" Barra said.

"Did you see her at Founders Day?" Timo asked. "Is she Primus?"

"My new master forbade me from attending," Barra replied. "Most Journeymen and Apprentices were told not to go."

"Why . . . ?" Timo stopped. It didn't really matter to him who was at Founders Day—he was a Guild runaway. "Just don't tell anyone you saw me."

"I need to go," Barra said. "I need to make a good impression." She looked away. "You know how it is."

"Sure," Timo replied, but she was already through a door. He muttered his invisibility spell and hurried back to Yash and Wuls.

"Why did you talk to her?" Yash said.

He was angry, and Timo couldn't blame him. The feeling that something wasn't quite right returned in full force.

"I don't know," Timo said. "I shouldn't have because now we can't go to my mother's."

"Not after you told her," Yash agreed.

"I have another place," Timo said. "Follow me." He set off the way they'd come. They'd have to chance Rorik's quarters and assume that they hadn't been sealed off. He'd taken half a dozen steps when he realized he didn't hear anyone behind him. He turned to see that neither Wuls nor Yash had budged.

"Come on," Timo said. "It's just one corridor this way." The two brothers exchanged a glance. Finally, Yash shrugged, and they headed in Timo's direction.

Timo set off again down the familiar corridors. They were very close to Rorik's quarters, the place he'd called home for much of his life.

He wasn't sure why he'd stopped Barra. It wasn't as though they'd been friends, at least not since Barra had helped him get into the Hall of Records and his mother had found out. Had he simply wanted to talk to someone he knew? He couldn't undo what was done—all he could do was trust Barra not to tell anyone she'd seen him.

He ducked through a doorway and headed up the stairs, the Seyoyans silently following him. There was no trace of mage mist on the familiar wooden door at the top of the stairs and cautiously Timo pushed it open.

He paused. The house was quiet. Had the Server left after Rorik's death and his own disappearance? Leaving the two Seyoyans standing on the stairs, he squeezed through the door.

How long had it been since he'd been here, since Rorik's death? He counted back. Five nights—it seemed like so much longer. He glanced through each doorway off the entrance hall. The sitting room furniture had been disturbed. Who would have investigated Rorik's death? His mother for one, and probably Inigo. Which meant Hestor had been here—Inigo didn't go anywhere without his Journeyman. He paused. Hestor was a full Mage now; would that make him a more powerful ally for Inigo?

The door to Rorik's workroom was open, and carefully he peered in—the room was in shambles. The chair where Rorik had died was on its side, and Timo rubbed his eyes, trying not to see Rorik, struggling for air, as the spell closed his throat.

"Are we safe?"

Startled, Timo spun to face Wuls. The Seyoyan gestured towards the hallway.

"Will there be food?" he asked.

"We should be safe," Timo said. "Food? I'm not sure." Wuls' face fell, and Timo remembered that he'd been held captive for days by Inigo. Had he even fed his prisoner? "Let's see," Timo said. He led the way towards the kitchen.

There was a promising trace of mage mist circling the cold storage. Timo opened it slowly. A large block of cheese and an urn half-filled with milk were nestled inside. He picked up the cheese—it was cool to his touch. He tossed it to Yash, who caught it and grinned. Timo sniffed the milk. It was sour, too sour to drink. He closed the cold storage cupboard and opened the one beside it. Apples filled a small basket. He pulled it out and put it on the rough worktable.

"That's it, plus water." Timo gestured to the pump that sat along one wall of the kitchen. Wuls pumped it a few times, and Timo was relieved to see fresh, clean water flow from it.

"This is all?" Yash asked. "I expected a Mage to have more."

"The Mage who lived here died," Timo said. "Fish and bread were brought in every morning." He looked around the room. "There will be tea somewhere, but we can't risk a fire to heat it."

"Water will do." Yash grabbed an apple and bit into it. "We'll be leaving at dark anyway." He chewed slowly. "You are sure that this Mage is dead?"

"Yes," Timo replied. "I'm sure." *I watched him die—I killed him*—was what he thought but didn't say.

"Huh. There is no glory in stealing a boat from a dead Mage."

"As long as there's a boat to steal," Timo said quietly, hoping that the dock underneath was as forgotten as Rorik's quarters were.

TIMO SLEPT IN his own bed, something he'd never expected to do again. It was only for a few hours and it was daytime, but after everything that had happened in the past week his bed felt foreign. Wuls woke him when it was his turn to stand watch. The Seyoyan then joined his brother in Rorik's chambers. At first, they hadn't felt comfortable sleeping in the dead man's bed, but Timo had assured them that it wasn't where he'd died.

In the kitchen, Timo pumped some water into a mug. Like most things on Mage Guild Island, the water flowed by magic. Once, when he'd first become his Apprentice, Rorik had taken him to see how water was provided to the island. At first he'd thought it was some elaborate scheme his mother and the Primus had fabricated in order to keep him studying hard.

Rows of Mages brought sea water in through the base of the island while others purified it with magic. Still more sent it through the pipes that spider-webbed through the island to all the pumps and fountains and bathing rooms.

Rorik had told him that this was where Mages with minor talents were placed. They were part of the machinery that allowed those with real abilities to undertake the important work of managing the guild.

Other stations with similar purposes dotted the lower levels of Mage Guild Island, all doing their part to keep the island aloft and supplied with all the necessities—water, air, lights, heat. Timo had thought it a waste of Mage talent. Wouldn't it be easier to live on dry land where rivers naturally ran with clear, cold water? He hadn't said that to Rorik, of course. His mother would have been told and Timo would have been lectured yet again on how fortunate he was to have such a powerful mother and mentor and how he should be applying himself to his studies.

He walked from the kitchen to the eating area and peeked through the curtain. It was dusk outside—they should get ready to go. He left the mug on the table and headed for the door to the dock below, reinforcing his invisibility just in case anyone was below. He, Yash, and Wuls could all see each other despite the spell so it seemed sensible, though he was worried about using too much of his power. But it wasn't an issue so far and his short nap had re-energized him.

Timo unlocked and opened the carved, wooden door that led to the dock. The smell of sea water wafted up from the dark as he stepped onto the stairs and closed the door behind him.

He hadn't been down to this dock in a while. Rorik rarely went anywhere by boat and Timo had never been allowed to set foot off the island—and certainly not alone. The steep stairs seemed to go on forever, and Timo clutched at the railing as he slowly descended. A stumble could not only send him plummeting to the bottom, but the noise could also alert anyone in the area below Rorik's quarters.

With his feet even with the underside of the island, he crouched to look. When he accidentally looked straight at a mage light he blinked, his eyes watering. There were muffled voices so he eased down another step for a better view.

Boats bobbed in the water and thankfully one was tied up at the dock below. He stared out towards the sounds of voices. There were people on a dock a little way off. It wasn't close enough for a good view, and he squinted, trying to identify them, but they were too far away.

As far as he could see, there was only that one group below the island. Timo froze—and why was that? The few times he'd ventured down he'd been surprised by all the activity: boats filled with people gliding in the water; Servers cleaning docks; fishermen bringing their catch in to sell. But not today. Other than the one group he could see no one—no boats, no people. Was it this quiet because it was the day after Founders Day or did it have something to do with the tremors from last night?

He crept back up the stairs. He'd discuss this with the Seyoyans, but even invisible, he'd felt far too exposed to leave by boat when it was this quiet. The feeling that something wasn't right returned, and he shivered even though he wasn't cold.

"I THINK WE should go," Yash said. "There is a boat—that's all I need to know."

They were at the dining table. Pieces of wax from the cheese and a few apple cores littered the scarred wood of the table they sat around. Half a dozen apples remained in the basket, and Yash grabbed one and bit into it.

"Besides," he said around the apple. "We don't have enough food to last another few days."

"I know," Timo said. "But it makes me nervous. Even invisible there will be signs of us and our boat."

"And no one to see them," Wuls said.

Timo wasn't surprised the younger Seyoyan sided with his brother. It was a wonder they'd been separated long enough for him to be taken by Inigo in the first place. He didn't have a lot of experience with siblings. None of the Apprentices with brothers or sisters had acted like these two—like they were a team, looking out for each other—like they really cared about each other. Was this normal? Was this why Kara wanted him to live with her? Yash had risked his life to save his brother—Timo *thought* that Kara would be willing to do the same for him. Would he do that for her? Or Giona?

"What if they're looking for you?" Timo said, and Wuls looked up, startled. "I know the man who was keeping you prisoner and he's not going to give up easily. He has people, lots of people, including Mages, who do what he tells them." The entire council, Timo thought, but didn't say. He'd expected Inigo to search for Wuls magically, though, not by physically watching docks and boats. Except Inigo knew that Wuls could see magic—he might assume he could avoid magical traps.

"We can't let him find us," Wuls said. He looked at Yash. "I think he'd rather have me dead than let me go. You as well."

"This man, would he kill us?" Yash asked Timo. "Even if he could ransom us, would he kill us?"

"Yes." Timo nodded. "The only reason I'm still alive is because he doesn't know I can see the traps he's had set for me."

"Then we should wait," Yash said finally. "Until we can find out who is watching the docks below, we should wait." He looked from Wuls over to Timo. "Can we get more food? It might be a few days. Maybe we can steal some from a house?"

"That's too risky," Timo said. "We might be invisible but we still need to open doors to get in and out."

"Can you ask your mother?" Wuls asked.

"No," Timo said. His mother had never helped him before; he couldn't assume she would now. "I can talk to Barra again, the girl I met last night."

"If you think it's safe," Yash said. "If you think you can trust her."

"I think so," Timo said when what he meant was he *hoped* so. It was a chance he'd have to take. He needed more information. Something was wrong and he needed to know what. "I'll send a spell to find her then I'll talk to her."

Chapter 9

KARA STARED OUT across the bay. The more distant Guild Islands were mere smudges against the sparkling blue of the water, while on the closer ones she could make out buildings.

Timo was on one of them—alone—probably frightened. They couldn't assume Mole would be able to track him down. Annya had given Mole a description of Timo in disguise but what if he had changed the way he looked once he left the ferry? They had no way of knowing what or who he looked like.

"Are you ready?" Santos asked.

She nodded and stepped closer to the railing of the loggia. The sun was just about to set. They would try to locate him now, while there was still daylight, and then again once dark fell. An exact location wasn't possible—they weren't high enough to see every island clearly—but they would get a general direction.

Santos reached up and over the railing, and a large bubble of grass green mage mist flowed from his outstretched fingers. It hovered in the air for a moment before it sped off. Kara watched it recede until it was just a speck. When she could no longer see it, she shaded her eyes and scanned the sky.

There—a flare of green mage mist list up the sky above . . . no, it couldn't be.

"I think there's a problem with the spell," Kara said. "It's over Mage Guild Island. Can you try another one?"

"It should have worked," Santos said. "It's not a complicated spell. I'm basing it on you, his sister. I'll try to refine it." He created another bubble of mage mist and stared at it intently before it rushed off.

The second flare of mist joined the first. "It's over Mage Guild Island again," Kara said. She frowned. "Could the amount of magic on the island be attracting your spells?"

"It never has before," Santos replied. "We're sure Timo actually left the island?"

"Annya was certain," Kara said. "She told Mole that when she left him he was in line for the ferry. If he'd been discovered she would have heard."

"Not if Inigo kept it quiet."

"There were dozens of Servers," Kara said. "I doubt even Inigo could keep news from spreading within Server Guild. Besides, you spelled him to tell the truth. Try again, please."

REO POKED HIS head up through the stairwell. "Did you find him?"

"No," Kara said.

"Yes."

Santos met Kara's eyes. "We've been at this for an hour. Every spell shows the same location. Before and after Giona was included in the conditions."

"Santos is right," Giona said. "It's a basic finder spell. There's not much that can go wrong."

"But he can't be there!" So much of Santos' mage mist illuminated Mage Guild Island that Kara could make out the towers.

"Can't be where?" Reo asked. He climbed up the last few stairs and joined her at the railing.

"Mage Guild Island," Santos said. "Every single spell has shown it as Timo's location."

"But he was off the island—he was safe," Kara said. "Why would he go back?"

"We won't know until we find him," Reo said. He pulled Kara to him, and she sighed. "But I believe Santos' spell tracked him. Mole started his search on Mage Guild Island. He'll find Timo and then they'll both be fine. Remember, most of the really powerful Mages have little or no magic."

"But we don't know how long that will last," Kara said. Why had Timo gone back? "Do you think he was caught? Did they catch him and take him back?" If Timo had been hurt she would make Mage Guild pay.

"That's possible," Reo replied. "And if that's the case, Mole *will* find him."

"At least we know he's alive," Giona said. "The spells wouldn't have gone anywhere if he was dead."

"You didn't tell me that!" Kara said. She'd been so certain Timo was on another island that she'd never even considered that he might be dead.

"We didn't need to," Santos said. "But we needed to know."

"So we wait to hear from Mole?" Kara said.

"It gives us some time to strengthen our defences," Santos said. "Before Mage Guild attacks."

"You think they will?" Kara asked.

"Yes," Santos replied. "So do you."

"Yes," Kara agreed. "My own mother attacked us for years. The current council will not hesitate."

"It's only a matter of when," Reo said. "Inigo and the council can either wait for their magic to return or harness the power of others."

"I could stop them," Santos said. "I could return as Primus. It would allow me a chance to find Timo."

"No!" Kara said. "They'll kill you." As much as she wanted her brother by her side, she did not want to sacrifice Santos. "Besides, you said you never wanted to return to that life, a life where you had to wonder whose way were you in, who might be trying to kill you." She turned her head to find Santos smiling. "It's not funny."

"No," he agreed calmly. "But I wouldn't have to wonder who was trying to kill me, would I? Not when all of them would be." His smile faltered. "But it might keep you safe. All of you."

"It wouldn't," Kara said. "Once they killed you we'd be worse off than now because we wouldn't have you."

"Giona is here," Santos said. "And you. And Timo will be here as well."

"He might not stay," Kara said. "Why would he want to live here? I've killed both his parents—he might not want to be near me. Besides, Mage Guild will want us all dead."

"Neither Arabella's nor Valerio Valendi's deaths were your fault," Reo said. "But we'll respect any choice Timo makes. We need to find him so he has the chance to make a choice. And we *will* find him."

"I hope so," Kara said. "Because I barely know what he looks like."

"That is not your fault," Santos said. "Your mother made sure you didn't get to know him."

"I feel like I failed him."

"You shouldn't," Santos said. "His mother failed him by not letting him see you."

"How she hated me," Kara said. Despite believing that she'd made peace with this long ago, she heard the bitterness in her voice. "Even before I was born she hated me. Otherwise how could she have left me behind?"

"She was ambitious," Santos said sadly. "And ruthless. Just as I was before Valerio cursed me. It was what the Guild required of me in order to become Primus."

"But you changed," Kara said, and Santos laughed bitterly.

"Only because change was forced upon me." He paused, and they both stared out across the bay. The far shore was dark now, with only a few lights marking the shoreline. "And by my own Journeyman, a man who lived under my roof, ate at my table."

Kara glanced over to see Santos frowning.

"Another Mage twisted by the Guild," he finished quietly.

"Are they all?" Kara asked.

"The ambitious ones, it seems so." Santos sighed heavily.

"I'm not sure Warrior Guild is much better," Reo said. "All Guilds seem to take away your choices."

"And it does not seem to matter whether you are highly placed in the guild or amongst the lowest," Santos said. "The unguilded here are better off."

"Yes," Kara said, thinking about people like her brother Osten. Born into Mage Guild but with no magical power and no connections, he would have been relegated to a short, hard life of drudgery. Instead he was an unguilded merchant, successfully trading at the market in Old Rillidi, happy and free to do as he pleased.

From a few paces away, Timo watched his spell meander through the lower passageways. This was the third spell he'd sent to find Barra. The first one had disappeared and reappeared moments later, apparently after finding Barra. The second spell had raced off far too quickly for him to follow. It had come back before he was even half way down the hall.

This third spell he'd deliberately slowed down and now he chafed with impatience as it nudged along the floor, pausing at each intersecting hall or door. He heard the sound of footsteps, and he stopped, his heart pounding, as a Server trudged past him.

Timo was invisible, of course, but that didn't mean he couldn't be bumped into.

The spell he was following—a faint line of mauve that trailed along the rough stone floor—pooled in front of a closed door. Timo let out a long breath. He recognized the door—had in fact used it many times. It led to the library, which meant that Barra was not at the home of the Mage she was assigned to as Journeyman.

With a quick check over his shoulder, Timo opened the door and slipped through. His spell flowed up the stairs and onto a landing, before disappearing around a corner. He hurried to catch up, not concerned that his footsteps echoed on the wooden landing. In all the years that he'd been using this set of stairs he'd never encountered another person. Servers had no reason to go to the library and anyone else had better-lit and better-travelled ways to get there.

After another turn a short staircase led down a few steps before turning yet again. Mauve mage mist slipped under the final door, a plain wooden plank that hung on leather hinges. Timo pressed his ear to the door. There were no sounds from the other side. He gently pushed the door ajar and squeezed through. This side of the door was a bookshelf. He carefully pushed it back in place, stifling a cough when he disturbed the dust that covered the books on one of the shelves.

He was in a small, rarely used room of the library. The first time he'd come this way he'd investigated but had found nothing but ancient journals, their leather covers cracked and flaking. Some of the journals had been written hundreds of years ago and the language was so archaic that Timo had strained to decipher it. He assumed that the people who'd written these journals had been important at one time, but now they were forgotten, along with the words they'd committed to paper—any wisdom they'd been trying to pass on was now crumbling and mouldering in obscurity.

But it was a good out-of-the-way place to meet with Barra.

Timo exited the room and headed towards the main area of the library. Barra had been using the same table for years—he hoped becoming Journeyman hadn't made her change her habit. He peered around a shelf. Yes, she was there, hunched over a table that was strewn with scrolls, his spell slowly winding around her feet. He made a quick hand gesture and his spell faded and disappeared.

He looked around and frowned. He had expected the library to be less busy. Apprentices and Journeymen were given a few days off during Founders Day celebrations and most of them spent that time anywhere but at the library, but not today. He could see at least a dozen people seated at the tables—many with their heads bent together, whispering. He eyed the unusual activity, wondering if they were talking about Rorik's death—or his own disappearance. He shrugged. None of that concerned him. He was here to see Barra.

Timo spied on a younger Apprentice who sat at one end of a table, his head down, fast asleep. A quick relocator spell put a page from the youth's workbook into Timo's hand. Another spell retrieved a piece of charcoal from the edge of the fireplace. Still cloaked in invisibility, Timo wrote a quick note to Barra. He stared at her as he sent the note to the table in front of her. Startled, she nervously looked around the room before picking it up and reading it. She looked up sharply, scanning the library. It was foolish, she couldn't see him, but he couldn't help holding his breath as her gaze swept over him. Timo stepped behind the book case and returned to the small room.

"Who's there?" Barra called softly when she entered the room. She held the paper out in front of her, obviously following the directions on the map he'd drawn. Timo removed his spell.

"It's me," he said. "Timo."

Barra gasped and backed away a step. "How did you do that?" she asked. "Invisibility isn't taught to Apprentices."

"Rorik thought it might be useful," Timo lied. He'd taught himself the spell based on notes he'd found in Rorik's workroom. He took a deep breath. "I need your help."

"My help?" Barra asked. She narrowed her eyes and looked at him. "Why do you need my help?"

"You must know that Rorik is dead," Timo said. He paused

and met Barra's eyes. She nodded. "I'm being blamed." Barra nodded again, this time more slowly, and Timo closed his eyes. "I didn't do it but I don't think that will matter."

"What do you want me to do?"

"I need food," Timo said.

"All right," she replied. Barra crossed her arms across her chest. "I can get you food. Where are you staying?"

"At Rorik's." Timo smiled wryly at her sharp look. "I figured it was the last place anyone would ever look." He paused and looked down at the ground. "That's the other thing. Can you find out if anyone besides my mother is looking for me?"

"I can ask around," Barra said after a short pause.

"Discreetly," Timo said.

"Discreetly," she agreed. "Shall I come later tonight?"

"Yes, thank you," Timo said.

Barra headed to the busy part of the library. Timo muttered the invisibility spell, turned to go—and stopped. What was that? A thin ribbon of pink mage mist led from Barra towards the far door. She paused to look behind her and frowned when she couldn't see him. When she started forward again, he could no longer see a trail of mage mist. Had she sent a spell to notify someone? It hadn't seemed focussed, like a spell. It was as though magic was seeping from her. Maybe her new Master had shown her some new techniques?

Still wondering about it, Timo pulled the shelf out and exited the room and library. A few minutes later he was back inside Rorik's quarters.

"Did you bring anything to eat?" Wuls asked as soon as the door was closed.

"No." Timo headed for the living area, Wuls trailing him. "Barra said she'd bring food later."

"Did you tell her about us?" Yash looked up from a book he was reading. Dark grey mage mist curled around the binding.

"Of course not," Timo said. "Where did you get that?" He already knew the answer to the question, though. The book was from the top shelf in Rorik's workroom, a stack of books Barra Primus had never wanted him to look at—a stack of books covered in Valerio Valendi's mage mist.

"From the old man's workroom," Yash said. "But it wasn't his. The mage mist is a completely different colour."

"Yes," Timo agreed. "It belonged to my father."

"Valerio Valendi was your father?" Yash jumped to his feet, letting the book drop to the floor. "Wuls, we need to get out of here." Yash said more to his brother in Seyoyan, and Wuls stared at Timo before he backed away a step, a worried frown on his face.

"I never met him." Timo dragged a hand through his hair. "He died before I was born."

Wuls said something in Seyoyan that sounded harsh, and Yash nodded. "My brother is not sure we can trust you," Yash said. "I agree."

"What do you know about my father?" Timo asked. "No one ever talks about him but I do know that he was not a good man. He cursed his mentor, the man he'd lived with and learned from for years." He looked up at them. "I didn't like Rorik much, mostly because he did what my mother wanted, but I would never have deliberately caused him harm."

"How did he die?" Yash asked. "This Rorik."

Timo sighed and looked away. "He was cursed," he said finally. "I could see the spell that wrapped around his neck."

"And this curse killed him?" Wuls asked.

"Yes. No," Timo said and then stopped. He sighed again. "I tried to remove it and that's when it killed him." He looked up at them. "He would have died soon anyway, but my meddling made it worse, much worse."

"Huh," Yash said and moved closer to him. He said a few words in Seyoyan to his brother, who looked at Timo with wide eyes. "Why would you think you could remove the curse?" He took another step closer and stared at him. "And why are you so sure that you affected it?"

"Because I did," Timo said. "I interfered with the spell and watched it kill Rorik. I was there, I know what I did." Yash sat down across from Timo and stared at him. Timo shifted under his gaze, eventually asking, "Why are you looking at me like that?"

"I only know one person who can manipulate spells," Yash said. "I met her years ago, when I was just a boy." He grinned. "Her husband is a good friend of our uncle."

"You know Kara?" Timo asked. "And Reo?"

Yash leaned back and continued to study him. "I've met them.

How do you know them?"

"Kara is my sister," Timo said. "Half-sister. We share a mother."

Yash's eyes widened. "So this mother you keep talking about is Arabella Fonti, Mage Guild Secundus?" Timo nodded. "You say she will not help you?"

"No," Timo said. "She won't. And the Guild Council blames me for Rorik's death. That's why I didn't want to return to Mage Guild Island."

"And yet you did," Yash said. "Why?"

"I need your boat," Timo said. "To get to Old Rillidi."

Yash nodded. "Are you invited? They have very strong defenses."

"I'm invited," Timo said. "I was hoping a friend would come for me but I tried to help Rorik before he came back."

"Who is this friend?"

"Reo's former Apprentice," Timo said. "An Assassin."

"Ah," Yash said. "For many years those Seyoyans who can see magic have worked with Assassins. Our uncle was such a one—he worked with Reo."

"That's how you met Kara," Timo said, and Yash nodded.

"Kara Fonti is held in high esteem by my people." Yash grinned. "It would help elevate my own standing to give aid to her brother. Much more than stealing a boat from a Mage would."

WHEN HE HEARD the soft knock on the door, Timo waved Yash and Wuls towards Rorik's workroom. He opened the door to an anxious Barra Eska. She looked around briefly before stepping into the hallway. She jumped when the door closed and Timo became visible. He took a heavy basket from her and set it on the floor.

"There's food for at least a few days," she said. "It was all I could safely take." She leaned against the door.

"Thank you," Timo said. He frowned at the faint strand of pink mage mist that trailed from her left foot, under the door and out into the hallway. In the library he'd thought it lacked focus. Now he wasn't so sure. "Are you all right?"

"I'm a little nervous," she replied. "I'll get in trouble if I'm caught."

"But you feel well?" She nodded, and he continued. "We'll be quick. Were you able to find out if anyone is searching for me?"

"I didn't feel safe asking," Barra said. "I can't chance getting into trouble."

Something about the way she'd answered him made Timo stare at her, but she looked away to avoid meeting his gaze.

"You've told them."

Barra started to shake her head and then shrugged.

"Is that why you have magic trailing from you?" Timo asked. "Is that a spell to make sure they know where I am?"

"There's no spell," Barra said. "I told him you were here."

"Who did you tell?"

"My new Master, Faron," Barra said.

"Faron?" Timo sucked in a breath. "The whole council will know. Why?"

"Why?" Barra asked. "Why shouldn't I? I'm his Journeyman, I need his trust in order to learn as much from him as I can. I told him when I first saw you—I said you were going to your mother's." She scowled. "But he didn't find you there, and he was angry with me. He'll find you now, though. He's already on his way."

Timo glared at her, but she looked away and settled against the door. "He knows that you can make yourself invisible so don't think that will help you."

"Yash!" Timo called. He felt some satisfaction when Barra paled. "We've been betrayed."

Yash burst from the workroom, Wuls behind him.

"Shall we kill her?" Wuls asked.

Barra glanced around, fear in her eyes. She couldn't see the Seyoyan but she heard his question. She shrank against the door.

"Too late for that," Timo said. "We need to get out."

Yash nodded, and he and Wuls headed for the door that led down to the dock. Yash pointed at Timo and then the other door. Timo nodded. Yash hadn't wanted to say anything out loud, not when Barra would simply tell Faron, but he wanted Timo to use the Server corridors. Yash and Wuls slipped through the door and were gone.

"You can't trust them, you know," Timo said. "Not any of them. Faron will use you until he's bled you dry, then he'll discard you." He paused. "I think he's already stealing your magic."

"It's not like I have much of a choice," Barra said, and Timo was shocked at the bitterness in her voice. "You ruined it for me with your mother. At least she wouldn't have expected me to share her bed for the privilege of becoming a Journeyman. That's right," Barra said when he stared at her. "I had offers from two Mages and both were very clear that I was expected to do more than simply learn magic. At least Faron is young and handsome." She spit on the floor. "Not like that pig Castio."

"I'm sorry," Timo said. "I had no idea."

"Of course you didn't," she said. "You were too busy feeling sorry for yourself. Feeling cheated because you'd been denied access to some of the most boring records ever created."

"That's not . . ." Timo started. He paused when he heard noises from outside. He waved a hand and mage mist wrapped around Barra and held her tight against the door. Another spell reinforced the door and locked it tight. Finally, he spelled himself invisible and leaned towards Barra.

"You're right," he said. "I *was* busy—busy trying to stay alive. Why do you think I was always bruised and battered? You should ask your friend Hestor about that. And ask him why he tried to hire an Assassin to kill me."

"That's a lie!" Barra said. "He wouldn't."

"He did. You can check Warrior Guild's records for proof. You can't trust those Mages, Barra." Then he ran for the door that led to the Server corridors.

TIMO SQUEEZED UNDER the table and wedged himself against the wall, his head on his knees. He'd been travelling the hallways for hours now, looking for signs of the Seyoyans but he hadn't come across them. Were they hiding somewhere, like him? He huddled at the back of the storage room, wondering what he should do next.

If Yash and Wuls had finally stolen a boat they were now far away from Mage Guild Island. Timo shook his head. No. Yash would do everything he could to take Timo with him when he left in order to gain standing with his fellow Seyoyans. Timo couldn't say the same about Wuls—the younger brother was more intent on getting away. But he'd been imprisoned by Inigo, a Mage who Timo knew had no compassion.

His stomach rumbled, and he thought about the basket of food Barra had brought, the one he'd had to leave behind in Rorik's quarters.

He sighed. No food, no water, no one he could trust. Maybe it was time to find his mother. Would she help him? Could she? If the whole council was aligned against her, she might not be able to. He thought about what Barra had said—that the offers to take her on as Journeyman had included bedding her mentor. Had his mother had to deal with that? Was that why she'd always been so cold, so distant with him? And was that why she had barely acknowledged Kara?

Arabella Fonti had been eighteen when she arrived on Mage Guild Island. She was virtually untrained at an age when most Mages with talent were midway through their Journeymen postings. She'd already had a child—Kara—and left her behind. Timo had never really wondered what it must have been like for his mother. Untrained and with no political ties, no Mage would have wanted her as their Apprentice. But she'd been beautiful and ambitious. She would have used any advantage she had in order to succeed, including bedding someone who could help her.

But Barra had wanted to avoid being forced to use her body to obtain a posting. No wonder she'd wanted Timo to talk to his mother. Unfortunately for Barra, he doubted Arabella Fonti would have sympathy for another woman's struggle. She'd tried to hire an Assassin to kill her own daughter, for Gyda's sake. And she had not softened in the years since.

Barra might blame him for ruining her reputation with his mother but there had never been a real chance that Arabella would have taken her on as Journeyman.

But would she help him now? Would Arabella Fonti use the powers she had as Secundus to help her son? He couldn't be sure. Which left him with no friends, no allies, no one within Mage Guild whom he could trust.

He refreshed his spells and lay down on the dusty flagstone floor of the closet, no closer to knowing what he should do than when he'd entered the room. His stomach rumbled again, and he ignored it, pillowing his head on his hands. He stared at the far door until his eyes closed and he fell into an exhausted sleep.

KARA LEANED AGAINST the kitchen wall and watched her son as he and Reo, their heads bent together, dug in the garden. Nando's small hand plunged into the soil, and he laughed as he pulled up a clump of dirt.

"That's a big one," Reo said.

Nando held the wriggling worm up before he dropped it into a small bucket.

"I'll catch a big fish," the boy said, and Kara smiled.

It was early; the sun was just rising above the trees. For days, Nando had been pestering his father to take him fishing, and Reo had finally agreed. Kara sighed, and the smile slipped from her face.

Her children could never meet their grandmother because *she'd* killed her. She would have to tell them one day—just as she would have to tell Timo. Unlike when she'd killed Valerio Valendi, she'd known what turning the spell back would do. She'd meant to kill—she just hadn't meant to kill Arabella Fonti.

She sighed again. Timo would probably despise her—she was responsible for the deaths of both his parents—but finding him was just as important to her now as it ever was. She would make sure he got to choose how he lived his life. If he chose to live it somewhere without her, well, that had always been a possibility. But he hadn't lived years knowing his mother wanted him dead. And perhaps she'd saved him from that. If Arabella and Inigo had become Primus and Secundus, they would have used all of Mage Guild's resources against Old Rillidi even if Timo was living here. So someone was going to die and she couldn't be sad that it wasn't those she loved. But she was angry that she'd been forced to kill.

There was nothing to be done about Mole, Reo had told her, not for another two days. They'd all agreed, including Mole, that no one was to try to track him down unless five days had passed without word from him. At that point, she, Reo, and Santos would go after him.

She watched as her son found another worm and giggled as he brushed his dirty hands on his trousers. Nando was the exact same age as Mole had been when she'd first met him, and the contrast between the two was startling.

Where Mole, quiet, solemn Mole, had never been comfortable in the light, at times Nando seemed like a child born of sunshine and smiles. Reo looked up and she met his gaze over the top of their son's head. She smiled sadly and glanced away. Two more days before they would go after Mole and Timo. Two more days of pretending to live her life, pretending that part of her family wasn't missing, that part of *her* wasn't missing. Kara sighed and stared out past the garden to where the sun sparkled on the waters of the bay. Two more days and they would go. Because she knew that something had happened to Mole.

Chapter 10

TIMO'S MOUTH FELT dry and gritty. He licked his lips, moistening the cracked skin, as he opened the door and stared out into the empty hallway.

He'd lost track of time. He thought he'd slept for five or six hours—that it was now around midnight. He couldn't be sure, but he couldn't wait any longer. He had to find water and food.

While he'd slept, his subconscious had done what he couldn't do awake. He was now certain that he could not approach his mother. Barra had sent Faron to Arabella Fonti's quarters—he realized now that it was her dock he'd seen people on. Whether by choice or by force, his mother was helping Faron and the council. Which meant that she was aligned with Inigo, a Mage who wanted him dead. He could not trust his mother.

He watched the hallway for a few minutes before he eased out into it. He gently closed the door behind him and stood with his back flat against the wall. After a few moments of quiet, he readied a spell. He wasn't leaving without the Seyoyans.

THE MAUVE FINDER spell slowly trailed along the floor, moving ever closer to the centre of the island. A few corridors earlier, Timo had passed the hallway that led to his mother's house. It was quiet, like the rest of the corridors he'd been travelling for the past hour.

Up ahead the mage mist slipped under a door, and Timo

stopped in front of it. He placed his ear against the wood, hoping for some sense of what was on the other side but he didn't hear anything. He took a step back. It was a door like many others that lined the hallway.

With a deep breath, Timo slowly pushed the door open. The light from his mage mist exposed a few steps—then it was gone, leaving the stairs in darkness. After a quick scan of the hallways behind him, he stepped through the doorway and onto the steps. The mage mist from the spell that kept him invisible cast an eerie glow as he started to climb the stairs.

He counted a total of twenty-two steps before he was blocked by a solid wood door. Faint mage mist traced the outline of it but the spells were old and not very strong. With a quick wave, they faded to nothing.

He pushed the door, eventually leaning his whole body against it before it shuddered open enough for him to squeeze through.

He was in yet another dusty storeroom. The dim light from mage mist revealed discarded furniture stacked almost to the ceiling. He pushed the door shut and dragged a broken table in front of it to hide the tracks in the dust. There was a second door on the opposite side of the room. He crept across to it and pressed his ear against the wood.

Muffled sounds came from the other side of the door. Timo slid down to the floor. It would be morning by now, and if he was in someone's living quarters the household would be rising for the day. He tried to swallow but his tongue was thick in his parched mouth. He needed water now. He could not wait until the night, when the house was settled.

Timo strengthened his invisibility spell and gently opened the door. The hallway was empty, so on hands and knees he scuttled out and quietly shut the door behind him. With his back to the wall, he stood, took a step towards an open doorway, and peered in.

He pulled his head back in shock. It wasn't a kitchen, and there were no Servers. He craned his neck to see into the room again.

"If you tell me what I want to know I'll let your friends go," a man said roughly. His back was to the door but Timo recognized the thatch of blond hair and the arrogant voice—Faron, one of the council members. He also recognized who he was speaking to.

Mole.

Mole called out in a language Timo recognized as Seyoyan. There was a faint response from beyond another door before Faron's fist plowed into Mole's right cheek and the Assassin's head snapped back.

"You can do better than that," Mole said. He looked up at Faron, his right eye already starting to close. "Or maybe you can't. Kara took away your magic, and you're weak without it."

Faron's arm rose again.

"Stop," a woman said, and Timo was startled when Barra walked into view. "He's trying to make you angry."

"Don't tell me what he's trying to do!" Faron turned towards Barra, furious. "I want to know how that witch did it, how she drained a room full of the most powerful Mages in Tregella of their magic."

"Why would he know?" Barra said. "He's not a Mage."

"No," Faron said quietly. "He's not. And neither is she. So how did she do it?"

When he turned to watch Mole, Timo saw that he was being held by spells. Pink mage mist wrapped around his arms and legs, securing him to the chair he was sitting in. The chair was anchored to the floor with more pink mage mist—Barra's colour.

Timo frowned. How had she gone so quickly from trying to secure her Journeyman position to capturing and torturing a man? And what did they mean, Kara took away magic? Could it be done? Then he noticed the line of pink mist that connected Barra to Faron. He'd asked Barra about it but she'd claimed there was no spell. Barra took a step away from Faron and the mist stretched but still tethered the two together.

Without thinking, Timo waved a hand towards the pink mist. It wavered, and Faron glanced around in surprise.

"What was that?" he asked, peering around the room.

"I didn't hear anything," Barra said.

Timo held his breath, not daring to even move enough to duck outside the room. Faron spun around, his right arm in the air, faint pink mist clinging to his right hand.

Faron was draining Barra's magic from her and using it himself! *She* hadn't secured Mole to the chair, *he* had, using magic he'd stolen from her. Barra would *never* have allowed him to do this. Taking power from another, even if they agreed, was one of the few Mage Laws that was punishable by death. Barra didn't know Faron was stealing her power.

Timo looked past Faron and Barra to Mole. Who blinked and nodded once in his direction. Did Mole know he was here? Mole smiled and nodded again. Yes, somehow Mole knew that Timo was here.

He concentrated, and a spell dripped off his hand onto the floor. Slowly it slid across to Mole. As it circled up his right leg, the pink mage mist dissolved. Mole shifted slightly and flexed a finger as Timo's spell released his right hand before travelling across his body to his left hand and then down his other leg to his ankle.

The tread of boots on stone pulled Timo's attention away from Mole. He ducked into the hallway and shrank down beside the door, trying to make himself as small as possible. A cloaked figure strode towards him, and he held his breath. Cloth brushed against him as the newcomer swept past him into the room. Another figure, following the first, paused in the doorway, forcing Timo to remain hunched where he was.

"Master Faron," a voice said. "I understand that you have captured one of Kara Fonti's accomplices."

"Ah, Inigo," Faron said. A chair scraped across the stone floor. "How nice of you to stop by." Faron's voice was closer now, but he didn't seem pleased at the interruption. "And who's out in the hall?" Timo shrank for a moment, panicked that somehow he'd been seen, but it was the Mage who stood in the doorway who answered.

"Hestor Galina, Master Mage." The Mage beside him stepped through the doorway, and Timo took advantage of the rustle of his robes to stand up. He craned his neck to see past Hestor and into the room.

"Of course," Faron sneered. "A full Mage and yet I see you're still Inigo's lapdog."

"Just as you've found your own," Inigo gestured to Barra, who stood beside Mole, her eyes fixed on the floor. "Ungrateful wretch," he muttered, and Barra's shoulders slumped and she collapsed into herself.

"She has her uses," Faron said. "And now I insist that you leave."

"No," Inigo said. "The man you've captured is council

business, he comes with me." He glared at Faron. "We will be grateful. You are, of course, welcome to attend his interrogation in the council room."

Faron flicked a hand, and pink mage mist flew from his fingers and wrapped round Inigo's throat. "He stays," Faron said.

Inigo's hands flew up to his neck, and his fingers scrabbled at his throat. Another flick of Faron's hand and the mage mist faded into nothing. Inigo sucked in a gasping breath and took a step towards Faron.

"I wouldn't," Faron warned, his hand in the air. "It seems I'm the only one with any magic after the debacle at Founders Day."

Inigo stopped struggling, and then Timo heard Barra gasp.

"I think we both know that's not true," Mole said. He stood with Barra clasped to his chest, one hand around her throat. "How long will your magic last once your source is dead?"

"Long enough to kill you," Faron said, facing Mole.

Timo made a small gesture and the rope of mage mist that linked Barra to Faron snapped. Barra's eyes flew open in surprise, and Faron grunted. Mole's smile widened, and he dropped his hand from Barra's throat.

"Even with her magic I doubt you'd have time to kill me," Mole said. "But now that it's gone . . ." His eyes flicked around the room, pausing on each Mage for just a moment. "I don't expect any of you to be much trouble."

"What do you mean?" Barra asked quietly. "What just happened?"

"Your Master didn't mention it," Mole said. "But he's been stealing your magic. He must have started before Founders Day." He smiled. "Once Kara took their magic he hasn't been able to create a single spell using his own power."

"Kara Fonti took his magic?"

"Another thing your Master forgot to mention," Mole said. "No Mage who was in the room that night has any magic left." He paused and looked directly at Inigo. "Kara thinks it could be permanent for some."

"Ridiculous," Inigo said. "My power is returning already."

"It's not," Mole said.

Timo had to wonder at Mole's confidence. Was it a guess? Timo stared at each Mage in the room, but as hard as he looked he could find no trace of magic except for Barra's. Even now the stolen power was thinning around Faron.

"I'm sure he'd like everyone to think it was," Mole said. "But only this girl has any magic." He called out a few words in Seyoyan. "I will be releasing the others in a moment," he said quietly. "Then we will leave."

"You won't get far," Inigo said. "We'll find you and kill you."

Mole stepped toward Inigo, pulling a frightened Barra with him. "I would kill you now," he said softly. "But I promised Kara Fonti that I would not do anything to jeopardize my mission." Mole relaxed slightly and retreated. "But don't think I don't know what you did." He stared at Inigo. "Arabella Fonti is dead because of you," Mole said.

Cold spread along Timo's limbs. His mother was dead?

"I was at Founders Day. You attacked Kara, and she sent your spell back to you. But you used the Mage Guild Secundus as a shield and she was killed by your spell. The one you meant for Kara," Mole finished.

Timo's legs felt weak and he slumped against the doorway. He looked over at Barra, who seemed afraid, but not surprised at this news. Had she known all along? Yes, he could see it in her eyes. She'd spoken to him and hadn't said a word about his mother being dead, she'd even gone so far as to let him believe she was alive and well.

"I really don't care," Faron said. "The truth is I do have more magic in this room than anyone else. Right, Barra?"

Timo's anger at the girl evaporated when he saw the terror in her eyes. She actually shrank against Mole, who still held her captive.

"That's actually not true," Timo said. He stepped into the room and dropped his invisibility spell. "I have more magic than Barra." He met Faron's gaze. "Besides, she won't use her power on your behalf."

"Timo," Hestor said. "Thank Gyda. Stop that man. He's threatening to kill us."

Timo strode over to Mole's side. "That's funny coming from you, Hestor. How many times did you try to kill me over the years—five, ten? And let's not forget that you tried to hire an Assassin."

"No, let's not forget that." Mole nodded. "Although we know you were asking on behalf of someone else," Mole said. He looked at Inigo and grinned. "I wanted to take the commission just to part you from your Guilders. I'm still sad that I was outvoted."

"Assassin contracts are governed by Guild Law," Hestor said. "You'd be forced out of the Guild if you didn't fulfill it."

Timo snorted and met Mole's eyes. "Mole isn't Guild," Timo said. He looked at Hestor. "But you've all but confessed to trying to arrange my death." His gaze shifted to Inigo. "And I believe Mole was speaking the truth about the death of my mother." His lips tightened. He and Arabella Fonti hadn't had an easy relationship, but she was still his mother. He turned to Mole. "I'll get the Seyoyans."

Mole nodded, and Timo stepped past him. He glanced at Barra as he went by, and she dropped her gaze, but not before he saw the panic and defeat in her eyes. He sighed as he made his way to a door at the far end of the room.

Would he have done anything differently in her position? It hadn't felt like it at the time, but his mother and Rorik *had* protected him—Barra never had that. And the one thing she'd hoped would save her, to be assigned as Journeyman to a woman, he, Timo had spoiled. Or so Barra believed. And she wasn't wrong, not really. If Arabella Fonti hadn't had her son to protect, she might have taken on an Apprentice or Journeyman. And she might have wanted to teach a woman.

The door led to a short hallway lined with four more small doors. Pink mage mist swirled around three of them.

"Yash," Timo called. "Wuls, where are you?"

"Timo," came the reply. "Back here."

Timo followed the voice to the third door. He waved the spell away and grasped the latch. The door swung open, and he saw Wuls lying flat on stone the floor. Pink mage mist covered him from the neck down.

"When I move it gets tighter," Wuls whispered. The mist seemed to sink into him, and he gasped.

Timo knelt down and studied the spell. Using Barra's power, Faron had created a strong and very vicious spell. He glanced around the room and frowned. It looked as though Faron made a habit of keeping captives. Thick chains were attached to bolts in the wall, wisps of pale blue mist still clinging to them. A small chair was propped up against the wall beside the open door. Did he come and watch his captives? Torture them? Timo shook his head in disgust. No wonder Barra had preferred Mole to Faron.

"Hold still," he said to Wuls. "I need to know what I'm dealing with." He wasn't about to repeat the same mistake he'd made with Rorik. He didn't want to trigger an even worse spell while trying to remove this one. He poked a finger at the spell, and Wuls sucked in his breath. Timo met his eyes and Wuls blinked once, telling him to keep going.

Timo closed his eyes and tried to *feel* the spell. He nodded. There was power in this spell but it weakened right . . . here. He poked a finger into the pink mist and willed the spell towards him. Slowly it started to unravel. He copied what he'd seen Kara do so long ago and trailed his finger along the floor, drawing the mage mist with it. Wuls' breathing became harsher and then he gulped in a raspy breath.

"Thank you," Wuls said. He sat up, and the mage mist seemed to run off him onto the stones of the floor.

"You're welcome," Timo said. He flicked his hand, and the mist faded away. "Where's Yash?"

"Next room," Wuls said. He stood up, leaning heavily into the wall. "I haven't heard anything from him since Mole was caught." He stumbled through the door, Timo close behind him.

"You know Mole?" Timo asked. A quick wave and the mist that clung to the next door dissipated.

"He introduced himself," Wuls said. "In Seyoyan." He pulled open the door. "Yash," he called out. He said more in Seyoyan and then launched himself into the room.

Timo followed to find Wuls sitting on his knees beside Yash, who was laid out on the floor covered in the same pink mage mist. He didn't move even when Wuls leaned into him and spoke directly into his ear.

"Stand back," Timo said. He bent down over Yash. "He's breathing, but barely."

Timo knelt beside the Seyoyan. This spell was more powerful than the one he'd removed from Wuls. He tentatively reached a finger towards the mist but snatched it away when it seemed to wind tighter. Yash's shallow breathing became a wheeze, and Timo met Wuls' worried gaze.

"Do it," Wuls said. Then he closed his eyes.

Timo nodded and swept his hand over Yash, *pulling* at the spell as hard as he could. The pink mist lifted off Yash in one big sheet and flew towards Timo. He rocked back on his heels and fell over backwards when the mist struck him. Then it slowly sank into him.

"Yash." Wuls leaned over his brother, cradling his face. Yash shuddered and then sucked in a breath. He opened his eyes and croaked something in Seyoyan. Wuls replied and gently touched Yash's face.

"Thank you," Wuls said to Timo. He held out a hand, helping Timo up from where he'd tumbled to the floor. "What happened to the magic?"

"I'm not sure," Timo said. He flexed his hands and stared at them. Was there a tinge of pink to his mage mist? "I think I absorbed it." Was that what Kara had done? Was that how she'd drained the Mages of their power? But she wasn't a Mage—could she even absorb magic?

"Let's get Mole and get out of here," Timo said. He'd worry about what had happened later, when they were safe. Wuls helped Yash to his feet, and they followed Timo out to the main room.

"You got them, good," Mole said. He still stood with his arm on Barra, but to Timo it now seemed more protective than threatening. The three Mages were tied together in the middle of the room.

"You won't get far," Inigo said. "The council initiated extensive patrols after Founders Day."

"And this one," Wuls toed Faron, "has his own traps laid out." He turned to Timo. "That's what caught us. We could see it coming but we couldn't outrun it." He looked over at Barra. "It was her magic though. Why isn't she tied up with the rest of them?"

"She's coming with us," Mole said. His eyes narrowed, and he stared first at Wuls and then at Yash before settling on Timo.

"Barra," Timo said as he took a step towards her. "Is that what you want? I couldn't help you before, with my mother, but I—*we*—can help you now."

"They'll kill me if I stay, won't they?" She looked up, searching his eyes. Timo nodded, and she sighed and straightened her shoulders. "Then I have no choice."

"We can't trust her," Wuls said. "I say she stays."

"I don't know you," Mole said. He leaned towards Wuls, and

Timo would have sworn that Mole, as compact as he was, towered over the Seyoyan. "This is my mission. I say she comes."

"Wuls." Yash placed a hand on his brother's arm. "This is not the time."

Wuls shook Yash's hand off but he stepped back to let Mole lead Barra out the door. Yash and Wuls followed, with Timo in the rear. Once out in the hallway, Timo shut the door and locked it with a spell.

He turned to face the others.

"We need to find a place to rest," he said. "It's day, and I, for one, need food and water."

"I know a place," Barra said. "It's not far."

"Good," Timo said. "Let's go."

Barra, followed closely by Mole, headed off down the hallway. Timo gestured to Yash, who simply shrugged and looked at his brother. Wuls folded his arms over his chest and glared at Timo.

"I don't trust her," he stated.

"I do," Timo said. "She didn't do any of this by choice." He looked down the hall, where Mole and Barra had stopped. "We don't have time for this now. We have to go."

"We'll go our own way," Wuls said. "We can avoid any magical traps by ourselves."

"That's your choice," Timo replied. "But we know how well you've done up until now. If you don't trust my judgment then trust Mole's. He's trained to know."

"Mole," Wuls spat. "He was right, we don't know each other."

"I thought you said he introduced himself to you?" Timo asked. He slapped Wuls' shoulder. "Come on. Mole is the one who was coming for me—he was Reo's Apprentice." Timo ignored the look that passed between the Seyoyans and walked by them. He heard their footsteps following behind him long before he'd caught up to Mole and Barra.

BARRA SET A fast pace, leading them along narrow, dark passageways to a corridor that ended at a tall wooden shelf.

"I'll go first," she said softly. "In case anyone's there already."

Mole placed a hand on her arm. "I'll go with you."

Barra nodded. She wedged her left hand between the shelf and the wall, easing the warped wood a few inches away from the stone. Mole reached across her and pulled. The base of the shelf swung out, and Barra squeezed through the hole in the wall and was swallowed by darkness. Timo wondered briefly why she didn't use a mage light. Then Mole shrugged and winked at him and followed Barra.

"I don't like this," Wuls whispered after a few moments.

"You don't like anything," Timo said. He heard Yash stifle a laugh, and Wuls turned his glare away from Timo and onto his brother. "It's Mole. They'll be fine."

"Of course we'll be fine," Mole said from the darkness. "Hurry up. It's clear."

Timo had to turn sideways in order to fit through. His shirt caught on the old wood of the shelf and ripped as he forced his way through. He felt his way forward, hearing the others staggering after him.

"Mole?" he called out in the dark.

"Go three steps forward and then one step left," Mole said from behind. "I'll close this up."

A shadow was outlined in the wedge of light from the corridor. It dipped for a moment and then the light narrowed to a sliver before it disappeared. Timo threw his hand out in front of him, mauve mage mist showing him a narrow corridor that ran between rough stone walls. He shuffled forward until he saw the passageway jog to the left.

Yash leaned over his shoulder. "We can see too if you keep your hand up high."

Timo nodded and raised his hand, trying to keep it high enough for the others to see as he snaked around the corner. After a few more steps, the narrow passage opened up. Barra knelt beside a pile of cloth, her hands fumbling with something. Then he had to squint against the glare of a lamp.

"Why not a mage light?" he asked as he stepped over to her.

"This is where I come to get away from magic." She stood up but wouldn't meet his eyes. "I keep it stocked with food and water. Just in case."

"In case of what?" Timo's question was lost in the noise of the others arriving.

Barra moved over to a small shelf along the wall and took a jug from it. She quickly lined up two battered metal cups and filled them. She handed one to a grateful Timo and the second one to Mole.

"In case she needs to stay out of the way for a few days," Mole said.

"Why would she need that?"

Mole gave him a long look. "You of all people shouldn't have to ask that," he said. "You know what Mages are capable of."

"Yes," Timo replied. He did, so why was he so surprised that Barra needed a place where she felt safe? Because she'd always seemed so strong, that was why. He sipped his water. It was warm and had a slight metallic taste to it, but it was clean. His mother had always seemed strong too, and they'd killed her. He looked over at Barra. Her shoulders were slumped, and she seemed tired—too tired and dispirited for someone so young. This was what Mage Guild did to its young, he thought angrily. It drained them of hope and joy and forced them to do things they hated, *become people* they hated, just to survive.

He handed the cup back to Barra so she could refill it for one of the others. He'd been much the same as her until he'd met Kara, Santos, and Reo two years ago. Even *with* the knowledge that there was a better future for him, that there were people who cared about him, he'd continued to feel lost and alone and without hope.

"You'll be safe once we get to Old Rillidi," Timo said. Barra looked up at him, but her eyes were dull. "We all will, right, Mole?"

"Yes," Mole said. He touched Barra's shoulder, briefly. "Santos will be happy to have another Mage to train."

"Santos?" Barra looked frightened. "Is he a Mage?"

"Yes," Mole said. "Santos Nimali—he's the true Mage Guild Primus."

"I won't work with anyone who's Guild," Barra hissed. "Keep him away from me." She shrugged away from Mole and went to the back of the room.

Mole looked over at Timo, who shook his head sadly. "Let her be. She's been through a lot." He leaned closer to Mole and whispered, "Faron wouldn't take her on as Journeyman unless she bedded him."

Mole clenched his hands into fists before he turned towards the door.

"Where are you going?" Timo asked.

"To find some food," Mole replied, his voice tight. "And to

finish something." He paused just before he pushed the door open. "I won't be gone long."

"Do you want me to make you invisible?" Timo asked.

"No," Mole's smile was grim. "I want him to see who kills him."

TIMO WALKED OVER to Yash, who, following Barra's directions, was reaching up to the top shelf. He pulled a wrapped package down.

"Where's Mole?" Wuls asked, coming to stand beside Timo.

"He went to find food."

"And now we're left with her?" Wuls gestured towards Barra. "I don't trust her, and now the only reason Yash and I came with you has left."

"He'll be back," Timo said.

"Sure," Wuls said. "We only have your word that he was Reo's Apprentice. He could be anyone, even an enemy."

"He speaks Seyoyan."

"Yes," Wuls said. "But so do some of our enemies."

"You're free to leave any time you want to," Timo said.

"Yes," Wuls said. He glared at Timo and joined his brother who, with Barra, was unwrapping the package.

IT TURNED OUT to be dried meat. Timo had never seen anything like it, but Barra said that one of the servants in her mother's house had shown her how to dry and preserve the meat. It would keep in the waxed wrappings for years, she said. Preserving food with magic would have been much easier, Timo thought, but Barra seemed to have an aversion to using magic, especially in this room.

"Mole didn't need to go look for food at all," Wuls said. "That doesn't sound like a real Assassin, leaving before he's sure of the need."

Timo ignored Wuls' comment, instead concentrating on chewing the tough meat. They were all sitting with their backs to the wall, facing the door. There was only the one small lamp, and the two Seyoyans' white braids glowed weirdly in the flickering light.

"If he returns with some fresh bread, I don't care if he's a real Assassin," Yash said. "Although I think he is." He looked over at his brother. "I've met one before."

"Be quiet," Wuls said. "Just because you're two years older doesn't mean you know everything."

"I know more than you," Yash replied.

Wuls looked ready to reply when Barra hushed them.

"Stop it," she said. "Do you want to be found? This room is in a little used part of an estate but it doesn't mean someone isn't near enough to hear us."

Wuls glared at Barra. "I don't take orders from you."

"That's enough, Wuls," Timo said. "You will be quiet." He raised his hand, letting the Seyoyan see the mage mist that snaked around his fingers. "Or I'll spell you quiet."

"You won't," Wuls said. He shook off Yash's hand and stared at Timo.

"I will," Timo said. "This is not a game. If we're found, they'll kill us." He looked around the room. "All of us. And you two," he pointed at Yash and Wuls, "will not have an easy death. Did you even wonder why Faron was holding you?"

"He was going to ransom us," Wuls said.

"No." Timo turned to Barra. "There was no plan for ransom, was there?"

Barra took a deep breath and let it out slowly. "Faron wanted to know what makes you able to see magic." She looked at each of the Seyoyans before her gaze settled on Timo. "He thought that if he could understand it with the Seyoyans then when he finally caught you he'd be able to take that ability from you."

"But he wasn't planning on being gentle," Timo said.

"No." She shuddered. "I didn't know any of this before I became his Journeyman, but he's been experimenting for years with lesser magic wielders. He mostly uses those born outside of Mage Guild but who have some power—enough to bring them to the island. Everyone thinks they are put to work at some of the more mundane tasks like supplying fresh water and lighting the city, but Faron . . ." Barra's lips tightened. "Faron, he would take some of them and . . . try to find the source of their magic." The look she sent Timo was haunted. "He . . . took them apart." Her voice quieted. "I found his notes. He'd cut off their limbs one by one to see if their magic changed." She drew in a ragged breath. "He did it while they were alive and awake."

"Worse than I thought," Timo said. Right now he was very

glad that Mole had left to attend his unfinished business. He looked over at Wuls. "You will be quiet." The Seyoyan nodded solemnly, his braids glowing in the dim light.

The next hour passed in silence. With Wuls and Yash watching the door, Timo stretched out on the floor to try to sleep. They would either be found or they wouldn't, watching the door was not going to change that. But if he was rested he might be able to fight off an attacker.

Timo jerked out of a deep sleep, clutching at the hand that covered his mouth.

"Quiet," a voice said close to his ear. "I didn't want to wake the others."

Timo blinked up at Mole before he relaxed and nodded. The hand dropped from his mouth, and Timo scrambled up to a sitting position. He looked around the dimly lit room. Barra was curled up in a corner, and Yash was sprawled beside the shelf, and Wuls—Timo grinned and shook his head—Wuls lay stretched across the entrance, fast asleep. Mole must have stepped right over him.

"We need to talk," Mole said. He sat down beside Timo and tossed a loaf of bread at him. It was warm, and Timo couldn't help closing his eyes and breathing in the doughy scent. How many days since he'd done something as simple as enjoy fresh bread?

"We can't stay here much longer," Mole said. "Once the Mages are discovered they'll send spells to find us."

Timo nodded. "Faron?"

"Dead."

"Good," Timo said. He met Mole's surprised look. "He deserved to die. The others?"

"Alive," Mole replied. "And still tied up." He paused. "I am sorry about your mother."

"Is that really how she died?" Timo asked. "Inigo tried to kill Kara and then he hid behind my mother?"

"Yes."

Timo shook his head. "He must have read about my father's death. He knew she could deflect his own spell back on him."

"Don't blame Kara," Mole said.

"I don't," Timo said. "It wasn't her spell. Was my mother really working with Inigo?"

"They'd agreed that he would be Secundus to her Primus. They invited us to Founders Day—they wanted Santos to approve their appointments. We came because your mother promised Santos that he could see you."

"She lied about that," Timo said. "She knew I was gone. She told me to find Kara."

"Sure, sure," Mole said. "That must have been before she struck her bargain with Inigo. Although he admitted that your mother wouldn't have been Primus for long."

"No, I don't suppose she would have," Timo replied sadly. His mother must have known how dangerous any deal with Inigo would be—why couldn't she have left Mage Guild Island? From everything he knew about his sister, she would have welcomed their mother on Old Rillidi. Instead, she'd chosen to stay and play a deadly game with a treacherous Mage.

"Now what?" Timo asked.

"How many days has it been since Founders Day?"

"What? I'm not sure . . ." Timo started counting the days in his head. "I think four. Today is the fourth day after Founders Day."

Mole nodded. "That's what I count. If they don't hear from me by tomorrow, Kara, Reo, and Santos will make their way here. I don't want that."

"But they can help."

"Maybe," Mole said. "But it's too dangerous. Too many people want them dead."

"People want us dead too," Timo said.

"Yes," Mole agreed. "But not the whole Guild. We need to get off this island today, before they come."

"Do you know how?" Timo asked. "We were planning on stealing a boat, but now . . ."

"We'll still need a boat," Mole said. "But we have to be further from the centre of the island than we are now." He rubbed a hand across his face. "We may need to use force in order to leave."

"Force . . ." Timo repeated. "You mean magic?"

"Yes." Mole nodded. "Most of the strongest Mages are without magic, thanks to Kara. A few, like Faron, will have stolen magic, but the others? We don't know if—or when—they will regain magic. We need to leave now."

Chapter 11

Kara dropped her pack on the table in front of Reo.

"Can you check and see if I'm missing anything?" she asked. "I want us to leave by noon."

Reo put down the knife he'd been sharpening and looked up at her. Lisha and Nando were at the main house, being schooled by Pilo, so they were alone in their small cabin.

"It's only been four days," Reo said. But he pulled the pack over to him and looked through it anyway.

"I know," Kara said. "But I need to go now." She paced in front of the window, staring out past the trees to the blue water of the bay. The barrier was as secure as they could make it and had been for days. Besides, she'd drained the power from most of the Mages—she doubted any of the council had magic.

"You've packed everything I can think of," Reo said. He rose and handed her the pack. "I'll grab a few things of my own, and then we'll get Santos."

"Thank you," she said. But he had already disappeared into their bedroom. She sighed again and rolled her shoulders, grateful that Reo hadn't insisted they wait another day—that they follow the plan they'd laid out before Founders Day. But the events of Founders Day had changed things. Her mother was dead and for some reason Timo had returned to Mage Guild Island. She slipped her pack over her shoulder and went to fill her water skin. And there had been no word from Mole.

They should be on Mage Guild Island by dusk. She only hoped

they hadn't waited too long.

"But we'll be safer if we're invisible," Yash said.

"Not if Barra and I lose you," Mole replied. They were sitting in a circle on the floor. Mole had declared it almost dusk, though Timo had no idea how he could possibly know that.

"We should split up anyway," Wuls said. "Timo can spell Yash and me. We'll get ourselves off this island."

"That might be better," Timo said. "That could split up the searchers."

"That won't matter," Mole said. "There are more than enough lesser Mages to conduct a thorough search. The Seyoyans can do what they want—they are not my responsibility." He glanced over at Wuls. "But we need to make sure they cannot tell anyone our plans."

"We won't be caught," Wuls said.

"Sure, sure," Mole said and turned back to Timo. "We'll change our plan once we separate. They *will* be caught, and they *will* talk. I'm not willing to take the chance that there isn't at least one Mage left with the skill to pull the truth out of them." He smiled grimly. "It won't be pleasant."

"What if everyone but me was invisible?" Timo said. "If anyone notices me, I'm already dressed as a Server. Yash, Wuls, and I can see everyone. You and Barra can see me." He really didn't want them to separate, didn't want to think about the Seyoyans being tortured because of him. And Mole was right— they would be caught. He didn't understand why Wuls, who'd been captured twice already, thought he could evade Mages— especially now that the entire population of the island was probably looking for them.

"That should work." Mole was nodding. "If we run across anything unexpected Timo can make himself invisible too and everyone else can stay in place until all is safe again. I will be able to scout ahead and take care of anyone in our way."

"Take care of?" Barra said. "What do you mean *take care of*?"

"He means he'll kill them," Wuls said with a sneer. "Right, Assassin?"

"If I have to," Mole agreed softly. "If leaving them alive puts us in jeopardy."

"But you didn't kill Faron or Inigo," Barra said. "Doesn't that put us in jeopardy?"

"No," Mole said. "The search was already in place, and I thought that killing them might make things worse. They could decide we're too dangerous to try to capture and simply send killing spells after us." Mole met Timo's eyes across the lamp. "But I went back."

"Did you kill them?" Wuls asked.

"Just Faron," Mole said. He turned towards Barra. "He deserved to die. Timo agreed."

Barra closed her eyes briefly, and when she reopened them Timo saw relief in them. She sent him a grateful look, and Timo decided that she didn't need to know he'd agreed with Mole *after* the other man had already killed Faron.

"Now they'll want us dead?" Wuls said.

"Possibly," Mole said.

"I think they want us dead anyway," Timo said. "I don't think this changes anything at all. We have to assume that any traps, magic or otherwise, are lethal."

"That's *always* my assumption," Mole said. "All right. Timo will spell everyone except himself invisible, and I will lead. We'll keep to the corridors and sometime before dawn we'll go below and find a boat. If all goes well, we'll be on Old Rillidi by dawn."

"You make it sound easy," Timo said.

"Let's hope Gyda takes pity on us and keeps it easy," Mole said with a laugh. "It won't be as interesting but we won't have to miss any more meals."

EVEN THOUGH HE could see the others, Timo, as the only one visible, felt exposed and alone. Mole sidled along the wall to an intersecting corridor. He looked each way before he waved them forward. Timo, hunched over to keep as low as possible, shuffled towards Mole, Barra right behind him and Yash and Wuls a few steps behind her.

"We go south." Mole indicated one of the intersecting corridors, and again Timo wondered how he knew these things— the time of day, the direction—without any visible clues.

"I'll signal when it's clear," Mole continued, and Timo nodded.

Mole had said the exact same thing every few minutes for the past few hours—they all knew what was expected. He glanced back at Wuls and Yash. The Seyoyans were getting increasingly impatient at the slow progress. Perhaps Mole's comments were less for him and Barra and more for them.

Mole slipped around the corner and trotted down the hall. Timo waved Yash to his side. Since they were invisible, the Seyoyans had been taking turns watching for Mole's signal.

"How much longer?" Wuls whispered. He had leaned past Barra in order to speak to Timo, and startled, she shrank away from Wuls. Timo gave her a reassuring nod, and she relaxed.

"It's only been a few hours," Timo said. "Dawn is still three, maybe four hours away." When they'd first left Barra's hiding place, they'd had to defuse a few magical traps, but it had now been hours since they'd seen one.

"I think we should find a boat now," Wuls said. "We'll be safer on the water."

"Neither you nor I have spent much time underneath the island," Timo said. "Mole knows his way around down there the best. We need to trust him."

"Why should I?" Wuls said. "He's the one who decided we should bring her, and I *do not* trust her." Barra flinched at Wuls' statement but she didn't say anything.

"I trust her," Timo said. "She didn't do anything she wasn't forced to do. And Mole has been safely coming to see me for months. You can leave anytime you want, but I'm going with him."

Wuls frowned and glared at him, but in the end, he settled in to wait. Timo glanced at Yash, who still had his head poking out into the intersecting corridor, watching for Mole's signal.

"Has Mole really been coming to see you?" Barra asked.

"Yes." Timo nodded. "He was keeping an eye on me until Founders Day, when I felt I could leave." He laughed, but there was no humour in it. "Gyda knows I should have gone sooner." He looked over at her. Barra's head was on her knees, and she looked weary beyond her years. "You knew my mother was dead the first time I spoke to you." He tried not to make it an accusation but she bowed her head just the same.

"Yes," she replied. "I'm sorry. I had already decided that I had to tell Faron I saw you. Talking about your mother would have made it harder for me to do that." She looked over at him. "She didn't deserve what happened to her."

"No," Timo agreed. "But neither did I, nor you. I don't blame you."

"You should," Barra said. "I could have made different choices."

"Yes," Timo said sharply, and she looked up at him. "You could have made *worse* choices. You could have become like Hestor. He tried to kill me, more than once, simply to gain favour with Inigo."

"I might have become like Hestor in time," Barra said softly. "I was on that path. I knew Faron was going to hurt you, yet I still told him where to find you. All to, as you say, *gain favour*. You wouldn't have done that."

"Don't be so sure," Timo said. "I've had my mother and Rorik protecting me ever since I was born." And he'd never once considered what that must have cost them—what it eventually *did* cost them both. "And I have my sister. Two years ago she gave me hope that there was a safer place for me, that I could make different choices. You didn't have that." He paused. "And when Mole started visiting I didn't feel so alone. You didn't have that either."

"I did," she said. "A little. Hestor tried to protect me as much as he could. I knew he was doing it because he was hoping for more than friendship, but he never pushed me. But the other? Hope for a different sort of life? No, I did not have that." She was silent for a few moments. "Do I have that now?"

"Yes," Timo said. He was absolutely certain that Barra would be welcome on Old Rillidi. "I've been told that Santos wants more Mages to teach. Besides, Mole has decided that you're coming with us. I'm not willing to cross him, are you?"

THEY TRAVELLED FOR another two hours before Mole decided that it was time to head down to the docks.

"If we get too far from the centre we run the risk of not finding a usable boat," Mole said.

"I think we should try nearer the shore," Yash said. "Won't there be fishing boats?"

"Not tied up," Mole replied. He stared at a set of double doors that were set halfway down the hallway they were crouched in. "Not around here, anyway."

"There must be," Wuls said.

"No," Timo said. "You don't understand the Guilds. Fishing is not a Mage Guild task. Someone else does that. They may fish in the waters around Mage Guild Island but they won't be Mages, and they won't live here."

"I wouldn't fish near here if I wasn't a Mage," Yash said.

Timo had to agree with him. The view of Mage Guild Island he'd had when he'd taken the ferry had unnerved him. It seemed so much more unnatural than Arts Guild Island, though the same magic sustained them both. He wouldn't come anywhere near this island if he didn't have to, and he didn't think fishermen would either.

"Wait here," Mole said, and he slipped towards the doors. He opened one side and seemed to sniff the air. After a moment, he closed the door and scurried over to Timo and the rest.

"I smell the sea," Mole said. "And it's quiet. I'll go in. If I'm not back in twenty minutes you're to keep going. Find another way down."

"What?" Timo said. "No. We won't leave you behind."

"You will," Mole said. "If I'm not back it means I've been caught or I'm dead."

"Then take me with you," Timo said. "I'll make myself invisible. I can watch for any magical traps and use magic to stop any Mages."

"No," Mole said. "I won't risk you. I'll take one of the Seyoyans. They can see any traps."

"But they can't undo them," Timo said. He leaned in to whisper in Mole's ear. "Besides, I'm not sure they fully realize the danger we're in."

Mole frowned and looked past Timo to the Seyoyans. "All right," he said. "But stay close. Remember, I won't be able to see you." He turned to the others. "Timo's coming with me. Stay here until we return."

"What if you don't return?" Wuls asked.

"Then may Gyda's luck be with you," Mole said.

Timo spelled himself invisible. Wuls looked angry, and poor Barra looked scared. He reached out and patted her shoulder.

"We'll be back," he assured her, and she nodded. Then Mole was off down the hallway, and Timo had to hurry to keep up.

Mole slid to a stop in front of the doors. He sniffed. "You stink," he said without turning around. "And you breathe heavy. I'll be able to find you if you stay back a few paces." He eased the left hand door open and squeezed through, Timo right behind him.

Shutting the door cut off the light from the hallway, and Timo had to rely on the glow from the mage mist that enveloped them. Mole stood still, so still that Timo wondered if he was even breathing.

The air in the corridor by the doors was dank, and in the dim light, Timo thought he saw a dark patch of moisture on the stone blocks of the ceiling. That told him that they were in a part of the island where lesser Mages stayed. Such poor upkeep would never be allowed where the powerful Mages lived and worked. Here there must be fewer guilders for Servers and less magic to keep the structures pristine.

Mole moved forward slowly and peered around a corner. Timo flattened himself against the wall. The stone felt cool through his tunic and he shivered. When Mole disappeared around the corner, Timo leaned out to look.

There was an open door. And when Mole reached it, he paused and looked in. He turned his head towards Timo and shook it, then trotted towards a second door. He stopped, and Timo thought he saw him gesture to him so he rounded the corner, trying to make as little noise as possible. He reached the first door and was about to walk past it when he heard a noise and froze.

Mole was waving frantically and backpedalling towards Timo, so he reached out a hand before the smaller man bumped into him. Mole stopped, grabbed Timo's hand, and pulled him into the room.

There was just time to register the cavernous size of the room before Mole forced Timo to his knees and shoved him against the wall. Somewhere out in the hallway a door was unlocked and opened. It was shut and relocked and footsteps headed towards them.

"I doubt they've made it this far," a man's voice said.

"Let's hope not," was the reply. "The son of the Secundus who was Apprenticed to the Primus? He's like to have more power than both of us together."

"The council wants him bad though, him and his companions. I never seen a Seyoyan before. Do they really have fins?"

"Nah," replied the second man. "I seen one once, long time ago. He had real long white hair and dark skin, but regular arms.

Asides, we're not gonna see them. Patrolling is a waste of time."

"But it beats being on the work crew," the first man said. "Should we look in on them?"

The footsteps paused at the open doorway, and Timo held his breath. He could see Mole tense, ready to pounce if he needed to. There was a grunt from the pair near the door and then they left.

"Strange to see them like that," one of the men said as they headed towards the double doors. "And stranger to think that it's usually us down there too."

"If we caught some of them fugitives maybe we wouldn't have to go back to it."

"Might be worth the risk," was the reply. A door opened and closed, followed by silence.

Timo breathed a sigh of relief before he realized that Barra and the Seyoyans were in the path of the Mages.

He turned to Mole, but the other man clutched his tunic and motioned for him to keep quiet. Gently Timo turned around to face the room. And his jaw dropped.

Mage mist illuminated the huge room—rivers of it, in every colour of the rainbow, streamed down the middle of each of the four aisles and collected at the end, feeding into a wide, dark opening in the wall.

Each aisle was lined with long tables that were dotted with lumps covered in loose, dark cloth. One of the lumps moved, and Timo realized that they were people—lesser Mages—harnessed to draw out their magic to power the city. He'd seen a workroom before but it had been brightly lit with fresh breezes blowing in through high-set windows—not this dank, dark cellar. There the Mages had been alert, talking and laughing, eager to meet the Mage Primus and his Apprentice. Here the lesser Mages stared blankly across the tables at their workmates, or lay with their heads on tables. From each one a different coloured thread of mage mist streamed, pulling their energy out of them and merging into the thicker strands that exited the room.

There was a low current of sound, and Timo realized that it was the accumulated noise of laboured breathing interspersed with the odd snore or cough.

"We can get out through that hole in the wall," Mole whispered, barely raising his voice. "You make sure they stay asleep."

Timo nodded, and then realized that Mole couldn't see him. "All right," he replied. "Are you sure that's a way out?"

"It has to go somewhere," Mole said. "I'll backtrack to get the others."

He left, and Timo continued to stare at the scene in front of him, at the dozens of men and women who were literally being drained in order to supply Mage Guild Island with their magic.

Were they even aware? The two Mages who had looked in as they patrolled the hallways had said that they were usually in this room. They had that to look forward to, bleeding their energy so that others with more power, with better political ties, could have the comfort of whatever these people paid for. At least they couldn't see the mage mist, at least to them it was simply a room full of people in a stupor.

Were the lesser Mages in this room tired and lethargic after they completed their task? Would they rouse at dawn to go to whatever homes their power bought, and would a second group sit down and be drained of their magic? He leaned out into the corridor, looking towards the double doors. They were shut tight. There was no sign of Mole or the others. Had they run into trouble with the two Mages who'd been patrolling?

It was too early to go looking for Mole. Besides, the Assassin would be able to manage the two Mages—he was invisible, he had an element of surprise, and he not would hesitate. Not like Timo. He'd never killed or even seriously hurt anyone. He wasn't sure he could do it unless someone was trying to hurt him.

He looked out over the workroom. Time to make sure these Mages didn't wake up any time soon. He studied the flow of magic for a few moments before deciding what to do.

Timo held one hand out in front of him and concentrated on the threads of power that were being drawn from the Mages. One at a time—using their power to conserve his own—he sent the mage mist towards its owner, wrapping it in a small spell to send each one deeper into sleep. Half the Mages were now spelled. He peered out of the workroom door and looked at the double doors again. There was still no sign of Mole.

He sent a few more Mages to sleep, and the river of mist flowing towards the hole in the wall slowed.

Suddenly the mage mist in the aisles reversed direction. But instead of reversing towards the lesser Mages it swept up towards *him.* The mist swept past him, through the door and out into the hallway. The door to the room slammed shut, and he pressed against the wall. The dozen Mages he had not yet put to sleep looked around in confusion.

"The alarm went?" said one Mage close enough for Timo to hear. "Why'd the level drop?"

"Hey, I can't wake up Lennat." The shout came from the far end of the room. "Nor anyone else." Other Mages tried to wake their neighbours, their panic rising when they couldn't rouse them. A few jumped from their seats and fanned out along the aisles, warily scanning the room, wisps of mage mist clinging to their fingers.

Timo huddled by the door, hardly breathing, worried that the lesser Mages had enough skill and magic to cast spells. He didn't dare open the door to try to escape—the lesser Mages in the room would notice. Besides, he'd triggered an alarm. Guards were probably on the way. He might not be able to evade them in the narrow hallway.

And worse, Mole and the others were at greater risk of being caught. Would they leave, now that Timo had tripped some kind of magical trap? They should, he hoped they did. Mole could still get the others out to safety. Timo would have to do the same for himself.

He slunk towards the farthest corner of the room, away from the door. Suddenly mage lights appeared, and Timo squinted. Reinforcements were on their way. He had to find a place to hide, quickly.

In the bright light, Timo spied a rickety wooden shelf along the back wall. He gingerly climbed to the top shelf and stretched out across it, pressing himself against the stone wall. He concentrated for a moment, creating a barrier of mage mist in the air in front of him. Invisible, no one could see him, and now any reaching hands would meet what felt like the stone wall. As long as anyone searching didn't pay attention to the depth of the shelf, he should be safe.

After finding no immediate threat in the room, the lesser Mages had relaxed. Some of the others had started to wake despite Timo's spells, and they huddled in the aisles talking in hushed and nervous tones.

They were waiting for something, Timo thought. There was a

sound from out in the hallway. The mage mist around the door faded and it swung open. A guard entered with his sword drawn. He was followed by a Mage who Timo recognized from the council. Medium height and big-bellied, he cupped reddish-brown mage mist in his hand, ready to cast a spell.

"What's happening here," the council Mage said, his voice booming across the now silent workroom. "Why has the work been interrupted?"

"We're not sure, Master Mage," one of the men said. "The alarm went off." He looked nervously around the room. A few lesser Mages had not yet woken up. "Some of us didn't wake up right away."

"And no one saw anything?" the Mage asked. He frowned. "Of course not, you're entranced here, aren't you?" He turned to the guard. "Check the room. Perhaps it's the fugitives we've been looking for."

Timo held his breath while the guard searched the room. Twice he came close enough for Timo to reach out a hand and touch him, but each time he found nothing unusual and passed by.

Once he'd finished searching, he returned to the Master Mage's side.

"Back to work then," the Mage said. "Back to your seats. I'll reset the spell. Can't have the island without water for long, can we?"

The lesser Mages dutifully sat down at their tables, many of them dropping their heads onto their hands. The Master Mage's rust-red spell snaked amongst them, and in a few moments, they were once again enthralled. Another spell drew their magic out of them, and it streamed along the aisles towards the back of the room. In moments, the streams of mage mist looked the same as it had when Timo had entered the room with Mole.

"Gyda curse that witch and Founders Day," the Mage said. "Since I was the only council member not there, all these mundane tasks fall to me."

"I'd do it if I had the power," his companion said.

"Of course you would, you wouldn't have a choice." The two turned to leave. "I have to report this to Inigo. I almost wish they'd killed him along with Faron. At least then I'd have some peace."

Chapter 12

KARA LEANED OVER the prow of the small boat as it silently parted the waters of Pontus Bay. She clenched her hands into fists and then opened them, trying to relax afters hours of tense waiting. Santos and Reo had insisted they wait until dusk and now the sliver of a moon hung over them in a cloudless sky, the faint light of Santos' spell of invisibility casting an eerie glow over the water. She looked back and met Reo's eyes. They'd been right to wait, she knew, but it didn't help ease her fear and worry.

She sighed and faced forward. Mole was capable, she knew that. He'd always been self-sufficient; even the little boy she'd first met had taken care of himself. Once they'd found a safe place to live, he'd followed Santos around for a while. But after a few years he'd concluded that he would never have magic and so could never be Santos' Apprentice—that's when he'd turned his attention to Reo.

Reo hadn't wanted to train anyone, not to be an Assassin, but Mole had been insistent. Reo said he was good, and Kara hadn't been surprised. Mole had always liked the dark, always preferred being awake at night, and had been more inclined to watch than join in. What Reo forced Mole to do was talk, become more socially aware. Because an Assassin had to be an expert liar.

Eventually Warrior Guild had an assignment for Mole. One they either couldn't or didn't want to officially fulfil. Up until then, although by then a Journeyman, Mole hadn't taken a life.

After he'd successfully completed the task, he was considered a true Assassin, although not Guild.

Kara hadn't liked it—that the boy she'd watch grow up was a killer—but Mole had wanted to put his training to use. Now it comforted her. She *knew* Mole was capable of doing whatever was needed in order to get himself and Timo to safety.

A moment after silently gliding under the bridge that joined Mason and Merchant Guild Islands, their destination came into view. Had the glow of Mage Guild Island dimmed since her trip here on Founders Day or was it only wishful thinking? The Mages she'd drained of power would want her dead, and she could only hope they hadn't recovered enough magic to pose a threat. They were all counting on that.

They rounded the shore, heading south for a few minutes before Reo steered the boat under the edge of the island. The smell of dank earth hit Kara, and she shuddered, knowing that the hulking mass of the island was above her. In the past she'd boasted that she could sink this island, strip away all of the spells that kept it aloft. Now, while she was underneath it, she wondered if Timo could as well.

Mage lights were sparse in this remote section and there were only a few dilapidated docks. Flashes of green mage mist swept past her, and Kara looked back to see Santos, his hands in the air, casting spells. Mage mist crawled over the docks that were visible, testing, she knew, to see if they were stable. Finally, in the distance, all the spells converged on a single dock. Kara pointed and Reo lined up the prow of the boat with her hand.

The first dock, although stable, did not have a safe entrance to the hallways or grounds above. It took two more tries before Reo and Santos were satisfied. By the time they had all stepped out of the boat, Kara worried that it was too close to dawn to travel unnoticed, even invisible.

The stairs led them up to a ramshackle hut. Santos waved his hands, and green mage mist—the invisibility spells—settled on them. Kara huddled beside Santos while Reo slipped outside to scout the area. When Reo re-entered the hut, she reached for him, drawing him close to her and the Mage.

"We're in a poorer section," Reo said softly. "None of the houses are much better than this one, but I didn't see anyone around. We have a few hours until dawn."

"I'll set the tracker then," Santos said. "Are you ready Kara?"

"Yes," she replied while signalling him by tapping his arm twice.

Grass green mage mist flared, and then a ball the size of her fist hovered in the air before her. Concentrating, Kara gently drew it to her. She studied it for a moment before pushing it away. It drifted a few feet ahead of her and then stopped, as though tethered to her. She rose and stepped towards the spell and it floated a foot or so away, keeping the distance to Kara steady.

"There's only one," Kara said. "I thought we were tracking both of them?"

"I set two spells," Santos replied. "They must be together."

"Thank Gyda," Kara said. Mole had found Timo. She took a deep breath, relieved. "Let's go," she said and reached down to help Santos up.

Reo was already at the door, easing it open. Once outside, the ball of mage mist settled over her shoulder, pointing towards the towers of Mage Guild Island.

"This way," Kara said, and she stepped forward, following Santos' finder spell.

EVENTUALLY TIMO THOUGHT it safe enough to move. The council Mage and the guards had left long ago, and the lesser Mages were once again still figures slumped over the tables. Every once in a while someone shuffled their feet or coughed—otherwise it was unnaturally quiet as the magic was drained from the room's occupants.

He climbed off the shelf, scrambled down to the floor, and crept over to the door.

He was going to search for the others, of course. While he *hoped* that Mole was getting the rest to safety, Timo wouldn't leave the island until he was certain.

He peeked out into the hallway—there were no signs of anyone, but the double doors were shut and edged in reddish mage mist. He cast a simple spell to find Mole, and it floated towards the doors.

Timo studied the reddish mage mist. It didn't feel malevolent, but it might trigger a warning for the council Mage if he removed it. He gently *pushed* the mist over to one side of the door and tugged the other side open. The hallway was dim, lit only by mage mist. He carefully closed the door and turned to watch the rust red spell. When no thread of mage mist detached itself, he relaxed, slightly. In a few moments the mist once again covered both doors. Relieved, Timo turned and followed his finder spell back to the corridor where he and Mole had left Barra and the Seyoyans.

He flicked his hand, and another spell flared briefly. Mole had found them. Or had they all been caught together? He peered down the hallway, hoping to see some sign, something that would tell him his friends were still free.

He paused and studied the quiet hallways. If they'd been found by the two lesser Mages, Mole would have killed at least one of them. And Barra had more power than the lesser Mages— he thought she'd use it to save herself and Mole. But there were no traces of a struggle, either physical or magical.

Besides, if the council Mage caught them after Mole left the workroom, an alarm would have been sounded and more guards would have been sent to investigate. He had to assume Mole and the others were still safe.

Timo waved his hand, and the finder spell headed down the corridor in the direction opposite from the double doors. Maybe Barra and the Seyoyans had moved before Mole came back for them? Was he looking for Mole, who was looking for the others?

HE NO LONGER had the corridors to himself. Timo wedged himself into a corner while a half-asleep woman trudged by, her head down and a clean white apron draped over her arm. She rubbed an eye as she shuffled past him. A few feet further on, she lifted the latch on one of the wooden doors that lined the hallway and disappeared through it.

He slid down the wall until he was sitting on the flagstones, his knees tucked up under his chin. Should he try to find a place to hide for the day or should he continue searching for Mole and the others?

He ran a hand through his hair and leaned his chin on his knees. It was still early—there should still be another hour or so before the hallways became busy, but he would have to be even more careful—and slow.

Mole's path was leading him back into the centre of the island, back to where the most powerful Mages lived. Was he doing it on purpose or was Mole confused? Timo shook his head. He couldn't imagine Mole being confused, of not being sure of his course. He had to assume the Assassin had a plan and knew exactly where he was going.

The finder spell hovered at head height near the wall of an intersecting corridor, and Timo heaved himself to his feet. He'd keep going, but slowly. He couldn't chance someone bumping into him or hearing his footsteps.

But he might be able to muffle any sounds he made. Concentrating, he created a small spell, mauve mage mist pooling on his open palm. The mage mist gently stretched to envelope his whole body before sinking into and merging with the invisibility spell.

Timo reached out and slapped the wall. There was no sound. He stamped his foot on the floor. Again, nothing. With a grin, he hurried over to the finder spell. As soon as he was within range, the spell bobbed around the corner and headed down the hall. Invisible and soundless, Timo trotted after it, confident that no one would be able to hear him coming.

But he couldn't hear anyone else either. He turned another corner and found himself face to face with a guard and he had to scramble in order to keep from colliding with the man. The guard, a Mage carrying a sword, stopped and stared around him. He sniffed once and Timo held his breath wondering if forgetting yet another sense would be his downfall. It had been days since he'd been really clean and Mole had confirmed that he smelled a bit. He took a slow step backwards, his eyes on the Mage, who now scanned the hallway. The Mage smiled, and Timo's heart stopped. He'd been found.

"Master Mage," came a voice from behind Timo. "I was hoping I'd see you this morning." Timo flattened himself against the wall as a round woman with a Server Guild patch stopped in front of the Mage.

"Were you?" the Mage replied, and the woman smiled widely.

"I was," she said. "It's glad I am to know that you're here keeping my Guildsmen safe." She paused and leaned over, letting her hand drop to the Mage's arm. "Server Guild is very concerned about Mage Guild's recent troubles."

"I personally appreciate your concern," the Mage said. He

gently removed her hand from his arm. "But Mage Guild is more than capable of managing our own affairs."

"Of course you are," the woman replied. "I would never say otherwise. Here," she lifted the cloth off the basket she was holding. "Have a sweet bun. They're fresh from the oven."

"Thank you," the Mage said. He flashed a genuine smile and reached out to grab a bun.

Timo was grateful that he couldn't smell it—just the sight of the brown pastry glistening with sugar and dotted with raisins made his stomach growl. How long had it been since he'd eaten a proper meal? Two days? Three?

The two exchanged a few more pleasantries before the Server headed off down the hall. To find and try to bribe another guard? Did they do this everywhere they Served? Gather information about the secrets other Guilds were trying to keep? Someone would pay for that information, but more importantly, it might allow Server Guild to navigate the treacherous politics that surrounded the more powerful Guilds—Warrior, Guider, Masons, and of course, Mage Guild.

Eating his treat, the Mage guard headed in the direction opposite to the one the Server had taken.

Once again alone in the corridor, Timo looked after the guard and then the Server. He needed to know if Mole and the others had been caught. If he was right about the Server, she would learn that before the guard did. He stepped away from the wall, and the finder spell trailed after him. His stomach rumbled. Maybe he could get close enough to steal a sweet bun from the Server.

HE DIDN'T MANAGE to steal a bun but he knew where quite a few Mages were stationed. The Server led him to each of them as she handed out treats and carefully probed for information. And she was very good at that—so good that Timo was convinced that it was part of her duties for her Guild. Now both the Server and he knew that Mole and the others had not been found.

There were more people travelling the corridors now. Timo created a new spell to find him a safe place to hide. He bound the finder spell to him before following the second spell down a narrow corridor to a small door that looked less polished than the others he'd passed.

He tugged the door open and peered in. The spell hovered in

the centre of the room and in the weird light of mage mist Timo could see cloth-covered stacks. His arm dimpled in the cool air from the room, and he breathed in the musty smell. His stomach rumbled as he slid into the room. He took another, deeper breath as he gently closed the door behind him. With a quick wave of his hand a spell traced the door. He attached the finder spell to it—the spells would let Mole into the room, but no one else.

He lifted the cloth off the nearest stack. Cheese—finally, something to eat—the room was full of great rounds of wax-covered cheese. He dropped the cloth and headed towards the back of the room.

He sat in the corner and gnawed on a fist-sized piece of smooth, creamy cheese. He shivered and pulled the rough burlap tighter over his shoulders. The room was cold, colder than it had seemed when he'd first entered. He dragged another piece of burlap from a nearby stack of cheese and slid it beneath him, buffering him from the cold of the flagstone floor.

He finished eating and huddled into the burlap that covered him. With his hunger satisfied, Timo leaned his head against the cool wall and closed his eyes.

KARA SCANNED THE well-manicured garden. Dawn was a few minutes away but the cloud cover meant that the sky had barely brightened. She hoped no one would set foot into the garden so early on a dull day like this. The shrubs they crouched behind had been shaped like sea creatures, and when she peered in between their branches, she could see wisps of mage mist still clinging to them.

She didn't think anyone on Mage Guild Island would have magic to spare for gardening anytime soon, not after she'd drained so many of them of their magic.

"No spells?" Reo asked softly from her left.

"No," she replied. "Except for Santos'." The finder spell still hovered above the side door to the manor house. It looked like it was time to head for the hallways and corridors below. Past time, really, they should have been inside before dawn hit, but the spell hadn't brought them to a promising way in until now. Even so, this entrance was risky. A big manor would have a large staff—even invisible it would be difficult to get through to the passageways below.

"Oh no!" she said as the spell split into two. One ball of mage mist continued to hover by the door while the other sped off along the side of the manor and disappeared around a corner.

"Did something happen?" Reo asked, worry in his voice.

"Yes. The spell, it divided into two," Kara replied. "Mole and Timo must have split up." Why would they have done that? Were they in trouble? Had they been caught?

"Which one do we follow?" Reo asked.

"The one I can still see," Kara said. "Only one spell remains tethered to me."

"How do we know who we're tracking?" Reo asked.

"We're not leaving without them both," Kara said. "So it doesn't really change things."

"You're right," Reo replied. "But it would be nice to know what skills we'll be adding to our group first." He shook his head slowly, a movement only Kara could see. "Let's find out who we're tracking," Reo said. Still in a crouch, he hurried to the door. He opened it and listened for a few moments before he waved in their direction.

"Come on," Kara said. She slipped inside the house, Santos right behind her.

Inside, the glow of mage lights lit a small vestibule with two closed doors and an open hallway. The spell hovered above the door directly across from them. Kara leaned into Reo and told him the location of the spell.

At the sound of footsteps, all three of them flattened against the exterior door. Reo unwound a thin rope from his arm and stretched it between closed fists.

The door directly across from them—the door the spell indicated they must go through—opened and a heavyset Server, a basket filled with eggs slung over one forearm, stepped through. Kara caught a glimpse of lit stairs heading down before he closed the door and turned the corner into the open hallway. Once he was out of sight, Reo pulled her towards the door the Server had just exited.

Reo carefully opened the door, and after a brief pause, he slipped through it. When he was halfway down, he looked in her direction and nodded, once.

Kara slipped through the door, tugging on Santos' arm to follow. The two reached the bottom of the stairs just as Reo pulled his head back in from another door.

"No one's around," Reo said, and he opened the door wider. "Come on."

Once in the hallway, Kara took the lead, Reo's hand on her left arm while Santos held the other end of Reo's rope. The spell led them along dimly lit hallways, past several doors and intersecting corridors. A few times they had to pause to let Servers, carrying various baskets and bundles, go by. Once they had to sneak past a guard—a Mage who was watching the corridors. Kara wondered if that was in response to her visit on Founders Day or because they were looking for Timo.

A few hallways past the guard, the finder spell stopped in front of smaller door. It was wooden, like the rest they'd passed, but it had an air of disuse about it. Kara signalled to Reo and all three of them flattened themselves against the wall. She leaned over and spoke softly into his ear.

"I think he's in there."

Reo nodded. He didn't ask who "he" was—they wouldn't know which of them they'd found until they opened the door.

"Careful," Reo said, and he dropped his hold on her arm.

Kara nodded even though she knew he couldn't see her. She knew what Mole was capable of.

She edged over to the door, her back flat against the wall. A shuffle came from down the hall, and she stopped, not daring to breathe. A Server headed their way, a thin woman bent over by the stack of linen she carried. Kara held her breath until the woman passed. She turned to Reo—he nodded, and she exhaled softly.

She opened the door, and the finder spell surged inside. She paused in case there was a defensive spell, but she didn't see any mage mist.

The finder spell hovered in the back corner, just past a few rows of shelves that were stacked with dishes and old pots. Kara leaned into the room.

"Timo, Mole," she whispered.

"Kara!" came the reply, and then Mole stepped out from behind a shelf. The finder spell bobbed after him.

"Thank Gyda," Kara said. She leaned out into the hallway. "It's Mole."

It took only a few steps to reach Mole, and then Kara wrapped her arms around him. He stood a little stiffly, and she grinned. Mole was never one for hugging.

"I was hoping to be off the island before you started your search," Mole said when Kara stepped away from him.

"But you're safe," she said. She pushed him back into the room. "Make room for Reo and Santos."

Mole's shoulders slumped. "I should have been able to do this myself," he said.

"But we're here now," Reo said. His hand groped around until he found Kara's arm. Santos closed the door to the hallway, throwing the room into darkness, except for the mage mist.

"Where's Timo?" Reo asked.

"I don't know," Mole said. "We got separated a few hours ago. I hope he's made his way out."

"Not likely," came the response from behind the furthest shelf. Kara felt Reo tense up beside her.

"You can come out now," Mole said. He looked in Kara's direction and shrugged. "Can you see them?"

"See who . . ." Kara started to say when a head peered over Mole's shoulder. A head covered in white braids. "A Seyoyan?" she gasped in surprise.

"Timo and I managed to pick up a few others along the way."

The Seyoyan stepped out from behind Mole, followed, to Kara's surprise, by another one.

"Is that really Reo Medina?" the first Seyoyan asked.

"That's Wuls," Mole said. "His brother Yash is around here too."

"I see them both," Kara said. She leaned over to Reo. "Two Seyoyan youths, about fourteen or fifteen are against the wall at the end of the aisle. They've been spelled invisible."

"Greetings," Reo said in Seyoyan. "I am Reo Medina. Do I know you?"

"I'm Yash Samma," the older boy said. "And my brother Wuls Samma is here as well. We have met before, Reo Medina, a long time ago. Our cousin is Chas Honess."

"Yash Samma," Kara said. "Do you see magic, like Chas?"

"We both do," Wuls said. "That's how we can keep together."

"Of course." Kara stepped towards the pair, bringing Reo and Santos deeper into the room. "I'm Kara Fonti. It's an honour to meet relatives of Chas'." The group was much larger than she'd expected—it would be harder to remain undetected. But with the two Seyoyans they could split up into two or even three groups. Maybe they could even send messages—mage mist messages— that she and the Seyoyans could read. But without Timo they only had one Mage—Santos. Kara stopped.

"But there are two colours of mage mist," she said softly. The mist that swirled around Mole was soft mauve while the Seyoyans were covered in a soft pink mist.

"Sure, sure," Mole said. "There's one more. Barra, come meet Timo's sister, Kara."

A pretty girl, no, a young woman, tentatively came out from behind the shelf. She glanced around, her eyes not focussing on anything or anyone and Kara knew that she couldn't see them. Pale pink mage mist trailed from her fingers.

"Kara, this is Barra Eska," Mole said. "She's coming to Old Rillidi with us."

Mole's chin jutted out, like he expected a fight, and Kara glanced from him to Barra, who had grabbed hold of Mole's hand and was clutching it tight.

"Is she a Mage?" Santos asked. "I would dearly love to have more Mages to teach."

"Yes," Kara and Mole said together, and Kara saw Mole relax, just a little.

"I've just made Journeyman," Barra said softly.

"Excellent," Santos said. "Are there any more of you hiding that we need to meet? I'd like to get off my feet and we need to decide what we're going to do next."

"That's everyone," Mole said. "Come, there should be enough room in the corner." He paused. "I'll stand watch."

"Nonsense," Santos said. "We need your knowledge. I'll create a small spell." His hand flicked out, and green mage mist sped towards the door.

KARA TOOK A sip and handed her water skin to Barra. A small mage light hovered above them, and all of the spells keeping them invisible had been removed. Santos' *small spell* was keeping the door to the room hidden, much as he'd hidden Kara and Reo's cabin for so many years.

"Thank you," Barra said. She took a sip and passed the water to Mole, who hadn't left the young woman's side.

They huddled in the corner of the room, sitting on the cool flagstone floor, propped up against walls or shelves.

"Is it true that you took away their magic?" Barra asked. "At Founders Day?"

"Yes," Kara replied. "They're lucky that's all I did. I was very angry." She glanced over at Reo, who looked up from his conversation with Mole. "My mother was dead. Inigo attacked us then used her as a shield."

"Oh, of course," Barra said, surprised. "Arabella Fonti was your mother. I'm sorry . . ." Barra paused. "She didn't deserve to die."

"No. Not like that," Kara said, her mouth a grim line. "Did you know her?"

"Me? A little," Barra said. "I had hoped to do my Journeyman studies with her." Barra looked down at her hands and sighed, a soft, sad sound.

"She was Secundus," Kara said. "I expect there was a lot competition to be placed with her."

"No," Barra said. She looked up at Kara and frowned. "She always made it clear that she had no interest in teaching. I had hoped she'd make an exception for me."

"Because you were a friend of Timo's?" Kara asked.

"No," Barra said. She glanced away for a moment. When she turned back to Kara, she slumped a little. "I haven't always been nice to Timo. No, I was hoping that Arabella Fonti would take me because she was a woman, and I so desperately did not want to take any of the offers I'd received." She shut her eyes. "Men expect much more from a female Journeyman than they do of males." She opened her eyes, and the look she gave Kara was haunted.

"I see," Kara replied softly, and she did. Barra Eska had had to make a terrible choice, one that wasn't really a choice at all. "Who did you end up with?" Kara asked casually. So I can make sure he dies a slow death, she finished silently.

"It doesn't matter," Barra said. She looked over at Mole. "Mole killed him."

"Good," Kara said. She watched as Mole caught Barra's glance. He smiled shyly. As he turned to answer a question from Reo, he met Kara's eyes and blushed. Mole and Barra Eska? That made her decision even easier. She caught Mole's comment about where they should go to look for Timo.

"No," Kara said. All eyes turned her way. "First we're finding a way off this island."

"Without Timo?" Mole said. "We can't leave without him."

"We won't," Kara said. "*I won't.*" She'd lost her mother to Mage Guild, she wasn't about to lose her brother. Mole must have seen the determination in her face, because he nodded and settled his back against a shelf.

"There are too many of us to continue searching for him safely," Kara continued. "And some who are not trained to fight." She inclined her head towards Barra. "That puts all of us at risk."

"But Barra's a Mage," Mole said.

"Not fully trained," Kara replied. "She is an asset, but her strength and talents are unknown. It's the same with the Seyoyans."

Reo turned to Barra. "Could you kill?" he asked the young woman. "With magic? Would you be able to kill someone you know—someone you think of as a friend? It may come down to that."

Barra clutched Mole's hand tighter, but she didn't reply. Reo turned to his former Apprentice. "Kara is right. We need to get Barra and the Seyoyans off the island. You will take them to Old Rillidi. Santos, Kara, and I will find Timo."

Chapter 13

HIS SHIVERING WOKE him up. Another violent spasm wracked Timo, and he clutched at the rough fabric that draped his shoulders, pulling it tighter. Faint light from the mage mist that blanketed him illuminated the aisle he lay in, rounds of cloth-covered cheeses stacked high. He sat up and pulled his knees into his body, trying to keep warm. He shivered again and rubbed an eye with his knuckle.

He stood and stretched out kinked limbs before he reached for the cheese nearest him, the one he'd cut into, and ripped another chunk off it.

He had no idea what time it was—or what day, for that matter, although he thought it couldn't be much more than twelve hours since he and Mole had been separated. That would make it late afternoon or early evening. Almost time to emerge from his hiding place and resume his search.

He chewed slowly, forcing himself to swallow despite the dryness of his mouth. The cheese had some moisture, but it was also salty. He'd need water soon.

He swallowed the last bite and brushed his hands on the burlap wrapped around him. It was time to decide.

Ever since he and Mole had parted, he'd been wondering what the Assassin had done. If he thought Mole had taken the others off the island then Timo needed to leave as soon as he could—if he thought Mole was still here, he needed to keep looking for him.

He shook his head. No matter how much he wished that Mole had safely left the island—hoped that following Mole's trail would lead to a dock or a ferry—he didn't think the Assassin would leave without him.

He tossed the rough burlap he'd wrapped himself in over the half-eaten cheese. While he was searching for Mole and the others, they would be looking for him. Should he stay in one place and hope they found him? It was dangerous travelling the corridors, even invisible, but he thought it even more dangerous to stay in one place. If he could use a spell to track Mole, somewhere there was a Mage with enough power left to use a spell to track Timo.

Startled by that train of thought, Timo hastened to the door. He'd been so used to waiting for evening that he hadn't even considered, until now, that Mages would be more likely to search during the day. He had to leave this storage room right now.

He cracked the door open and peered into the hallway. It looked empty, at least from this vantage point. He cursed himself for not finding a room that was more out of the way, one that wasn't on a main corridor. There was nothing he could do about that now.

He squeezed through the door and once in the hallway, closed it and leaned against it.

A ball of rust-red mage mist hovered a few feet away, and then suddenly a cloud of dense mage mist settled on him. When he tried to repel it, the spell tightened, the way Inigo's curse had tightened around Rorik. Timo stopped struggling, and the spell loosened a little as it settled. It felt clammy and cool on his skin, and he couldn't move.

There was a shout but he wasn't able to turn his head to see who or what was coming. Timo carefully worked on the spell again, this time concentrating on slowly dissipating it. The mage mist started to thin—enough for him to turn his head. The council Mage who had investigated the workroom hurried towards him, trailed by two guards. And beyond them were Inigo and Hestor. Timo redoubled his efforts to remove the spell, and finally it fell away.

"That's him," Inigo yelled. "Get him. Now!"

Timo ran. He must have dispelled *all* of the spells on him, including his invisibility spell, because now his enemies could see him. He waved a hand at the ball of mage mist that hovered above his head. It faded to wispy strands of rust-red, and then it was gone.

Timo sped around a corner, skidding as he bumped into a Server. He careened off her and kept running, trying to reach the next corner before the guards caught up. He muttered the invisibility spell just as he reached the intersecting corridor. As soon as he rounded the corner he slowed and tried to calm his breathing.

He was in a major hallway now. It was wider than the one he'd left, and half a dozen Servers, carrying various bundles and baskets, travelled in both directions. He jumped in front of one, letting their footsteps cover the sound of his own. He looked back—the guards and the Mage were at the intersection, looking first in one direction, then the other, then again in the first direction. The Mage waved his hand and a ball of mage mist flew towards Timo. He flicked a hand and it thinned and disappeared. But he must have paused because the Server behind him bumped into him, dropping the basket he was carrying.

The Server shouted, and Timo grunted and stumbled to his knees. By the time he regained his feet, the Mage and the guards were halfway to him. A spell flew towards him, and Timo dove to the floor and slid along the wall. The spell slammed into the Server behind him, and the man gasped and fell. His head hit the flagstones with a sickening sound, and his body crumpled to the floor. The man's eyes were wide open and vacant just a few inches from Timo.

Timo closed his eyes as bursts of mage mist swept past him down the hall, and Servers screamed as they attempted to flee.

The air smelled of singed cloth and burnt flesh. Steps came towards Timo, and he opened his eyes to see the guard turning over a body a few feet away.

"A woman," the guard said, and straightened.

"And the others?" the Mage said. He stood a little behind the guard, a look of distaste on his face.

"Servers," the guards said. "Server Guild will want compensation."

"That's Inigo's problem," the Mage said. "Not mine. He's proclaimed himself Primus, and he told me to use whatever force I had to in order to stop Timo Valendi." He looked down the hallway, his eyes sliding past the spot where Timo lay hidden by his spell. The Mage flicked his hand and then shook his head. "The finder spell isn't here. The boy must have been able to evade it. Get someone else to clean this up and then follow me." The Mage stepped past a body and headed off down the hall.

"Master Mage Jinaro," the guard said. "I don't think you should carry on by yourself."

"Pah," Jinaro said, turning around. "He's just an Apprentice, and not a very powerful one, I hear. I'll manage."

"But Primus Inigo said . . ."

"Follow me when you've arranged to have this cleaned up," Jinaro said. "That's an order."

"Yes, Master Mage," the guard said. He stared after Jinaro as he strode down the hallway. "Inigo thinks the lad might have some of his sister's skill," the guard muttered. "It would serve you right if he took your magic away, like his sister did." The guard headed towards the intersection of the corridors.

Timo sat up, rubbing his elbow where it had hit the floor. He should go before they came to remove the bodies. When that happened the corridor would be too busy for him to slip away unnoticed.

In the end Timo stayed where he was. He studied the dead Server beside him before casting a spell. Mage mist crawled over him, covering his body from head to toe. He looked down at his chest—like all spells, he saw through this one. He had to trust that it was working.

The corridor was empty. All the Servers had fled and no others had come this way since the Mage had attacked.

Timo removed the invisibility spell, leaving the second spell in place. He closed his eyes and slowed his breathing—he had to trust his magic. Footsteps echoed down the hall, and he heard a guard giving instructions to remove the bodies.

Booted feet hurried past him—probably the guard trying to catch up to Jinaro. Good. The others might not know how many Servers had been killed, might not realize that there was one extra body. He felt himself being prodded by a boot.

"Let's get this one," a voice said from above. "Be careful, there's a lot of blood." Then he was grabbed by the arms and feet and half-carried, half-dragged down the hall. He was pushed onto a cart of some kind, where he lay with his face pressed against wood. Other weights—the bodies of the Servers who'd been killed—were piled in beside him. Eventually the cart started to move. He sucked in a breath, almost gagging on the smells of death that travelled with him—blood, piss, shit. He didn't know where he was being taken but for now he was safe.

KARA LOOKED AROUND the room. She'd never been in her mother's home—not even as a child. She trailed a hand along the top of a chair upholstered in velvet. There were a few books stacked on the table beside the chair. She opened the top one, and her eyebrows lifted in surprise. Her mother had been reading one of Santos' old journals. She'd thought she'd hated the former Primus.

Reo entered the room, and she looked up and met his serious gaze.

"We have to wait for dark, of course," Reo said. "Then we'll see Mole and the others safely off. Santos thinks he can hurry the boat along without making it noticeable."

Kara nodded. "And Barra Eska?"

"Santos is teaching her a few defensive spells," Reo said. "He seems pleased."

"And Barra?"

"She's nervous, but determined." Reo held out a hand, and Kara walked into his embrace. "I think she's afraid to disappoint Santos." He kissed the top of her head. "Mole hasn't left her side."

Kara sighed and settled into his warmth, enjoying the feel of Reo's body against hers, enjoying this brief respite before they once more entered the dangerous corridors of Mage Guild Island.

They'd decided on her mother's house because they were certain that it was empty. They also thought the council would have already looked for Timo here. Kara had removed a spell on the door that led up from the hallways below—one that was probably set to alert the Mage who cast it that the house had been disturbed. Then Santos had not simply spelled the door shut, he had blocked it from the inside. Anyone opening the door from the hallway would find a blank wall. And *that* would trigger a spell to let Santos know someone was there.

"Reo Medina, Kara Fonti," Yash said formally from the doorway. "Santos Nimali has asked that you join him in the workroom."

Kara sighed and stepped out of Reo's embrace. He kept hold of her hand as they left the room.

Kara stood in the doorway with Reo, looking into the workroom. It was not a large space, and there were no windows so a couple of mage lights illuminated the room. Santos sat in a straight-backed wooden chair, and Barra sat on a small stool in front of him, her hands folded in her lap, pink mage mist trailing from her fingers. Mole stood by a plain fireplace, a scowl on his face. Kara felt Yash Samma back away from the room, and she smiled. She thought she knew what was coming and thought it wise for the Seyoyans to stay out of it.

"You *are* leaving with them," Kara said.

Mole looked at her, startled, the scowl replaced by a pleading look.

"You have to, Mole." She almost felt sorry for him. He'd thought he could argue with Santos, and maybe even Reo—but he knew he wouldn't win against her.

"I came here to save Timo," Mole said stubbornly. "I plan on doing that."

"You've done your part," Kara said, trying to soften the decision. "But your responsibilities changed when you and Timo decided to help the others. I have no doubt that you both willingly accepted that responsibility but with Timo gone you're the only one who can fulfil it."

"But . . ." Mole started. He paused to look over at Barra, who stared down at her hands. "*You* could take them to safety. That way I can stay and help Santos and Reo."

"You know that won't work." Kara shook her head. "My skills will be needed here. Besides, although I want to help Barra, Yash, and Wuls, you're the one who promised them. Am I right?"

Mole stared at her for a moment, clenching and unclenching his hands. Finally, he relaxed. "Yes. I did promise them. Timo and I both did."

"That's settled then," Reo said. "We'll help you as much as we can, then it will be up to you to get them all to Old Rillidi."

THE CART HAD been stationary for a while, and the men who'd pulled it had shuffled off. Judging it safe, Timo opened his eyes and lifted his head. Disturbed by his movements, flies scattered and buzzed in circles around the contents of the cart, looking for a place to land. He flicked a hand to shoo them away from his face. He'd become used to the smell of the corpses but when he lifted his head, a cool wind ruffled his hair, and he gulped in fresh, salty air.

The cart took up most of the space in the small room. The stones of the floor and walls were rougher than those of the corridors, and green moss grew in the corners. The wooden braces of the cart rested on the top of a wooden half door. From beyond came the sounds of water lapping at wood.

He sat up. Beneath his spell, his clothing was mottled with blood. Not as much as the spell had covered him with, but this was real—black and sticky and slightly coppery smelling. He looked over at the bodies of the Servers. Four dead, all because of him. He shook his head, his lips tight—*he* wasn't the one who'd recklessly sent killing spells down a hallway full of people. *He* wasn't the one who'd killed them. But he was sad that they had died, that the spells meant to kill him had instead killed them. But he didn't regret that he was still alive.

Now he knew for certain that Mage Guild wanted him dead. That made other decisions easier. If he came across Jinaro—or Inigo or Hestor—he'd have to be ready to kill them. If he was the enemy of Mage Guild, then all Mages were his enemy. He took a deep breath and thought of Mole's face when he'd returned from killing Faron. He'd have to be like that, cold and calculating. He could do it, he hoped.

Timo eased himself up and out of the cart. Once on the ground, he undid the spell that disguised him as a dead Server and cast the one to make him invisible.

He leaned out over the half door. The dark water below him looked cold, and he didn't see a boat. Far off, a mage light illuminated a shabby dock, and even further away he thought he saw a difference in the colour of the water. Was he close to the edge of the island? Could he make it out from underneath it safely?

He ducked into the room. He might be able to get away but he had to find Mole and the others. He'd promised. He sidled around the wagon until he was in front of the wide doorway that led back into the hallways and corridors. He peered out. The rough hallway was dark, which hopefully meant it was empty. Through the gloom he saw a short hall that ended in a closed set of double doors. A sliver of light seeped out from under the doors.

He crept into the hall, keeping his back to the wall as he slowly made his way to the door. Mage mist from his spell illuminated each step, helping him avoid the loose stones and bits of wood that littered the floor. When he was halfway there, the light coming from under the door changed. It was no longer steady—now it bobbed and flickered—and it was getting brighter.

Timo flattened himself against the wall as footsteps scuffed the uneven floor. The wooden doors rattled before one side swung open and mage light spilled in. By the time Timo's eyesight adjusted to the light, the man carrying it was beside him.

Small and wiry, the middle aged man shut the door behind him. The Server Guild crest was prominent on his chest but his clothing was a better cut and quality than that of the dead Servers in the cart. Timo stayed pressed against the wall as the man walked past him towards the wagon. He heard an inarticulate cry of grief before the man raised his voice.

"Gyda cursed Mages," the man spat. "Throwing their spells around, killing good honest Guildsmen. We'll make 'em pay, don't you worry. Oh no!" Even more grief tinged the man's voice. "Vina, not you!" His voice broke into a sob. "I'll pull the Guild from this island, that's what I'll do."

There were rattling sounds and then a gust of salty air swept past Timo.

"We'll get you home first," the Server said. "Then I'll tell the Guild to pull us *all* off."

Waves slapped against wood, and something bumped into the wall.

"Straighten that boat up," the Server called out. "I'll bring the whole cart across."

"How many?"

"Four," the Server said. He stepped in front of the cart and picked up the poles. He grunted as he started to drag the cart out of the room. In a few minutes the half door was closed. Gruff voices talking in low tones faded, and then there was silence. Timo waited a few more moments before making his way to the double doors. He tugged one side open and stepped out into the hallway.

If Server Guild really did remove all of their Guildsman from Mage Guild Island it would cause chaos. Let the men who ran the council live without both magic and Servers! He could only hope that both situations lasted a long time. He paused at the thought of power returning to the Mages, especially Inigo and the rest of the council. He had to find Mole and get them all off the island before that happened.

Kara followed Santos down to the dock. Santos' green mage mist enveloped a small boat and cast a greenish glow over Reo, Santos, and Mole.

"The boat's ready," Santos said. "Time to make their path a little darker." He flung a spell out across the water. Mage mist slowly wound its way past the docks and boats that were scattered throughout the darkness.

"I can only do this as far as I can see," Kara said.

"That should be far enough," Reo replied. He stared out in the general direction of Santos' spell. "You can see for a long way down here—at least as far as the poorer section of the island. There probably won't be many lights there anyway."

Kara nodded. She *could* see a great distance. As the mage mist continued its slow journey along the surface of the bay, illuminating the path for her, she focussed on the mage lights that dotted the ceiling. One by one their brightness faded. Here and there she left one at almost full strength, and a few she let go completely dark. When she could no longer see the green mage mist, she stopped.

"That's it," she said. "I've tried to make the route as inconspicuous as possible."

"Well done," Reo said. "I can barely make out that it's a path, and I know where to look. Mole, go get Barra and the Seyoyans. It's time for you to go."

"Barra knows how to signal?" Kara asked Santos.

"Yes," he nodded. "I showed her how to cast the spell." He smiled broadly. "She's smart and has a decent talent. She'll be a pleasure to teach."

"As long as we all make it home to Old Rillidi," Kara said. They couldn't afford to look beyond their next task, not when they still had to find Timo, not when they might have to deal with the Mage Council.

"We will," Reo assured her. "We've done it before, we'll do it again."

"With Timo," Kara said.

"With Timo," he agreed.

Yash quietly came down the steps, followed by Wuls, Barra, and finally Mole. All four stepped into the boat, Yash confidently taking a seat at the tiller. Mole sat in the middle, with Barra beside him and Wuls stretched out with his head hanging over the prow.

"See you back at home," Kara said, and Mole nodded solemnly.

Santos waved a hand, and the boat slowly set off along the path Santos' spell had created a few minutes ago.

Kara wrapped her arms around herself. Mole wasn't happy—but he was safe. Now they had to make sure Timo was safe too.

"Come on," Reo said and took her hand. "We need to get off the dock."

SHE WAS TAKING yet another aimless walk around the sitting room when the spell burst into the room and hovered above her. Her shoulders dropped, and she sighed in relief.

"Santos, Reo," Kara called. "They've made it. Barra's spell is here, and there's no sense of urgency or danger. They've made it out from under Mage Guild Island."

"Excellent," Santos said. He held a cup in his hand, a trail of steam wafting above it.

Reo stood beside him, a satisfied look on his face.

"The finder spell for Timo is ready," Santos said. "Let me know when we can leave." He turned to look at Reo at the same time that Kara did.

"It's late enough now," Reo said.

They didn't expect anyone to search Arabella's rooms once they were gone but Reo had suggested they remove all visible traces of their stay anyway. It would be better if Mage Guild never knew they'd been here, if possible.

Kara stepped into her mother's bedroom. She'd deliberately stayed out of it until now—it had seemed too intrusive. After all, she'd only seen her mother a handful of times in her life.

But the few times she had seen her, she'd always been impeccably dressed, her clothing rich and expertly tailored and her hair smooth and controlled. Had she had to make the same choices that poor Barra Eska had? The first time she'd met her mother was when Arabella had visited her at her home in Larona. She'd travelled there with Valerio Valendi. Kara had always assumed that her mother had bedded Valendi because she loved him, in her own way. Now she wondered if it was more for the protection and opportunities he had offered.

Kara had been young and extremely naïve about the realities of the world, but she'd recognized the lust and desire in Valendi's eyes. Had her mother seen that? Had Arabella Fonti's place in Mage Guild been so precarious that she'd sent her daughter to almost certain death in order to secure her own safety and security? In order to keep Valendi from choosing Kara?

When Reo had misguidedly taken her to see the woman who wanted her dead, Arabella, pregnant with Timo, had gloated about it being Valendi's child. And when Kara had told her Valendi was draining her power, Arabella had dismissed it. But maybe she'd been too afraid to confront the Secundus? Maybe her safety—her life—was dependant on her *not* confronting him?

What would her mother have become if she hadn't born Valerio Valendi's child? If she hadn't had the advantages that came with being the Mage Guild Secundus' woman? She certainly wouldn't have become Secundus herself—Arabella achieved that position through the support of Rorik, Valendi's puppet, and political power she gained through association with Valendi.

Without Valerio Valendi her mother might have become a council member, but she would have needed to be allied with at least one other member. How many times had her mother had to make Barra Eska's choice and bed a man for protection and position?

Kara focussed on the jewellery box that sat on top of the dresser. She opened it and scanned the various necklaces and earrings and bracelets. There, that would be an appropriate keepsake of the woman who'd given her life, but had wanted no part of it. Kara picked up the gold brooch, turning it over in her hands.

The purple stone winked in the dim light, and she smiled. Much the same colour as her mother's mage mist, it reminded her of the brooch her mother had pressed into her hands as she urged Kara to flee all those years ago. That brooch was gone, traded long ago for supplies of one sort or another. Now she had another one to replace it, to remember Arabella Fonti by. Kara pinned the brooch to the underside of her shirt, next to her skin. With one last glance at the room, she left, closing the door gently behind her. She would not be coming back to this room, to her mother's quarters. She hoped she never had to return to Mage Guild Island. Not once they found Timo and found a way off it.

Chapter 14

CONFUSED, TIMO WATCHED the spell. He'd created it almost half an hour ago and it had yet to move. He took a step closer to the ball of mage mist. He'd created the spell exactly the same way he'd created the other finder spells. Exactly. Hadn't he? He poked a finger into it, not really sure what to expect, but the spell didn't change. He waved his hand to drive the spell away and it languidly floated a foot in front of him before it stopped and hung in the air. With a grimace, he dispelled the magic and sat down with his back against the door.

What was wrong? Had something—maybe a spell that was sent while he was asleep—affected his magic? But he *always* enhanced his ability to repel magic while he slept in case Inigo and Hestor tried to kill him in the night. It was an automatic gesture, one he'd done without fail ever since he'd figured out how to do it. Unfocussed spells wouldn't affect him, but ones directed at him could.

And he'd created that spell, hadn't he? He ran a hand through his hair and sighed. He couldn't remember. It was something he did without conscious thought so he couldn't be sure that he *had*. He stared down at the floor. Was his magic contaminated? Could he trust his invisibility spell?

He created a small mage light—his magic worked for that. A relocation spell also worked. He took a deep breath and ran through a few of the exercises he'd been forced to do daily as an

Apprentice.

After a few minutes, he leaned against the wall. He could find nothing wrong with his magic so it must be that particular spell. Unless . . . Would his spell still find Mole if he was dead? Quickly he created a spell to search for Barra. It too stayed within the small room. He tried to create a spell to search for her body, but it did the same thing. It sat in the middle of the room, not moving. Nothing changed when he cast spells to find Yash and Wuls.

Timo waved his hand, and the spells dispersed. He couldn't find them, not with this spell. He'd have to try something else.

He was so used to the spells not moving that he was surprised when the next one did. He jumped to his feet and pressed his ear to the door as the spell slid out into the hallway. Timo carefully opened the door and crept out. The spell was a few feet along the corridor, bobbing slowly as it moved. He caught up to it, keeping his back pressed to the corridor wall as he followed the spell. If he'd cast it correctly, it would lead him to the last place he'd seen Mole. From there he'd begin his search again.

Instead of taking him to the workroom where he'd become separated from Mole, the spell was leading him closer to the centre of the island where the most powerful Mages lived.

The spell stopped a few feet ahead of him, and he frowned. What was wrong with his magic? Why couldn't he get a simple finder spell to work? Angrily he waved his hand to disperse the spell. He had to figure out what was happening, why his magic was failing him. He looked around at the very familiar corridors. He was in the hallways he'd travelled every day on his way to the library from Rorik's estate.

These hallways, the library—even invisible they were not safe for him. But Barra's hiding place was close. He could rest there and decide what to do next. There might even be some water and dried meat left.

He walked quickly, turning corners and passing through halls until he finally reached the door. He opened it just enough to squeeze through and gently pulled it shut. Mage mist lit the small space, and Timo squinted, trying to see through it before he realized that the mage mist was the wrong colour.

Someone grabbed his arms. He flung an attack spell, and the grip on him loosened. Rust-red mage mist swept over him and clamped his arms to his sides. His attacker held him tighter as

Timo repelled the spell. But as soon as one spell was gone, another took its place. Muscled arms lifted him off the floor, and he was pinned between the wall and his attacker.

"Keep fighting me and I'll be forced to hurt you," a low voice said in his ear.

Timo ignored it—if he didn't get away he'd be dead soon. He cast a spell and was out from his attacker's arms, but another spell slammed into him, and he dropped painfully to the floor. His eyes fluttered closed just as a pair of slippered feet appeared beside his head.

Gyda his head hurt. Timo felt rough flagstones beneath his cheek, and he grunted when his arms were yanked behind his back. The hands that clutched him stilled, holding his wrists in a painfully tight grip.

"Hurry," said a voice. "Get the ropes on him."

The pressure on his wrists worsened as rope was looped and cinched. He was dragged to a seated position. His head dropped to his chest in pain, and he sucked in a couple of ragged breaths before he opened his eyes.

A Mage stood in front of him, the one called Jinaro—a Mage who was powerful enough to sit on the council. A Mage who had *not* been affected by Kara at Founders Day.

"You are more than you seem," the Mage said. He bent down and looked Timo in the eyes, and Timo knew that his invisibility spell was gone. "Only accomplished Mages even attempt relocating themselves." He straightened and looked over Timo's head. "I thought you said he had little power?"

"That's what we were told, Master Mage." It was Hestor.

Barra must have told him about this hiding spot. Timo was only grateful that Hestor hadn't brought the council here earlier, when they were all here.

"Bring me a chair," Jinaro said.

Something was dragged across the floor, and then Hestor came into his view. He placed a chair in front of Timo, and Jinaro sat down heavily.

"Still doing someone else's bidding I see," Timo said.

Hestor flushed and glared at him.

Timo looked up at the Mage Jinaro. "Inigo will kill me," he said calmly. "And then my sister will destroy Mage Guild."

"Your sister," Jinaro said thoughtfully. "Remind me who that is?" He frowned and looked over at Hestor. "Inigo hasn't been very forthcoming about why he wants you."

"My sister is Kara Fonti," Timo said. "The woman who drained everyone's magic."

"Hestor, is this true?" Jinaro asked sharply. "Don't bother answering—I can see by your face that it is." He turned back to Timo. "I dislike it when Inigo doesn't tell me the truth."

"He and his friends killed Faron," Hestor said. "That part is true. I was there."

"And our mistake was not killing you and Inigo while we had the chance," Timo said. "It won't matter. Once I'm dead none of you will last long." He repelled the spells that surrounded him.

"Hold him," Jinaro yelled.

Arms clamped around Timo so tight he struggled to breathe. A new spell wrapped itself around him, more rust-red mage mist.

Jinaro sat back in the chair. "It's good that I brought along non-magical guards. Keep a tight hold on him." He eyed Timo. "You must be very powerful if you can override one of my spells. Did Rorik know?"

Timo nodded. He wasn't about to tell this Mage that he hadn't overridden his spell—he'd eliminated it—and that it had taken very little effort. But he didn't bother doing it again. Jinaro had obviously created triggers to let him know when something went wrong with his spell.

"Does Inigo know?" Jinaro's gaze settled on Hestor, who shuffled nervously. "And don't lie to me, or I'll tie you up beside your friend."

"I don't think so," Hestor said. "At least, he never warned me."

"Politics," Jinaro said. "I hate them. That's why I wasn't at Founders Day in the first place, and now Inigo has embroiled me knee deep in his burro shit."

"Let me go," Timo said. "I'll leave Mage Guild Island, and no one will see me again. You'll have to kill Hestor to keep him from saying anything to Inigo, though."

"That would suit me," Jinaro said. He smiled at Timo, and Hestor paled. "And I would if I thought I could." He sighed. "No, I will have to hand you over to Inigo." He looked past Timo to the guard who held him. "Now."

Timo felt a damp cloth pushed in front of his nose, and the guard held his mouth closed. He held his breath for as long as he could, but finally he drew in one deep, sickly sweet, breath. His head sank to his chest.

Kara stopped and gripped Reo's arm to let him know that something was wrong. She heard a muffled curse from Santos and turned to see him step back—he'd bumped into Reo. She would have found that amusing except that the finder spell was no longer moving forward. Instead, it had slowed to a crawl, and now, after a few minutes of that, it had completely reversed direction. She leaned over and spoke into Reo's ear.

"The spell's heading in the direction we just came from," she said.

"All right," he replied. "Timo must be on the move."

They'd left Arabella's apartments before true night had fallen. The risk of encountering anyone awake had been outweighed by the advantage of travelling before Timo stirred. Obviously he was moving now.

Kara retraced her steps. The finder spell picked up speed, and she hurried after it with Reo and Santos trailing her. She didn't want to spend another day hiding out—she wanted to find Timo and leave before dawn.

A few corridors later the spell took a sharp right. Reo held her back when she would have followed it.

"Stop," he whispered. "That leads to the heart of Mage Guild."

Kara stared down the hall. She desperately wanted to follow the spell to Timo, no matter where he was, but they couldn't simply charge in blindly. She sighed, and Reo relaxed his grip.

"We need to hide," Reo said. "Until we can find out more and make a plan."

It wasn't much of a hiding place—a small vestibule that led to some stairs. They weren't planning on being here long so Santos created a few spells to hide them and keep anyone away.

Kara thinned out the invisibility spells just enough that Reo and Santos could see through them.

"I'll investigate," Reo said.

"No," Kara replied. "You can't follow the finder spell. I'll go."

"Santos can make it visible enough for me to follow," Reo said. "It's a risk, but it's our best option."

"No," Kara said.

"I'm going," Reo said. "Please don't argue. Why would Timo

return to the centre of the island?"

"They don't have him," Kara said.

"They might," Santos said. "And if they do, only Reo has the skills to free him."

"But what if he comes across a Mage with power? He won't be able to stop the magic."

"I won't have to," Reo assured her. "They won't know I'm there. If I feel they are a threat, I'll eliminate them."

"Kill them?" Kara asked.

"If I have to, yes," Reo said. He met her gaze and held it for a few moments.

Finally, she looked away. "All right," she said. She hated when he had to kill but she also knew he might have to in order to save Timo and keep them all safe. All she wanted was to live her life in peace on Old Rillidi, surrounded by family and friends. Why was that such a difficult and dangerous thing to make happen?

"Be careful," she whispered to Reo. "I need you to come back."

"I will," Reo assured her, and she wasn't sure which plea he was answering.

Reo and Santos spoke quietly for a few moments, and then Reo was gone. Kara slid down to sit on the floor, her back against the rough stone.

"He'll be fine," Santos said. He slowly lowered himself to the floor beside her. "He was doing this sort of thing, with less magical aid, long before he met you."

"Yes," she agreed. "But that was years ago. And even then he knew he wasn't going to come back one time."

Santos patted her knee. "It won't be this time," he said. "I promise."

Kara leaned her head against the stone wall and closed her eyes to wait for Reo to return. She hoped Santos was right, that Reo would be fine, that Timo would be safe, but she felt helpless.

"HOLD HIM," a voice said.

Timo's arms were wrenched so far behind his back that he grunted in pain.

"He's waking up," the voice continued. "Jinaro, another spell."

Timo sucked in a breath, tasting the sickly sweetness of whatever they'd drugged him with. He was lying face down on some kind of mat. His left cheek was mashed against rough fabric, and he felt the weight of someone—the person who was pulling on his arms—on his back. He struggled to lift his head and open his eyes but his arms were wrenched again. He gasped in pain and dropped his head down.

"Don't kill him," the voice said. "At least not yet."

He was almost too numb to care. At least if they killed him he wouldn't hurt so much. Once he felt his way past the agony in his arms, his head pounded and his hip felt bruised where he lay on it. He couldn't feel his fingers so he figured that the rope or whatever they'd tied him with was too tight. What did they care, they were planning on killing him anyway. He was surprised they hadn't done it already, they'd been trying for so long.

"Lift him up," the voice said. "He's awake."

Timo was roughly pulled up to a sitting position. His hair was grabbed from behind and his head yanked up off his chest. He was too tired to fight and simply let himself be handled. Footsteps came towards him and then stopped.

"Look at me," the voice said.

Timo shrugged but kept his eyes closed. It didn't matter to him who stood before him—they would kill him and his sister would make them pay.

His face was slapped so hard that his head snapped to the left and his eyes opened in response.

"You will obey me," the voice said again.

Timo looked up. Inigo. He wasn't surprised. He glanced past him and met Hestor's gaze. At least the journeyman had the grace to look ashamed. Jinaro stood on the other side of Hestor. He was frowning, but he held a ball of mage mist, ready to cast a spell.

"Thought you didn't want to be involved in the politics," Timo said. His voice was weak, and his lips were cracked and dry. He wondered how long he'd been unconscious.

"I do what I must," Jinaro said calmly.

Inigo's eyes had narrowed at this exchange.

"Yes," Inigo said. "They all do what they must, what I tell them." He peered down at him, a small smile on his lips. "We have your friends," he said, and Timo closed his eyes in pain. "The Seyoyans and the others."

Timo waited for Inigo to continue, waited for him to say that they'd killed Mole, because he knew without a doubt that they'd have to. Mole wouldn't let either himself or Barra be taken alive.

When Inigo didn't continue, Timo opened his eyes and stared right into his.

"No, you don't," he stated.

Inigo's eyes narrowed, just a little, and Timo knew it was the truth. They hadn't found Mole and the others, they didn't even know who Mole was. He started to laugh then, a painful choking sound. It took Inigo a few seconds to realize what it was—then he slapped Timo hard enough that his head snapped to the other side.

Timo tasted blood. At least there was moisture in his mouth. He started to giggle, and then he stopped. No sense making it easy for Inigo to beat him to death. He looked up at the Master Mage.

"You don't even know who I was with, do you?"

"Two Seyoyans, the Assassin, and the Eska girl," Inigo said. "She's no concern of mine. She has little magic and even less sense."

"She's why Faron is dead," Timo said, and was rewarded when Inigo flinched. "Thought you might want to know. Faron made her bed him, and my friend took exception to it." Timo looked away and saw Hestor's pale face. "I guess he should have killed all three of you."

"The Assassin?" Inigo asked. "He said he was part of Kara Fonti's delegation on Founders Day."

Timo shrugged. "He's likely gone now, but I don't expect him to forget." He looked up at Inigo and smiled. "Neither will my sister. I would think that they'd be formidable enemies."

"I'll kill them," Inigo said confidently. "Just as I'm going to kill you."

Timo laughed even as he braced himself for the blow that came.

"You tried for years but couldn't even kill *me*, a half-trained Apprentice. Do you really think you can kill the Mage Primus, a Master Assassin, and my sister, who can drain your magic?"

"I've already killed one Mage Primus," Inigo said. "I expect I'll have little trouble with this one."

"So you *do* admit it," Timo said. "You killed Rorik, the Acting Primus. I also hear you were responsible for my mother's death." He looked over at Jinaro. "The Council finds this acceptable? Inigo's admission should be cause for his death."

Jinaro shrugged. "I really don't care what the Council thinks. I simply want to be left in peace."

"You'll be next," Timo said. "Neither you nor Hestor can be allowed to live with this knowledge." He looked over his shoulder at the guard who still gripped him. "You might be last, after you've killed the other two, but one day soon you'll have an accident that will take your life. No one will connect it to this, of course, because of the five of us in this room, only Inigo will be left alive."

The guard pulled his arms, and Timo winced at the pain.

"You have no idea what you're talking about," Inigo said smoothly. "Of course nothing is going to happen to my friends here. In fact, they will all be rewarded for helping me catch and kill such a dangerous enemy of Mage Guild."

"Then you'll all pay the price," Timo said. "Once my sister knows the truth."

"Your sister," Inigo spat, "has no magical talent. I checked the records. She was tested and found wanting, for years and years." He smiled down at Timo. "No wonder her own mother rejected her."

"But she took *your* magic," Timo countered. "On Founders Day. She walked into a room full of Mages and reduced you all to non-mages. Because she doesn't have magic, she has *unmagic*." As do I, he finished silently. His head was starting to clear and he could feel himself getting stronger.

"Unmagic," Ingo said. "What uses does it have? So she temporarily took away my magic. It's returning even as we speak." He held his hand up as if to show Timo his power but there was no trace of mage mist anywhere on Inigo.

Timo smiled. Maybe he would never get his magic back.

"She can undo spells," Timo said. "*Any* spells."

"I repeat, what can she do with it?"

Timo started to laugh again. Inigo raised his hand but Timo couldn't stop laughing. The last few days had taken their toll, and now that he had nothing left to lose, he couldn't stop laughing.

"What keeps Mage Guild Island aloft?" Timo asked. "What keeps the water running and the lights on?" Inigo's hand struck him—hard. The last thing he saw was Jinaro's horrified face.

HE ACHED. HIS head throbbed, his arms felt like they'd been

pulled from their sockets, and he tasted his own blood, but as bad as he felt, at least it was proof that he was still alive.

He sucked in a breath and opened his eyes. One eye, at least; the other was swollen shut, either from the blow or the fall to the floor. A foot shuffled into view—the guard, from the look of the boot. Timo braced himself for more pain—a blow, a kick, more wrenching of his shoulders, but nothing happened.

"Keep still," the guard said.

Timo nodded. He wasn't sure he could move anyway. The boot edged away from him, and when Timo looked up, the guard was leaning with his ear against a wooden door.

"I say we let him go," a muffled voice said from the other side of the door. "We can't risk the island."

"She can't undo all the magic." That was Inigo speaking, Timo would recognize his tone of superiority anywhere.

"How do you know?" Jinaro said.

"It's not possible," Inigo said. "No one could do that."

"Before Founders Day we would have said that draining the magic from over a hundred of the most powerful Mages wasn't possible. And yet it happened. I will not risk it."

"It's not your decision." Inigo was yelling now. "I'm Primus now. I say we kill him."

"No, we need him alive. We can negotiate with his sister—Timo for her promise to leave us alone."

"Jinaro, I'm warning you . . ."

"Or you'll what? Kill me? He was telling the truth about that, wasn't he? It's better for you if none of the rest of us survive."

"How can you even think about listening to that boy's delusional ideas? Didn't you hear him laugh? He's insane."

"In that case, I'll leave. I want no part of your decision. When his sister comes asking questions—and I do think she will—I'll be able to say that I couldn't talk you out of it. That it was all your fault."

"I can't let you leave."

Timo had to strain to hear Inigo's voice.

"You can't make me stay," Jinaro said. "I'm the one with magic."

After a pause, Inigo spoke again. "I don't want us to fight about this. Why don't we let the full council decide?"

"That's acceptable," Jinaro agreed. "I can just as easily blame the full council as I can you."

"Guard, bring the boy," Inigo called.

The guard stepped from the door just as it was opened from the other side. Timo was hauled to his feet and slung over the guard's shoulder. He grunted as his bruised ribs met the guard's shoulder, and then he was being carried through the door, his hands still bound behind his back.

Timo carefully dispersed all the spells that Jinaro had placed on him—a new one formed just as an old one faded, and he dispersed that too. He held his breath. He couldn't see Jinaro, but there was no shout or exclamation from him—he must not have included a warning spell this time. Exhausted, Timo strained to cast a rudimentary healing spell. By the time they reached the first turn in the hallway, his ribs no longer ached and his head was relatively clear.

Chapter 15

HE WATCHED THE solid stone blocks of the floor pass beneath him as he was carted through the dimly lit corridors. Timo tried to shift his head to see past the guard—to see the path they were taking and determine who was with them—but all he managed to do was strain his already sore neck. He relaxed and let himself hang limply as the guard strode forward.

Was Jinaro still there? Inigo's decision to involve the whole council confused Timo—there would be no chance to keep his death a secret. Or would he try to kill Timo along the way? Inigo could lead the guard directly into a trap that would kill both him and his burden.

Panicked, Timo strained his neck, struggling to see around the guard's body. He felt something in his shoulder shift and he bit down against the pain. Ignoring his throbbing shoulder, he maneuvered his head so he could see between the guard's body and elbow.

The way forward was clear of mage mist. *Of course it was.* Inigo had no magic to waste, not since Kara had drained him during Founders Day. Timo relaxed his neck and let his head bump against the back of the guard. With a deep breath, he gathered his power and closed his eyes.

He heard footsteps up ahead, two, no three sets of feet scuffing the flagstones—Inigo, Jinaro, and Hestor. The leather strap that held the guard's sword creaked when he moved, and he panted as he carried Timo down the hall.

One set of footsteps receded into the distance slightly, and Timo held his breath. Did Inigo already have a trap set along this path? He had to rely on his instincts, but those instincts had been honed over the past two years—two years spent avoiding all kinds of traps—two years of staying alive despite the increasingly determined efforts of first Hestor, and later Inigo, to kill him. Right now those instincts told him that Inigo had no intention of parading him before the full council. He had something planned, some trap was readied that he expected would kill Timo, probably the guard, and even possibly Hestor and Jinaro.

He heard a subtle click. Timo released his spell and *shifted* the guard—and him—about five feet ahead. The guard swore and stumbled to his knees, dropping Timo. He landed on his sore shoulder and sucked in his breath, staring down the corridor.

"Gyda cursed brat," the guard muttered. He leaned over Timo, his hand raised, ready to strike him.

"Look behind us," Timo said, his voice nothing more than a croak. "I could have saved only me."

The guard followed Timo's gaze along the path they'd been about to travel. He dropped his hand and stared. His eyes hardened, and he looked at Timo. One quick nod—that was the only acknowledgement he gave his saviour. Then the guard gripped Timo, more gently than before, and pulled him into his arms.

"What's happening back there?" Jinaro called.

"I tripped is all," the guard said. "And dropped the boy. But we're both no worse for wear."

"Then get moving," Inigo said.

Now cradled in the guard's arms, Timo could see the corridor ahead—and the Master Mage. He was hovering behind both Jinaro and Hestor, no doubt hoping to be the first to see the disaster he thought they'd find in the hallway.

Timo glanced up as the guard took one last look behind at the taut wire strung across the corridor, reflecting the light. Waist high, it would have sliced right through both of them if Timo hadn't relocated them. When he turned and looked forward, Jinaro was watching him with narrowed eyes. The Mage turned and headed down the hallway.

Eventually Inigo led them through a doorway and up some

stairs. They were close to the council chambers—Timo recognized the corridors they travelled now. Had Inigo given up trying to kill him or would he dare to use a trap so close to their destination? The guard walked more slowly and now lagged half a dozen steps behind Hestor. The new Mage glanced back, quickly, and then trailed his left hand along the wall. The guard grunted and stopped.

"What'd he do?" he asked softly. "Ah, I see it." He shook his head and dropped to his knees, setting Timo on the ground.

That's when Timo saw it. Another wire, set at shin height this time. There was a faint line in the dust of the flagstone floor where the wire had been buried. The guard unsheathed his sword and jabbed at the line, cutting it. There was a whoosh and something bounced off the walls and hit the floor. Steel tipped arrows, four of them.

Once again the guard bent over Timo and gently picked him up. "Is it all of them?" he asked softly.

"No," Timo replied. "Just Inigo and Hestor. The rest of the Mages aren't involved." At least he didn't think they were.

"Am I dead?"

"No," Timo said. "Not if we make it to the council chambers." He looked up and met the guard's eyes. "But you'll need to leave Mage Guild Island as soon after that as you can."

"Gyda," the guard swore. "And go where? I'm Mage Guild. Four generations, not that it's done me any good. What about you?"

Timo shrugged. He could feel his magic building, but physically he was weak. He wouldn't be able to run—he wasn't even sure he could walk.

"They won't kill me right away," Timo said. "Besides, I have friends on the way." He thought he did. He *hoped* he did. How long ago was Founders Day? Were Kara and Santos on their way? Five days, Mole had said, and then they would come looking for them. But would they find him? And if he was being held by the council would they *dare* rescue him from here?

They rounded the final corner, and Timo grinned. A nervous looking Hestor fidgeted outside of the door to the council chamber. He paled when he caught sight of them.

"Sorry to keep you waiting," the guard said. "Had to fix my boot."

He swept past Hestor and into the room and didn't stop until he'd carried Timo all the way to the very front. A dozen Mages milled around, and Inigo and Jinaro stood near the head of the table. Inigo looked up when the guard stopped in front of him and gently set Timo onto his feet. The guard ignored Inigo's motion to leave, instead settling one hand on Timo's sound shoulder, steadying him. His other hand dropped to the rope around Timo's wrists and quickly untied it. Timo kept his hand behind his back and closed his eyes, focussing his power. He used some of his magic to help his hands and shoulder heal enough to be usable. The rest, he let build around his hands.

When he opened his eyes, the Mages in the room were manoeuvring around the table. Older Mages sat down, the younger ones like Hestor, along with some Journeymen, stood nervously with their backs against the wall. When everyone was settled, Inigo swept his gaze around the room, ignoring Timo.

He'd told the guard that he'd be all right if they made it to the council, but any confidence Timo had disappeared as he watched Inigo. He looked like a man who had every expectation that his orders would be obeyed.

Jinaro was staring at his hands, wisps of rust-red mage mist eddying about his fingers. He didn't care whether Timo lived or died—he only cared that he escaped blame in case Kara came demanding answers. A council decision to execute Timo would allow him that.

Of those present, almost half had mage mist. But besides Jinaro, only one other seated Mage had magic, and to Timo it looked thin and weak. It was the younger Mages and Journeymen, the ones leaning against the wall, who had what looked like their full powers. Timo smiled. The council members didn't trust each other—they'd decided to bring along their own sources of magic. He studied the ones still with power. He could change that, just like Kara had changed it on Founders Day.

He clenched his hands at his side and slowly called the magic in the room to him. He was surprised when the mage mist actually started flowing to him. At first the strands were thin, but after a few moments, mist as thick as his wrist was streaming from every single active Mage in the room. When the mist reached him he simply absorbed it. He could feel himself growing stronger with every wisp of power that flowed into him. His shoulder pain vanished, and he could see out of his eye.

Buoyed by the absence of aches and pains he automatically started to straighten up, and then caught himself. He didn't want to alert them yet—not until he'd drained every single Mage in the room of all of their power—so he remained slouched beside the guard.

He glanced down at his fists. Mage mist circled them so densely that he couldn't see his hands, and the hairs on his arms stood straight up. The guard behind him grunted in surprise and his hand dropped from Timo's shoulder. He chanced a glance backward. The guard lifted a single eyebrow, and Timo blinked once, quickly.

"Council members," Inigo said. "Master Mages and Journeymen. I apologize for the last minute request to convene, but it is a matter of urgency." Inigo paused. "And Justice. We are here to pass judgement on this Apprentice."

Timo looked up and met Inigo's gaze. The Mage's face was calm, his eyes clear.

"Timo Valendi is accused of killing our Primus—his own mentor—Rorik."

Voices buzzed around the room, and Jinaro reclined in his chair, a thoughtful look on his face.

"As well, Master Mage Faron, one of our fellow council members, is dead," Inigo continued. "We suspect that this Apprentice was complicit in that death as well!"

None of the Mages would meet Timo's eyes. His glance fell on Hestor, and the Mage looked away, a flush spreading across his face.

"Hestor knows I didn't kill Faron," Timo said. "And Inigo boasted about killing Rorik a few minutes ago in front of both Hestor and Jinaro."

"Be quiet!" Inigo bellowed. "I will not tolerate your insolence."

"Am I not permitted to answer the charges against me?" Timo asked.

A few heads around the room nodded, but most of the Mages simply looked on in silence.

"You will be quiet or I will be forced to gag you!"

"How do you plan on doing that?" Timo asked. He took a step away from the guard, towards Inigo. "By asking the guard behind me to cover my mouth? The man you would have happily let die on the way here as long as it meant *I died*?" Timo turned to face the rest of the council. "Two traps were sprung along the corridor." He turned to Inigo. "Did you think I wouldn't see them? I've spent the better part of the last two years avoiding traps like those—and worse. You'll have to do better than that if you want me dead."

"Guard, seize him," Inigo shouted.

"No," the guard replied. "What the boy says is the truth. There were two traps. The first one would have sliced us in two. The second was triggered by the skinny Mage called Hestor."

"I did not," Hestor protested. "And you'd do well to not accuse your betters."

"I may not have magic but I'm full Mage Guild same as you," the guard said. "And my eyesight is just fine. You triggered the second trap."

"Enough," Inigo said. "You are not a Mage—you have no right to speak in council."

"I'm Mage Guild," the guard replied.

"But not a Mage!" Inigo yelled. "You will be silent."

Timo looked around the room, but the Mages and Journeymen lining the walls refused to meet his eyes. They would let Inigo get away with this. Only a few still had trickles of mage mist draining from them, the rest, including Hestor, showed no traces of magic. Timo felt power still building—his skin prickled with it.

"What of the guard's charge?" Jinaro asked. "That a trap was triggered in the hallway?"

"If there was a trap, there should be proof," Inigo said. "You, near the door. Backtrack down the hallway and check for any traps."

A small man sprinted out the door and into the hallway. Timo didn't even have to wait the few minutes it took the man to return to know there would be no proof. Inigo and Hestor would have made sure of it.

"Nothing in the hallway, Master Mage," the man said when he returned, slightly out of breath. "No traps, nothing that might slice a man in two."

"They were there," the guard protested. "I swear to Gyda, they were there."

"And yet no evidence," Inigo said. He looked around the room.

"I think this Apprentice has made some sort of deal with the guard. He's shown himself to be devious and untrustworthy." Inigo paused. "We have no choice," he continued. "He is guilty of crimes against both Mage Guild and Guildsmen and must be put to death immediately." Inigo looked directly at Timo, his lips spread into a triumphant smile.

Timo clenched his fists even tighter, fighting to hold onto the magic that threatened to spill from him in anger. "Where's your proof?" he asked. He turned to face the crowded table and back wall. "If I need to show proof of my accusations, why doesn't Inigo need to show proof of his?"

"We have an eyewitness," Inigo said. "Both Hestor and I saw the man who killed Faron. Your accomplice—a man you helped escape us earlier."

"That doesn't prove I had anything to do with it."

"You are found guilty by association," Inigo said. He turned to the Mages. "This Apprentice is guilty of these crimes, and he is sentenced to death. If any council members disagree with these findings, speak now."

Timo peered around the room. Hestor's smirk slipped when he met Timo's eyes, but Jinaro shrugged and settled his hands across his belly.

"Stay behind me," Timo whispered to the guard. Then louder, he said, "I was there when Rorik died."

"You see," Inigo said. "He admits to his crime!"

"I played a part in the Primus' death," Timo agreed. "But it was Inigo's curse that killed the Primus. Rorik died when I tried to remove it."

"How could you know he was cursed?" a council member said.

"Like my sister," Timo said. "I *see* magic."

He smiled when Inigo paled. "And I can tell who cast the spell. Inigo cursed Rorik with a spell that worsened when tampered with. I hastened his death by a few hours, maybe a day at most."

"You cannot be like her," Inigo said. "You've been tested."

"You mean all the traps Hestor set for me over the past two years? I fooled you," Timo said. He glanced at Hestor and smiled at the look of horror on the Mage's face. "*All* of you."

"*We forced the truth from your mother!*" Inigo screamed.

"Ah, my mother," Timo said calmly. "*She* fooled you too. Despite the truth spells you used on her—the spells *you* convinced the council to use on the *Mage Guild Secundus*—she was so good at lying to herself that lying to you was easy. About me, about my father." He shrugged. "Did you know that my father caused Santos Nimali's madness? The great Valerio Valendi cursed his own mentor." He lifted his hand up. "None of you can see it, but I have amassed a great amount of magic." Timo smiled. "*Your magic.* You see, I'm like my sister in another way. I have drawn out every trace of magic from everyone in this room. But I can use this myself."

"Guard, restrain him!" Inigo yelled.

Timo met the guard's calm gaze. The man stepped back a pace and crossed his arms across his chest.

"I hadn't made a deal with him," the guard said and motioned his head towards Timo. "At least not until now. You capture him yourself."

"Council Mages!" Inigo called. "Restrain this prisoner."

A few Mages and Journeymen tried casting spells but when nothing happened—no magic came forth—they looked around in confusion.

"They can't," Timo said. "At least not with magic." He lifted his left hand, and a ball of light flew up to the ceiling and hovered there. "I'm the only one in this room with magic."

"Hestor, Journeymen," Inigo called again. "If anyone of you has hopes of becoming a member of this council, you'll kill Timo Valendi."

A few Journeymen started forward. Hestor hung back, but after glancing at Inigo's furious face, he joined the others as they started towards the front of the room and Timo.

"Stop," Timo said.

He raised both hands, and a wave of multi-coloured mage mist flew out. He reached his arms out, and the mist fanned, growing denser as magic streamed into the spell.

The mist reached the table and slammed into the wood. The table screeched along the floor as the desk was pushed. Mages who were sitting were shoved backwards—men and chairs tumbling into the Mages and Journeymen behind them. There were screams of pain as the spell pressed the table back and pinned them against the wall.

Horrified, Timo dropped his hands, hoping to stop the rush of the spell. No new power was added but the wave of mist continued to push people and furniture against two of the walls in the room. But he couldn't stop the power from draining from his hands. Without direction or intent, it pooled on the floor in the centre of the room—a multi-hued rainbow of mist that continued to grow.

"Stop it!" Inigo screamed at him. He still stood behind another table that had slid partway to the back wall.

"I can't," Timo said.

He could barely hear himself over the cries and screams. He reached a hand out, hoping to draw the magic away. There was a pause and then an audible sucking sound as the magic reversed direction.

Released from the spell's grip, Mages and Journeymen dropped to the ground, some broken and bloody.

When Timo took a step back, he bumped into the guard. The spell was coming towards him, gaining speed.

"Take it easy," the guard said, his hands on Timo's shoulders, steadying him.

"But it's coming," Timo whispered. Would it kill them? Kill *him*? Panicked, he willed the magic towards the floor in front of him. The heaving mass grew bigger. Timo slashed one arm down, and the mage mist started to spin. The spell picked up speed, spinning faster and faster, sucking all the magic in the room into it. Timo felt drained and when he looked at his hands, only his own mauve mage mist still flowed from them. Carefully, he stemmed the flow of magic, slumping in relief when it thinned out and stopped.

But the magic in the room continued to spin, flashes and sparks now illuminating it from within.

"Move back," Timo said to the guard behind him, to the Mages and Journeymen, to Inigo—to himself.

He regretted his boast from earlier—that he could drain their magic and use it. *It* was using *him* now. What could he do with it? How could he disperse so much power? Frantically he scanned the room. Everyone had their eyes fixed on the spell, and Timo realized that though they couldn't see the mage mist, they could feel the power and see the sparks.

He squared his shoulders. It wasn't going to simply go away so he'd have to *send* it away. He took a deep breath, closed his eyes and concentrated on the mage mist, on slowing it down, on getting control over it. The parts of the spell that were made up of his magic responded, but the rest fought him—much like the Mages who'd bled their power into him were fighting him.

He opened his eyes. A thick band of mauve mage mist surrounded a swirling mass of multi-hued mist. With his right hand, he directed his spell down. The flagstone floor seemed to bend beneath a great weight and then, in a burst of shattered stone, the floor gave way and the magic dropped through it.

Moments later there was another crash as the spell ruptured the floor below. The sea was next, Timo thought as he hurried over to the edge of the hole. He peered down, praying to Gyda that no one had been in the corridor below when the spell had burst through the floor.

The floor just below him was shattered and cracked, and far below that, past another jagged hole of twisted and melted stone, he could see light—mage mist—glinting off water. The sea glowed for a moment and then it went dark. Timo sighed in relief. It was gone. The spell—the wild mass of magic that he'd unthinkingly accumulated—was gone.

He shivered. He'd warned that Kara could destroy Mage Guild Island but now he *knew* that he could too.

"We have to go," the guard whispered at his side.

Timo looked up. The guard crouched beside him, and he looked worried, and a little afraid. Of him. Timo couldn't blame him. He'd lost control of magic and put them all at risk.

"Now," the guard said. "Before they regain their wits."

He nodded towards the Mages, most of whom were still freeing themselves from behind toppled furniture. Hestor stared at them, his eyes blazing with hatred. Timo grabbed the guard's outstretched hand and pulled himself up.

There was debris in front of the door and more than a few Mages between them and it. Timo flexed his right hand. He still had some magic left, enough to get them out of here, he hoped, but not enough to get them off the island.

"Stop them." It was Inigo, his voice weak but still with the power of command behind it. A couple of Journeymen stepped away from the wall, sidling towards Timo and the guard.

The door rattled and then a crack appeared as it slowly opened inward, pushing debris as the bottom of the door scraped along the floor.

Gyda, please don't be more guards. Timo raised his hand, readying a spell.

The two Journeymen scowled at him and moved towards the partially opened door. One was close enough to look through it. He had just enough time to frown before the door slammed into him, sending him stumbling into his companion. Both men tumbled to the floor, sliding to a stop a few feet away. A man stood in the doorway, tense and ready to fight. He was covered in a layer of grass green mage mist.

Timo dropped his hand and grinned, loosening his grip on the spell.

"Reo?" Timo said.

Reo nodded. "Hurry. We need to get out of here."

"Yes," Timo agreed. He took two steps towards the doorway then stopped and turned, looking back at the guard. "Are you coming?"

"I heard someone but I don't see them," the guard said. He looked at Inigo, who was still calling for Mages to stop them. "But it's got to be better than this lot."

"Yes," Timo said. "I told you I had friends on the way. One's here now."

He stepped past Reo and out the partially open door. Once the guard slipped by him, Reo grabbed a broken chair leg, slammed the door shut, and wedged the chair leg into the gap between the door and the floor.

"Can we trust him?" Reo asked.

Timo turned to find the former Assassin staring at the guard, whose unfocussed eyes nervously looked in his direction.

"Yes," Timo said. "I'd be dead if it wasn't for him."

"All right," Reo said. "He comes with us. But I don't trust him."

"He'll be fine," Timo assured him.

"Yes. Otherwise he'll be dead." Reo turned and started to trot down the hallway.

Timo reached out for the guard's hand. "Follow me," Timo said. "My friend's invisible but I can see him."

"He wasn't so friendly with me," the guard said.

"He's my sister's husband now," Timo said. "But he used to be an Assassin."

"Gyda help me," the guard muttered as he followed Timo down the hallway.

Chapter 16

REO CHASED A faint ball of green mage mist down the hallway, and Timo followed, dragging the guard behind him. Reo signalled for them to stop before he turned a corner. A few moments later, he looked into the hallway and waved them forward. Timo rushed around the corner and then stopped so suddenly that the guard bumped into him and almost sent him sprawling. Right on top of the two bodies that slumped against the wall.

"Gyda," the guard hissed.

"Let's go," Reo said from a few paces further away. "There could be more."

"Come on," the guard said. This time it was he who drew Timo along in his wake. "These two was mean. Not sad they're gone."

Dragging his eyes from the two dead men, Timo stumbled down the hall after Reo and the grass green spell that was leading them all, he hoped, towards the Mage Primus. And his sister.

Reo crouched beside a small wooden door the mage mist had stopped in front of. Timo and the guard caught up and flattened themselves against the stone wall.

"Mole," Timo gasped. "We have to get him."

"He's fine," Reo said, not taking his eyes from the door, not even breathing hard after the sprint down the hallway and killing two men. "He should be home by now."

Timo clutched at Reo's sleeve. "And Barra? The others?"

Reo sighed and glanced at him. "All fine. All gone from this

Gyda cursed pile of rocks." Reo pressed an ear to the wood of the door for a moment before he turned a grim face to Timo. "Later we'll discuss what the Mage Guild was doing to a couple of Seyoyan youths."

"Nothing good," Timo said and shivered.

"That's what I thought," Reo replied. He eased the door open. "Give me five minutes then follow me. Lock the door behind you if you can."

This time Timo barely glanced at the body—another man—as he pulled the guard up the stairs and past it.

They spent another half hour following Reo around corners and through doors. Finally, they reached a hall lit only by a mass of mage mist that was layered against one wall. Grass green mage mist. Reo reached a hand out, feeling along the wall.

"Right here." Timo had caught up to Reo and pointed towards the mage mist.

The Assassin nodded and his hand disappeared into the wall, followed by his head.

"Got him."

Reo's voice was muffled, and at first Timo thought he was talking to him. Then a head poked out from the wall—Kara—and he realized the Assassin had been talking *about* him.

"Thank Gyda," Kara said.

She grabbed his hand and pulled him through the mage mist and into a small alcove. The guard crowded in behind him. The spell cast an eerie glow over his sister's face but the relief on it was apparent.

"Timo, are you all right?" she asked.

"Fine," he replied. "At least I think so."

"If they've hurt you . . ." Kara's voice trailed off.

She peered into his face with such fierceness that Timo finally understood how she could love an Assassin. She would kill to keep those she loved safe—to keep *him* safe—just as readily as Reo would.

"I'm fine," Timo repeated. "Just drained, tired. Can we get out of here?"

"Yes," Santos said from the corner. "I hate this island. I didn't realize it until I left it and came back again, but it drains me."

"Of your power?" Timo asked, curious. Could the island have become so layered with magic that it sucked it from those who had it? He studied Santos from head to toe but there was no mage mist seeping from him.

"Not my power," Santo said with a shake of his head. "Of my calmness—of my ability to think rationally. I almost feel as though the madness is returning."

Santos and Kara exchanged looks.

"There's mage mist almost everywhere," she said. "Do you think all that magic is affecting you? Why didn't you say anything earlier?"

"Because there's nothing to be done about it," Santos replied. "We'll leave as soon as we can, and I'll either be better or I won't."

"Is it because you were cursed?" Timo asked. "Or could it affect everyone who lives here?" The few days he'd spent on Arts Guild Island he *had* felt lighter but he'd assumed that was because he'd felt safe. Safer than he'd ever felt in the house he grew up in, anyway.

"I suppose it could," Santos said, a thoughtful look on his face. "That might explain how progressively corrupt Mage Guild and the council have become over the past few decades."

"Excellent," Reo said. "Not only do the Mages want us dead, they all might be half-mad. We need to go, now. There's no telling what they're capable of."

"Santos," Kara said. "Can you spell us invisible?"

"I can do that," Timo said. "Let Santos conserve his power."

"You're sure?" Kara asked.

Timo nodded, and she smiled.

"Good. Who's your friend?"

"Oh," Timo said. He'd forgotten about the guard. He turned to him. "Sorry, I don't know your name."

"It's Elman," the guard said. "Guildsman Elman."

"Do you have any magic, Guildsman Elman?" Santos asked. He'd left the corner and now stood beside Kara, brushing dust from his robe.

"No," Elman replied. "Who's asking?" He glared at Santos.

"I promised him he could come with me . . . us." Timo said. He met Santos' steady gaze. If the Primus was feeling mentally unsteady he wasn't showing it.

"That's fine," Santos said. "But we still need to know what skills he has. Reo?"

"He can move quietly," Reo said. "And he knows some of the

guards." Reo glanced at Elman, a smile hovering on his lips. "He didn't like them much so I think we can trust him at least enough to help us get away. And he's wearing the right uniform in case we need it. Can you use a sword?"

The guard looked from Santos over to Timo and then to Reo.

"Again, who's asking?"

"I told you," Timo said. "They're friends of mine. My sister Kara Fonti, her husband Reo and that," he pointed to Santos, "is Mage Primus Santos Nimali."

"Santos Nimali," Elman repeated. "The Primus who supposedly died years ago and returned on Founders Day?"

"Yes," Santos said.

Elman looked over at Timo. "No wonder the council hates you." He paused and his glance settled on Kara. "The deaths of Primus Rorik and Secundus Fonti were bad business, and Gyda knows I can't trust Inigo, so yes, I can use a sword. And yes, I'm on your side. I'll be happy to get off this island, if you'll take me with you."

"Good," Reo said. "Then we need you to tell us everything you know about where we are, what guards and Mages might be around, and anything else that might help us get away safely."

ONCE REO WAS satisfied with Elman's answers to his questions, the guard led them to a small room that was tucked behind a hallway that led to what he called the work areas. From the guard's descriptions, Timo knew it was where he and Mole had been separated, near where the minor Mages were being drained of magic to power the island.

The room they were in barely needed Santos' concealment spell, and Timo believed Elman when he said that only a few guards knew of it. It was dusty and choked with cast-off furniture but it seemed a safe enough place to rest.

Timo sat with his back against the wall and let his exhaustion sweep over him. It had been hours since he'd slept or ate or drank, and the small spell he'd used to make them all invisible had sapped his energy more than he'd counted on.

"Here."

He opened his eyes to find Kara kneeling beside him, holding out a water skin. He drank deeply before handing it back to her.

"I am so very sorry about our mother," Kara said. She sighed and slid to the floor beside him.

"Mole said you deflected Inigo's spell," Timo said. "And that Inigo hid behind her."

"Yes," Kara agreed.

"I don't blame you for Inigo's actions." He raked a hand through his hair. "Or our mother's. Was she really willing to have Inigo be her Secundus?"

"So she told Santos," Kara replied. "Although . . . after, when Santos spelled him to tell us the truth, Inigo admitted that he planned on killing Arabella anyway."

"Probably another curse," Timo said. "That's what he did to Rorik." He looked down at his hands. He knew so much more about his unmagic now he could probably save Rorik from that curse, instead of hastening his death.

"We need to know what happened," Kara said. "With the council." She placed a hand over his, as if to take hold of it, but instead she let her hand hover a few inches above his. Slowly, wisps of different coloured mage mist were pulled from his hand towards hers. "And how good you are at drawing out magic."

"Good?" Timo laughed. "I didn't know it could be done until Mole told me that you had done it on Founders Day. Today I was desperate enough to try it myself." He rubbed a hand across his eyes, blocking out the light. But he could still see the destruction—feel the power course through him. "I couldn't control it though. Almost ruined the room. And I think I killed people."

Her hand gripped his and squeezed.

He looked up into her eyes. "I know they wanted to kill me, so it should make it better, but it doesn't." Were they innocent, the people who'd died in that room? They'd been following orders given to them by their superiors. Gyda, most of them were simply trying to get through each day without losing their place—which in Mage Guild meant your life. Could he blame them?

"No, it doesn't make it any better," Kara said gently. "And it doesn't get easier." She glanced over at Reo, who was talking with Elman and Santos. "I have that from an expert."

"He had to kill in order to get us here safely," Timo said. "I never would have thought an Assassin would be troubled by that." He met her eyes. "But he is, isn't he?"

Kara sighed. "It's not the life he chose for himself—that's the one he has with me—but he makes an effort to keep his skills sharp. He knows that not everything can be settled with words."

"No," Timo agreed. "For years my mother tried to convince the council that I wasn't a threat." He looked down at his hands, which were now clenched in his lap. "And now *I am* a threat, partly because they left me no other role."

"Sadly, yes." Kara got to her feet. "Once we get to Old Rillidi you'll be able to choose a different role."

"Will I really be safe there?"

"As safe as you can be. It's your home, after all."

Timo took Kara's outstretched hand and let her help him up.

"How is it my home? I've never been there."

"Santos discovered years ago that our mother was related to Paolo Santini," Kara said. "But he never told anyone and his madness caused him to forget it. But Santos, me, my children, and you are all heirs—so we own Old Rillidi. Not even the guilds can take that away."

"I . . ." Timo stopped and grinned. "I have rights to a place the guilds can't ever control? That's more than I ever expected."

Kara nodded and stepped over to Reo, who absently pulled her against him.

Timo felt a knot of tension disappear. He'd been thinking of Old Rillidi as a haven, but one where he would live by someone else's grace. To know that he had a right that even the guilds couldn't deny him made him almost light-headed.

Would his mother have left Mage Guild if she'd known? He shook his head. No. Arabella Fonti would have seen leaving as a sign of weakness, as giving up. Besides, she never believed she was in danger, even after Rorik was killed—after *he* told her that the Primus had been killed by a spell. She never would have left Mage Guild for an uncertain future with the daughter she'd never acknowledged.

But she might have sent *him* to Old Rillidi earlier if she'd known he was an heir to the First Guildsman. Especially since she wouldn't have had to admit that she'd done it to keep him safe. She would have been able to justify it because it meant that he would have what no other Guildsman in Rillidi could—land not controlled by any guild.

Timo sighed and leaned against the cool stone wall. Knowing he had a right to safety on Old Rillidi didn't mean getting there would be any easier.

"We're ready to leave," Kara said, returning to him.

Timo looked past her to Reo, who pulled something from under his collar. He wound it around his arm, overtop of his coat sleeve.

"Can you create a finder spell?" Santos asked him.

Timo nodded.

"Good."

"Five is too many to travel together," Kara said. "You and I must split up so that both groups can see, and send, magical messages. I'll be with Santos, and you'll go with Reo and Elman."

Reo joined them, trailed by Elman.

"Elman thinks the safest way to the surface is through a workroom," Reo said. "Mages being drained of their magic should be easy enough to bypass."

"We're going to the surface?" Timo asked. Other than his mother's and Rorik's gardens, he'd never spent much time outside. The amount of mage mist had made it almost impossible for him to pretend he didn't see it—something neither his mother nor his Master had wanted to know.

"We'll come back down and find a boat if it's safe," Reo said. "Otherwise we'll head to the ferry docks. It doesn't much matter where we go as long as it's off Mage Guild Island."

"Won't guards be watching for us?" Timo asked. He wished he'd paid more attention to the planning. He felt as though he'd missed something important.

"We'll be invisible," Kara reminded him. "They won't be able to see us."

"Guards with any usable magic were called in by the council after Founders Day," Elman said. "And the rest won't do anything without a direct order."

"You're sure?" Reo asked Elman. "The guards at the ferry won't try to stop us if they do see us?"

Elman shrugged. "Without magic they can't better their position within the guild, and as long as they don't ignore an order, they won't be disciplined."

"Good." Reo nodded. "Hopefully we'll all be on the same ferry but if not, go to the nearest Warrior for help."

"They'll help?" Timo asked. "They were looking for me—along with Mages."

"Warrior Guild has been looking for you on our behalf ever since Founders Day," Kara said.

"And I'll be with you," Reo continued. "But even if we're separated, they'll help."

"They won't hand me over to Mage Guild?"

"No."

Reo, Santos, and Kara all spoke at the same time.

Timo looked from one confident face to another. He wanted to believe them—it was similar to what Mole had told him—that Warrior Guild would do as Kara and Reo asked, but it was hard to believe that any guild would deliberately obstruct Mage Guild.

"If we get separated I will contact the nearest Warrior," Timo said, vowing to stick close to Reo. Warriors would help the former Assassin, but an unknown Mage Apprentice? Not only was Mage Guild powerful, but magic was essential to the existence of all of the guild islands, including Warrior Guild's. Could he trust that they would jeopardize that for him?

TIMO PEERED AROUND the corner—Elman was at his back, one hand on his shoulder. Reo trotted down the hall to an intersecting corridor, paused to look each way, then waved Timo forward.

"It's clear," Timo said over his shoulder. "Up to the juncture."

Timo padded along the corridor, Elman close behind. An hour had passed since they'd left their hiding place. Santos and Kara were a few minutes ahead of them. They would regroup at the workroom and split up again once they'd made it outside.

"We go right," Elman whispered when they reached Reo. "The workroom is through the door about halfway down the next corridor. It's the only one on that wall."

"Timo," Reo said. "Any sign that Santos and Kara have made it?"

Timo poked his head into the next hallway. A patch of grass green mage mist swirled in front of a closed door. "Santos left a marker by the door." He squeezed between Reo and Elman.

"Good," Reo said. He settled his back more firmly against the wall. "We'll give them a few minutes in case they set off an alarm."

"Kara would have seen a spell," Timo said. "And Santos would have sent us a warning."

Reo glanced over at him, and even though Timo knew the former Assassin couldn't see him, he still couldn't quite meet his eyes.

"Mages," Reo said. Then he grinned, ruining the seriousness of the moment. "There are other ways to warn people, even on Mage Guild Island." Reo looked past Timo to where Elman sat hunched against the wall.

"How would you warn Guildsmen?" Reo asked. "If there was danger?"

"What danger would there be?" Timo asked. "Mage Guild Island is safe."

"So speaks a Mage," Elman said. "The rest of us would listen for the bells. There's different rings for different events. Like when the Primus died," he looked over at Timo. "And the Secundus."

"I didn't hear anything," Timo said. Bells had been rung for his mother? Why hadn't he known that? It helped, a little, knowing that her death had been acknowledged by the inhabitants of Mage Guild Island.

"It's not for you," Elman continued. "They can't be heard down here anyway. But we who don't have magic—we keep an ear out for the bells."

"I've never heard them," Timo said. "I didn't even know that they existed."

"Like I said," Elman replied. "It's for us who don't have magic. Partly so we can protect ourselves from those who have it."

"I heard them once," Reo said. "A long time ago."

"Did someone die then too?"

"Yes," Reo said. He paused and stared down at the floor. "Your father."

"My . . ." Timo stopped. His father had been Secundus when he died—when Kara had killed him in self-defence. Reo must have been on the island in order to hear the bells. Kara must have been too.

KARA STOPPED JUST inside the door, stunned. Santos and Timo had described it to her but she still couldn't quite fathom what she was seeing.

The cavernous room was filled with rows of tables lined with people sitting slumped over tabletops or with their heads leaning back as they stared blankly up at the ceiling.

Ropes of mage mist—some so faint that she could hardly see

them, others as thick as her wrist—flowed from the people to merge and stream between the tables out through a hole along the far wall.

"That's the way out," Santos whispered over the noises of dozens of unconscious people—a low rumble of wheezing and snores punctuated by coughs.

"Will we fit through it?" Kara asked. After the confined hallways, she was having a hard time adjusting to the sheer size of the room. She brought her gaze back to the people slumped across the tables. The ones sitting close to the hole would easily fit through it.

"We should," Santos replied. He smiled at her. "It does take some getting used to. I remember the first time I was sent to monitor a workroom. I had nightmares for weeks after." He shivered. "Not a life I would want to live."

"Are they hurt?"

"No," Santos replied. "But in a way their lives are stolen from them. For half the day they are unaware of anything around them. But it's not restorative like sleep. Can you see their magic being drained?"

Kara nodded and lifted a hand to shield her eyes from the brightness.

"It drains their energy as well as their power," Santos continued. "When they are released from the workroom they are so exhausted that all most of them can do is go home to bed. When I was Primus, we took to feeding them in the workroom before and after their duties because some of them were too tired to eat. They became extremely weak. A few even died."

Kara forced herself to look at the closest table.

"And they're full Mages? Full Guildsmen?"

"Aye. They are the unlucky ones—they have power but either don't have enough to do magic or they are not able to learn how to use it." Santos turned haunted eyes her way. "During the lucid periods of my madness this is what I was most worried about. To be trapped underground and have my magic drained away each day only to renew it and have drained away again."

"They would do that?" Kara asked.

"Oh yes. It's likely that some of the Mages here are mentally unbalanced. There's no other use for them, the council would say."

"But it's a horrible life," Kara said. As much as she hated the clammers, even she wouldn't want to be responsible for sending them here.

"Yes," Santos agreed. "A horrible life, if this is living. Thankfully I was not sent here."

"Because you're the heir to Old Rillidi?"

"And I was too powerful, too unpredictable." Santos stared out across the room. "Can you imagine the death and destruction I would have caused here?" he added softly.

Kara shivered. Yes, she could imagine it. She'd seen the devastation Santos' uncontrolled spells had wrought on Old Rillidi—the burnout, the damage to his estate—but a powerful spell confined in small space like this? Santos could have obliterated a whole section of the island, or started a fire in the underground hallways.

"But their magic, it's only used to power the island. I mean, Inigo can't just take their power, can he?"

"No," Santos replied. "It's against Guild law to use another's power for yourself, although there are always those who try it. But it's dangerous. Tapping into someone else's power leaves you open to them."

"If you know they're doing it," Kara said.

"Yes," Santos agreed. "But even if they don't, all power is imbued with the intent, or personality, of its owner. There are reports of Mages going mad by tapping the power of multiple other Mages."

"Not something most Mages would risk," Kara said. Although Valerio Valendi had risked it with her mother.

"I wouldn't," Santos said.

"Should we wait here for Reo and Timo?" Kara asked.

"Let's move closer to the bottom," Santos said. "I dislike the idea of the five of us navigating past these Mages at the same time."

Kara nodded and followed Santos down the few steps to the workroom floor. By the time they'd passed three tables, the light from the mage mist that flowed past them was so bright that she had to shield her eyes and turn her head to the side. She grabbed onto Santos' arm and let him lead her further into the room.

The light suddenly dimmed, and startled, Kara lifted her head to look for the cause. A wall of mage mist soared up past the tables and engulfed them.

With a cry, Santos fell to the floor, and then Kara was surrounded by mage mist so dense that she couldn't even see her own hand. She stumbled into something on the floor and fell to her knees, hard. Her hand landed on something yielding and with a shock she realized that it was Santos. She felt around and encountered an arm. Right or left? She fumbled up the arm to the flat surface of his back. He'd fallen face forward. With increasing panic, she rolled him onto his back and leaned over him. Then the mage mist swept past them, up the stairs and out into the hallway, taking any spells that kept the lights on with it. The silence that followed was broken by a few groans.

"Santos?"

Kara reached out to Santos' head and gently turned his face towards her.

"Are you all right?"

Santos' nose was flattened to one side of this face, and his once twinkling eyes stared blankly at the ceiling.

"Santos!" Kara cried. "No!" She shook him by the shoulders, trying to revive him, trying to force life back into him. "No!" She dropped her head to his chest and sobbed, once, the sound of it loud in the still room.

"Reo!" Kara whispered. She struggled to her knees. Had they been far enough behind them? Had whatever spell they'd unleashed travelled far enough to hurt Reo?

Kara scrambled up the stairs on hands and knees and lurched towards the door. She had to get to him. *Reo!* He had to be alive, he had to be safe. She sobbed, grabbed the door frame and swung out into the hallway. They were there. Kara sprinted towards the figures huddled in the middle of the hall. Three figures—two crouched over the third that lay on the floor, not moving. *Reo!*

"Gyda!" Kara rushed towards them. It *was* Reo on the floor. She slid to her knees beside him.

"Kara."

Reo weakly grasped her hand, and she blew out the big breath she hadn't known she was holding.

"It came too fast," Timo said. "I tried to deflect it but it came too fast."

He knelt on Reo's other side. Elman leaned over him, one hand clutching Timo's shoulder.

"Is he all right?" the Mage guard asked.

"I'll be fine," Reo said. His voice was hoarse, and the hair on the left side of his head was matted with blood. Reo touched a hand to it and grimaced. "Knocked me down and I hit my head."

"I felt a wind or something go past," Elman said. "But it didn't touch me. Why?"

"You were holding onto me," Timo said. "Unless specifically targeting me, magic tends to go around me. Kara too, I think."

"Yes," she replied absently, studying Reo's face for further signs of damage. "I saw it go right past. Santos . . ." she trailed off.

Reo gripped her hand, and she continued.

"He's dead. In the workroom. Somehow we triggered a spell. It was so sudden . . ."

"We need to go," Reo said. He started to sit up but grimaced and dropped to the floor. "They'll be coming. Elman, help me up."

Kara stood aside as Elman carefully helped Reo to his feet. Her husband sucked in a breath and closed his eyes before trying to put weight on his right foot. He grimaced again and hopped a step, holding onto the guard's shoulder.

"Come on," Timo said from her side. "We need to go. The invisibility spell was destroyed by the trap, so anyone can see us right now. Whoever set that trap will be here soon."

"We'll go when Reo can move!" Kara snapped. Then she took a deep breath and reached for Timo's hand. "Sorry. I'm just . . ." She waved a hand. "Reo, and Santos . . ."

"I know," Timo said. "But the Mage council will not stop. We have to get away from here."

"I'm ready," Reo said. "A few cracked ribs, a strained ankle. If I can't keep up then you are to leave me behind."

"No!" Kara said. "Either we both get out of here our neither of us does. Lean on me." She wrapped an arm around him, careful to keep it low, away from his ribs. She turned Reo towards the workroom, and they slowly headed there. "This is still the way out," Kara said. "And I'm not leaving without you."

TIMO POKED HIS head into the workroom and let out a breath. The mage lights hovered close to the ceiling, illuminating the broken bodies that littered the tables and spilled onto the floor. Santos lay in an aisle, his bloody face pointed towards the ceiling. The furniture was undisturbed except for the few chairs that had been toppled by their dying occupants.

The spell had been set to kill, then, without damaging the room. A more subtle spell would have spared these workers and only targeted intruders, but the council couldn't be bothered. *Mage Guild* couldn't be bothered. He shook his head in disgust. The council would probably have this room filled with more Guildsmen and be draining their power by morning. More people they felt were expendable.

He carefully went down the stairs, searching for more mage mist. By the time he reached the back wall and the opening that would lead them out of the room, he was furious at Mage Guild. *Gyda curse them for treating these people so cheaply.* Some of them were no older than he was—practically children—sacrificed because the Mage who had set the spell couldn't spare the time and energy the keep these people—these *Guildsmen*—alive. They had their power taken from them, were forced to sit in dark rooms and be drained so the guild could keep the island aloft and lit—so that the precious few with significant power could live in splendor and comfort.

And those with power? They didn't even spare a thought or care for the Guildsmen whose lives they used up as they went about their days, squabbling over politics and currying favours as they jockeyed to see who could lie and cheat their way to more power. They disgusted him! He pounded on the table nearest him, then stepped back when the body of the poor soul who'd died there slipped to the floor.

Timo rubbed a hand across his face, saddened by all the deaths that had happened because Mage Guild wanted *him.*

"It's safe," Timo called out. "No sign of any more spells."

Kara stepped into the room, Reo leaning on her. Elman followed, keeping his gaze low as they headed towards Timo.

"They didn't deserve this," the guard said. He stopped beside Timo and looked out over the room, a sad frown on his face. "Thank Gyda they wouldn't have been aware of anything, not entranced like they were."

"No," Timo said. "They wouldn't have known. Wouldn't have had a chance to escape."

"Are any left alive?" Kara asked quietly. "I didn't check."

"No one's alive," Timo said. "The spell made sure of that." He shook his head angrily. "They didn't have to kill everyone!"

"If Mage Guild will kill both the Primus and Secundus, then no one is safe," Reo said.

"Can we bring Santos with us?" Kara asked. "He deserves to be taken to Old Rillidi. I know it's what he would want."

Reo glanced over his shoulder at Santos' body then turned to Kara, sadness etched onto his face.

"I'm not sure we'll be able to manage," Reo said. "Not with my injuries."

"I'll cast a spell," Timo said. "To make him float."

"Could you send him back to Old Rillidi alone?" Reo asked. "Assassin boats are spelled to go to a specific location. Could you do that with Santos?"

"I'm not sure," Timo replied. "I've never done a spell like that." He glanced over at Kara. "And I've never been to Old Rillidi. I don't think I have the skill to send him somewhere I've never been."

"We should try to bring him with us anyway," Kara said. "Even if Santos doesn't make it home I don't want to leave him down here."

"All right." Timo closed his eyes to concentrate. Floating and barely visible, so they could all see him. When he opened his eyes, Santos, encased in mauve mage mist, gently rose from the floor to hover at the same level as the table tops. "You should be able to nudge him higher or lower if you need to," Timo said.

"Thank you." Kara left Reo's side and reached out to tug on Santos. "Elman, you'll need to help Reo so I can manage Santos."

"Do we want to be invisible?" Timo asked. "Should I redo that spell?"

"No," Reo replied. "It's more important for us to keep track of each other. I don't want to be blind to all of you."

"All right," Timo said. "I'll lead, in case there are more traps." He was pretty sure he had the most experience detecting traps. Would Santos still be alive if he'd been with him instead of Kara? He shook his head and stepped through the hole and into a dark tunnel. He couldn't think that way. It wasn't his fault that Santos was dead. Absently, Timo flicked a hand, and a mage light bobbed overhead.

They'd been in two separate groups for a reason—he'd been travelling separately from Santos for a reason—so that each group could see and do magic. Besides, there was no reason to think the outcome would have been different if he'd been there—if they'd all been travelling together—other than the possibility that both Elman and Reo might be dead too.

Timo took a few more steps into the tunnel to make room for Kara, who pulled Santos' body behind her. If Reo had died along with Santos he wasn't sure Kara would have been able to move forward as calmly as she was doing right now. And he didn't think he'd have been strong enough to lead them to safety. Mage Guild would truly have won.

Chapter 17

TIMO SLIPPED AND fell to one knee, again. The tunnel wasn't meant for travel, that much was certain. So far the floor, far from flat, was sloped and strewn with rubble and rocks they had to scramble over. It had taken them almost half an hour to get past the bend they'd seen when they'd entered.

And in the centre was a stream of mage mist. Multi-coloured at the edges, but white in the centre, it flowed along the floor of the tunnel. But unlike a real stream, the mage mist flowed up, the same direction they were travelling.

Now a wall of rock taller than Timo blocked their path, mage mist flowing up and over the rock like a reversed waterfall. Keeping to one side, away from the magic, Timo reached up, grabbed hold and pulled himself high enough to see over the edge. The tunnel continued on and the floor flattened out, though it still sloped upwards.

Elman boosted Timo up and over the edge. A second stream of mage mist came from a hole that was set low in the tunnel wall and joined the main flow. Careful not to step directly into the magic, Timo inched close enough to peer through the hole.

Another workroom, smaller than the one they'd entered through. The hole was smaller as well. He might be able to wriggle though it, but a fully grown man would have difficulty. He hurried back to the ledge.

"We need to be quiet," he whispered. "There's another

workroom. The opening is small, but someone in the room could be awake."

Elman bent to one knee, and Reo stepped onto his thigh. Timo grabbed the Assassin's outstretched hands and pulled. Reo dropped onto the tunnel floor with a grunt, then quickly rolled away. A dark spot glistened on the rock where he'd landed.

Timo leaned over the edge. Kara pushed Santos' floating body towards him and he grabbed it, settling it against the tunnel wall, out of the way. He helped Kara scramble up and then the two of them hauled up Elman.

"Reo," Kara called softly, worry in her voice.

Startled, Timo looked down the tunnel. Reo lay with his head near the small opening, peering through it. Most of his body was submerged in mage mist.

"Get out of there." Kara scrambled over to Reo. "You're covered in mage mist."

Reo glanced around before he wriggled away from the opening.

"I didn't see anyone awake," Reo said. He took a breath before grabbing Kara's hand and struggling to his feet. "I can breathe more deeply." He tested his weight on his sore foot. "And my ankle feels a little better. Did the magic do that?" He looked at Kara before his gaze settled on Timo.

"I'm not sure," Timo said. He bent down and tentatively reached a hand into the river of mist. Power surged up his arm, and he snatched his hand back. "Gyda!" His hand still tingled but when he raised it he didn't see anything different about it.

"It's pure power," Timo said. "But unfocussed. There is no intent in this magic—not good, not bad. I've never seen anything like this before. I've never *imagined* anything like this."

"No intent?" Kara asked, puzzled.

She bent down to study the mage mist, and Timo was struck by how odd this must look to the others—he and his sister studying and discussing something that only they could see.

"But Santos said that magic *always* has intent," Kara said.

"But this doesn't," Timo replied. "Maybe it has something to do with the trance the Mages are put into? Or because each Mage has so very little power?" He turned to Reo. "I think this magic helped heal your ankle."

"Is it dangerous?" Reo asked. "I can walk but I can't fight, not with my ribs still so sore."

"No," Kara said. "I don't trust it."

"I have to try," Reo said to her. "If there's a chance I can be healed, I have to take it." He looked over at Timo. "Do you know why it worked?"

"No." Timo shook his head. "I can only guess that this magic is so pure that it automatically fueled your body's own healing power." He looked over at Kara. "You have more experience with the intent of magic. Can you feel anything?"

She shook her head. "I still don't like it. It could be doing anything."

"Including healing me," Reo said. Deliberately he stepped into the middle of the tunnel. "Am I in it?"

Timo nodded. "But it's only as high as your knee."

Reo nodded, dropped to the floor, and stretched out, fully submerged in the mist.

Kara clenched her hands nervously until Reo sat up. He sprang to his feet, patting his ribs.

"Much better," he said. "I still feel a twinge but it's as though the injury is weeks old." He rolled his shoulders. "Let's go. We've been here too long." He grinned. "But we should be able to travel more quickly now."

Timo led the way through the tunnel, past a third workroom that directed even more mage mist into the tunnel. Now it was impossible to walk without stepping into the magic. By the time they reached a fourth room, Timo's body hummed with power and mage mist crawled over him.

Had any Mages ever done this before? Walked through the rivers of power that they collected to run the island? He had to believe not, otherwise they'd all be teeming with power, or at least Inigo would be. He'd never heard his mother or Rorik talk about this—he had to assume that if a Mage had ever known about this they had kept it to themselves. Just as Timo had to keep it a secret from Mage Guild. He shuddered. What would a Mage like Inigo do with so much pure power? Or a man such as his father had been?

He looked back and met Kara's worried gaze.

"I'm not even doing anything," Timo said. "It's just . . . collecting in me."

Kara reached a hand out. Where her hand brushed his arm,

the mage mist retracted.

"Why doesn't the magic withdraw from me?" Timo asked. "It usually does."

"Perhaps it's the intent," Kara said. "Without intent behind a spell, power might simply be attracted to you because you have your own." She shrugged. "Or maybe because you can use it?" She looked over at Santos' body. "I don't think he knew about this."

"Neither do I," Timo said. "And *none of them* can ever find out."

He met Kara's solemn gaze, and she nodded, slowly. "No one in all of Tregella would be safe."

Timo slid down the wall to sit beside Kara. Santos' body hovered just down the tunnel, and Reo and Elman were scouting ahead, searching for a way out.

According to Elman, the power from these workrooms went to the surface where minor Mages used the magic to control the water system. The Mages at the surface were awake—and had enough magic to create small spells. The group needed to find a way out of the tunnel before they reached them.

By now Timo was so used to the mage mist that swirled along his body that he only noticed it when it reacted to Kara's presence and retreated from her.

"Do you think it's night yet?" Timo asked.

Reo had been adamant that they not leave the tunnel until it was dark outside. The light from the mage mist flickered and cast odd shadows on Kara's face.

"Close," Kara replied. "I think." She studied the bottom of the tunnel at their feet. "Do you see the colours?" she asked. "Of different Mages' magic?"

"Yes." Timo paused. Other than with Yash and Wuls Samma he'd never really talked much about his abilities. "Santos' mage mist was green."

"Grass green," Kara replied sadly. "To me it was the colour of hope."

"Hope," Timo repeated. "I suppose I might have come to think of him that way too." He glanced at her. "Although you were the one I hoped to find."

"Even though I killed both your parents?"

Timo sighed and looked away. "I found some old documents

that my father had spelled," he said. "In Rorik's study. Even after so many years I didn't want to touch them, the spells were so malevolent. My father was not good."

"Nor was our mother," Kara said. "Although I didn't want her dead."

"Our mother had to force herself to believe her own lies in order to live with the things she'd done." He shrugged. "Does that make her better than Valerio Valendi?" He dipped a hand into the mage mist that pooled by his feet. "If she'd known about this source of power, I don't think she would have used it for her own gain. At least not as ruthlessly as my father would have."

"Or the council," Kara said.

"No luck." Reo joined them and crouched on the other side of Kara.

Elman stood a few strides ahead in the tunnel.

"We went as far as we dared," Reo said. "There is no exit before the workroom of minor Mages."

"I can direct enough power to create an exit anywhere we want it," Timo said.

"How would we know where to make it?" Kara asked.

"Elman?" Reo turned to the guard. "Do you know where we are? What might be beside or above us?"

Elman walked a few steps along the tunnel, peering up at the ceiling. He shrugged.

"Are we east of the minor Mages? I think there's a park above us. At least I remember walking through one in order to get to the workroom up there. But I've only had that duty a few times. If we're east."

"We're east," Reo said. He pointed towards the side of the tunnel. "Timo, can you burrow through here? On an angle so we can walk up it. And make the walls solid so that they don't cave in on us."

"I'll try," Timo said. He walked over and placed his hands on the tunnel wall. The dirt felt rough and damp beneath his palms. He closed his eyes and concentrated on the feel of the earth and the magic that coursed through his body.

He'd said that he could do this, but he'd never tried anything like it before. Up until now most of his magic had been spells either assigned by Rorik or stolen from him. Spells that he knew worked because so many others had cast them before him.

Most Mages didn't create new spells until they were well into their Journeyman years. But just as he'd taught himself to feel the intent behind a spell, just as he'd taught himself to evade the traps that had been set to hurt or kill him, Timo knew that he could do this. Because he had to, there was no other choice, so he *would*.

With his feet placed firmly in the stream of mage mist, he started to gather the power and direct it towards the wall in front of him. The rock and dirt before him slowly started to crumble and fall away. Mage mist swept it down the tunnel, back the way they'd come. He felt his companions shift until they were upstream of the earth that was flowing faster and faster.

The river of mud and dirt avoided Timo, skirting past his feet as it flowed downhill. He took a step forward, past the original tunnel wall, and still the earth kept sweeping past him. Another step and then another. Eventually he had to drop to his knees and crawl as the height of the tunnel diminished. His feet were no longer in the stream of magic and yet it still answered to him, still continued to excavate earth at his request.

Eventually the flow of dirt faltered and then stopped. Roots dangled above his head and a worm wriggled free and dropped onto his shoulder. Timo brushed it away and quickly retreated out of the new tunnel.

When he stepped back into the flow of mage mist he felt power surge through him, replenishing what little he'd used to dig the way out.

"I didn't break through to the surface," he said as he joined the others. "But it's close. If anyone were to walk above it they might fall through."

"I'll look," Reo said. "To see if it's dark enough. And make sure no one is there to see us exit." With that he was gone, quickly scrambling out of sight.

Timo clenched his hands and turned towards Kara.

"He meant that he'll kill anyone up there, didn't he?" he asked. "When he said he'd make sure no one sees us."

"If he has to," Kara replied, her face grim. "In order to keep us safe."

Timo nodded and leaned against the wall of the tunnel and looked at Kara, the sister he'd never had a chance to know. She was worried that her husband, the father of her children, would need to kill again. To keep them safe, she'd said. But would it? Would one more death keep them safe? Would Old Rillidi be the safe haven he'd been promised now that Santos was dead? Or would Timo's presence put them at even greater risk?

He had magic, as did his half-brother Giona. And Barra Eska, if she stayed. But one freshly trained Mage and two Journeymen would not be able to hold off all of Mage Guild forever. One day the Mages of the council would regain their powers—either their own or by using others. Or worse, they would realize they could use the pure magic for their own ends. Inigo would not hesitate to let the island and everyone who lived on it sink into the bay if it meant he could use this magic.

He looked down at the magic that eddied around his feet. Someone had to stop them—stop Inigo, stop the council, stop the endless succession of Mages, each more ruthless and power mad than the last, who would do anything, sacrifice *anything*, to have enough power to control everyone else.

Only Santos had been free of that arrogant ambition. And now he was gone and someone else had to stop them.

IDLY KARA SWUNG a foot towards the flow of mage mist. It ebbed away from her, then rushed into the space her foot left when she swung it back. Reo had only been gone a few minutes. *Too soon to worry.* She pushed her hair out of her eyes and sighed. It was never too soon to worry. He'd return, he always did, but if he'd had to kill again a little piece of him would be gone. And as always, she'd try to fill the empty place it left with love and laughter, but this time, without Santos, it would be harder. She glanced at Santos' body—it floated just out of the way. Dirt was piled almost to the Mage's back, making it look as though he was resting on the ground rather than being held aloft by magic.

What she'd said to Timo was true—the colour of Santos' mage mist had always been the colour of hope. And now that it was gone—*he* was gone—she had to find something else to give her hope. Timo was part of that, but it wasn't fair to him for her to pin all her hopes on him.

He was the same age she'd been when she'd left her mountain home in Larona all those years ago, and Gyda knew she'd been timid and naïve and totally unprepared for what the world would send her way. She'd grown up fast, because she'd had to. So would Timo. He already had. Both his mother and his mentor were dead—killed by the same people who had been trying to kill him for months.

"We can go."

Reo was at her side. As usual, she hadn't heard him. She looked into his eyes and nodded in relief. Whatever he'd found at the end of the tunnel, he hadn't had to kill.

"It's dark, close to midnight," Reo said as Elman and Timo crowded around him. "There was a guard but I told him I was with Elman and he promised to stay away."

"Who was it?" Elman asked. "Did he say?"

"He gave his name as Callub."

Elman grunted. "I know him. Not well, but I think we can trust him."

"He'll do what he said?" Kara asked. "Stay away? And not tell the guild?"

"I think so," Elman said. "Those of us without magic look out for each other. He'll help, for my sake."

"Good," Kara said. She went to Santos' body and gently tugged it forward. "I'll follow Reo with Santos. Once we're outside Elman and Timo can come through. Timo," she turned to her brother. "Can you fill in the hole after us? We don't want anyone to follow our path." Timo was right; they could not afford to have Mage Guild discover this source of power and what it could do. Without Santos to protect them, it could mean the death of everyone on Old Rillidi.

Timo nodded.

"Let's go," Reo said.

Kara followed him up the rocky path. His wariness spread to her, making her flinch at the odd shadows the mage mist illuminated along the path. Staring at Reo's tense shoulders made her ball her hands into fists, one wrapped around Santos' robe as she pulled him along after her.

Yet another night spent on Mage Guild Island, trying to escape with their lives. The last time, she and Reo had outrun her mother and had to kill Valerio Valendi. Now her mother was dead and Valendi's son—her brother—was as desperate to escape as she and Reo had ever been. She hoped it was easier this time.

Timo followed Elman along the newly created tunnel, mage

mist trailing his footsteps. He'd need power to close the tunnel off once they were out and was concentrating on siphoning off a single thread of power from the main artery.

Ahead of him, Elman dropped to his knees, and Timo copied him, dirt and rocks beneath his hands and knees as he scrambled through the tunnel. Elman disappeared, and then Timo's head jutted up and out of the earth. He grabbed hold of Reo's outstretched hand, and the Assassin pulled him out of the tunnel.

Timo brushed his grimy hands against his trousers. It was night but there was enough mage mist for him to see the dirt-smudged faces of his companions.

"I'll be a minute," Timo said. He turned to the pit they'd climbed out of. "I need to bring some of the earth up along the passageway."

"We'll wait there," Kara said, pointing to nearby some bushes. She gripped his shoulder before she reached out for Santos' body.

It was an eerie sight. The faintly visible body floated waist high, and the mage mist that covered it cast long shadows on the faces of the other three.

Timo reached out with his right hand, pulling the power to him. He focussed on drawing it from deep underground, on bringing the recently dislodged earth with it and returning it to its original resting place—making the island whole where he'd torn it apart.

"Elman? Is that . . ." the voice trailed off.

By the time Timo swiveled his head to look, Reo had his hands on a man's neck.

Timo took a few steps towards them, unsure what was happening, what, if anything, he should do.

"I thought you were going to stay away," Reo whispered.

"It's Callub," Elman said. "Let him go."

"Elman," the new man, Callub said. "I'm sorry."

Timo joined the group in time to catch the look that passed between Reo and Kara.

"Sorry for what?" Timo asked.

"He's reported us," Reo said harshly. "Despite his promise not to."

"Callub, what have you done?" Elman grabbed the other man's shoulders and shook him. "Why?"

"I didn't think it was really you," Callub said. "Heard you been missing and when this one said your name I thought he'd killed you." He looked at Reo, his eyes wide. "Why else wouldn't you have been the one to approach me?"

"Who'd you tell?" Elman asked. "Did you just report it to the minor Mages?"

Callub looked to Elman and then nervously back at Reo, who still held him by one arm.

"I went to, but one of them council Mages were there," he said. "He weren't too happy about me interrupting, and he didn't seem to be in any rush. That's why I came back, to keep an eye out like."

"You saw where Reo first exited," Timo said, his heart sinking. This man could lead a council Mage to the tunnel. The tunnel full of power so pure that a council Mage wouldn't be able to keep himself from using it. "Did you tell him?"

"Ah, Callub," Elman said. "Why couldn't you just wait 'til I got here?"

"Sorry," Callub said. "I thought you was dead." He glared at Reo.

Timo couldn't blame the man, really. Reo looked like what he was—dangerous. If he'd seen him appear out of nowhere, in the dark, asserting friendship with a missing man, he might have assumed the same thing. He sighed.

"This changes things," Timo said.

"No," Kara said sharply. She grabbed his arm and spun him around to face her. "This changes *nothing*. We need to move as quickly as we can and get off this island."

He looked at his sister, at the stubborn set to her jaw, the way she'd squared her shoulders and balled her hands into fists, and he shook his head. She knew. She already knew what had to be done, what only *he* could do to keep them safe, to keep Mage Guild from finding—and using—the pure power.

"You know this changes everything," Timo said softly.

Kara's arm dropped from his. A sob broke free from her throat, and Timo almost faltered. Reo looped an arm around her and drew her to him.

"I have to destroy the guild," Timo said. His voice was calm, much calmer than it should be considering his heart felt like it was beating fast enough to jump right out of his chest.

"No," Kara said. "Please. We can leave."

"It won't help," Timo said. "They'll have the power to destroy

Old Rillidi."

"Because Santos is dead," Reo said flatly. "You think we won't be able to keep Old Rillidi safe."

"We won't," Timo said. "But not because Santos is dead. With *this* source they'll have more than enough power to destroy Old Rillidi—and they'll do it. Now is our best—maybe only—chance to destroy Mage Guild." He looked over at Elman. "But I'll have to destroy the island as well."

"We can come back," Kara said. "When we're better prepared. The Mages won't regain their power for weeks, maybe months."

"We don't know that," Reo said. "Not for sure. That's what happens to the clammers, who you say have little magic to start with. We don't know how long the effects will last for powerful Mages."

"Especially if they find this source of pure magic," Timo said.

"You can't go destroying Mage Guild Island," Elman said. "Thousands of people live here, folk who have no say in what the council does. You'll kill them too."

"I know that!" Timo shouted. He *hated* that he would be responsible for the deaths of innocents. "I probably care more about those people than any single Mage on the council does. But what do you think will happen to them when—not if—but *when* the council discovers that there is a way to use another's power without going mad?" The hole that led to the tunnel was partially filled in, but finishing the job wouldn't help, not when a council member knew where to look.

Elman looked at the hole in the ground. His shoulders drooped and he seemed to shrink in on himself.

"Callub," Elman said. "Go ring the warning bells. People need to leave the island."

"But," Callub said. "I . . . I can't just walk into the tower room and start ringing the bell."

"You have to," Elman said. "I promised to help these people get home, and I'm going to keep my promise."

"I won't do it," Callub said. "You're gonna kill thousands."

"Most of them will die anyway," Elman said, sadness etched into his face. "Once the Mages realize that they can use the workrooms to feed their own power, they'll use up anyone with a spark of magic." He spat on the ground. "At first they'll tell us it's to fight Mage Guild's enemies. Old Rillidi will fall first, then the other guilds."

"Warrior Guild will be next," Reo said flatly.

"Probably," Elman agreed. "But it won't much matter *here* because anyone with magical power who's not strong enough to keep themselves out of the workroom will be used up. Their energy will be sucked up until they die. The council will destroy every guild they think is a threat. Which is most of them." He looked at his fellow guard. "Callub, you know they won't stop there."

"No," Callub said. "Then they'll do what they've always done. They'll turn on each other."

"They'll kill each other off, like they've always done," Elman agreed. "But this time it's us—the poor, the weak, the untrained— who will power their fight. And we'll die doing it."

Timo held his breath when Elman paused and stared down at his feet. If they could at least warn the Guildsmen, at least give some of them time to flee to safety, his heart would be a little lighter.

"I know how I'd rather die," Elman said. "Up here in the open, fighting to get away." He spat on the ground again. "Better than sitting unconscious in the dark while someone drained the life out of me."

"Gyda," Callub said. He rubbed a hand across his face, smearing the glint of tears away from his eyes. "I'll go ring the bell."

Timo grabbed a hold of the guard's arm, preventing him from turning away from him.

"How long," he asked. "From the time you ring the bell to when we can expect most people to be on their way, how long will that be?"

"'Bout an hour," Callub replied. "Maybe two. Folk know what the bells mean. Most will run with what's on their back." He sneered. "It's the Mages who'll think they have time to pack."

"Good," Timo said. "I should be able to hide for at least an hour or so." He let go of the guard's arm, and Callub loped off into the night.

"We need to go," Reo said. "Kara, Elman, and I." He peered off to his left. "Someone's coming."

"Then go," Timo said. "I'll come when I can." He clasped Reo's outstretched arm and was surprised to be pulled into a hug.

"Yes," Reo said. "You have to. She'll never forgive you—or herself—if you don't."

Reo stepped aside, and Timo was engulfed in Kara's arms. Tears tracked down her face but she didn't make a sound. She kissed him on the forehead and then let Reo lead her away.

Timo sighed. Alone, as he'd always been. He stepped back towards the hole in the ground. A quick spell made both him and the disturbed earth invisible. Now it was time to see which council Mage was investigating. And whether they had any magic left.

Chapter 18

"I just found him," Kara whispered.

She crouched behind Reo, Elman behind her.

"I know," Reo said. He gently pushed Santos' body beneath a hedge.

They had to leave Santos behind. To Kara it felt like one more betrayal, but as much as she wanted to deny it, Timo was right—things had changed. She said a silent goodbye to the Mage who had befriended her so long ago. He'd been more than a friend over the years. He'd given her a home and helped her learn about her talent with unmagic. She would miss him. But he of all people would tell them to do everything they could to save themselves. And that meant letting Timo try to destroy Mage Guild.

Because Timo was right about that too. The Mages *would* find out how to use that power source. And they *would* destroy Old Rillidi. That was the only reason she hadn't fought to change his mind. All was lost if Mage Guild wasn't shattered.

Reo half-turned to her. "If anyone can do this, Timo can," he assured her.

She gave him a half-smile. "Yes," she agreed. But did that mean he really had a chance?

"Remember what Mole said," Reo said. "Timo's hard to kill."

"I know," Kara said. She wished he hadn't had so much experience dodging spells meant to hurt or kill him.

"And he has plenty of power to fuel his spells," Reo said.

"Yes," Kara said.

Reo backed away from the bushes, keeping low, and Kara and Elman followed.

But that worried Kara too. Timo had access to a lot of power but it was not unlimited. If the Mages realized that Timo's power came from the workrooms they could cut off his source of power. Timo knew that as well—he'd need to act soon, before the Mages could interrupt him.

He had one chance to destroy Mage Guild and he would take it. That was why he was staying behind. And he would use all of the power he had available. Would he assume he could not survive—would he *plan* on not getting out alive?

Reo gestured to her, and she nodded, scanning the park in front of them. Once past this park, Elman would lead the way to the nearest ferry. They hoped to be there before the bells rang. Once the alarm sounded there would be chaos. It would be easy to lose themselves in the crowd, but much harder to be sure that they had safe passage off the island.

Reo sprinted across the grounds, not pausing until he reached the far side. Kara waited until she saw his raised arm before running towards him, keeping low.

She reached his side and sat, breathing heavily, as she waited for him to signal Elman to join them. Without Santos and Timo, they had no magic on their side. They would have to rely on Reo's considerable skills and Elman's knowledge to get them to safety. Kara shook her head. For a woman who'd spent the early years of her life lamenting her own lack of magic, she'd become incredibly used to having access to it. Mage mist ghosted close to Reo, and absently she waved it away. Even she'd become reliant on magic—but once Mage Guild was destroyed everyone would need to learn how to live without it.

THEY WERE STILL ten minutes away from the ferry when the bells started to ring. Elman picked up the pace, and Kara had to jog to keep up.

People came out of their houses and milled in the streets, worriedly looking at the sky, obviously wondering what was happening.

Kara caught up to Elman, who had been slowed by a crowd thronging the mouth of a small alley. Reo wedged in beside her, one hand on her elbow. He leaned over her shoulder, closer to Elman's ear.

"How much farther?" Reo asked.

"Another few blocks," Elman said. He grunted as he shouldered his way past a burly man in a tattered robe. "Stay close." The guard pushed past another group, this time a family hurrying in the same direction as them—two small children were being towed by a sombre man and distraught-looking woman.

Elman turned into a quieter street. A few people hurried from the side door of a manor house as a well-dressed man, obviously the owner of the house, stood on the steps, hesitation on his face. He recognized Elman's uniform and called to him.

"You! Stop and tell me what's going on," he said. "Why is everyone running?"

"It's the bells," Elman replied. "The alarm to get off the island."

"Get off . . ." the man started to say, then he stopped talking and shook his head. "No, I've heard no such thing. My sister's husband's cousin is on the council. I would have been warned."

"Then stay," Kara muttered as she followed Elman past the man. As they turned into another street, Kara looked behind her.

The man still stood on the top step, looking up at the sky as though the pealing bells would give him a different answer, one he liked better. Kara shook her head and then she was around the corner.

People thronged the area around the ferry docks. Kara bumped into Elman's back where he had stopped at the edge of the crowd. Reo made his way to her side.

"Can we get on?" Reo asked.

"Should we?" Kara replied.

A woman struggled past them, one baby on her hip and a young boy clutching her hand. A man a few steps ahead spotted the woman and grabbed her hand, towing her closer to the ferry.

"These people have nothing. Can we take space on the ferry from them?" she continued. "From their children?" She looked around at the crowd. She wasn't sure what she'd expected, but it wasn't this seething mass of people trying to escape. She supposed she'd thought more people would react like the man at the fine house had—with skepticism and disbelief.

"You should have said so earlier," Elman said. "I would have taken us somewheres else. Not sure we have enough time now."

"Is there somewhere else?" Reo asked. "I'm not sure we'll be able to board a ferry anyway. This crowd has its own idea of who's leaving first."

Kara peered over Elman's shoulder. Reo was right. She'd assumed that the man who had taken hold of the woman with the two children had been a relative, but now he was passing her off to someone else ahead in the crowd. As she watched, the woman and her children were ushered to the front of the crowd. Kara lost sight of them when they passed through a narrow gate. When she scanned the crowd, she noticed more women and children being passed forward. There was a stir behind her, and she turned in time to see the mob surround a man at the edge of the crowd.

"Let me through," the man shouted. "I'm a fully trained Mage. I take precedence over any of you."

He pulled his hand back, and Kara watched in horror as mage mist enveloped his fist. Without thinking, she reached her own hand towards him, *pushing* his magic away. Greyish blue mage mist spiralled upwards. The man grunted, surprised. He flung his hand forward trying to activate his spell. Those nearest to him shrank away from him but when nothing happened, they surged forward, shoving the Mage towards the edge of the crowd.

Reo grabbed her hand, pulling it down.

"I'm glad you did that but we don't want to expose what you can do." He softened his words with a smile, and Kara tucked her hand down at her side.

Elman studied her and then looked over the crowd.

"We won't get on this ferry or the next," he said.

"And we don't know if there'll be time for another," Kara agreed. "But there is another way?"

"Yes," Elman said. He took her hand and started pulling her through the crowd, Reo trailing her. Once they reached the edge, they skirted the mob and headed east.

"There's a boat dock," Elman said. "For guards. Don't think anyone ever used it—least not that I ever heard—but we had to check it, keep it ready. Me, I used to like the walk. Got me out in the air." He smirked. "And away from Mages."

He led them down a narrow laneway, pausing once to let a group of people pass.

"There'll be boats there," Elman continued.

"No one else would have taken them?" Kara asked. It seemed unlikely that desperate people would ignore the promise of safety the boats would hold.

"Nah," Elman said. "The Mages don't trust anyone. The way in to the boats is spelled. I used to have to take an amulet with me or the spell wouldn't let me in." He looked at her from the corner of his eye. "I figure you can get us past that."

"Yes," Kara said. She smiled for the first time since they'd left Timo. "I can get us past that."

THE MAGE MIST was thick—a sure sign of Mage Guild's paranoia. Why would they care so much about these boats? Kara studied the mist—almost all of it a single, dull turquoise colour that pulsed up and then down the steps that Elman assured them led to the boats.

"This was done by one Mage," she said. She waved the mist down the stairs but it quickly surged back up. "And they really wanted to protect these boats." The spell wasn't the most malevolent she'd ever come across, but would probably do something unpleasant to anyone who entered without protection. And it was extremely stubborn. She put more force into pushing it away but it recoiled to almost the same spot.

"Been here for years," Elman said. "I think the Mage who done this is long ago dead. Had some notion of sending out trained Mage guards to attack Mage Guild enemies, from what I heard."

A few people stopped in the street behind them—an elderly couple and three youths.

"Are you gonna get the boats?" the woman asked. "Can we come with you? We can't make it to the ferry. Not with my husband's leg." She gestured to the man beside her. He leaned lopsidedly on a rough stick, his other side supported by a lad about Timo's age.

"Elman," Reo whispered. "Is there enough room in the boats?"

The guard nodded. "These boats were planned to carry an army. There's lots of 'em and each one holds at least twenty men."

Kara looked up from studying the mage mist. In just a few moments a small crowd had gathered, and she wondered where they'd come from and how they knew that the boats would be available.

"We should be able to take all of you," Reo said. "Just as soon as we get the boats free from magic.”

Kara didn’t seem to be able to send the spell away so she stepped towards it and plunged her right hand into it, willing it to dissipate. It took much longer than she’d expected, but finally, the mist started to thin. In a few more minutes it was gone, at least at the top of the stairs. More mist swirled at the landing.

“This is a stubborn spell,” Kara said to Reo. “I need to get rid of it in stages.”

“I’ll keep the crowd back,” he replied.

Kara stepped through the door and onto the landing, once again plunging her hand into the mist.

It took three more passes before the mage mist was completely gone. She’d taken a few steps and now she was in a large cavern. Not far away she could see the edge of the island. Sunlight glinted on the waves of Pontus Bay.

Rows and rows of boats bobbed in the water, tied to long docks that jutted out towards the island’s edge. She counted twenty, thirty, fifty boats. That was one thousand people, if each one held as many as Elman guessed. More than ten ferries could carry, Kara estimated. The island shook, and she almost lost her footing on the bottom stairs.

She hurried back up the stairs. They were running out of time. She felt another tremor and refused to think about what that meant for Timo.

“Close to fifty boats,” she gasped as she dashed outside. “And the spell is gone. Let’s get these people down there.”

Reo nodded and faced the throng. Just as at the ferry, women with children were shepherded through the crowd to the front. Elman led them through the doorway and down the stairs.

“We need some men too,” Kara said.

“You there, go with them,” Reo said. He pointed at about a dozen men who had shuffled aside to let the women and children pass.

The men all shook their heads.

“No,” one said. “We look out for those who can’t.”

“They won’t be able to row the boats fast enough,” Kara said. “The first boats have to leave before the rest can move.”

The men hesitated, and she glared at them.

“There’s room for everyone here,” she said. “*We can save everyone.* But not if the first boats can’t get out from under the island. Now go!"

The group of men looked at each other. One stepped back and pointed to a younger man behind him.

"I hurt my arm last year, and it never quite healed up right," he said. "Let someone more able go first."

The younger man stepped forward and followed the rest as they headed through the doorway.

Kara shook her head in disgust. An island full of the best healers in Tregella and this Guildsman hadn't been healed. Why did Mage Guild treat its own people so badly?

The island trembled, and she clutched Reo's arm to steady herself. That's what Timo was doing—making sure Mage Guild couldn't steal power from its people to fuel even worse atrocities against them.

She turned to help people down to the boats. The island shuddered again, and she closed her eyes for a second. Timo had promised to give them as much time as possible—but he'd also promised to follow them off the island. Could he keep both promises or would he be forced to choose one? Kara knew which one she wanted him to keep. She desperately wanted her brother safe and sound, living a happy life on Old Rillidi—or anywhere he wanted, really. But his only chance at that meant Mage Guild must be weakened or completely destroyed.

TIMO HUDDLED NEAR the opening to the tunnel. Invisible, he'd been carefully filling the hole in, leaving just a narrow shaft that he could squeeze down if he needed. Or draw more power through. A thin stream of mage mist led to him and a pool of power lay just beneath the earth. He could actually *feel* it, almost as though it was calling to him. He hoped that was because he had unmagic—that he was the only one who could feel this pure source of power—and use it. Although it was possible it had been discovered—maybe by a minor Mage in a workroom—but been kept a secret. Or did a Mage have to be powerful already in order to use this pure power?

There was a shout and half a dozen guards ran through the park area, cutting through the bushes that surrounded the grassy area. One stumbled and fell, cursing. His curse turned into alarm when he realized he'd tripped over something. It was the barely visible Santos.

Timo settled onto the ground. Callub had said that the council Mage hadn't been in a hurry, but he would come now. One guard headed back the way he'd come while his companions hurried towards the sound of the bells.

A shrub grew just a few feet from the entrance to the tunnel and Timo crawled over to it, taking deep breaths to calm his breathing. After a few moments he felt more stable, almost ready to face whichever council Mage would be arriving.

Footsteps pounded across the lawn and two guards ran up to where Santos' body was still tucked into the hedge. One guard peered around the open space while the other reached around and found Santos.

"It's a body," the guard said over his shoulder. "Like I told you."

"But whose?" a voice said. Then Jinaro stepped into view.

Timo sucked in a breath. The Mage stopped a few steps away from Santos' body, warily eyeing his surroundings. A blanket of white mage mist ghosted around him. He flicked a wrist, and white mage mist covered Santos, and Timo's spell faded until Santos was completely visible.

He knew! Jinaro knew about the pure power—he'd tapped into it already! Timo clenched his fists. There was no choice now, no more uncertainty—he had to destroy Mage Guild Island. Jinaro might not have shared his discovery but it was only a matter of time before someone like Inigo questioned his ability to create spells after Timo took away his magic.

"Santos Nimali," Jinaro said. He stared at the body. "I suppose this means Inigo truly is Primus."

"I don't see any intruders," said the guard as he scanned the area. "What should we do?"

"Take the body to Inigo," Jinaro said. "He'll want proof that his little trap worked."

One of the guards gripped Santos' arm and tugged him, still floating, towards the far end of the garden.

Jinaro stepped closer to the remaining guard.

"You and I will take another look around," the Mage said. He flung a hand up, and a large mage light appeared. Jinaro moved a finger, and the light floated above them, lighting the dark night. At a signal from the Mage, the light headed out into the garden. Jinaro and the guard followed.

Timo left the shelter of the shrub. He might be invisible, but the branches disturbed by his body weren't. He'd rather be out in the open anyway, in case he had to run. Silently he trailed Jinaro as he searched the garden. The Mage and guard passed a small building. Timo was still a few steps away from it when he felt the tug of pure power. A tendril reached out towards Jinaro, who paused and took a deep breath. The wisp of mage mist was absorbed by the Mage, who smiled and continued after the guard.

Did Jinaro even know where his power came from? Timo skirted the building, pushing the mage mist away from him. He certainly knew he had the use of magic—he'd created the mage light.

Suddenly the bells stopped ringing.

"Finally," Jinaro said. "Now I can think. What was that, a signal?"

"Warning bell," the guard replied. "The call to leave the island."

"Ah, very devious," Jinaro said. "Trying to get the workroom Mages to leave their posts." He turned to the guard. "See that whoever rang the bell is taken to Inigo."

"Yes, Master Mage." The guard nodded and headed off across the park.

"They wanted me to be without all the lovely magic," Jinaro said to himself. Then he giggled.

Timo closed his eyes, and his shoulders drooped. The Mage *did* know where the power came from. But had he shared his secret?

Jinaro flung a hand up, and the mage light spun up into the sky. He chuckled and reeled it towards him and continued to search.

Jinaro was a few steps away from the hole in the ground when he stopped. A smile split his face, and Timo knew that he could feel the power just below the surface.

"Here's where you came out," Jinaro muttered. He knelt on the grass and swept a hand out in front of him. Dirt and small pebbles, hidden by Timo's invisibility spell, skittered under the Mage's hand. He swept the ground again, and a stream of power snaked through the small hole left in the earth and headed for Jinaro.

Timo moved a little closer, pushing the power down into the

ground. Jinaro frowned and held his hand out. Even the pure power that enveloped Timo strained towards the Mage. Timo clamped down on it, hard.

How was he doing that? Drawing the power to him? Timo took a step back and the pull from Jinaro decreased.

"Come on," Jinaro crooned. "I know you're down there. Come fill me up!"

"Fill you up with what?"

Timo spun at the same time as Jinaro. Inigo stood a few feet away, the guard behind him.

"Fill you up with what?" Inigo repeated. He looked up at the mage light that hovered over Jinaro. "How did you manage the light?"

Jinaro shrugged. "My magic is returning, that's all."

"Really?" Inigo said.

As he stepped past Timo to reach Jinaro, the pure power that coursed through Timo *arced* to Inigo. The Mage stopped, startled, as power swirled around him. Timo struggled to control the power surge, cutting the link between Inigo and him, but it was too late. The Mage raised a hand to his face in wonder.

"I can feel the power," he said softly. "I can feel the magic. What just happened?"

"I'm not sure," Jinaro said. He stared at the ground where Timo stood.

He raised his hand to cast a spell, and Timo relocated himself a dozen feet away.

Jinaro's spell hit the ground, and a blast of rock and dirt spewed up. Inigo, who had been standing close to the spot, whirled on Jinaro. He swept a hand out, and a spell hurtled towards the other Mage.

Timo hid behind a hedge. A ragged crater stood where Jinaro had been but the Mage was alive, hovering a few feet in the air. Pure power now streamed from the hole in the ground—one thick river leading to Jinaro and a second to Inigo. A third, smaller stream wound its way to Timo.

"You always were planning on killing me," Jinaro yelled as he let another spell fly. "You couldn't just leave me alone."

Inigo, fueled by hatred and pure power, rose into the air, deflecting the spell. It smashed into the ground a few feet away, at the feet of the guard. The man was swallowed up in the explosion, and a pit was left where he'd been standing. Neither Inigo nor Jinaro seemed to even notice that the guard was dead.

Frantically, Timo tried to sever the streams of pure power leading to the two Mages, but it was too strong. The best he could do was siphon some of it to him.

Inigo and Jinaro continued to battle, screaming at each other. Both Mages hovered in the air, shielded by white mage mist so thick that Timo could barely tell them apart. Blast after blast damaged the garden until there was nothing left except ragged pits and craters and burning shrubs and trees.

The stream of pure power was growing weaker, and Timo wondered if the Guildsmen who were unwittingly supplying it were unconscious—or dead—from fueling the fight between the two Mages. It's what he'd expected—why he'd decided he had to destroy Mage Guild Island.

The flow of pure magic dwindled to a trickle and then finally stopped. The Mages didn't even notice as they continued to fling less and less powerful spells at each other. When they had only tiny amounts of power left, Timo reached a hand towards each Mage, drawing what was left of their power to him.

The pure magic fought him, and he was sweating by the time the thin trails of power reached him.

Inigo tried to cast a spell but when nothing happened, Jinaro laughed.

"You fool," Jinaro said. "You've used up a power source you have no idea how to reproduce."

"And you do?"

"Yes," Jinaro smiled. "And once I replenish my power, I will kill you. I'll have to since you will never leave me alone after this."

"I'm Primus now," Inigo said. "I'll have you detained and tried for treason."

Timo took a step back. Now that the fighting had stopped it was safe for him to return to the tunnels and figure out how to *undo* Mage Guild Island. With his eyes on the Mages, he took another step. He stumbled into a crater and pitched backwards with a cry.

"Who's there?" Inigo called out.

"It's them," Jinaro said. "I thought someone else was here. That's who I was aiming at but then you tried to kill me."

"Who is it?"

Unsteadily, Timo rose to his feet. The pure power was surging towards the two Mages again, and he fought to control it.

"It's the Valendi brat," Jinaro said.

Inigo stepped towards him, and Timo, desperate, relocated himself a few steps away.

"He shouldn't be able to do that," Inigo said. "He's stronger than we were told."

"I can feel the power he's holding," Jinaro said. He took a few steps towards Timo. "I want it!"

"Why?" Timo asked. "So you can drain the life out of more Guildsmen? How many died for this?" Timo gestured to the destroyed garden. "Twenty, thirty?"

Jinaro paled, but he reached an arm out to Timo, calling the pure power.

"If Guildsmen died it was because it's their place to serve us," Inigo said calmly. "Those with lesser talents always sacrifice for those with greater ones."

"No one deserves to die to fuel a fight between Mages who think they're better than everyone else," Timo said. "You're supposed to take care of Guildsmen!"

"You sound like your friend Santos," Inigo sneered. "Wanting to help the lesser Guildsmen. *We are not all created equal,* despite what Gyda's teachings say."

"No," Timo agreed. "We're not. But that doesn't mean those with less exist to serve those with greater abilities."

"You're so young," Inigo said. "So naïve. Your mother was smart and ambitious. She understood what it took to get and keep power."

Inigo took a step towards Timo, who retreated carefully, keeping both Mages in view.

"Is that why you wanted her dead?"

"She was in my way," Inigo said. "I couldn't become Primus with her still alive." He snarled a grin. "But she was keeping secrets, wasn't she? She and Rorik. Not the fool I thought he was, but he's dead all the same."

"Because you cursed him."

"A spell I learned from your father," Inigo said. "One he learned off Santos himself, so he told me." Inigo chuckled. "I do like the symmetry of that. You triggered the spell, of course, but don't blame yourself—he would have been dead by Founders

Day."

"I don't blame myself," Timo said. "As soon as I saw Rorik, I knew what had been done to him. And by whom." Inigo seemed eager to talk, and if it would allow a few more people to flee to safety, Timo was inclined to let him.

"You know he won't allow you to live," Timo said to Jinaro.

The Mage was still edging towards him, his hand outstretched. It was as though he'd forgotten about anything other than the pure power.

"He doesn't care," Inigo said. "He's intoxicated by the power. I can feel it in you but you barely seem to notice. Why is that?"

"I've always been surrounded by magic," Timo said. "For every single waking hour that I've spent on Mage Guild Island, I've seen magic. It's all around us. All I have to do, all I've ever had to do, was call it to me. This isn't so much different." He shrugged. It was different—more pure, more powerful, more volatile—but he wasn't about to tell Inigo that. "And I can control it." At least he hoped he could.

"To what end?" Inigo asked. "I can give you political power beyond your imaginings. I can make you Secundus to my Primus. At sixteen! It's unheard of! You could do whatever you liked with those who tried to harm you."

"Except you," Timo said.

"Except me," Inigo agreed. "No one would follow you without me there to vouch for you."

"It's not what I want," Timo said. "That's something even my mother never understood. Power, Mage Guild, living on this island—none of it's what I want."

"Of course it's what you want," Inigo said, smiling. "What else is there?"

He swept his arms out, and Timo thought he was simply showing the island; instead, a cloud of mage mist sped towards him. Timo stood his ground, and redirected the spell so that it swept past him.

"How . . ." Inigo started. "What did you do?"

"Not much," Timo said. "That's the thing. I don't need to do very much in order for magic to shy away from me. But I can *call* it. And then I can control it. *All of it.*" Now it was Timo's turn to sweep his arms wide. This time he sent all nearby residual magic spinning away into the night until there was one simple mage light left hovering overhead. The lack of magic surrounding them jolted Jinaro, and he stumbled to his knees.

"What have you done to it?" Jinaro asked. "All that lovely power. It was mine, it called to me."

"It belongs to the guild," Timo said. "And the Guildsmen it's been bled from. And now I'll use it to give them the only thing I can. Freedom from Mage Guild—freedom from the guild that should nurture and protect them but instead harvests them— steals their power and their lives." Timo sank to his knees and placed his hands on the broken landscape of the garden. He wove a quick spell of protection around himself and then closed his eyes and *reached* out to the magic. All of the magic. Slowly, like something being woken up from a slumber, he felt it responding to him—felt Mage Guild Island responding to him.

There was a ping against the shield he'd built.

"Why can't I touch him?" Inigo asked. "What's he doing?"

"I think he's doing what he warned us his sister would do," Jinaro said. "Destroying Mage Guild Island."

"That's not possible," Inigo replied. "Get some guards. Guards! Guards!"

Timo felt the flurry of fists beating against his shield, and then he was lost in the vast web of spells that made up the island. Years and years of Mages had used power from Guildsmen—alongside their own magic—to create the buildings and passageways of the island until it was more than a lump of earth that floated in the sky. It seethed with the joys and ambitions and despairs and needs of those whose life magic had imbued it with power.

He stumbled and fell to his side. A guard raised a fist to him, but before he could do more than cock his arm, Timo had relocated himself out or reach. He rubbed a hand against a sore temple. He must have dropped his shield wall while he was immersed in the magic.

The guard flailed at thin air, recovered, and scanned the garden.

"Over there," Inigo said, pointing towards Timo.

Sword drawn, the guard started forward. Jinaro fell to his knees in the spot where Timo had been, his hands scrabbling at the earth.

"Stop it!" Inigo kicked Jinaro, and he fell onto his side, his hands still weakly digging into the earth. "Any magic here is mine!" Then the head of the Mage Council knelt and reached down to the ground.

Timo cast a protective spell just as the guard reached him. The man slashed at him with his sword but the blade bounced off the spell and plunged into the soft dirt. Straining, Timo drew a tiny bit of power from the ground beneath Inigo, taking magic out of the man as well.

The new Primus sagged briefly, before straightening.

"You won't be able to stop everyone," Inigo said. "I'll order hundreds, thousands of guards and Mages to attack you. And they will."

"If you can find them," Timo replied. He looked up at the guard who glared at him from the other side of his protective barrier. "Didn't you hear the bells? It was the signal to get off the island."

The guard looked over at Inigo and shrugged before meeting Timo's eyes. "I was told it was a drill, a test. No harm's coming to the island."

Timo sighed. "Does this look like no harm?" He gestured to the ruined garden around them. "A man named Callub assured me that people would leave."

"Callub you say?" The guard sent a nervous look towards Inigo. "I weren't told Callub rung the bells. Where is he?"

"On his way off the island," Timo said. "I hope. That's what he said he'd do. You should do the same."

Timo stood up, his protective spell stretching around him. He'd delayed as long as he could. Inigo was right. With enough people—guards and Mages—pursuing him he wouldn't be able to complete his task. It was time he found a safe place to work with the island's magic.

Once invisible, Timo closed his eyes and concentrated on sealing the tunnel and burying the remnants of pure power that still called to him from deep under the earth. Then, to keep Inigo and Jinaro from accessing any power, he forced all magic in the area away, towards the outer edges of the island. The island shook for a moment, and then settled. The buildings nearby went dark as mage lights were extinguished.

He set off towards a small garden on the other side of the library. His mother's garden, although he'd rarely seen her in it. She'd once told him that it reminded her of the mountain home she'd grown up in. At the time he'd thought it had pleased her but years later he'd come to understand that she despised the garden, just as she despised having been born in a rural mountain villa. Inferior—that's what she thought it said about her. Timo grimaced. Now he knew her bloodline—the talents passed on by her—were superior, not inferior.

Chapter 19

KARA SCANNED THE grounds just outside the gate. The last of the crowd was being ushered down to the boats.

A while ago the bells had stopped ringing, and later the island had finally stopped trembling and shaking, but that hadn't been a comfort to her. Was Timo still alive? They couldn't wait for him even if he was. He would have to find his own way off the island. Kara wiped a tear from her eye. She'd only just found him!

Reo stopped beside her.

"The boat is ready to go," he said. "There are still half a dozen left in case others find their way here. In case Timo finds his way here."

"Good." And it was, really. If they hadn't been here—if *she* hadn't been here—none of these people would have been able to get to the boats. But Timo wouldn't know about these boats, wouldn't know that there was a way off the island here. Sadly, she turned towards the gate but movement caught her eye.

"Wait." She placed a hand on Reo's arm. "I think someone's out there." She peered out beyond the gate towards a small laneway. There, she saw it again. "Come on," she said to Reo. She headed toward the lane, and he silently followed her.

"Hello?" Kara called softly. "We're leaving the island now. Do you want to come?"

She heard a scuffle from behind a low fence. Before she could take two steps in that direction Reo had vaulted over the fence. A shrill scream turned into a yelp of outrage.

"Lemme go," a voice yelled.

"No," Reo answered.

When he straightened, Kara could see him over the top of the fence. He turned to face her, and she glimpsed a small form writhing in his arms. The girl wasn't more than five or six—the same age as her own children—and she did not like being held captive.

Kara darted around the corner and stopped in front of Reo and his squirming burden. The child stopped struggling when she met Kara's gaze.

"Shhh. We aren't going to hurt you," Kara said. "But we can't let you run away."

"I won't run away," the girl said.

She went limp, as if to prove her point. Kara met Reo's eyes and smiled. Their own children often tried this just before trying to break free.

"I'll keep hold of you, just the same," Reo said softly.

He carefully set the girl's feet on the ground, keeping a firm grip on her shoulders. She lunged, trying to break free, but he held her tight against his legs. When she stepped down on Reo's booted foot, Kara turned her head away to keep from laughing out loud.

"We won't hurt you, truly," Kara said. She knelt down in front of the child. "We have two children of our own, just about your age."

That caught the child's attention and her head swiveled from Kara, up to Reo, and back to Kara.

"You're married?"

"We are," Kara replied. "Our son Nando is six and Lisha is four. I think you're a bigger girl than Lisha."

"I'm five," was the reply.

"What's your name?"

The girl eyed her suspiciously for a moment. She crossed her small arms and settled them on her chest before she shook her head and frowned.

"Is your family close by?" Kara asked.

The girl stared at her feet, her lips clamped shut.

Kara stood up, wiping her hands on her trousers. "Hello?" she called out. "Is someone missing a five-year-old girl? Hello?"

When there was no answer, she shook her head. "We can't leave you here. Reo, take her to the boat."

"No," the girl cried. "Leave me alone!"

"We can't," Kara said. "Did you hear the bells?" The girl nodded, and Kara continued, "Do you know what they meant?"

Hesitantly, the small head shook back and forth.

"They were telling everyone to get off the island," Kara said. She gestured to the empty streets around them. "Something bad has happened, and it's not safe here anymore."

The island shuddered, and the ground buckled beneath their feet.

"We need to go," Reo said.

"We can't leave," the girl said softly. "Not without mama." She stared at Kara, her eyes wide with worry.

"Where is she? Is she hiding?" Kara asked.

"She's sick. She didn't get out of bed today."

"Show us," Kara said.

The girl nodded solemnly. "This way." She trotted down the alley and slipped through a gap in a wooden fence.

"I hope she's not just running away from us," Reo said.

He reached the fence and instead of trying to squeeze through the gap he grabbed a loose board and pulled. The fence swayed for a moment before the board came loose with a squeal. Reo dropped it to the ground, and Kara went through the gap. The girl had paused a few feet ahead. When she saw Kara, she turned and ran left around a small shack. Kara reached the front of the building in time to see the girl enter another alley a few doors down.

Kara sprinted, trying to keep up. Was the girl really trying to show them or was she simply escaping? Once in the alley, Kara stopped. Reo caught up to her, and she slammed her hand on the side of a building.

"Gyda! She's gone." Kara spun, looking in all directions, but there was no sign of the girl.

"Can't blame her for not trusting us," Reo said. "I'll look left, you look right. Surely one little girl can't outsmart the two of us?"

"She already did," Kara muttered. But she paced along the left side of the alley anyway, hoping for a sign that the child had gone through the fence or into one of the shacks that lined the alley.

"I think her mother really is sick," Reo said.

"I do too." The child's statement had had the ring of truth. Why else would a girl so young be out alone in the streets? Although she knew her way around well enough that it could be a habit.

"Shhh," Reo said.

He'd paused beside a hut. The wood was greyed and splintered, and a small window was set up high in the wall, the shutters hanging loose.

Kara joined him, her head cocked. A low moan came from within the building.

"Someone's inside," she whispered. "We need to try to get them to leave. Let's hope it's the girl's mother." She didn't want to think about others left behind, those too old or sick—or stubborn—to react to the bells.

Quietly they made their way to the front of the house. There was another low moan and then a whimper of pain. The front door opened, and the little girl crept out, her hands over her ears. She huddled down beside the door, facing the side of the building.

Kara gently reached out and pulled the girl to her.

"Make her better," the girl cried. "Make mama stop crying." Tears tracked the child's face, and she buried her head in Kara's shoulder.

"We'll do our best," Kara said. She hoped they could help, but without a Mage, she wasn't sure what they could do.

Reo opened the door and led the way inside.

It took a few seconds for Kara's eyes to adjust to the dim light. Another low moan told her where the woman lay. A rickety cot was pushed up against the wall, and a figure huddled there, a thin blanket covering her.

Kara set the girl down onto the ground and knelt beside the cot.

"Panna? That you?" The woman rolled over.

When she saw Kara, she recoiled, scrabbling backwards a little. The blanket fell to the floor.

"Reo, she's not sick, she's having a baby. We won't hurt you," Kara said to the woman. "But you can't stay here."

"I heard them bells," the woman said. "But I can't walk to the ferry."

"We'll help," Kara said. "And we're not going as far as the

ferry. My husband will carry you."

"Your husband?" The woman stopped talking and moaned, her hands clutching the edge of the cot.

"They have two children my age," the girl, Panna, said softly. "Least that's what they told me."

Kara nodded. "We do. And I know from experience that a second baby comes faster than the first. Come on, we don't have much time."

"All right," the woman said. "It can't be worse than staying here by myself." She took a deep breath and swung her legs over the side of the cot. "At least Panna'll be safe."

"Reo," Kara said.

She moved out of his way, pulling little Panna with her.

Reo bent down and reached around the woman, pulling her up and into his arms.

"Let's go," Reo said. "What's the fastest way to the boats?"

Panna led the way, Kara close behind her. It took them longer since they had to travel through the streets instead of by way of Panna's shortcuts, but they made it to the square. Elman stood outside the gate, a worried look on his face.

"The island's starting to sink," Elman said. "It's slow, but we need to get out from under it as soon as we can."

They all filed through the gate, Kara holding Panna's hand as they headed down the stairs. The bottom step was slippery from the water that now washed over it.

A few steps along the dock a boat sat, half-filled with Guildsmen.

"Derry," one older woman called. "We thought you'd left already. Give her here, lads."

Reo handed Panna's mother off to a couple of men in the boat. They set her down and soon three women huddled around her. Reo grabbed Panna and swung her into waiting hands.

Kara stepped in, followed by Reo, and Elman pulled out his sword and slashed the thick rope that tethered them to the dock. He pushed the boat out before he jumped over the gunwale.

"Man the oars," Elman called. He made his way to the centre of the boat and sat down. Another three men settled beside him, each pair wielding a long wooden oar. The boat jerked, and Kara fell against Reo, who steadied himself against the side of the boat.

Kara stared at the dock they'd just left. Water covered it,

lapping against the second stair from the bottom. The island was sinking. Was Timo safe? Was he even alive?

"He's smart and he has very strong magic," Reo said. "He'll make it out."

"I hope so," Kara said. She rested her head on Reo's shoulder and sighed, letting the rhythmic pull of the rowers lull her.

A few moments later they were out from under the island, sunlight glinting off the gentle swells of the bay. Boats of every description were scattered ahead of them, carrying refugees from the sinking island, refugees from the politics of Mage Guild.

Kara turned to watch the island. From this vantage point she couldn't tell that it was sinking but *she* could see a difference. The tall spires of the buildings in the centre still rose majestically into the sky, but they no longer glowed with layers upon layers of mage mist. Even as she watched, the mist seemed to evaporate, thinning first near the top and then closer to the ground. Slowly, one spire sank, forever altering the skyline of the island.

A man behind her muttered a prayer to Gyda. A scream split the air—Panna's mother, bearing another child of Mage Guild.

This would be the first child born outside of Mage Guild. A good omen, Kara decided, a new life with a chance to live free of the guilds. She hoped the child was able to live the way it was born.

TIMO LEANED AGAINST the low garden wall and closed his eyes against the sun. It was a beautiful day. A day he was going to fill with destruction—and death.

He hadn't found any pure magic, not close enough to be used by him or the council Mages. He could only hope that those who usually manned the work rooms had heeded the bells and left the island. There would be others who had stayed—the ill, the elderly, and some just too obstinate to believe the message the bells were sending. Most of the council would stay—they were too busy securing their political lives to worry about their physical ones. And they were so accustomed to using magic that some of them might not remember that right now, they had none. By the time they realized their mistake Timo would have sent them below the waters of the bay.

His earlier encounter with pure power had left him even more sensitive to the swathes of magic that infused Mage Guild Island.

He'd spent the last ten minutes pushing some of that magic away from the centre of the island and out towards the less magically dense edges. Now, even with his eyes closed, he could sense the layers and layers of spells that enveloped the island from the tops of the tallest spires to the underside docks where boats bobbed on the waters of the bay.

The oldest spells—the ones that had started the process of creating and raising the land mass—felt purer, *more generous*, than the more recent spells. Mage Guild Island had been built with good intentions but over the years Mages had poisoned it with their viciousness and cruelty. Now it was up to Timo to tear the heart out of all that malevolence. Starting with the most powerful Mages—the council.

He hardly even had to call the magic, it came to him so willingly. A spell rushed into him, at first overwhelming him, before he unmade it and let the power merge with his own. A rumble brought him out of his trance, and he looked up to see the library tower slowly sink out of the sky. After that he was more careful about the spells he called to him—he planned to take the island apart in stages in the hope that more people would escape before the final foundations for the island were destroyed. That's why he'd sent magic to reinforce the edges. He didn't want to undermine that by being careless now.

A late thought made him erect a barrier around the garden—and he had to wonder if he had secretly wanted to be found before he could complete his terrible task.

He cautiously teased magic out of the spells that surrounded him, and soon he had amassed enough power to do what he planned. He closed his eyes and concentrated on the centre of the island where the most powerful Mages lived and worked. The council room, Rorik's home, the library, and Faron's cells—they were all located within the area he pictured. He made sure his mother's home, the garden he sat in, was not included and then he channelled the magic to surround that section. He forced it down, into the earth, until power encircled that part of the island from sky to sea.

"Gyda forgive me," Timo said. Then he closed his eyes and released the largest relocation spell he'd ever created. The island shuddered and dropped a few inches before everything fell silent. Timo exhaled and leaned over his knees.

It was done. He'd moved the centre of the island a few miles south, out over open water. Without most of the spells that kept the island aloft and without Mages capable of immediately creating them, that part of the island was even now sinking into the bay. He had just killed people he knew—evil people like Inigo but also misguided ones. And there were others who had been— not friends—but at least not enemies. Now most of them were probably dead.

SHE WOULD HAVE missed it if she hadn't been trying to count the boats that were scattered across the bay. Suddenly, clouds of multi-coloured mage mist towered over the water. Then a huge mass appeared and immediately dropped into the sea.

In the few seconds that it took to sink below the surface of the bay, Kara caught glimpses of dirt and buildings. Moments later an enormous swell lifted their small boat, causing the rowers to scramble to hold onto the oars. Then the wave was past them, heading towards the rest of the islands of Rillidi.

"What was that?" Reo asked.

"Timo," Kara replied. "Following through on his promise to destroy Mage Guild Island." She looked over at the island. The skyline was different—many of the highest towers could no longer be seen, and the amount of mage mist that swirled around the island was diminished. "At least some of it."

Where the land had dropped into the bay, the surface of the water swirled with debris. A few boats near the area headed towards it.

"Should we look for survivors?" Kara asked. "After Timo sent them to their deaths?"

Reo placed a hand on her shoulder and squeezed. "Yes, we have room, the other boats may not."

Kara sighed and closed her eyes. They would help who they could, and if Inigo was one of the survivors, they'd deal with him separately.

In the end they picked up just two bedraggled and confused men, neither of whom had any magic. Other boats rescued people as well but Kara was too far away to know if any of them were Mages she knew—Mages who it would be dangerous to let live. She had to be content with the knowledge that most of the powerful Mages had little or no magic. Perhaps any who did escape would hide, or find a way to use their gifts to benefit others?

Their small boat paused once, to let the men rowing trade places. Fresh rowers bent to the oars, and they resumed their journey to Old Rillidi. The shoreline of Merchant Guild Island was littered with broken boats and debris—damage caused by the wave that had swept past them—and when they slipped under the bridge between Merchant Guild and Mason Guild Islands, the water mark reached almost to the underside of the bridge.

On Old Rillidi, the old boat at the docks had been pushed further up on the sand, but there was little damage this far from Mage Guild Island.

Kara was grateful to see that both the old manor house and her small cabin were undamaged. Figures waited along the shore, and when the boat got closer, she recognized Mole and Giona.

Mole waded into the water, grabbed the prow of the boat, and dragged it into shore. Reo and a few of the men jumped out and helped, and soon the boat had been hauled up onto the beach. Kara took the hand Mole extended to her and stepped out onto Old Rillidi.

"Where's Timo?" Mole asked.

"He stayed behind," Kara said. "To finish it."

"With Santos?"

Kara shook her head and blinked to keep the welling tears from falling. "Santos is dead," she said.

"Gyda." Mole looked down. When his head lifted again, there was a grim smile on his face. "I thought that old man would live forever."

"So did I," Kara agreed. "We weren't able to bring him home." She would always regret that, but Santos would have understood.

"So Timo's alone?" Mole asked.

"He said he'd follow as soon as he could," Kara said. "And we had to leave." She gestured to the confused people who were climbing out of the boat. "We released dozens of boats. The rest were filled completely."

Mole nodded, his mouth a tight line. "He'll be happy to hear that." He looked out towards the bay.

"What news?" Reo asked. He placed an arm around Kara's shoulder, and she leaned into his steady warmth.

"Giona's using spells to try to hear what's happening," Mole said. "But he's never met Timo, so he hasn't been able to find him. All we've heard is a general confusion." He rubbed a hand across his face. "But a while ago something big happened."

"I pinpointed it to the centre of the island," Giona said. "It just went . . . silent."

"It was Timo," Kara said. "We think he moved a big section of Mage Guild Island and dropped it into the sea."

Mole's eyes brightened. "So he's really doing it? Sinking the island?"

"We think so," Reo said. "If Giona's right, then the centre is gone. I think we can assume Timo's targeting the Council."

"Kara?" Elman approached her, eyeing Mole warily. "Is there a place to take these folk? The women say Derry's time is soon, and she needs a warm place to have her child."

"Of course," Kara said. "Mole, can you take her up to the manor?"

"No. Sorry," Mole said. "I'm going to get Timo."

"You can't," Kara said. "The island is sinking."

"And with the Mages gone, Timo will let it sink slowly."

"It's too dangerous," Kara said. "I won't let you."

"If I don't go, you'll never see Timo alive," Mole said. "He won't even try to leave."

"He will," Kara said. But in her heart she knew Mole spoke the truth. She knew because she would feel the same way. She'd killed Valerio Valendi in order to save her and Reo's lives but it had taken her a long time to be able to live with that. Would she have wanted to live if she'd been forced to kill hundreds, maybe even thousands of people? Especially since some of those who would die were victims themselves?

"Go," she said to Mole. "Bring him back if you can, but don't sacrifice yourself if you can't find him. I need you to come back."

Mole nodded. He turned and grabbed a surprised Giona, and the two of them headed up the beach, leaving Kara and Reo to deal with the refugees.

KARA SAT BESIDE the bed that held the sleeping mother and infant. One of the women from the boat poked her head through the door. When she saw Kara, she smiled and gently closed it.

Once they'd gotten Derry settled into a room, it had been an uneventful birth, thank Gyda. Little Panna had worriedly hovered near her mother until Reo had taken her to play with their children. The baby, a healthy girl, had been born a short time later.

"Thank you," Derry whispered from the bed. "For everything. Saving Panna and me. And now my baby."

Kara smiled and met the woman's eyes. "You're welcome." She leaned over and gently lifted the cloth that covered the baby's face. "She's beautiful. Do you have a name in mind? Maybe the father's?"

Derry scowled. "She's got no father," she said. "Neither does Panna. They're my girls though the Mage as got them on me didn't give me a choice."

"Shh," Kara said. "Of course they're your girls. No one here will ever try to take them from you." She settled back into the chair and sighed. Poor Derry had suffered the fate Kara herself had escaped so many years ago. But they were safe now, and would be able to make their own choices.

She'd introduce Timo to Derry and her children when he made it to Old Rillidi. People like this were why Mage Guild had to be destroyed.

Chapter 20

THE GARDEN WAS eerily silent. No birds sang, no insects buzzed. It was as though they knew that danger lurked here.

Timo closed his eyes against the fading sun and felt his way through the island to the magic. The newer spells—those that were years rather than decades old—had been concentrated in the very centre of the island, the very part that no longer existed. He'd used that magic to fuel the spell that relocated that part of the island out to sea. Only wisps of spells devoid of purpose were left behind. He gathered them to him, feeling his own power rebuilding as he absorbed each partial spell.

The ground shuddered. Timo opened his eyes and blinked. The island was sinking, a little bit every hour. Left alone, it would take days, maybe even weeks, for it to fully submerge. Plenty of time for even the most foolhardy to realize what was happening and leave. Now that he'd ripped out the black heart of Mage Guild, he was tempted to simply let nature take its course, let the already weakened spells falter—as they eventually would. But that meant *he'd* have to wait weeks as well and he wanted this over.

He'd give them a day, maybe a day and a half before he started draining the power from the oldest spells—the original spells that had created the island and lifted it up out of the bay.

That's how they'd done it, so many years ago. The shape and feel of the power that was still contained within those first magnificent spells, told him that the Mages who had created this island had swept dirt and mud and plant life from the bottom of the bay, dredging it miles from the south to this spot. They'd lifted it up out of the water and then others had formed it into a mass of land that could be lived on—built on.

What a sight that must have been! How proud those Mages must have been—*should* have been—to create something so wondrous out of nothing but their talents, determination, and vision.

But in the years since that glory, the heart of the guild became poisoned and twisted with power until Timo had no choice but to destroy it. He sighed. Kara had agreed with him. Santos would have too, if he'd lived. But that didn't stop him from wondering if he was just the same as the rest of them, just as power-hungry and ready to dispose of anyone in his way.

The council was corrupt—evil—and Inigo felt he had the right to use Guildsmen in any way he wanted. Even if it killed them. *He* would rather be dead than have someone drain his power like that, and he had made that same decision for hundreds, thousands of people. Did that make him any different from Inigo?

Timo awoke with a start. He'd slid down against the wall, his body twisted against the now cool stone. He shoved himself upright and dragged a hand through his hair.

A few hours had passed, and it was dusk now. He stood up and stretched, automatically searching for magic. And froze. A powerful spell was close and it was moving towards him. Would it tell whoever had sent it where he was? He scrabbled away from the wall and headed to the small door to the kitchen. Once inside his mother's house, he barred the door and set a series of spells around the entrance to keep intruders out. They would know he was here, but it would give him more time.

He stared out at his mother's garden while he poked at the mist that was steadily heading his way. It was pure power. The spell sucked at his magic. He pulled all his senses back from the spell. Only Inigo and Jinaro knew about pure power.

They were in the garden now. The mage mist was so bright that Timo had to shield his eyes. Ah, now he could see. It *was* Inigo and Jinaro. And they'd brought Hestor. Jinaro's hand was clamped on his wrist, and spells coiled tightly around the younger

Mage. His face was slack, and he didn't seem aware of anything around him—and he was incandescent with pure power. Timo's eyes took a few minutes to adjust to the brightness but then he saw two lines of mage mist snaking from Hestor—one to Jinaro and one to Inigo. The Mages stopped outside the kitchen.

Inigo had gone from using the power of the workrooms to enthralling a full Mage even more quickly than Timo had expected. Not that Hestor didn't deserve some punishment for trying to kill him all those years, but this? How long before Hestor's power was depleted? Would they drain him until he died? Inigo would only care that his source of power was gone—would Jinaro? Timo surveyed the glassy, fevered look in Jinaro's eyes. The Mage seemed so intoxicated that Timo doubted he would even notice that he'd helped kill someone.

Carefully, Timo reached out and gently drew power to him—and was thrown against the kitchen table. He stumbled and fell to his knees, grasping the edge of the table. He steadied himself and looked out the window directly into Inigo's eyes.

The self-appointed Primus smiled and made a sharp downward gesture with his hand. A flash of mage mist flew towards the window, shattering it. There was a burst of white light when the spell hit Timo's defenses.

Timo covered his eyes a moment too late. The flash temporarily blinded him, and he had to feel his way to the back hallway. He tested his defensive spells and grimaced. The pure power that Inigo was feeding into his spells was more powerful than the old magic Timo had put into his own. He wouldn't be able to hold them off for long.

The dim light in the hallway seemed too bright for his sensitive eyes as he hurried to the door that led to his mother's sitting room. He quickly drew power from the many spells still active around the house. Then he sat in his mother's favourite chair and shielded it.

He could feel turmoil through his connection to the magic but it was quiet in the sitting room. He built up small stockpiles of magic before he blocked any threads of power that fed into the room. If Inigo entered the room, he hoped to trap him and prevent him from accessing more pure power. Inigo would be forced to use what magic he had to break through Timo's barriers, hopefully leaving him vulnerable. The worst of Mage

Guild council had to be dead before he sank the rest of the island.

When they burst through the door, they were bright with magic—so bright that Timo knew they had another source of pure power. He squinted against the light of the mage mist and tried to see past the glowing figures.

He easily identified Inigo and Jinaro—they were ablaze with magic, as was the shuffling figure of Hestor. But beyond them were three more figures he'd missed seeing before, three figures feeding pure power to Hestor, who in turn was feeding Inigo and Jinaro.

"Gyda!" Timo swore. He'd missed the figures earlier because they were smaller than the rest. *Children! Inigo and Jinaro were feeding off the energy of children!*

"Monsters!" Timo said, surging to his feet. "You're hurting children!" He pushed a spell towards Inigo's group to hold them at the edge of the room.

"It doesn't hurt them," Jinaro said. He giggled and shook Hestor's arm. "See? He doesn't feel a thing."

Hestor's face remained blank, and he shuffled sideways a step in order to stay on his feet. But one of the children looked up at Timo, his gaze full of terror.

Timo looked away from the child and met Inigo's smiling face.

"He hasn't found his talent yet," Inigo said. "None of them have. But I have. Such raw power, such purity! And not tainted by being able to tap into it themselves. It's so much better than the adults'."

"Lovely," Jinaro agreed. He reached out to stroke the head of the child closest to him. The girl—no more than seven—trembled and looked away, but although her whole body seemed to try to strain away from his touch, she remained rooted where she was.

"You are immoral," Timo said. "Feeding off children."

"Immoral?" Inigo said. "These children belong to the guild, and I am Primus. They and their talents are mine to use as I see fit. It has always been that way."

"No," Timo said. "At one time the guild served its members, not the other way around."

"Is that what Rorik told you? Or your mother?"

Inigo sent a burst of power against Timo's shield. It weakened slightly, and Hestor groaned and fell to one knee.

"Or maybe it was that degenerate Santos," Inigo continued.

"You shouldn't believe anything *he* told you. He was the most ruthless of us all at one time. How else do you think he became Primus?"

"He changed," Timo said. "That's why he never returned to the guild. But it was the old spells that told me. I can feel their intent, feel what they were meant to do—build a safe home for Mage Guild, provide shelter and food and comfort so that Mages could concentrate on mastering their abilities. But in order to do good, not evil."

"You can't know that," Inigo scoffed. "Every Primus for the last century has been ruling the guild in the same way—by increasing their own power."

"And not one of them would have been able to create the spells that lifted the guild islands up from the sea floor," Timo said. "Because none of those spells were created by a single Mage. They were created by teams of Mages, all working together, with one goal in mind—building a safe place to live."

"Teams of mages," Inigo said. "I don't believe it. Mages were not created to work in teams—we hold and use power as individuals. Like this."

Inigo sent a blast of magic towards Timo, a great, dense cloud of white mage mist that sparked and roiled where it met the mauve of Timo's defensive spell. Timo shuddered and fed more power into his spell, pushing the white back slightly. He reached for the magic below his feet, the old spells that kept the island aloft, and pulled that power to him. The island shook and the floor buckled once, twice, before it steadied.

But Inigo didn't give up. His face contorted with rage as he threw both hands forward, a pure white spell issuing from them. Hestor dropped to the stone floor, his face now twisted in pain and his mouth open in an eerily silent scream. The wall of mage mist thickened as Inigo continued to push pure magic at Timo.

Jinaro screamed and tried to strike out at Inigo, but the Primus flicked a wrist and Jinaro's head snapped up. He clutched his throat as mage mist covered his face, suffocating him. He fell to the floor, writhing, but after a moment his body stilled.

Timo gritted his teeth and fed more power into his defenses.

Then the children started screaming, high-pitched wails of pain and terror.

"Stop!" Timo yelled. "You're killing them!"

"Mine to use," Inigo said through teeth clenched with effort. "Any way I want to."

"No!" Timo pushed his spell forward, hard, and it slammed in to Inigo, severing his connection with the three children and knocking the Mage to his knees. But he'd used too much force, and the spell continued past the Master Mage, blowing a jagged gash in the wall. The island shook again, this time with enough force to throw Timo to the floor. He crawled over to where the children lay, still and silent, but breathing, thank Gyda.

With the last bit of power he had, he created a spell to keep them safe. Then he stood up and hobbled over to Inigo.

He was still alive. Timo drew in a shaky breath and pulled every last bit of magic out of the Mage. It wasn't much—just enough to steady his trembling legs. The room shook again, and he dropped to his knees. A hand grabbed his ankle, and he felt a sharp pain in his thigh. Inigo raised his hand, the knife he held wet with Timo's blood.

"I came prepared," Inigo said.

Timo scrambled to get out of the way as Inigo plunged the knife down. The blade hit the stone floor and skidded a few inches. Ignoring the pain in his leg, Timo dragged himself away, leaving a smear of blood on the floor. On his knees, Inigo advanced towards him.

Frantically, Timo tried to pull more magic from the island but he was too weak now. The blood that pumped from his leg was taking his energy with it. Inigo lurched to his feet and took a step. Timo looked behind him for something he could use as a weapon. A vase sat on the table near the door to his mother's workroom. He started to drag himself towards it but Inigo reached Timo first and leaned over him.

Desperate, Timo grabbed any wisps of magic left in the room and created a weak barrier to protect his head and neck. Inigo's knife slid off it and plunged into Timo's arm, rather than his neck. With a grunt of pain, he rolled out of the way as Inigo raised the knife again.

Timo lashed out with his good leg, kicking Inigo's exposed ribcage. The Mage shrieked, and his arm dropped, the knife clutched in his lowered hand. Timo kicked again, and the knife flew across the room.

While Inigo scrambled after the knife, Timo gripped a chair

and hauled himself up. Dragging his injured leg, he stumbled to the table and grabbed the vase. He turned in time to see Inigo pick up the knife.

Panting and dizzy, Timo leaned against a wall.

"Even if you kill me you've already lost," Timo said. "I've already destroyed Mage Guild Island."

"I have enough power to fix it," Inigo said. "There are still people—Mages—that I can tap into."

Timo closed his eyes and searched for power, but all he could find was a few old spells—so old that their power had faded.

"Not close enough for you to use," Timo said. He gathered the old spells and used some of the magic to staunch the flow of blood from his leg. He wanted to live after all.

Inigo took a few halting steps towards him, waving the knife. "Maybe not," Inigo said. "But I still have a knife."

"And I still have magic." Timo slammed the vase against the table, shattering it. With the last of his power, he sent the shards hurtling towards Inigo. The Mage raised his arm to shield his face, and the knife fell to the floor.

Inigo grunted. Flecks of blood peppered his arm, and it dropped away from his face. Blood flowed from his eyes and down his cheeks. Hands waving in front of him, he staggered around the room.

On unsteady legs, Timo limped towards the Master Mage. He stooped to pick up the knife and then stepped in front of Inigo.

"Should have done this long ago," Timo said. He plunged the knife into Inigo's left eye and stumbled back a step.

Blood spurted from the Mage's wound, and without a sound, he crumpled to the floor.

Timo skidded on a pool of blood and fell backwards, hitting his head on the floor.

Someone was shaking him—his body trembled from the force of it. He lifted his hand to shoo the person away, but there was no one there. He opened his eyes. He was alone in his mother's bedchamber, lying on her bed. The bed shook, and he watched as a small crack in the ceiling travelled a few inches towards the door.

He sat up, or at least he tried to. Dizziness forced him down onto the bed. His thigh throbbed, and when he reached down, he felt a thick wrap on it.

What had happened? He didn't remember waking, or dragging himself here.

Slowly he half slid, half fell off the bed, struggling until he had the foot of his good leg on the floor. Steadying himself against the bed, he shoved himself upright and hopped towards the door. Another tremor threw him off balance, and he grabbed the door handle to keep from falling.

He smelled them from the hallway—the smell of blood and shit and death.

Inigo lay in a pool of blood, the knife still sticking up from his eye. Jinaro was just beyond him, his face blue and his hands at his throat. Hestor lay beside one of the children, but the other two were gone. Were they alive?

Timo felt nothing but anger at the three dead Mages, even Hestor, who'd been used by men he'd tried to emulate. But the children had deserved none of this.

"I've taken the other two children to the boat already," a voice said from behind him. "They're breathing, but that's about all."

Timo spun around. "Mole, what are you doing here?" Timo asked. His voice was scratchy, and his throat was parched.

"Came for you," Mole said. "Wasn't sure you were planning to get out alive."

Timo looked at the bodies. "They were *feeding* off them," he said. "Inigo deserved a slower, more painful death."

"Sure, sure," Mole said. "But thanks to you he's dead and you're alive, along with two of those children." Mole hooked his thumbs into his waistband. "I'm impressed."

"Impressing you always seems to have something to do with death," Timo said. "Me either dealing it or escaping it."

"I am an Assassin," Mole replied. "And you haven't escaped it yet. Do you want to?"

"I hadn't been planning on it," Timo said. He spread his hands out. There was dried blood—Inigo's blood—on them. He looked up and met Mole's eyes. "But yes."

"Good. That means I don't have to tie you up and drag you." Mole smiled. "Trust me, you do not want to cross Kara."

The island shuddered violently.

"We need to go," Mole said. "Now." He headed for the door to the dock.

Timo nodded and hobbled after him.

Mole's boat was the only one Timo could see underneath the island. It was tied up to his mother's dock, the children settled in-between the two seats with blankets carefully tucked around them.

"Will they be all right?" Timo asked. Mole had so much more experience with life and death than he did—though he was catching up, he thought darkly.

"If we get them to Giona in time," Mole replied. He jumped into the boat and steadied it with one hand on the dock.

"How did you know where I was?" Timo asked. He stepped into the bow of the small wooden vessel and settled in. The mage lights that usually lit the underbelly of Mage Guild Island were dim, and if he'd stood and reached up, he'd be able to touch the dirt above them.

"I figured you'd go to ground somewhere familiar, where you felt somewhat safe," Mole said.

"Not a big list," Timo replied. He'd chosen his mother's place because he knew it, and he knew it would be empty. But did he feel safe here?

"No," Mole replied, and Timo thought he saw a ghost of a smile on the Assassin's face.

Mole untied the rope and shoved the boat away from the dock. He grabbed the oars and gestured towards the pair that lay flat near Timo.

"Unless you have enough magic to speed us up we better get rowing."

Timo fumbled getting the oars into the oarlocks. Mole had powered them past four docks before he was able to aid their escape. He concentrated on rowing, on keeping up a steady rhythm that helped rather than hindered their progress. He looked up from his task and wondered at the pool of sunlight he could see off to his left. Then he realized what it was—the hole in the island, the empty space left when he relocated the centre section out over the bay.

The island shook and clumps of earth splashed into the water beside the boat, sending eddies off into the distance. The underside of the island was closer to them. Now he wouldn't even be able to stand up without bumping into it. Timo bent to his task, trying to put all his strength into rowing. He looked over his shoulder, trying to determine how far away the edge of the island was. Too far. He stilled his oars.

"We won't make the edge," Timo said, his chest heaving as he turned to look at Mole.

"We have to try," Mole said. "It's our only chance."

"No," Timo replied. "It isn't. We should make for the centre. I hollowed it out, hoping to remove most of the Mages." He pointed to his left, and Mole followed his finger.

"Is it safe?" Mole asked.

Timo shrugged. "At least we'll die looking at the sky."

Mole laughed. "Gyda, I hate being under here."

THE HOLE IN the centre of Mage Guild Island was bigger than even Timo had imagined. Mole whistled in appreciation as the boat skimmed out from under the dirt into the pre-dawn sky. The edges of the hole were crisp, as though they'd been cut with a knife.

Timo looked up at buildings that were sliced down the middle, the hallways and rooms open to the air. And beyond that was the blue of the sky. He'd been joking when he'd said they could die looking at the sky, but looking up at it now, he was comforted.

"This is bigger than all of Santos' estate on Old Rillidi," Mole said. "Including the grounds. And you did this? Moved it?"

"Yes," Timo said. "I'm the cause of so many deaths."

"People were going to die," Mole said. "Mage Guild would have taken everyone slow—this way those who die go quick."

"I know," Timo said. "But *I* made the decision that everyone would die quick. I'm as bad as Inigo."

Mole pointed to the children in the bottom of the boat. "You think these little ones would have wanted to live being slowly drained of life?"

Timo looked at Mole, surprised at the fury in his face.

"I think they'd rather be dead. I know I would," Mole finished.

Timo looked past Mole to the destruction he'd caused. When Inigo and Jinaro had been draining them, the children had been terrified. He had saved them—and countless others—from that. Even the dead boy was better off, wasn't he?

"How do I live with what I've done?" Timo asked.

"You remember that others—like these two here—are alive because of you," Mole said. "They now have a chance at a better life than they ever could have hoped for because of you. *Because of those deaths you're the cause of.*"

Timo nodded and bent back to his oars.

"Is there any magic left?" Mole asked. "Can you do one more spell?"

A few tendrils of mage mist hung from the surrounding buildings, and Timo gathered them to him, but the major spells, the old magic that kept the island aloft, couldn't be reached. Not with the small amount of power he had right now.

"I can do a small spell," Timo said. "I don't have enough to take us far."

"Can you keep us afloat?"

Timo nodded. "Probably. Why?"

Mole looked around and then up. "This island will take some time to sink—hours maybe—and we'll be pushed up like a cork as it does. I'm not sure what'll happen when the island finally goes under but I do know I want to stay afloat."

"I can do that." Timo wove the small amount of mage mist around the boat, reinforcing the boat's design and construction to magnify the magic as much as possible. "It's done," he said.

He turned around to face Mole and bent over the two children. They were pale but at some point the girl had stuck her thumb into her mouth. Timo sighed in relief at this small sign of recovery. Then he settled in to wait and watch as Mage Guild Island sank around them.

"Do you ever get used to it?" Timo asked. They were in the centre of the opening. The island had sunk enough that they were even with the lower level corridors. Timo hadn't seen any bodies, but he was preparing himself. People had died—people he'd killed— and he couldn't stop thinking about it. "Killing people?"

Mole gently swept an oar in the water, keeping them centred. "No. And you shouldn't, not according to Reo." The Assassin looked up from his task. "But some don't care and others even get to like it." He paused. "I suspect Inigo was the last."

Timo nodded. "I'm not sure it even registered that he was taking a life." He looked at the sleeping children. "And right or wrong had nothing to do with it. It was all about power."

The surface of the bay was choppy, and Mole used his oars to keep the boat centred. Pieces of wood and small buckets and platters swirled around them. Something bumped into the side of the boat, and Timo clutched at the gunnels. The mage mist that ghosted around the boat solidified as the spell worked at keeping them afloat.

Timo unlatched one of his oars and shoved it against a small two-wheeled cart, pushing it into the swirling water. It got caught in the current and slammed against the stone of the hallway ceiling. It broke apart before being sucked under the stone.

Now the corridors were under water and the boat sat even with the lowest levels of the houses. When he looked up, Timo saw the edge of a garden or park. Soon they'd be even with it, and only the towers would be still above water. Would the island sink faster then? He swung the oar out and swept away a small table.

"Another hour," Mole said suddenly.

Timo grunted. Not long until the island was fully submerged.

The island was definitely sinking faster now. The lowest level of the homes was already fully submerged. Timo looked into an opulent living area—plush settees and carved, oak chairs swept up by the eddying water floated around the room. Some of the furniture washed towards them.

"Watch out!" he called to Mole.

Timo raised an oar above his head and grunted as a falling chair slammed into it, pushing the oar into his stomach. The chair rebounded off the wood and splashed into the turbulent water. He doubled over and tried to suck in a breath.

"You all right?" Mole asked.

"Will be," Timo managed to get out between gulping breaths.

The room the chair had come from was now empty of furniture, and Mole rowed them closer to it.

The boat spun, and from this new view Timo saw just how tilted the island was. The churning water was dotted with furniture and other debris that swirled towards the centre of the open area.

"We need to keep near the edge," Timo called. "My spell won't help if we get pulled into the whirlpool."

Mole nodded, his face grim as he struggled with the oars.

The sea was rougher now, and water splashed over the gunwales and into the bottom of the small boat. The children didn't move despite the water that had seeped onto the blankets. Timo pulled the fabric away from their faces, tucking it around small hands.

Timo swept the oar at debris to keep it from crashing into them. He tried to put more power into his spell but it was still weak—it would not keep them safe if the boat was in pieces.

The sun shone brightly, and cottony clouds skidded across the sky, but down in the hollowed centre of the island there was no wind, just the constant churning of the water and the sounds of crashing and splintering wood as debris and household items crashed into each other. Timo felt something change, and he looked up in alarm.

"What's wrong?" Mole called out over the sounds of the water.

"Not sure." Timo cocked his head and looked across to the swirling mass of debris that circled the whirlpool. "Hold on!" Timo yelled. He gripped the gunwales tight and mentally threw all of his magical energy into the small spell he'd created for their boat. The mage mist responded and shrank in on itself, wrapped tightly around the boat.

Suddenly the island dropped into the sea, taking the whirlpool and all its swirling debris with it. The boat rocked and bobbed as water churned and then spouted up under them. Waves crashed over Timo's head, soaking them, but the water didn't sink the boat. In the stern, Mole clutched at the oars, still trying to navigate them through the turbulent water. Timo pulled the children up, making sure the water in the boat didn't drown then.

The boat was tossed and battered as the bay waters tried to suck them down. A few moments later, the boat settled, and a bubble of water filled with debris lifted it up. With a whoosh, the water gushed out from under them, and they dropped. The little spell did its work, and the boat bobbed on the surface though both blanket-wrapped children had been tossed towards Mole. He had his arms stretched across them, holding onto the sides of the boat.

Timo hunched in the bow, his eyes fixed on the farthest edge of the hole in the island. It had tipped up as the side closest to him sank, and furniture, carpets, and other household items slid across floors and into the sea. Beyond the interiors he could see towers slowing tilting towards them. One building snapped in two, and a shower of stone blocks and bricks rained down. A tower crashed to the ground, its spire leaning out over into the bay. Then the island sank lower, and in moments, the tip of the spire was submerged.

There was a loud, grinding noise and an almost intact roof burst upwards, propelled by a gush of water. And through it all the small boat was tossed and spun and bumped around the swirling vortex that was at the centre of the hole in Mage Guild Island.

With one final rumble, the island sank below the bay. A huge wave slowly rolled away from it, a giant swell that lifted their boat up and sent it hurtling down into the trough on the other side. By the time Timo could determine the direction, the wave had increased in size and ferocity, heading out to sea. Another, smaller wave swept in towards the rest of the Rillidi Islands.

"So that's it," Mole said. He sat up and carefully moved the still unconscious children back into the middle of the boat.

"That's it," agreed Timo. At least he thought it was. He pushed all thoughts of the dead who now lay at the bottom of the bay out of his mind. "Let's get these children some help." Mole was right. It was better to focus on the living, those he could help save—those he *had* saved—rather than those he'd killed. He picked up the one oar and started paddling.

Chapter 21

HE'D EXPECTED THE surface of the bay to be calm and clear, not this endless expanse of tangled debris. Planks and furniture and casks and even the odd bed collected into jagged islands they had to navigate around.

Mole steered them well away from the remaining guild islands but there were numerous boats out on the bay. A few seemed to be picking through the wreckage, but most just floated aimlessly—witnesses to the destruction, Timo thought. He was glad that none of them came close enough to ask questions of the lone boat heading *away* from Mage Guild Island. Mole might be convinced that Timo had done the right thing but Timo doubted the rest of the guilds would be so quick to agree.

"We're close now," Mole said.

They'd been rowing for hours. At least Mole had. Timo was grateful for the Assassin's unflagging energy since he was as useful as the two children sleeping under the blankets. He waved away the last wisps of mage mist and leaned out, staring at the shore.

Old Rillidi. He'd been dreaming of it for two years—ever since he'd first met Kara Fonti and she'd told him he would always be welcome there. Mole had renewed energy, and the boat picked up speed. The rocky shore slipped past them, and Timo mentally reached out to try to get a feel of the place.

There was no magic. At first he wondered if he simply

couldn't feel it because his own magic was so depleted—but he felt the remnants of the spell on the boat. No, there wasn't even a whisper of underlying magic. Even on Arts Guild Island—because it had been created by spells—magic lay below every surface, under every speck of dirt, every stone block, and every tree. But here there was . . . nothing. He laughed at the absence of magic, delighted in this feeling of blindness, lightness.

"There's no magic here," he said in response to Mole's questioning glance.

"We have Mages," Mole replied. "Santos while he was alive and Giona. And now Barra."

"Yes, I expect there will be spells but there's no *magic*." He swept an arm out towards the shore.

"Why would there be?" Mole asked. "What would be the point, unless you want to make it a nicer beach or something."

"Exactly," Timo agreed. "No one feels the need to make this nicer, to change it into something else, something unnatural, by using magic."

"Maybe we like it the way it is."

Timo shook his head. He liked it the way it was too—unspoiled, clean of magical tampering. He hadn't realized just how oppressive living with so much magic had been.

Was that why Mage Guild had become so malicious and cruel? Had living amongst so much magic changed the people who lived there? It was sad to think that the best intentions of those long-ago Mages had been the first step towards the insanity that Mage Guild had become.

It would be a worthwhile thing to know, and he wished he had someone he could discuss it with. To find out what went wrong so they could stop it from happening again.

They rounded a spit of land and Timo saw two boats heading towards them. Seyoyans rowed the first boat—he recognized the blond braids. He grinned. Wuls and Yash waved frantically from the bow. Timo waved back. In the second boat, with a more sedate wave but an even more welcome sight, Kara Fonti.

The next few hours were a blur. Timo remembered Wuls hopping into their boat and taking over the rowing duties from Mole, who wearily moved aside. In no time they were ashore, his feet firmly on the unmagical soil of Old Rillidi. Kara swept him into a hug before handing him off to a young woman named Pilo, who showed him to a room in the huge manor house. Pilo said that Kara was looking after the two children they'd brought and would see him later, once he was rested and clean.

So he took advantage of the steaming tub of water that arrived and the soft bed that had been turned down. Sometime later he woke. The tub had been removed, and his sister sat at his bedside. She smiled solemnly.

"I wish it were under happier circumstances but I am glad that you're finally here."

"As am I," Timo replied. "Are the children all right?"

"They're recovering." Kara said. "Giona spent quite a lot of time with them. He had to—how did he call it? Infuse them with life, they were so depleted." She frowned. "He said they'd been emptied."

"By Inigo," Timo said. "He was . . . using them to feed his power."

"So Mole said." She paused. "He also said you killed him."

"Yes. He was trying to kill me," Timo said. "Inigo didn't even see anything wrong with using those children, draining them—it was his right as Mage Guild Primus to use any lesser Guildsman in any way that he wanted, he said."

"I'm glad he's dead," she said softly. "And that Mage Guild Island is gone."

Kara sat quietly for a few moments before she spoke again.

"Thousands of Guildsmen left when the bells rang," she said. "Many are here on Old Rillidi. Warrior Guild has been helping us set up camps and find food and water."

"Good."

"Barra Eska has already started to look, but I must ask you to help her when you're able. We need to know if any full Mages, especially any council members, are hiding amongst them."

"Will you kill them?"

"Not if they abide by our rules," Kara said.

"They might," Timo nodded. "Now that they're away from Mage Guild Island." He looked up at her. "I wish Santos was alive. I really think that living with so much magic made things worse—made bad people worse."

"I wish Santos was alive as well." Kara's smile was sad. "But what you just said will fascinate Giona. Oh! I almost forgot. He's blood to you much as I am. Do you want me to fetch him?"

"No," Timo said. "He's been busy healing the children. I'll meet him another time."

"So you shall," Kara said.

Timo's eyes drifted closed, and he barely heard when his sister left the room.

Acknowledgements

Thanks to my editor Margaret Curelas and everyone at Tyche Books for their hard work and for taking a chance on me. And special thanks to Ryah Deines for not holding poorly placed sticky notes against me.

About the Author

Jane Glatt loves that along with creating original worlds, writing fantasy allows her to indulge her curiosity about an eclectic group of subjects. So far she's researched synesthesia, medieval guilds, tidal rivers, cities atop bridges, pirates and privateers, plants used for healing and the history of spying. For that last one she blames a visit to the International Spy Museum (yes it's a real place), in Washington D.C.